THE DEATHLESS SONS

Books by Brendan Noble

The Frostmarked Chronicles:
A Dagger in the Winds
The Trials of Ascension
The Daughters of the Earth
The Deathless Sons

Frostmarked Tales:
The Rider in the Night
The Lady of Rolika

The Realm Reachers:
The Crimson Court

The Prism Files:
The Fractured Prism
Crimson Reigns
Pridefall
White Crown

For our cats, Bryza and Lyna, who were by my side or on my lap for most of my time writing this book. No, Lyna, it's not dinner time yet.

Author Note: Trigger Warning

The Deathless Sons contains elements that may be triggers or traumatic to some readers, so please proceed with caution if any of the below are so for you. I have done my best to treat these serious topics carefully and with respect.

- Mental illness
- Self-harm
- War/War Trauma

Godly and Demonic Marks

Marzanna - Frostmark
Winter, Disease, and Death

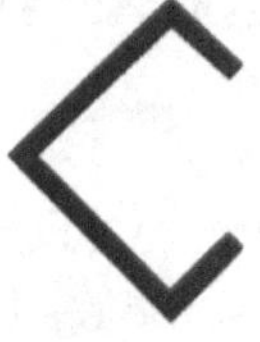

Dziewanna - Bowmark
Wilds, Hunt, and Spring

Jaryło - Springmark
Spring, Agriculture, and War

Mokosz - Mothermark
Women, Divination, and Earth

Perun - Thundermark
Thunder, Justice, and War

Weles - Serpentmark
Underworld and Lowlands

Czarnobóg - Darkmark
Death, Darkness, and Corruption

Dadźbóg - Sunmark
The Sun

Otylia - Moonmark
Endings and Moon

Wacław - Eclipsemark
Storm Demon (Płanetnik)

Pronunciation Guide

Characters

Wacław Lubiewicz: Vahtswahv Luubeeayvihch
(Little Name) - Wašek: Vahshehk
Otylia Welesiakówna: Ohtihleeah Vehlehseeahkohvnah
(Little Name) - Otylka: Ohtihlkah
Narcyz: Nahrsihz
Andrij: Ahndrey
Koschei: Kohshay
Baba Jaga: Bahbah Yahgah

Gods

Marzanna: Mahrzahnah
Weles: Vehlehs
Dziewanna: Djehvahnah
Jaryło: Yahrihwoh
Mokosz: Mohkohsh
Perun: Pehruun
Dadźbóg: Dahdzbohg
Czarnobóg: Charhnohbohg
Swaróg: Svahrohg

Other Terms

Žityje: Zhihtyeh
Krowik(ie): Krohvihk(ee)
Szeptucha: Shehptuuhah
Płanetnik: Pwahnehtnihk
Naw(ie): Nahv(ee)
Żmij: Zmee
Kwiecień: Kvihehchehn
Grudzień: Gruudjehn
Jawia: Yahveeah
Nawia: Nahveeah

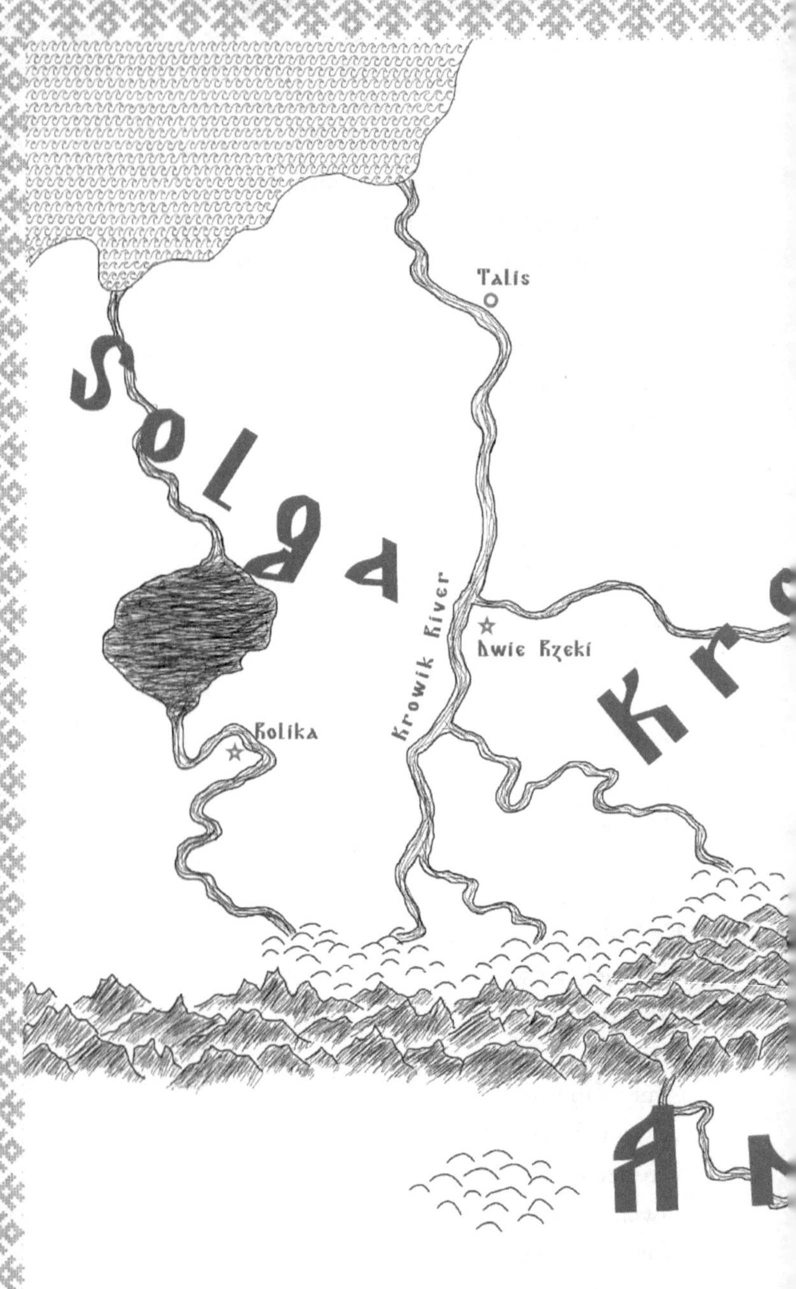

Talis
Solga
Krowik River
Dwie Rzeki
Kolika
Kr
A

WIK
vora
Astiw
Vastroth
Frostmarked Horde
Klist
Mangled Woods
Bustelintin
Narrow Pass
Wyzra River
ałe Wzgòrze
Kynnytsia
Behmir River
Huebia
uthern Hills
Tior River
Sheresy
Télem

THE FROSTMARKED CHRONICLES 4

THE DEATHLESS SONS

BRENDAN NOBLE

Part 1
The Wild Goddess

1

Wacław

Will Jawia ever bloom again?

DEATH CLAIMED THE LIVING REALM.

Marzanna's blizzard obscured my foggy breaths as ice and snow crunched beneath my boots. Frost crept up to mid-calf, snatching me with every step before I finally broke free of its frigid grasp. Shivering, I pulled my furs tighter. There was no end to the snowfall in sight.

The winds circled me, as if begging for me to wield them as a Naw płanetnik—a half-mortal, half-demon of the storm. We shared that desire, but in the weeks since the Huebia Revolt, each wintery tempest had fought my control of our flight. One like this would make it near impossible to even hold myself aloft, let alone fend off the demonic chały that lurked in the dark clouds.

I yearned to be free.

With the waxing moon above covered by the storm, only the twinkling of our campfire ahead offered any real light. Luckily, I didn't need sight. The tether binding me to Otylia pointed the way to her, growing tighter with each haggard step.

Her shadowed form blocked one side of the fire. Black hair hung freely down her back, covered only partly by the silver fox pelt she draped over her shoulders to warm her neck. One hand clutched her fur coat shut as she stared into the flames. She didn't sit, not when I was away. It was hard enough to get her to rest when I was by her side, trying to calm her nerves as we grew ever closer to finding her mother, the wild goddess Dziewanna.

Even from here, I sensed Otylia's anticipation. Our souls' bond prevented much in the way of secrets. That didn't stop us from trying, and she hadn't told me everything that had happened in the last few moons. I let her hold back. The walls around her heart and mind were strong, requiring care—not force—to be brought down.

It was that bond that alerted her to my presence amid the noise of the gales. She looked at me over her shoulder, her ivy green eyes alight against the campfire and her thin lips curled into the slightest of smiles.

The chill's clutches melted away at the sight of her.

I collapsed into Otylia the moment my feet slipped onto the thawing mush around the fire. My thighs throbbed from pushing through the snow. My face stung from the hail. The fire slowly dulled that ache, but it was nothing compared to her silent embrace.

We'd traveled hundreds of miles since leaving Vastroth, and each day wore us down more than the one before. Our support for each other was the last flame keeping us moving forward. Dziewanna had to be close. We would save her, and then she'd help us end Marzanna's winter over the living realm of Jawia. If it could be ended at all.

"You're rarely this quiet after scouting," Otylia said, pulling down my snow-covered hood and running her warm hands over my ears. They'd been numb, and when their feeling returned, so did the pain. A pin prick compared to the demonic hunger she quieted with her touch.

I gave a solemn smile and rested my eyes for a moment. Black and red danced across my eyelids with the flames. "The storms are getting worse. I'm worried for Mom and for Kuba and the others. You can survive from offerings and me from animal blood, but the crops are dead. Game is scarce. If we don't find Dziewanna soon, it won't matter what Koschei and the Frostmarked Horde do. They'll conquer our tribe's skeletons."

"Krowik exiled you."

"They feared me." I pulled back, circling the fire. Its constant motion held my gaze, some primal part of me not wanting to look away. "Huebia proved they were right to."

She crossed her arms and gave me a warning glare. "Don't do this again, Wašek, not tonight. You're tired. That's it. Tell me what you saw and then we can rest."

"A dead forest, like all the others." Having rounded the fire, I stopped beside her, taking her hands. "There's a river to the east of it and another to the west, so maybe this is the one we're looking for?"

We'd agreed one of us would scout ahead during the blizzards bad enough to stop both of us from flying. Going alone was dangerous, but she'd needed the time to recollect her strength through offerings from her worshippers. She despised drinking the blood from her moonlight altars. We had little other choice with the risk of demons and Horde patrols ahead. For a few hours of scouting, though, a goddess and demon were each plenty capable of handling a few enemies without the other. Our bond allowed us to call for help through our minds anyway if the situation escalated.

A larger group would've made the journey easier. I missed Kuba and Xobas, and Otylia had smiled so much more around Ara, the nymph Sabina, and the Mothermarked Vastrothie girl Ta-naro. With the blizzards growing ever more brutal, though, we'd had little choice but to leave them with the Vastrothie army, who'd used Mokosz's szeptuchy to travel through the mountains and toward Dwie Rzeki. We barely slept between treks. Every step and flight between those rests was met with Marzanna's frigid wrath. No mortal or nymph would've survived at the pace we were going, and through our marks, our friends would ensure we remained in touch with our allies—no matter how far.

"Vida and Jaryło's memories showed two rivers meeting at a

bridge before her palace on the frozen bay," Otylia said, nose wrinkled. "This could be it, or it could be just another dead end."

The Frostmarked szeptucha known as Minna had controlled Vastroth until Otylia discovered she was actually Vida, a girl we'd thought had died during the szeptucha initiation rituals almost five years ago. Vida had chosen to kill herself rather than remember what had happened to her. The rumor was that she'd been brought back from death multiple times by Marzanna. I feared what that did to a person, and what it meant if Vida wasn't the only one.

"Your Thread of Life still shows northeast?" I asked Otylia. As the goddess of endings, she saw the connections that bonded us to those we love and heard whispers of ends both future and past. The power frightened and fascinated me at the same time.

Our Threads appeared as Otylia's eyes flashed pure white. Stretching from our chests to those we loved, they glowed brilliantly—hers green and mine light blue. We'd followed the single green strand traveling north. It had to show us the way to Dziewanna.

"Mother's Thread hasn't moved since I discovered I could see it," she said. "We're going the right way, but when does the land end?"

"I have no idea. Zorza Wieczorna's evening gate in the sea was a long way west, but it *feels* like we've traveled further from Vastroth."

Her eyes returned to normal as the Threads disappeared, and the pulsing of our shared mark on my forearm faded with them. It reminded me that seeing the Threads with her was a gift only I had. "Weles claimed Jawia is far larger than Nawia, but I didn't even see the entire realm of the dead. The tundra could go on forever."

"Then we'll follow it forever," I replied, pulling her close and resting my forehead against hers. She was warm, and despite weeks of travel and her Ascension, she still smelled of wild herbs burnt in offering to her mother. A scent I'd known so well when we were little. "I'm sorry. I wish I could take the pain of her loss away."

For a moment, Otylia didn't react at all. We stood still with our heads touching and our souls sharing both love and loss. Silence was her choice, so I let the crackle of the fire and the howls of the dying blizzard replace our voices. She'd talk when she was ready. Until then, I shared her pain.

She stepped back when the fire smoldered to little more than orange ash and the sun's dull glow appeared in the east. Neither of us moved to restore the flames. Without the storm's cover, the daylight would expose its smoke and alert any nearby Frostmarked to our presence.

"Rambling won't save her," Otylia said, her head tilted down as she looked back at me. "We should rest until then."

I nodded. "Then tomorrow we fly."

2

Otylia

Where are you, Mother? I don't care who or what Marzanna has guarding you. I'll bring you home. I swear upon my moon and your wilds. I'll bring you home.

FOR THE FIRST TIME IN WHAT SEEMED AN ETERNITY, I awoke to the light of the setting sun as I emerged from the shelter we'd dug in the snow. No clouds. No blizzard. It was as if Marzanna had forgotten to swallow us whole.

Her frozen wasteland dwarfed us anyway.

White extended for as far as I could see, amplifying the sun's rays and making me squint as I stared to the northeast. The distant forest Wacław had scouted the night before was obvious now. It was leafless like all the others before it, but could this be the one I'd seen in Jaryło's memories on the night Marzanna captured Dziewanna? Part of me wanted to hope. But I couldn't. My hope had been beaten out of me by the combined efforts of Weles, Jaryło, Marzanna, Czarnobóg, and seemingly every other god and demon in the Three Realms. Spite drove me on now. To prove my enemies wrong, and to bring them Dziewanna's wrath.

Wacław's unruly blond hair and bleary-eyed face peeked out of the shelter. It was a short and narrow space, barely offering enough room for the two of us to lie next to each other. He liked that more than he was willing to admit. So did I.

"Hopefully that forest has some animals," he said with a stretch before kicking himself out of the shelter with the grace of a newborn pup. "I'm starving."

"You have enough *žityje*?" I asked, half-knowing the answer already.

He wiped the snow off his wide-brimmed płanetnik hat and put in on as he gave a tired smile. "Yeah, but—"

"Then you're fine. Mortal hunger can't kill us."

His smile grew, and I resisted the urge to smack it off his face. "Remind me why Jaryło forced you to pledge that you'd marry him? A god like him sure as Oblivion would hate to miss breakfast."

I smacked him anyway.

"Mention that bastard again and I'll make sure your other cheek is red enough to cover your dark veins."

Wacław's eyes widened as he wiped dark demonic blood from his lip. I'd hit him hard, but in the emotions we shared, all the regret was his. "Don't worry," he said, thumbing the black dagger sheathed at his hip. Thunderstone, capable of draining *žityje* and killing a god. "I don't need to speak his name to stab him the next time he shows his stupid golden face."

To quiet his rage, I swooped in for a kiss before grabbing my travel bag and pulling up my hood. "Glad the demon left you some guts. We'll need them if Marzanna knows I'm coming for Mother."

"Think Czarnobóg is actually guarding her?" He shouldered his own bag. "It seems like a waste for Marzanna to free a dragon from Oblivion just to have him guard her unconscious sister."

"I don't know how much of Death's Trial was real, but we have to be ready for anything. If Czarnobóg really was the first żmij, he's as ancient as Perun and Weles."

"And most of that time was spent trapped in Oblivion."

A gust circled us as Wacław flexed his hands beside him. Eight winds, the grandchildren of the god Strzybóg, each with their own *unique* personalities. I'd spent enough time with Kyustendil, the northwest wind, to know that even the youngest gods had their surprises. I shuddered just wondering what one of the eldest was capable of—if Czarnobóg could be considered a god at all.

"Let's go," I said, taking Wacław's hand. "It'll be another hour before the moon shows up. I'm not waiting that long."

He gave my hand a squeeze before leaping into the air. The gusts brought me with him, and I was grateful for the trousers beneath my slit dress as my skirt and coat flapped around me.

Using his winds to fly still unnerved me. End's force pulled me with the moon's power when I flew, controlled and direct, but Wacław's winds battered me. Each time, I gained newfound respect for birds' abilities to dive through the narrowest gaps with ease. Wacław's too, as he didn't hesitate or care about the winds' shifts. He just pulled down his hat and stared at the path ahead. A master of the winds. With black veins crossing his skin and his fur-lined coat drifting behind him to expose Marzanna's Thunderstone dagger, he surely gave the appearance of a storm demon. But his eyes held their bright blue. My Wašek was still in control, even if his demon had left its mark.

The winds carried us quickly over the forest. Starting at the bend of a north-flowing river, the trees crossed from its eastern bank to a second river. Here, the snow covered all but the tallest underbrush, but no tracks pierced its surface. We'd traveled far to the north. Were animals capable of living here in normal conditions, let alone the brutal terrain this land had become?

A howl answered my thought.

Wacław glanced at me for confirmation, and when I nodded, we dove toward the sound. Darkness crept over us with the descent. The wolves reveled in the night.

The winds silently caught us just above the snow, creating a surface beneath us that *almost* resembled solid ground. Wacław crept across it with ease. I moved slower. Each step felt like it could send me sprawling, but the winds held.

A short metallic sound broke the quiet. The last rays of light reflected off Grudzień's jagged black Moonblade streaked in colors as Wacław looked ahead with narrowed eyes. Seven wolves gathered at the base of a massive oak, two pups nuzzling into their mother in a nook of the tree as four others broke into another howl. They hadn't seen us yet.

Plenty of žityje for breakfast, I quipped to Wacław through our bond.

But he turned to me with worry in his gaze. *"They aren't Marzanna's,"* he replied. *"No glowing blue eyes. These woods are nearly dead already without me slaughtering the last of its animals."*

They're hunters like you. Mother said that's the way of the wild, and demons are no different.

"Wolves rarely kill an entire flock of their prey. Neither will I." He rose slowly, taking a long breath. *"Stay here. I'll go invisible and make this quick."*

The winds weakened beneath me, and the tips of my boots struck the snow as he took flight. Mortals and animals alike couldn't see him when he chose to be invisible in his soul-form. The wolves noticed the gust, though. Heads raised, they sniffed the air. One growled as Wacław drifted nearer, and both wolf and demon lunged at once.

Grudzień found flesh in a single strike.

The wolf had smelled Wacław's presence, but without sight, its teeth missed as Wacław tore through to its heart. *"One,"* his voice said in my mind as he devoured the heart and the *žityje* in its blood. *"One is enough."* It sounded like he was trying to convince himself more than me, and when he finished, I sensed the thrill in his soul for another.

Listen to your mind, not the hunger, I told him. *The demon's control is gone.*

He looked at me with blood covering his chin and gloved fingers. A beast. I fought my instinct to believe that. A beast would satiate its hunger until none remained, but Wacław forced himself to show mercy, to control the demonic urges. They'd lessened ever since I'd taken part of his demonic corruption in Huebia. That couldn't change what he was.

Most of the other wolves whimpered and backed away from the invisible threat. One advanced, and I expected Wacław to accept the second kill nature handed to him. Instead, he took flight and rushed upward, his winds dragging me with him.

We rose together as the sun disappeared over the horizon. Nightfall replaced it, and I grinned at the rush of power that came with the force of endings, bound to the moon. My skin released a dull glow. It rose from my fingers in white wisps that joined with End's colored ones for each creature nearby—for now just Wacław and the wolves in a vapor that spiraled through the night.

I broke free from the winds and grabbed hold of the moon's pull. It tore me upward, straight and faultless as I climbed ever higher. Breathing grew harder with each moment I climbed, but I needed to fly, to see Jawia from the above. This was the first time since we'd left Vastroth that clouds couldn't obscure the view, allowing me to rise to the stars as another flickering soul in the night sky. Then I saw it.

Water. Water!

I nearly screamed in glee at the sight of the moonlight reflecting off the sea's waves. The two rivers converged upon a bridge at the forest's end before splitting again and pouring into a small bay. A ring of ice encircled the land after that bridge, and my chest ached at the memory of Mother lying in the black dragon's shadow.

"We found her…" I whispered to myself before scanning the sky for Wacław. "Wašek! Come here! I see it."

The winds rushed through my hair and coat as he appeared beside me, his eyes wide. "This is actually it? Where's the palace?"

"Czarnobóg destroyed it." Our words were distant. All I could focus on were the spikes of ice forming a dome over the place Dziewanna had fallen, where Mother was trapped. My hand found her bone Bowmark amulet hanging at my collar. I couldn't breathe.

Wacław cupped my cheek, forgetting his bloodied glove and smearing crimson across my face. "Otylka, are… are you okay?"

I clenched my jaw. A spear of cold silver manifested in my open hand as I stared down at the fallen palace. The spear's light pushed back the darkness and my fear, replacing it with a need for revenge. I didn't care what kept her trapped there. I would kill it and free my mother, my goddess.

"Not until she's free." I met his gaze, and his eyes reflected my anger. *Good. Let Marzanna see what happens when he's unleashed.*

We charged north without another word. Wacław knew I needed action. Reassurance would've only redirected my fury at him, and no strategy could prepare us for whatever lay ahead.

Whoever guarded the palace remnants would see us quickly as we approached, but it didn't matter. Stealth was irrelevant. There would be no hiding within the circle of ice, and that was fine by me. I wanted nothing more than to tear apart the fiends that entrapped Mother, that kept her from me. She suffered.

So would they.

My power would reveal anything living, but there was nothing until a new puff of vapor appeared beside Wacław's wisp. The soft brown of a willow's bark, it drifted, slow compared to the excitement of the others.

It's her!

I opened my vision to the Threads of Life. My bright green Thread wrapped around me before shooting in each direction: one strand binding me to Wacław, others heading southwest toward Ara, Sabina, and Father, another dropping to the rivers and Weles in Nawia, and a final one stretching toward the far end of the ice ring.

In the darkness, I couldn't see her, but Mother was there. End's force confirmed it.

I removed my glove when her wisp stopped before me. So many questions wrapped themselves around my mind, and my hand shook as I raised my fingers toward the wisp. Seeing other's ends, both past and future, was jarring. To know I was about to see Mother's own…

"You see her wisp, don't you?" Wacław asked.

"I do."

He held my spear-hand, offering a smile I knew was forced. "You can do this. I'll be right here."

I couldn't return his smile. End could show me what's ahead or give me some answer to what had happened to Dziewanna, to Mother, but did I want to know? Suffering lay in those visions—of what she'd endured and what battles would come. I'd seen the destruction brought by Wacław's fall to the Płanetnik in Huebia and had been unable to believe it.

Mother's wisp moved toward my hand as I raised it. I pretended she could see me, that she was reaching to touch me for the first time in over four years. Childish hopes. I clung to them anyway, but as my fingers met her wisp, End's force didn't tear me away.

Cold silence met me instead. Shooting from my fingers up my arm and into my chest, Marzanna's frigid grip tightened around my soul. I recognized it from moons before. Wacław had cast out her curse through his Frostmark and now endured permanently frostbitten fingers as a result. But this time, her power held no sway over me.

I released a burst of *žityje*, repelling the chill in a blinding flash. When the light faded, my shaking hand drifted through empty space. Mother's wisp was gone, and tears streamed down my face. No more willow brown. No more dynamic energy. Just darkness punctured by the light pulsing from my skin and rising in silvery strands.

I yelled through the night, my rage echoing for eternity. Then I dove toward my mother's prison.

Spear in hand, I crashed into the blue ice dome, and its silver tip plunged through the barrier, shattering it the moment I struck. Power surged from the weapon. Light and endings both as dark wisps collided with me midair.

Screaming, the vapored forms of a hundred demons passed through me in search of escape. Each brought another onslaught of visions. Of their mortal death. Of the unnatural elements tethering their undead souls to Jawia. And of Marzanna's promises to fulfill their desires for freedom. Oaths unfulfilled. Minds corrupted.

The towers of ice I'd faced in Death's Trial rose above the ruins. Sharp and unnatural, they encircled me for over fifty strides in each direction. The moonlight above fractured through what remained of the dome. The ice and snow seemed a hollow gray with only the cores of the towers offering blue to break the colorless void. What unfiltered light remained covered me. My glow no longer pulsed, instead absorbing the moon's power and growing with my anger. I'd kill Marzanna for what she'd done. I'd torture Czarnobóg for a thousand lifetimes more. Once I freed Dziewanna and restored her power, the dark gods would truly understand wrath when they faced mother and daughter together.

Yet the air hung still. Impossibly cold against my skin, it stayed, as if trapped in time. Wacław slowly descending to my side broke the motionless space, but the eerie sensation remained. End's wisps had shown the demons within the dome. Where were they?

I opened my mind to the Threads of Life, but there was only a single source beyond the two of us. A figure lay in shadows at the ruin's far end. Her dim Thread wrapped her body before stretching out in only a few directions. The brightest one connected us, and my tears began again as I stared down at Mother's crumpled body. My power confirmed she lived, but what had Marzanna done to her? Why was she left unguarded?

"Czarnobóg isn't here," I stammered through gritted teeth. "Why? Dziewanna is the only one who can stop Marzanna."

Wacław laid a hand softly on my back. His other still clutched the dagger. "I don't know, but I don't like this. Go to her. I'll watch to make sure there aren't any lingering demons."

I dismissed my spear into a puff of light before dropping to the snow strides from Mother. Her appearance was the same as during the Trial, tearing at my heart. A few stray dark veins like Wacław's crossed her pale face, and her crown of antlers was broken as her brown hair hung mangled over a ripped, deep green dress. Her skin and bare feet were bloodied when they'd once been unblemished. She was a queen stripped of her wild throne, a goddess drained and broken. She'd suffered here alone because of Jaryło's betrayal.

She'd never be alone again.

As I approached, the shadow over her didn't shift. There was no żmij. There were no demons. Marzanna had drained her and left her here to rot, and none of the gods had bothered to save her. Neither

her father Perun nor her husband Weles could turn from their simmering war. Cowards.

"Mother?" I pled, kneeling beside her and taking her hand in mine. It was cold and limp. Her chest rose with each breath, but barely. "Mother, it's me, Otylia."

No reply came. Sorrow crept into my rage, forcing me to choke on my tears as I screamed and begged for her to answer. For years, I'd wished to just see her again, but now that I could, I was forced to watch her suffer Marzanna's Curse for a second time.

"No," I muttered. "I couldn't save you before, but this is different now. *I'm* different now."

I squeezed my Bowmark amulet like I had so many times, allowing its sharp ends to jab into my palm until blood seeped free. *Żityje*-filled blood. Holding my hand over her lips, I forced the trickle into her mouth and whispered a prayer I'd used as a szeptuchy to make sacrifices at her altar. The words in the old tongue spilled from my mouth, sloppy and ill-timed. Power flowed through them regardless, and Mother's Thread slowly glowed stronger.

"Come back to me," I told her. "You taught me to fight, and I haven't stopped since you died. But I need you now. The wilds need you now. Please, Mother, *wake up*!"

With those final words, I pressed my hands to her chest and sent the force of a moonblast directly into her. The ground shook beneath us as the spell scattered snow and cracked ice. I sensed Wacław's concern through our bond, but he didn't intervene as my light faded slightly. My breaths became chilled, forced. Though the blast hadn't taken everything, a cold sweat clung to my skin and *żityje* no longer flowed as freely from my fingers. It was a last effort to wake her— one that had failed.

"Uh, Otylka?" Wacław called.

I shivered, unable to reply as I stared down at Mother's unmoving body. Light emanated from her core, but nothing changed. Then that light disappeared completely, enough to make me fall back with my knees tucked in like a weeping child. What else could I do? I'd Ascended and fought across two realms to save her, and none of it mattered. Without her, spring would never return. Jawia would perish, and everyone I loved would die with it.

What good is the end if nothing comes after?

Light burst from behind my tears. I scrambled to my feet, wiping my eyes as every part of Mother exuded radiant white light. The Threads connecting us shone brighter than any I'd ever seen, and her body lifted into the air as the air shook around me. I felt her power pulse with mine. A steady rhythm, it grew with every beat until she awoke with a gasp, dropping hard to the now snow-free earth and stumbling. I caught her, and her green eyes widened as she looked up at me with the smile only a mother can give.

"Otylia, my Otylia! You came!" She said, her voice raspy as she looked up at the ice towers nearby. "Did you kill them?"

"Kill who?" I clutched her as she squirmed. "Mother, Czarnobóg is gone."

She tensed. "Not him. *Them!*"

My joy faded as she looked at Wacław. Dark, lumbering figures surrounded him. They crawled from the cracks in the ice with limbs broken and darkness swirling at their feet—demons, hundreds of them. And they were coming straight for us.

3

Wacław

Of course she laid a trap

I CHARGED THROUGH A SEA OF DECAYING BEASTS, slashing with Grudzień in one hand and my dagger in the other. A dance of blades and talons, darkness and wind. No matter how many I felled, their claws raked across my limbs as I rushed toward Otylia and Dziewanna.

"We need to get out of here!" I shouted.

The ferocity of the unquiet dead surrounding me was unmatched by any demon I'd seen. They resembled zmory, with gray-black decaying skin and puss oozing from wounds scattered across their forms, but their ears were pointed and large feathered wings stretched from their backs. Some scrambled with misshapen limbs like their nightmarish cousins. Most, though, ran faster than the winds. They fought as a swarm, flashing fanged teeth and threatening to pull me to the ground.

I couldn't fight them all.

Black blood covered me, both the demons' and my own. I heard nothing but their snarls, saw nothing but their hideous forms. Beneath it all, a dull excitement pulsed in my core.

Grudzień sliced clean through a demon's neck, the sharp teeth upon its edge biting through flesh and bone with ease. It was a god's sword—a shard of the Alatyr Stone that had created dragons, gods, and demons alike—but in my hand, it was a butcher's cleaver. The mortal part of me hated such death. The demonic one thrived among the slaughter.

Control it, I told myself.

But I needed my demonic soul to survive. Monsters lunged at me from every side. It took all my skill with a blade and grip of the winds to just hold my ground. I considered taking flight, but they had wings. The ground protected me against attacks from below. In the sky, I'd be truly surrounded.

Otylia! I yelled through our bond. *I can't do this much longer.*

"*Mother's awake,*" she replied, tearful. "*But her power's gone.*"

A demon's teeth pierced my shoulder. My grip on the rage faltered. I unleashed it, biting my cheek hard enough to draw blood before turning and throwing lightning directly into the beast's chest.

Blue light streaked from my blades and scattered over the closest demons. The one that had bitten me shrieked as the bolt shot straight through its torso and into those behind. It arced between each, splitting into smaller bolts that stunned enough of my foes to give me a moment to breathe. A moment would have to be enough.

Fly her out! I told Otylia. *I'll distract the demons.*

"*Wašek, they'll kill you!*"

They'll surely try.

The lightning dissipated just as I leaped over the demons and flew toward the opposite side of the ice ring. Despite losing the ground's protection, this was our only chance. Otylia would struggle to fight while focusing on Dziewanna. With the demons flying after me, she could escape, and then I would outpace my pursuers once she was far enough… I hoped.

My view from above only revealed how dire the threat was. Demons filled the entire ring, and more climbed the towers, baring their teeth as I neared. Not hundreds, thousands. Czarnobóg no longer guarded the wild goddess's prison, but Marzanna had left an army.

The demons' owl-like wings extended as they followed me, filling the moonlit dome with a writhing mass of darkness. Alone at its center, I tightened my grip on my sword and dagger.

I'd drawn most of the demons to me, but as Otylia and Dziewanna rose in a dim glow, my heart sunk. At least twenty beasts followed them. At the attackers' head flew three larger ones, their bodies more intact with *żityje* emanating from their hands—Nawie.

This was a terrible plan.

The demons encircling me grew closer, trying to block my escape from above and below. There would be no chance to flee from an extended fight. I could join Otylia now and hope for the best or leave us to die separate. Why had I thought this was the right option? Separation had brought us nothing but pain.

I burst upward as the demons closed their trap. Grudzień cut demonic flesh, but their teeth and claws tore into me. *Żityje* and blood alike poured from me as I fought to free myself from their grasps.

It wasn't enough.

Each time a demon fell, another replaced it. They closed around me. Suffocating. Deafening. I couldn't think. Every movement was instinct from Xobas's trainings or simply my body's desperation to survive. I had no grasp on my remaining *żityje* nor how far I was from the cracks in the ice dome. All I knew was I had to fight to reach Otylia, so I embraced the storm in my soul.

Lightning cracked across my skin, the only light in the ball of darkness formed by the demons. I numbed to their bites that sucked my blood and claws that sought to pull me to my demise. I no longer felt the cold hilt of my dagger or Grudzień's pulsing, unreachable power. I lost myself to the storm. Entrapping it in my soul, I sensed everything the winds touched. The writhing demonic mass. The Nawie chasing Otylia and her mother. The blizzards rushing toward us. And finally, myself.

The moment the winds met my skin, I released the lightning through my veins. Sparks snapped across my skin. Burning pain came with it, but I smiled at the sound of screaming.

The demons touching me reeled back with their fingers blackened and charred. I'd lacked the *żityje* for another lightning strike.

Luckily, I'd only needed another moment to break free, and I took advantage. With one last spinning strike with both Moonblade and dagger, I rushed after Otylia.

Exhaustion crept over me as Otylia and her mother passed out of the dome. We'd come so far to save Dziewanna. Each step we'd taken had been to find her, but the sight of the antlered goddess fleeing severed my hope. She was powerless. If she couldn't defeat her sister and Czarnobóg, then we were no closer to victory, and the Frostmarked Horde knocked at Krowik's door.

That exhaustion only grew by the time I reached the rear of the demons that had followed them. Wearily, I readied my weapons.

These, though, showed little interest in me, even when I struck down the closest of them. Whether they sensed I was drained or were too focused on preventing Dziewanna's escape, I didn't know. I took a wide route either way, catching my wide-brimmed hat as it threatened to drift into the storm. A bad sign. The winds got clumsy when I was running out of *žityje*, but we had a way to go if we were going to escape.

Otylia glanced back at me when I caught up, her expression shifting from relief to frustration. "Any other ideas, or are we going to flee together like we should've in the first place?"

"I…" My attempt to defend myself faded as Dziewanna regarded me with interest.

Despite the blackened veins visible at her collar and cracked antlers that seemed to grow *from* her head, she had a stunning presence. It didn't matter how beaten down she was. It didn't matter that Marzanna had drained her power. Dziewanna was still a goddess, and she shared Otylia's sharp green eyes that bore into my soul.

"There's no time for arguing," she said, stifling a cough as we flew over the shadowed forest. We'd quickly left the ice ring behind, but when I glanced back, the demons showed no signs of giving up.

"You're right," I replied. "My *žityje* will run out soon. I barely have enough to fly."

Otylia shook her head. "I told you to track it better."

"That's probably true," Dziewanna said before glancing at the empty trees below. "But even with Wacław's power and mine, it would take an immense amount of *žityje* to defeat this many strzygi. They're foul demons, and our only hope is to escape their sight."

"Where?" Otylia asked. "We're faster than them, but they'll catch us eventually."

She was right. Though the dark forms of the strzygi were falling further behind, I could still clearly see the individuals among them, and their Nawie leaders had almost kept pace with us. Any thrill I'd felt from the melee disappeared. For once, I was the prey.

Dziewanna pointed toward a batch of willows alongside the western river. "Take me to the trees. I may lack my connection to my force, but the wilds will protect us. Hurry! I have no desire to return to that accursed palace anytime soon."

Otylia dropped instantly with Dziewanna, but I remained in the air a moment longer. Something held me there. Not a force or magic, but a desire in my heart. To see the other Nawie closely. To understand what we were and *why* we were. Our second souls were corrupted, yes, but I still didn't know why we'd been born with another soul at all. Was it just the blood moon? A part of me needed a reason more than coincidence. Surely, the timing of my birth alone couldn't have determined my life's fate?

The lead Naw stared at me as the others strayed after Otylia. This one had long fangs and owl wings of the other demons, but its eyes revealed a life within. Or *her* life within. The strzyga had long auburn hair that tangled and matted itself over her decayed skin, and she wore a ripped dress, unlike the undead of her kind. I wondered if she'd struggled against her demonic soul too, if she'd thought herself simply cursed before the rage overwhelmed her. Was this the end for all Nawie without a goddess to redeem them?

Otylia's voice called through our bond. I'd lingered too long, but I had no regrets. There was an understanding in the strzyga's gaze as I fled. I mourned for the life she'd once lived and for the mortal soul trapped within her. For now, though, there was nothing I could do to save her. I promised myself I'd find a way for others.

The goddesses landed along the shore of the river before tucking beneath the arcing branches of a weeping willow. Naked, the tree offered little protection. Dziewanna had been sure, though, so I landed beside them and crouched, waiting for some aid from the forest.

"Stay silent," she commanded with a hand on the willow's trunk. "This is not our home, so we must be invited in."

Her whispers in the old tongue drifted over us, and the branches swayed against the force of the oncoming blizzard. The trees here were dead. Neither fish nor ducks swam the waters. Yet beneath that willow, I felt the warmth of life like a beating heart. It grew faster and faster until a creaking surrounded us.

Roots shot from the ground and ensnared my ankles.

"Uh, what's happening?" I asked. They crept up Otylia's legs too, but as I prepared to swing Grudzień, Dziewanna raised her hand sharply.

"I said to be silent!" she snapped. "The mistress of this willow demands our respect. Remain still, and all will be fine."

I bit my tongue, but I had little choice to move anyway. The roots had already wrapped themselves around my legs and were pulling me toward the base of the tree. My feet disappeared into the earth. Then my calves.

I looked at Otylia, expecting her to feel the same fear as I did, but her eyes were shut. Though the roots grew over her neck and pulled her ever deeper, a smile twitched at her lips. She laid her head back.

Then she disappeared beneath the tree.

4

Otylia

Marzanna took her power... What's left?

DZIEWANNA, GODDESS OF THE WILDS and the mother I'd lost years before, knelt beside me on the frozen, dead earth that should've been the abode of an ancient nymph. Instead, it was dim as Mother's skin stung cold against mine. Life filled her eyes again, but they were tired with black rings sunken above her cheekbones.

My battle rage crumbled in her arms. Unfortunately, the strzygi weren't the pressing issue.

"Explain yourselves!"

A frail nymph's yell echoed through the small, circular room. Bark and vines formed its walls, and branches stretched across the tall ceiling that rose high above. I'd known about the existence of nymphs' homes, but it amazed me to finally be in one. They were supposed to exist somehow on Jawia yet not entirely within it, as even this cramped space was larger than the willow itself.

Mother rose to meet the nymph. Without *żityje* or any connection to her power, she lacked the radiant glow I'd come to expect from Dziewanna, but there was a force to her now. The roots below seemed to weave into the shredded ends of her earthen dress. She looked upon the nymph with a fierce, unwavering gaze.

"We thank you for inviting us into your home, mistress of the willow," she said, her voice cautious yet firm. "However, I am the Lady of the Wilds, and you will not shout at me."

The short nymph huffed and crossed her arms, her wings fluttering enough to raise her to Mother's eye level. "Dziewanna is dead. Don't you see what has become of me? I'll starve like the others before long, and now you bring this fiend into my trunk?" She pointed at Wacław. "Be glad I let you live."

I shot to my feet, any calm I'd felt around Mother gone in an instant. My silver spear fell into my grasp as I advanced. "Threaten us again and see what happens. My mother *is* Dziewanna, and I am Otylia, goddess of endings. You offered us kindness by taking us in. Let us return the favor with our story before you call us liars."

The nymph fluttered back into the wall. Fear filled her eyes, reflecting the moonlight pulsing from me. "You… You truly are goddesses?"

Mother pushed down my arm with a look that told me to back away. "We are, and we are no threat to you. My role is to protect your kind. I confess I've failed at that, but I was alone in my fight to stop this winter. Take your anger out on my bastard of a brother, Jaryło. He released the dark żmij and allowed Marzanna to break her binds." She offered the nymph her hand, cupping her cheek with the other. "What is your name?"

The nymph dropped to her knees, ignoring Mother's hand. "Liuda, my lady. I apologize. I couldn't sense your power; though, your daughter's is obvious enough."

"My force does not answer my call." Mother turned to me as tears suddenly ran down her face. "The wilds are dead, yet I live. Corruption taints everything *he* touches. Even me."

I ran my fingers over her blackened veins. They were far fewer than Wacław's, but she was a goddess. How could she endure demonic corruption?

She coughed and held my hands. "I see the questions in your gaze, my child. No, I'm not like Marzanna. Jaryło's betrayal corrupted her, but she let her anger consume her divinity. This… This darkness is a remnant of her power joined with Czarnobóg's. They took turns draining me of *žityje*, but there was something more. It was as if they stole fragments of my soul, leaving behind their corruption until they were whole again."

Wacław finally stood with his head bowed. "Lady Dziewanna, is that how Marzanna has extended her control beyond the equinox?"

"Yes." Mother studied him with pursed lips. "A curse weakens both Marzanna and Jaryło while the other lives. It prevented her from surviving the equinox for centuries. When Jaryło aligned his Moonstones with hers to release Czarnobóg, I was powerless to stop them both without my brother's aid. Jaryło has always been a coward, but he's gone too far this time. I knew his scheme, so he left me to die. I doubt he knew what Marzanna could do to me."

Liuda paced across the room, nibbling on what looked like a nut before looking up at Mother. "Excuse me, my lady, but this sounds as if everything has gone horribly wrong." She paused with a regretful look. "What… What does this mean for us? We're bound to these trees, and even if we leave, we'll perish with them when their last bits of life fade."

"Now that Otylia has freed me, I will do what I can to return life to the wilds. But much damage has been done. In order for the seasons to return, Marzanna must relent or die."

I took her hand, remembering the chill I'd felt touching her wisp. "End showed me what happened, but how could a goddess drain you entirely? We can only take *žityje* from offerings."

Mother sighed and leaned on me, suddenly shaky. Unlike the powerful goddess I'd followed and strong mother who'd raised me, her cheeks were sunken and her arms bony. I couldn't help but feel like a failure. I'd been her only szeptucha, and I hadn't even learned about her imprisonment until moons after the equinox.

"Żmij and corrupted Nawie face no such restrictions," she said. "I'm sure you've become familiar with Wacław's abilities if you've made it this far alive. Now imagine a being who shares a goddess's power and a demon's hunger, free from the restrictions Rod has placed on our kind. To Marzanna and Czarnobóg alike, I was a supply of *żityje* greater than any other they could find."

I scoffed. "And Jaryło just abandoned you."

"As did Perun and Weles, Strzybóg too—as he's ignored his responsibility to fly me to Marzanna's palace for decades. Lazy old man... I am not surprised my father would ignore my plight after I rebelled against him, but Weles had promised to protect me as his wife."

Mother shook her head and stared at the branches above. The light emanating from the tree exposed streaks of red slicing across her eyes like the cracks in a frozen river. "*He* chose to marry me. I was forced. The least Weles could do is leave Nawia for once instead of sending the god who stabbed me in the back to kill my daughter." Her cheeks reddened, the first color on her face since our arrival. "I will never forgive him for that."

Her anger in my defense stunned me. I didn't know how to accept that care, so I turned to Liuda instead. "Are the demons still outside? We can't waste time here. The Frostmarked Horde will reach eastern Krowik by the time we get back."

The nymph closed her eyes and sang like Sabina had when she'd used her magic. The tree pulsed with the rhythm, and catkins floated through the air, landing over Wacław's blond hair and bloodied clothes. I tried to smile at the demon covered in little white tufts. I couldn't. Between Mother's pain and the fight we'd barely escaped, I was wound tight enough to explode.

"The demons are gone," Liuda said with a relieved laugh.

I looked at Wacław. "Can you fly Mother? Waking her and flying out used too much of my *żityje*."

He gave a solemn smile and placed his płanetnik hat back on his head. A small thing, but I needed his calm care right now. "I have enough to help me find my next heart, little more. Are you sure you can fly even yourself? I felt how much you used to wake her, and if Sabina and Ara don't collect enough offerings, then—"

"They haven't failed yet," I replied, brow furrowed. "Both of them know what's at stake, and I have plenty of worshippers back in

Vastroth after we helped the Daughters of the Earth. Offerings not given to a szeptucha grant less *żityje* without the proper rituals, but it'll be enough for me to recover quickly."

He gave me a questioning look but offered no appeal. "If the demons are gone, then stay here and make a blood altar while I search for some to drain among their dead. Then, whoever has enough *żityje* can help carry Dziewanna."

"Because splitting up worked so well last time."

"Take the time to talk with her," his voice said in my head. *"You've been waiting four years for this. Gods know when you'll have the chance next."*

Before I could reply, Wacław turned to Liuda. "I'm sorry to trouble you further, but—"

The nymph waved her hands. "Yes, yes. I'm not used to helping demons, but if Dziewanna says so, then there you are."

Wacław started his thanks but never finished. The roots wrapped around him, and his eyes met mine as they pulled him under. *"I'll never get used to this."*

Stay safe, I replied. *Love you.*

"I love you too."

Then he was gone, and I was alone with a nymph and the woman I'd hoped to see for so long. There was so much to say. I'd believed she'd abandoned me for years, but Mother had always been there. My goddess. My protector. Where could I possibly start?

"Liuda," Mother said first, "if you wouldn't mind allowing us some privacy."

Liuda perked up at the excuse to leave. She threw down her nuts and smiled. "Of course. I was planning to forage anyway—not that much is left."

Once the roots had taken the nymph away, Mother grabbed me in a tight hug, clutching my head to her chest. "Come, my love. Let me hear about your struggles, and then I'll tell you all your father was too cowardly to speak of. Someone needs to tell you what it truly means to be a goddess."

5

Narcyz

You've gotta be kidding me. One break. ONE. That's all I wanted.

SNOW, ICE, AND THE GODS' COMBINED HATRED poured through the tear in the side of my leather boot. It stung like a dozen hornets. Or I assumed so. Never had been stung before, unlike stupid Kuba, who'd had welts on his face for a week after whacking a hive with a stick when we were little.

That iron mining jackal had the guts to laugh at me anyway.

"Aren't you the one always mumblin' about everybody else 'not respecting their gear'?" he yelled across the convoy of warriors from the Vastrothie desert, his long wolf-like snout sticking up in the air, waiting to get smacked.

Kuba had died once already. *Wonder what he'd come back as if I made it twice.*

Having his soul stuck in a jackal body hadn't shut him up at all. If anything, it had made him more determined to be heard. I didn't understand the underworld sorcery that had prevented him from returning as a human, but I sure as Oblivion needed rest and quiet so I could FIX MY BOOT.

But the convoy didn't stop for anyone. Led by the Simuk Xobas on horseback, his wavy black hair even more a mess than my boots, our army was five-thousand strong. The march stretched a long way along the narrow snow-covered trails just west of the Wyzra River. We were headed toward the Krowikie capital of Dwie Rzeki, but home seemed an eternity away.

I'd thought our village to be large once. It was the biggest in Krowik after all, but then I'd seen Huebia. Made us look like chumps. Vastroth had cities of stone with walls bigger than a warrior's ego while we built with wood and clay. Sure, we had *more* villages scattered throughout our lands, but that just made Krowik hard to defend. We'd have to try anyway. Home was home.

I stepped out of line to inspect my damaged boot. A deep split, basically tearing the whole thing in two with each step. I cursed. Pa would be disappointed when we arrived.

"Broken?" a gruff but excited voice said from behind me.

I turned to see Amten, a scorpion hunter Otylia had met and apparently befriended in Huebia, towering over me with a wide smile. He wore armor made out of giant yellow scorpion shells that clinked with every step. That was weird enough. Weirder still, Amten showed off his armor by putting it on over his heavy wool coat. Most warriors who wore armor—Krowikie rarely did as it weighed down the wearer—did so under their coat, so it actually fit. Not Amten. The result was the breastplate barely reaching the massive man's stomach as the knots connecting its pieces frayed.

"I've taken care of these boots for years," I replied. "Pa gave them to me when I finished my first hunt and earned the right for him to cut my hair and claim me."

Amten gave a single exaggerated laugh. "Silly tradition 'eh. Kids all got long hair before that?"

"It's a formality. Ma cut mine short all the time so I didn't singe it at the forge."

"Ah." He cocked his head like he didn't actually understand, but he moved on. "I fix yer boots, ya?"

I crossed my arms. "What do you want in return? Pa and me can make the best swords in Krowik, but you've already got that little needle thing."

He nodded and patted the short, thin blade at his hip. Despite his claims that it was effective at killing the smaller scorpions, I was skeptical. "They say you called thunder. Almost killed old high chief, ya? Show me."

"I would if I could." I flexed my forearm, where Wacław's red Eclipsemark formed the shape of the blood moon he was born beneath. "Don't know what happened. It could've been our thunder god, Perun, or something else."

"Work on it, ya? Then show Amten so I can test my armor."

I chuckled. The lines of warriors were now mixed with camp followers as Xobas's front guard gave way to the rest of the convoy. We'd need to catch up, but Kuba was up there, and I was enjoying talking to Amten more than I'd expected. "Deal. If I figure out how to channel lightning, I'll shoot you with it first."

"Aye!" He smacked my shoulder hard enough to leave a nice bruise. "Just let me know before letting it loose. Don't want charred bits lying 'bout. Ma wouldn't like that."

Then he marched past with some vague instructions to meet him after he'd thought about "how them boots gonna work best." I couldn't help but smile, and my foot hurt a bit less as I rejoined the group.

Maybe it'll be fine. Only a couple more days to Dwie Rzeki, and then—

The ground shook. Arrows darkened the sky as a deafening shout rang out from across the frozen Wyzra. Shirtless, spear wielding men rode hundreds of black horses from the forest and over the ice, right at our exposed flank.

"Shield wall!" I yelled in the shared clan and Vastrothie tongue as chaos spread among our ranks.

But the arrows fell as I raised my round shield. They ripped through our ranks, slaughtering warriors and civilians alike. In just a few heartbeats, I stood in a pool of red.

I wavered, my worry made worse as I realized I had no idea where Andrij had ended up. *Keep your head. Don't let them get to you.*

Two bone-tipped arrows had embedded themselves in my shield. They stuck out toward the charging Frostmarked as twenty Vastrothie lined up on either side of me. Shields overlapping and spears jutting through the bottom gaps, we braced for the impact of horse and rider. More shield walls formed along our entire convoy. They were too far away to connect in our scramble, so we'd have to hold ourselves. I hoped Andrij had found allies too.

The Frostmarked cavalry rolled forward like thunder. Hooves cracked ice and plowed through knee-deep snow with ease. Gray, dead skin peeled across the riders' uncovered torsos, and their eyes were fearless, empty.

Then they struck.

Their long bone spears plunged easily through the Vastrothie's hide shields. My wooden shield held, but I was no match for the weight of a charger. I had just enough time to impale the first rider through the sternum before his now riderless horse knocked me off my feet.

From the crimson ground, death's stench hit me as hard as the charge. I held my breath to avoid gagging, but vomit was the least of my concerns.

Our thin ranks were broken. We'd been at most two lines deep, and the cavalry had overrun most of the nearby warriors already. People fled everywhere, desperately dragging children and belongings away from the killing. But the Frostmarked saw no difference between warrior and innocent. Someone had to stop them. How?

So many others were better at playing the protector. Andrij would've known who to defend and how to lead the warriors around him. Wacław would've already saved the innocents and launched the cavalry away with the winds. Otylia would've killed the Frostmarked with a magic glare or something. They were skilled. I was just a warrior, a man who'd jumped the fire only moons before. My allies were in disarray, but I could only clutch my shield and spear without direction. I was no płanetnik, no sorcerer, no general.

A boy stumbled strides away. Short and clumsy, the snow reached his chest, and he cried out for his mother as a rider swooped toward him. His parents were too far.

I wasn't.

Leaping to my feet, I held my battered shield before me and met the charger in stride. A stupid strategy. A spearman was little use without a shield wall, but I had to try.

The rider's spear shattered my shield in a shower of wood shards. Pieces scraped my face and blocked my vision, but my defense delayed him. The rider rounded wide, gaze fixed on me instead of the boy. Good. If he was going to kill, at least I could make sure he'd fall too.

He charged, his mount kicking up snow of red and white with each stride. My fingers burned against the frigid shaft of my spear. My heart hit my chest like a hammer to hot iron. This was it. Albin always said warriors knew when the death blow was coming. A sixth sense. He'd claimed the only thing you could do was make sure you took the other bastard with you to bring Perun's justice.

I barely blinked before the charger arrived. Spears clashed. His horse huffed, its mouth foaming and its eyes wild as it trampled corpses underfoot. My thrust found the rider's heart, and I hoped at least Perun would smile at my victory. Because I sure didn't.

Pain consumed my mind. I dropped my spear, crumpling into the snow.

Everything was red. My blood? Something throbbed in my chest, and another wound seared across my shoulder. Every breath was agony. Blood filled my throat, forcing me to cough to avoid choking, which only brought more pain.

Screams rang out from far away. Or near. It all seemed so distant yet loud. A terrible taste coated my tongue, and I realized I'd vomited. I had no control over my body as it fought to survive. I wished to black out. I wished for it to end. But the battle continued before me in gruesome detail, deaths on both sides adding to the pile of bodies that had once been our shield wall.

Had the boy escaped? It had all happened so fast. He was no longer where he'd been, and I prayed to Swaróg of the forge that he shield the child with his armor. *I don't deserve a blessing. Just give it to him.*

Then the front line shifted. A line of dark-skinned warriors in tortoise shell armor came into sight as the ground itself entangled the cavalry and shielded the Vastrothie elites.

Ta-naro's short frame ducked and weaved through the fight. The Mothermarked szeptucha threw circular weapons made of three spiraling glass blades before channeling Mokosz's power to skewer riders with stone spears. Other szeptuchy joined her along with a group of water demons, female rusałki and male utopiecs, who Otylia had freed from their corruption. They were away from their element, but they were more than capable fighters.

As they swept past me, a familiar voice broke through the roar. "Narcyz, gods! Narcyz, stay still. I'll get a healer."

"Andrij…" I mumbled through blood and bile.

"Shhh. Don't push it."

He took my hand, worry filling his deep eyes. The battle disappeared in that moment. All I saw was his ruffled brown hair, that birth mark on his jaw that looked like a fisherman's hook, and the care in his gaze. I'd have given everything to have more time with him. To tell him how deep my feelings were.

"We managed to organize a defense in the front guard," he said, "but I didn't know where you went. Kuba said you'd fallen back to worry about your boot." He bit his cheek and took a deep breath. "When I saw the mid-lines in shambles, I thought I'd lost you."

Maybe you did anyway.

"You'll be all right, Narcyz. I promise. Looks like the spear just clipped you, but why did you think you could stand alone in front of a charger? It could've killed you!"

I focused on every word. They were all I had of reality—that and pain. It made my boot seem meaningless. A few minutes changed everything, and I wondered if I'd have even a few more.

"You sure you don't have any of that lightning?" Andrij asked, trying and failing to smile. Tears wetted his cheeks. A bad sign. "Wacław can't give you even that?"

My marked arm lay before me. I stared at that pulsing red moon, as bloodied as the battlefield. Its glow slowly faded. My vision went with it, and soon, mercifully, the end took me away. I hoped Otylia would be kind just this one time.

6

Ara

I get why Otylia was so obsessed with becoming a szeptucha.

MY HAIR BLEW IN THE BITTER BREEZE as I channeled Otylia's moonlight. Tense, my entire body ached from the effort. I'd rolled up the sleeves of my hunting tunic, and the chill burned against my extended arms.

I couldn't stop.

Nothing could match sorcery. I loved shooting my bow on any day, but even the satisfying *twang* of the bowstring was inferior to power radiating from my hands. Well, technically, it was Otylia's power. I controlled it now that I was her szeptucha, though, and it felt amazing!

Sorcery took more practice than I had time, unfortunately. Between advising Zakir on his decisions as marzban of the Simukie Clan and collecting offerings for Otylia, I'd ended up channeling deep into the night most days since our return from Vastroth. I felt bad that Narcyz, Andrij, Kuba, Ta, and Xobas had to walk back with the Vastrothie army when Sabina, Vlatka, and I could fly, but my other worries were greater.

The Frostmarked Horde was coming. Much of Krowik would burn, and it was up to me to make sure the clans didn't burn with it.

Sure, I wanted Krowik to survive too, along with everyone else who wasn't a bloodsucking undead. But priorities were priorities. As long as I was with Zakir, I would do whatever it took to ensure he succeeded as marzban of clan Simuk. It would be *very* hard for him to succeed with the entire clan dead.

"Your illusions have gotten better," my wavy-haired lover said from his seat across the clearing from me, shivering in his long woolen coat. His gaze remained fixed on the clay vial in his grasp. He'd agreed to step away from his alchemical tests only if I agreed to let him bring it, whatever it was.

"If only illusions could defeat an army," I replied with an exhausted huff that fogged the air before me.

Channeling took my energy as well as Otylia's. She claimed the deity lost more *žityje* than the szeptucha, but I doubted she was ready to faint from an hour of forming warriors out of moonlight. The potential diversion had been Zakir's idea. With Xobas away, leading the Vastrothie to Dwie Rzeki, Zakir's tactics were the highest commands. I was skeptical of their merit.

Zakir looked up from his potion, only for a moment. "You like hunting. Hunting isn't about power or superior numbers. You succeed by planning and waiting for your target to come to you."

I paused in the middle of forming another warrior's shield. I'd made nearly twenty men and women, but Zakir had hoped I could make enough for it to appear like a small army at night. "That actually makes a lot of sense."

"It is logical. Our scouts say we have fewer warriors than the Horde. Any head-to-head fight will lead to our defeat. That means we must make them fight the way we want to fight. Perhaps this is easier when they are undead warriors and demons led by a psychotic goddess."

"Did you just make a joke?" I laughed, pleased to hear a genuine attempt at something other than intellectual discussion from him.

He grinned. It was just a small curl at the ends of his mouth, but for him, that was beaming. "You liked it? I have been trying to watch people like you said. The commanders often comment about women making irrational decisions immediately before making their own irrational decisions. It is confusing, but I believe it is meant to be a joke."

That tore me from my moonweaving. Giggling, I stepped through the illusory warriors and gave him a kiss. "Those men are being stupid. They don't understand when they're being exactly what they mock."

"People are odd."

"We're better that way." I grabbed his potion from him. "Come. The Krowikie will be celebrating the solstice with Noc Kupały in a few days. We need to be rested, because the preparations will be chaos."

He cocked his head. "Celebrating a fertility festival ahead of a battle capable of destroying the living realm is an—"

"Illogical decision, yes."

"Then why do they celebrate?"

"Because, my dear," I said, pulling him to his feet and planting another kiss on his lips. "Keeping people happy is often as important as keeping them alive. We need reminders of what and who we fight for. Plus, their priests say it's the most magical night of the year, with spirits more powerful than ever. We could use some extra magic against the Horde if you ask me."

Following the hints I'd given him many times, he threw his coat over my shoulders and held my waist as we made our way through the canvas tents. Many people were still up, despite the late hour, and they greeted us in traditional Simukie fashion—two fingers pressed to the nose, then extended toward the other person. I'd been born Zurgowie, but I'd slowly picked up the customs of Zakir's clan.

Sleeplessness had become a common custom among both clans. Many feared their nightmares after the slaughters we'd faced outside Kynnytsia. King Boz of Astiw had killed thousands. I still heard the screams many nights, and only channeling managed to get them out of my head. In truth, I had it better than others. Most had lost family and friends, while my own family had been safe in Dwie Rzeki. They'd since joined us, but nowhere was truly safe anymore.

Torches lit our scattered camp. Simukie and Zurgowie lived among each other for once, our numbers too scarce for us to fight separately. More than that, we'd suffered together. That shared pain had bonded the clans more than old rivalries could divide.

We'd made camp in an open plain a day's ride south of Dwie Rzeki. Close enough to reinforce each other's armies but far enough to avoid quarrels among the people. *That* divide was one we still needed to improve, as differences of beliefs and languages were difficult to overcome. Many Krowikie saw us as eastern invaders that had led the way for the Horde. Even before the Horde, though, refugees like me had been outsiders, and I wondered if our peoples could ever truly live in peace without the Horde's threat to unite us.

As we neared Zakir and my tent atop a small hill in the camp's center, Otylia's Moonmark burned on my neck. I tensed. She'd been close to finding Dziewanna the last time she'd spoken through her mark. Had she found her mother?

"Ara, we did it," she said in my mind, her usually sharp voice now exasperated. *"We freed Mother from Marzanna's palace, but she's drained and disconnected from her power."*

What's she like? I asked silently as I pushed aside the flap and stepped into our tent.

"I can't describe it. She's my mother still, but she's different. I should've expected it since I know the truth about both of us now, but I served Dziewanna for years without knowing she was my mother. Every time I say something, I'm worried she'll disagree."

Children argue with their parents. It's what we do.

She sighed. *"I just… I want to prove to her that I'm worth all the pain she went through to keep me away from Weles. She's supposed to be the one to kill Marzanna, but without her power, is that on me now? How can I do what she couldn't?"*

All good questions, but no one expects you to solve them in a day.

I paced over the woolen rugs covering the tent's bottom. Zakir lit a small fire in its center, and the smoke curled through the gaps in the fabric above. I breathed it in, trying to figure out a reply when I had little understanding of Krowikie gods, let alone what it meant to have a goddess for a mother. So I settled on a mortal experience.

Mother used to try and make me weave with her, I finally said. *I was awful at it. My fingers wanted to move all the wrong directions, and my feet tapped, desperate to move. For a long time, I kept at it anyway. I wanted her to be proud of me. Until one day, she threw down her needles and pointed outside as Father was preparing for another hunting trip. "Go with him," she said. "You're a child of the bow, no matter how hard I try to make you otherwise." I thought she was upset, but then she wrapped me in a hug and thanked me for spending the time with her. Maybe that's what Dziewanna wants right now. Just to know the daughter she's missed for so long. I mean, she's hundreds of years old and you're the first she's ever had. Of course she missed you.*

There was a pause before Otylia replied, *"I hadn't thought about it like that. Thanks... I've missed you lately, but I guess one advantage of you becoming my szeptucha is being able to talk from far away."*

I smiled to myself, which caused Zakir to raise his brow. *Well, consider these conversations temporary replacements. We all want you back, and not just because you could moonblast the Horde to Oblivion.*

"I'll try." Her tone shifted, growing more serious. *"I wish I was reaching out just about my relationship with mother."*

Please tell me Wacław didn't have another episode.

"Thank the gods, no. My ritual in Huebia worked, and Zakir's żityje potions have helped whenever he gets desperate. It's about the Horde." Another pause. *"Wacław heard from Kuba. Some of the Frostmarked apparently crossed the Wyzra and attacked the army Vastroth sent us."*

I grabbed Zakir's shoulder quickly, speaking aloud to him, "The Vastrothie were attacked. You should gather the commanders... and Zhaleh. The Zurgowie need to know about this too."

"Will you come?" he asked flatly. If he was concerned, it didn't show in his eyes. "Meetings proceed better when you are there."

"Once I'm done with Otylia."

He nodded before approaching his few coats lying across our bed. Per usual, he avoided the one lined in wolf's fur that High Chief Mikołaj had offered him for coming to Krowik's aid, taking the more informal wool one again and strapping a sheepskin cape over his left shoulder.

"Good choice," I said. "You look like Katiôn did as marzban."

Zakir's head drooped. "That comparison is not fair to Grandfather, but thank you." He uncorked one of his potions and downed it, wincing at the taste. "I will see you soon." Still grimacing, he left the tent.

Sorry, I replied to Otylia. *I needed Zakir to alert the commanders about the attack. We'll have to get word to Mikołaj too.*

"I'll let Sabina know, but I wanted to talk with you first."

My chest tightened into a ball, and I sat on the bed, gripping the frame as I finally asked what I was afraid to. *Are our friends okay?*

"Xobas and Andrij are fine. Kuba took a slash to his side but will recover." *Narcyz?*

"He..." She paused, her voice raspy. "He almost died. A horse struck him when he stopped its rider from killing a child. I never thought I'd care about that brute being hurt, but he hasn't woken up since the battle. The Vastrothie lost a lot of people pushing back the attack, and this wasn't even the Horde's main force."

You're always a ray of sunshine, you know that? I took relief knowing my friends had survived, but it all felt so temporary. What were a few more weeks of life when the Horde was going to crush us anyway?

"Well, I am the goddess of the moon."

When will you be back?

"By Noc Kupały, as long as the demons don't catch us again."

I sighed. *Sounds like quite the story.*

"I'll tell you more when we get back. Just stay alive until then."

You too.

I warmed my hands over the fire for a moment before grabbing my coat and heading to join Zakir and the commanders. Some of them would question my trust of a Krowikie goddess, but whose gods were whose didn't matter anymore. Marzanna and Czarnobóg would slaughter us whether we believed in them or not.

"Gods help us," I muttered, pushing open the tent.

A swordsman met me.

Silver flashed in his hand, and the fire illuminated his blond hair as he threw me back into the tent. I fell into a heap, sending rugs sprawling. Before I could fight to my feet, he was over me, one hand gripping my shirt and the other holding his blade to my neck.

"Little szeptucha," Jaryło said with a savage smirk. "You are coming with me."

7

Otylia

They could find us at any time.

SLEEP WAS HARD MOST DAYS. It was even worse when I had to worry whether the strzygi who'd guarded Mother would find us.

I jabbed my knees in the back of Wacław's thighs as the snow creaked outside. One of the few advantages of sleeping in the daylight was seeing any threats immediately. There was no movement in End's wisps outside, but I kept my eye on the opening from across our snow bunker.

"What was that for?" Wacław whispered, wriggling to get comfortable again.

One of us needs to watch the entrance, I replied through our bond.

"It's been three days. They've had plenty of time to catch us if they were going to."

They have forever. They're basically immortal until we kill them.

He rolled over to face me. *"Good point."*

This close, our knees bumped into each other and his morning breath was rancid, but I just studied every inch of his face. Not the demonic veins crossing his cheeks or his ridiculously blue eyes. What was beneath. The faint sun freckles dotting his cheeks, the little hairs that tickled my lips when I kissed him, and the scattered scars he bore like a hardened warrior.

What did he see when he looked at me? I know he did often enough. Mother had said during our time in Liuda's tree that men had a habit of that, and she still couldn't tell when they were trying to understand us and when they were trying to unclothe us.

"Why are you grinning?" he asked. *"I thought we were in mortal danger."*

Nothing. I pushed my head into his chest, hoping he didn't insist on an answer. There was too much on my mind between Mother and the Horde. There was no time for worrying what Wacław thought about me.

He chuckled and ran his fingers through my hair. Against my instincts, I gave into the care, closing my eyes and listening to his breaths. *"I know you're lying,"* he said, *"but I love you anyway."*

Just because my eyes were shut, that didn't mean I wasn't listening. And when another shift came from across the bunker, I popped my head up again, only to see Mother stretching. She noticed me and smiled.

"You have the look of a wild cat, Otylka," she said with a soft laugh. "If Wacław is that frightening, I will happily tear him from your arms."

I blushed. How was I supposed to respond to my mother joking about our relationship? It was hard enough to have one already. "I just didn't sleep well," I said, prying myself from Wacław's embrace. He gave a disappointed groan, but I was far too self-conscious now.

"I can't blame you," Mother continued. "Life as a fledgling goddess is difficult enough without the responsibility of protecting your powerless mother and the rest of Jawia." She peered through the entrance and into the forest beyond. "However, you were never a calm child, always squirming and babbling to yourself late into the night. Dariusz joked that you were learning the old tongue already."

Mother had spoken sarcastically, but thinking of life before didn't make me laugh. I pulled my legs to my chest, allowing End's wisps to drift around me. Their distractions were welcome, and they let me see if anyone was near.

"How long until nightfall?" Wacław asked as he sat up and rubbed his eyes.

"We have an hour or so," Mother replied. "Dadźbóg is almost to the horizon, but I worry for him. He hasn't been himself lately."

"It's hard to miss him when he hasn't bothered to help us," I said. "Neither has Perun."

"Each of us has our own alignments," Mother replied.

Wacław pulled his coat over his shoulders—noticeably broader than when we'd left after the equinox. "Do you think Marzanna has done something to Dadźbóg? What if Czarnobóg corrupted him too?"

Mother scowled. "I don't dare think of it. My uncle is pure of heart and has done nothing but protect mortals while Perun and Weles fought for power. He is their brother, but he does not seek to rule." Then she pulled herself out of the bunker, not allowing him to reply.

"I'll follow her," I said after a moment of awkward silence. "Keep an eye out until sundown."

Wacław gave me half-a-smile through his stunned expression. I just rolled my eyes and followed Mother into the waning light. He'd stumbled over his words more than usual with Mother in recent days, and it had to be about our relationship. Ever since I'd taken his mortal soul, he'd become more assertive, so it was odd to see him returning to the cautious boy he'd been before. I loved him either way.

Mother's cheeks were already red from the cold by the time I reached her. Standing at the base of an alder tree, she held a hand to its trunk with her eyes closed. She still had Dziewanna's biting fury, but this woman was more sorrowful than both my goddess and mother. I didn't even know how to talk to her. How was I supposed to help her recover from Marzanna and Czarnobóg's torture?

"You okay?" I asked, stopping further from her than was appropriate. Even my words were too casual, and I'd been unable to be completely honest with her in the few times we'd been alone. Ara had tried to reassure me, but my gut told me I was doing this all wrong.

"No."

My heart ached already. Yet I kept my distance, my boots feeling like they were caught in snow deep enough to swallow me whole. "I'm sorry," I said through my cracking voice. "We should've come sooner. I tried, but when the demon took Wašek—"

"No, my *mała dziką*. You have done far more than anyone should have asked of you. Especially your mother."

I smiled at her calling me her little wildling again, and tears welled in my eyes for the thousandth time since her death. I wiped them away. Wacław was too far to hear, but he'd see me crying. There was a time for it. Not now.

"Why didn't you tell me?" I asked, stepping toward her. "About myself? About Marzanna? You said in the Lake of Reflection that you were trying to protect me, but how is *this* protecting me?"

She opened her eyes. Pain lingered in them, but she did not weep as she lingered in her thoughts for a moment longer. When she spoke, her voice was strained. "You deserve the truth, so here it is: Destiny told me the Sudiczki's fates for me when I Ascended. The first fate claimed I would inherit Jawia instead of Jaryło. The second decreed that despite my stubbornness, I would love another so greatly that neither I nor my power would be the same. The third…" She clenched her fists and looked away. "The hag spoke of you."

My own fates raced through my mind as I approached her. "Mine weren't much different." I checked that Wacław was far enough not to hear before I continued, "The first said I would be Wacław's queen—whatever that means anymore. The second foresaw me becoming the goddess of endings, and I think Destiny meant that she knew I would struggle with it. She was right about that much."

"And the hag?" Mother asked.

"You first."

She smiled, the warm kind that only a mother was capable of. "You are certainly my daughter. Weles was likely aghast at your attitude, but I find it best to keep him on his toes. He's a grouch otherwise."

I returned her smile, but it faded at the memory of my blood father shattering my bones. "That's putting it nicely…"

"It is, but you asked about the final Sudiczka." She wrinkled her nose and shook her head. "The hag foresaw that the one I loved would suffer beyond what words can describe. I didn't believe Destiny's claims about the Sudiczki for centuries until I birthed you."

Again, I mirrored her. "Oh."

"That's why I left you out of my plan. I believed if I could defeat Czarnobóg with Jaryło, then we could entrap Marzanna in Nawia until autumn as usual."

"But Jaryło betrayed you."

"Yes," she grumbled. "That selfish fool was the one to release the black dragon, but he underestimated Czarnobóg. Even together, we weren't enough to defeat him. I saw how great his influence was, and I feared Marzanna would fall under his control, pulling her deeper into her corruption. The rest… Ack! You saw what happened when I confronted both Jaryło and Marzanna on the equinox."

Mother took my hand and squeezed. "I failed you. Now, I have no understanding of how to reconnect with the force of the wilds."

"The hag's omen scared me too," I said with emotions swirling in my stomach. Why did this have to be so hard? "I pushed Wacław away because Destiny said his corruption would kill me, but that just made everything worse. It would've been better if she'd never told me."

"I'm sorry." She raised my hands to her lips and kissed them. "I wish I could have prevented your suffering, but that pursuit only made you endure more. Fate is a horrible weight to bear. It was cruel for Rod to place it upon your shoulders."

"I'm glad he did."

She raised her brow. "You are? Since you revived me, I haven't heard you say anything positive about End's influence over you."

I scoffed at myself. "You're right. Seeing people's ends, good or bad, is a burden, but my force allowed me to free the demons in Sheresy and children in Huebia. End has shown me that just because something ends, doesn't mean that it's finished. Ugh. Does that even make sense?"

"It does. My father believes in justice, but he fails to recognize the world's cycle. Every end is a new beginning, no matter how painful."

"Right." I glanced back at Wacław. Sleep would've made him shift between his body and soul-form once, and I remembered how different he'd once been as he paced between the shadowed trees and the light of the shadowed sun. "Moonblasts and flying are fun too, but I miss channeling the wilds with you. Back when I didn't have a promise to Death hanging over my head too." I still hadn't told Wacław about the deal I'd made to save him after the Trial of Death. I would… eventually.

"You've grown strong, Otylka. It was time for you to leave my nest, but I was too worried to see it. In the end, it matters not. The force you wield now is greater than mine or even Jaryło's if you search it to its deepest depths. Even Death may fear you then."

I winced, remembering the vision of Wacław and me in the dark whirlwind. Whose end had that been? Ours? Jawia's? "What if I don't like what I find there?"

Mother grinned and laid a hand on my shoulder as she walked past. "Then change it. Rod warns us against altering fate, but what is a goddess of endings without the strength to mend what's broken and slay what's evil?"

"Nothing."

"Exactly." She nodded toward Wacław. "He has waited long enough."

Wacław took the gesture as permission to approach, and he bowed his head slightly to Mother as he did. "With the Horde's attack against the Vastrothie, we need to hurry. Flying on my winds may be better until nightfall. I have plenty of *żityje* for now, and Otylia can carry me at night if I run low. Lady Dziewanna, if you are okay with a demon helping you fly, I—"

Mother swatted at him as sarcasm slipped the sorrow from her voice. "Quit the formalities. I knew you were a Naw before Dariusz drew his own conclusions. The priest would've killed you as your mother fled the longhouse if I hadn't stopped him. I also knew you loved Otylia before you understood what it was to be fond of a girl." She stepped forward, towering over him despite his superior height. "So, son of Lubena and that imbecilic high chief I won't bother to name, yes, you may use Strzybóg's grandchildren to fly me. Be careful, though. I *am* your Otylka's mother. You'll never get Weles's blessing, so you'll need mine if you ever want to wed our daughter."

I stifled a laugh as Wacław flushed bright pink—adorable, even against his blackened veins. He swallowed. "Yes, Dziewanna. Best we begin now."

The winds rushed around us, lifting all of us as I closed my eyes, exhausted in mind and body. But my heart was full for the first time since we'd rescued Mother. Trading stories of the Sudiczki's fates had revealed how similar our worries were, despite how different our relationship had become. We'd figure out how to restore her power. We'd figure out how to defeat Czarnobóg, Marzanna, and the Horde. And when the dark gods dared to show their faces, we'd make them wish for Oblivion.

8

Wacław

Two goddesses and a Naw. We're quite the traveling party.

THE WINDS ECHOED MY SNARLS as I stood atop a mountain far to the northeast of the range we called Perun's Crown. Another blizzard had struck just when I'd reached the peak. In the time I'd risen, though, I'd seen my worst fears.

Smoke, thick and black, rolled across the late-night sky in waves. It collided with the winter storm, turning hail to frozen ash and choking me with each breath. The west burned. Koschei and his Frostmarked Horde ravaged my homeland, and there was nothing I could do to stop it. I had slain a god and flown to Nawia, but Marzanna's blizzard trapped me far from my people now.

I'm coming, Mom. I promise.

After relaying what I'd seen to Otylia, I started my descent down the mountain. Unfortunately, the storm also prevented me from doing so with any grace. I had enough grasp on the winds to drift downward, but that control came and went without warning. Each gust battered my face as I clung to the cliff edges, waiting for my next chance to drop safely.

My delayed return would at least give Otylia longer with Dziewanna. Their discussion the day before had finally led to some comfort between the two of them. It was difficult to talk in the air, and they needed every moment together—without me.

It hurt a little to be left out of those conversations, but they deserved more time than they had. Otylia had been without her mother for years, believing her to be dead. I'd felt her pain through our bond. Nothing, though, could let me truly grasp the depths of that sorrow for four years. Even holding Mom's body for a single moment when I'd thought she'd died had been too much. That's all it had been, a moment. I'd channeled Kwiecień's Moonblade to save her, but Otylia had possessed no godly weapon as a child.

The blizzard weakened by the time I reached our camp in the valley below an hour later. The smoke had spurred me to scout in the first place, but now that I was sure of its source, I wished I hadn't.

Ara and the clans had seen Kynnytsia burn in the distance during their retreat over the last moon. Few of them mourned.the fall of the Astiwie capital after King Boz's ambush, but his people shared our tribe's bloodlines. Many, if not most, would die because of Boz's arrogance. I prayed Krowik would fare better. My half-brother Mikołaj had his own cockiness, but he'd listened to my warnings, sent through Narcyz. That reassured me he would at least not be blind like Mieczysław. It would be enough. Hopefully…

Firelight soon revealed Otylia's form through the swirling snow and hail. White covered her coat and the hairs that slipped free from her hood. There was new light in her eyes. Though her mother's had become dulled and muddy, Otylia's pierced the storm, straight into my heart.

We exchanged a small smile when I reached her, and she startled me by leaning in for a long kiss. Her fingers ran through my hair as I held her waist, our hips touching and passion rushing through our bond. We endured each other's pain at our worst. In these few glorious moments, we shared our joy and the thrill of being in the other's arms. I treasured my ability to fly and dance with the winds, but I'd surrender it all to be with her. She was the moon, and I was the night sky reaching for her light.

"You have no idea what this means to me," she said, glancing toward our sleeping burrow when we parted. "Mother is resting for now. Things were weird at first between us, but every moment I spend with her… It's all I've dreamed of for years. She understands how hard it's been to Ascend. She knows more about the Three Realms than I could've ever hoped to before."

I pressed my lips to her forehead. "You two belong together. Even when she raised you, she pretended you were both mortals so she could stay close to you. I'm glad you can finally get to know her for real."

"I've always loved each part of her—mother and goddess—but it's amazing to see her entirely. Even if she's powerless for now, she's still Dziewanna. She's still my mother."

Otylia's smile alone melted Marzanna's frost. This side of her was one she showed no one except those she loved, and even then she often had walls to protect herself. I loved how strong she was. But more than that, I loved when she didn't have to be.

Her smile disappeared quickly, and she laid her head against my chest. "I shouldn't be acting so excited when our tribe is threatened. You're letting me rant about my mother when yours is in the Horde's path."

"You deserve to be happy, Otylka," I said, slipping my hands around her waist for both warmth and care. "I'll see my mother soon, but I do miss her a lot. We barely had any time together after Bidaês's attack… I still can't believe that happened."

"Lubena is alive because of you, and I'm sure little Nevenka is looking forward to seeing you again."

"Is she?" I nuzzled my head into hers as I thought about my little half-sister. It hurt to remember the hurt I'd caused through the demon's rage, but she felt safe in a world trying to kill me. "The last time I was home, I nearly went into a rampage, and Nevenka saw all of it. It doesn't matter who I heal when I'm the one causing the damage."

She ran her fingers across my neck and met my gaze, her brow furrowed. "You channeled a Moonstone's power to steal Lubena from Death himself! Nawie aren't supposed to care. They kill. You're *good*, Wašek. Sometimes, you're too good, but I need that side of you. Mother sees how important you are too."

"What did you talk about while I was gone?" I asked, hoping for a more comfortable topic. "I imagine there's a lot."

She sighed and pulled her coat tighter, looking west. Dogoda's wind was usually kind from that direction, but now it blew with a great gust that threw Otylia's hood down. Her hair came free, unkept yet beautiful as it flowed over her reddened ears and through the air behind her. The silver fox pelt seemed to stare at me over her shoulder, unnerving.

"Mother wanted to hear everything that had happened since the equinox," she said. "Apparently, she'd fallen in and out of consciousness as Marzanna and Czarnobóg drained her. When she contacted you through the golden egg in the Mangled Woods, she didn't know what would happen to her. That was the last thing she remembered."

"She gave me the last of her *żityje* so I could live long enough to save you," I replied, guilt strangling my gut. "And all I've done since is surrender to my demon."

"You did what she asked. Gods rarely trust demons, but Mother trusted you to expel Marzanna's Curse from me and then rescue me from Nawia. She knew you're more than your corruption, and you've shown that too."

I turned away. Her reassurances couldn't fix the screaming faces I saw in my nightmares. All the people I'd killed…

"What did she think about our journeys?" I asked.

"She said she's proud of me." I couldn't see her smile, but I heard her relief and felt it in my soul. "She never wanted me to suffer without her, but she knew she had to try to end Marzanna's corruption instead of just killing her sister. Jaryło ruined everything for her and now for me too."

I winced at the reminder of Otylia's blood pact with Jaryło. In return for him not harming her loved ones, he'd forced her to agree to marry him. Ever since she'd ended the Płanetnik's control over me, I'd searched for holes in the oath. There was a single clear one: Otylia could not harm Jaryło, but nothing in the pact prevented me from doing so. I pictured myself ramming Marzanna's Thunderstone dagger through his heart. Perhaps it would serve her intended purpose for a second time.

"I'll kill him every time he dares approach you!" my voice thundered, throwing the winds over the fire and sending its sparks scattering through the snow. "Though Jaryło isn't corrupted himself, he's the source of all of this. No matter what happens with Marzanna and Czarnobóg, he needs to pay. I'll kill him again and again until we can take his Alatyr shards and make him endure an eternity of torture."

When I turned to meet Otylia's gaze, a grin pulled at her lips. "Mother said the same, but she can't fight until we figure out how to restore her power."

"Then I'll kill him for her too."

"Good, bec—"

Screams ripped through the storm. A dozen at least, they echoed off the cliffs surrounding the valley, making them difficult to track until Otylia's eyes flashed white.

"To the south! Demons are attacking a group."

I drew Grudzień. "I'll check it out. Stay with Dziewanna in case the Frostmarked were tracking us. Dadźbóg will rise soon, and I can't have you losing much of your powers mid-fight."

She protested, but I was already charging through the snow. If demons were attacking mortals, it was far from a fair fight. Luckily, I could grant them some aid as long as the winds obeyed.

The gales lifted me at my call, my power returning as the blizzard slowly passed. Most storms granted me strength. I missed them, as Marzanna's unnatural blizzards disconnected me from my power. The winds could usually scour the lands and air when I needed them too, but amid her snowfall they refused to listen once they were a few strides from me. I was entering a battle blind.

The melee soon appeared. Four human-like figures chased a group of unarmed people. The victims left behind sleds full of supplies as they ran, but the demons focused only on the slowest of the group, swarming like wolves. They lunged at the man nearest to me.

I released the winds completely, dropping between the demons and their prey a moment before they struck. Only the man seemed surprised. As he startled and ran, the demons turned their attention to me. Their eyes were slits, and they ran their tongues across their sharp fangs. Each wore black armor over decaying skin that peeled across their oddly human faces, both the brown of the eastern clans and pale of our tribes. Whatever the armor's make, it allowed their movements to be silent as they shrieked and struck.

I swept the winds across me to throw the first aside. The others attacked my flank, but I spun away to push another back with a gust. With two stumbling in the deep snow, I turned to a third... too slowly.

Its teeth pierced my neck as its claws tore through my side. I tried to kick it away, but it held tight, biting harder and sucking blood from my veins. Panic took over as I flailed. The three others were upon me before I could think.

So I stopped thinking.

Wrapping the winds around me, I held my power in a tight ball before letting go. A wave rippled through the air, and the demons shrieked as they crashed amid the scattered sleds.

I leaped after the one that had bit me. It bared its teeth from behind a full sled, my black blood dripping from its fangs and its exposed arms bulging larger with each breath. The winds pushed me faster, but by the time I landed on the sled's back, the demon had doubled in size. Bidaês had been a massive wilkołak. This monster made him look like a child.

The demon charged as I pushed the sled with both my legs and the winds. The two collided in a shower of shattered pots and woolen clothes.

The demon's shrieks turned from excited to vicious, but it had fallen, allowing me to jump the sled on the winds and land over it. Its claws met Grudzień as I drove my jagged blade at the demon's head. *Just die!*

A *crunch* in the snow behind alerted me to another demon. I released the one below me and spun, pulling and throwing my dagger into the second's forehead in a quick sweep. It groaned and died as

I yanked the hilt with the winds. The fallen demon had pushed to its feet behind me, but I whipped the dagger around and struck its heart—or where its heart should've been.

The demon lumbered on.

I growled, taking a strike from its claws across my arm and countering with a wind gust that sent it to the ground face first. The two others had recovered now. I needed to be quick.

A windblast at the advancing demons bought me time to finish the monstrous one. Grudzień sliced through the air, its streaks of light the only color beyond the gray moonlight. When it struck, it tore through the demon's thick neck.

The beast's head rolled free, and I yanked my dagger from its chest. The earth shook when it hit the ground, spanning the full distance between me and its allies. I huffed. *Good riddance.*

I became aware of my dwindling *żityje* then. How? I hadn't used hardly that much, yet each use of the winds stressed my soul more. There was no time to ponder further. Neither of the remaining demons seemed dismayed by their reduced numbers.

The fleeing people were far from sight now. I wished I could've learned more about these new demons. Even if Otylia had come with me, though, I doubted she'd have been able to redeem them as she'd done with the rusałki and utopiecs in Vastroth. Some demons had no Threads of Life left. I wondered if Oblivion or this existence was worse for them.

The demons attacked from both sides, shrieking horrifically with each stride. A decent flanking attempt, but I flipped up and over their slashing claws, landing behind them with my blades ready.

The right one fell with a quick slash across the throat—not enough to kill a demon. By the time the second turned, I called lightning to my fingers and drove a bolt directly into its skull. The bleeding one could barely stand behind me, and one stab with Grudzień ended what life remained.

Demons dead, I rocked back on my heels and took a long breath. Then another. *That should've been easier.*

My *żityje* had slipped away so quickly, and without the full power of the winds, the demons had been faster than me. That alone was jarring. I'd faced szeptuchy, nymphs, and even gods, yet the ferocity of those demons was unmatched, even by strzygi. Other demons seemed to hold some piece of humanity in them. These… These were something else. A single bite from one had almost drained me, and it had used that *żityje* to grow even stronger. What would they be capable of on a battlefield with thousands of warriors?

Black blood covered my coat and face as I knelt over the first demon to slice open its chest. Being this drained was dangerous. I still had enough life force to fly, but healing my wounds drew upon what remained.

I'd suffered from a lack of *żityje* enough to know I never wanted to again. Otylia had traded part of her soul for mine to save me the first time I'd run out, and only Dziewanna sending the last of her strength through the Golden Egg kept me alive the second time. It was easier to replenish *żityje* now that Otylia and I could exchange it freely through our shared marks, but to avoid being a burden on her, I preferred eating animals' or demons' hearts to take it from their blood. Each movement was a slog nonetheless until I bit into the first heart and felt the familiar thrill of power fill my soul.

I'm in control now, I reminded myself. The Płanetnik's anger lingered within me, but his hunger was far weaker. Otylia had mended my soul, mostly, by creating a new oath of unconditional love to replace Father's broken one. I was fine.

Movement.

The winds alerted me to the arrow faster than any mortal sense. It pierced the snowfall, now little more than fluffy flakes, and shot toward my head. I snatched it out of the air before it could find its mark.

The archer's jaw dropped. Clothed in a long gray coat tied shut across a seam from his left shoulder to right hip, tufts of his light brown hair crept from beneath his woolen cap. His bow curved heavily above and below one hand, and the other pulled the string back again. The bronze-tipped arrow matched the one in my grasp.

"I'm not your enemy," I called to him in the clan tongue. It felt ridiculous saying such a thing moments after consuming a demon's heart. To these people, I surely looked as much a monster as the ones I'd killed, and I cursed myself for not going invisible first. "These demons are hunting us too."

Please understand me. There was no way to know if these people shared a language with Xobas's Simukie and Ara's Zurgowie clans, but it was surely closer than Krowikie.

The man slackened his bowstring but didn't lower the weapon. When he spoke, none of his quick, deep words were familiar, and his frown deepened at my lack of reply.

I sheathed my weapons and raised my hands. The pose hardly hindered me from using my power, but it had to be less threatening than two *żityje* hungry blades. "I am a friend," I said with the calmest voice I could muster. Though Father hadn't taught me much, he'd made clear you could express intent with tone far better than words.

More people appeared alongside the archer as Dadźbóg's light crept over the eastern horizon. Adults and children alike, they looked from me to the slain demons with wide eyes. They wore an assortment of clothes, from furs to tattered coats or cloaks wrapped tightly around tunics and dresses. Grays and browns were dominant, but a few scattered through the crowd had leather gloves adorned with deep green pieces resembling the scales of the dragon-like aspid in Boz's palace. They were of every height and skin color. One thing united them, though: their bodies were little more than skin and bone.

A bearded, wrinkled man in a tattered gray robe shuffled forward, leaning heavily on a birchwood cane. The archer glanced at him and un-nocked his arrow when he raised his hand.

"It has been many years since the Nawie have walked this realm so freely," he said in perfect Krowikie. "One cannot be surprised at such things, however, when more terrifying beasts than you have returned."

"Returned?" I asked. "These things have existed before?"

He nodded slowly, his head hunched and barely reaching the

archer's elbow. "Upióry are among the most corrupted souls—tormented, their humanity reduced to nothing by the dark dragon." He waved a dismissive hand. "Such things can be discussed over a meal. You may call me Ira. You killed all but one of the demons, and our few guards were luckily able to down the final one. Our survival is worthy of celebration."

I raised my brow. "You'd eat with a Naw?"

"There is little use in casting you away. Based on the abilities you displayed, we would fall quickly if you were to attack us. That you have chosen to help us instead is all the proof I need."

"Then you can call me Wacław Lubiewicz. I will bring my companions," I replied over my rumbling stomach. Real food sounded amazing. "I should warn you that one is of my kind."

Ira huffed, fogging the air between us. "Good. We could use more folk able to give these Frostmarked a real taste of their own poison. Retrieve them and come to us here. After this attack, my caravan must make camp anyway."

9

Kuba

Well, this sucks.

EVERYTHING WAS COLD. I mean, of course it was—a crazy winter goddess was trying to kill us after all—but tonight was *really* cold. Life as a desert jackal was hard enough without dealing with my snow-covered fur literally freezing to my skin. Daytime wasn't so bad. Night… Well, let's just say Otylia's moon was about as warm as her personality.

Andrij eyed me from across the cart we'd borrowed to haul Narcyz. "You look chipper."

"You messed it up," I quipped back, laying my head on my paws before me.

"I don't understand."

I gave an exaggerated sigh. "I'm a jackal. You're supposed to say, 'Why the long face?' You know, because—"

"Yeah…" He leaned back against the cart's low wooden side, glancing down at Narcyz with the same silly look women gave their babies. "Yeah, I get it."

"Now who has the long face, huh?"

No reply. I just shook my head as a Vastrothie night patrol walked past. Their tortoise shell armor looked almost as ridiculous as

Amten's deathstalker one, but they lacked the scorpion hunter's much-needed sense of humor. Most people were *dull.* Not Amten.

I actually found myself missing Narcyz. Sure, he was still there and just as good of company unconscious as he was awake, but everyone had been in a bad mood ever since the Horde kicked our butts. Narcyz at least would've helped me laugh at the sheer insanity we'd found ourselves in. Andrij didn't seem to find it funny.

"You going to jump the fire with him on Noc Kupały?" I asked him. "Or are you two just going to stare at each other until I vomit?"

"The festival is the least of my concerns," Andrij replied.

"Oh, come on!" I scooted closer to him. "What's all this fighting about if we don't have someone to come back to when we survive with half our limbs? One of you needs to admit what's going on before you freeze to death apart."

His apathy turned to a glare that I chose not to heed. "He almost died, Kuba. He might still if he doesn't wake soon. Yes, I care about him, but if I can't lead like a commander should, then the only fires we'll be jumping are those of the Smorodina River."

"Which one of you will wear the wreath?"

"What?"

"Ya know! The one the girls send down the river. Or is that different in Astiw?"

He cracked a small smile. A great success. "Oh, yeah, I'm *sure* Narcyz would love wearing a bouquet of wildflowers."

"Wouldn't be hard to catch his wreath then." He cocked his head, so I clarified, "Ya know, because he'd be beating you to death with it."

"You're odd. You know that?"

I smirked and stretched out my four legs. The cart was getting cramped, and I wasn't feeling tired enough to shiver myself to sleep yet. "What gave it away? The fur or my terrific jokes?"

Then I hopped out of the cart, allowing him to mull over that deep philosophical question. "Better to leave people with questions," Father always said somewhere between his third and twelfth mug of oskoła. "That way you keep the upper hand."

I'd never been sure what "upper hand" he'd wanted to keep, but something made sense about it. At least to me. Other people had different ways of thinking. That didn't make them *wrong*, just boring.

Camp followers gave me space as I winded through the bedrolls, makeshift tents, and dug burrows of our caravan. It was depressing. Girls used to call me cute before I opened my mouth and ruined everything. Now, I never got the chance.

Thinking about these girls just reminded me of Maja, and that hurt more than anything. She'd probably heard that I died fighting Marzanna's cultists. A shapely, rosy-cheeked girl like her wouldn't last long before some brute took her hand. Most of our warriors had been in Solga for the past moon, though, and I hoped that could work to my advantage.

I shook my head. *Idiot. You're not even human.*

That tiny detail would make things more difficult. But couples could get over anything when they loved each other, right? Mother said her uncle had a club foot, and his wife stayed with him until he died. I mean, sure, there'd been rumors she bedded a sheep herder, but that was irrelevant. Maja and I could overcome anything. Yup…

I stopped outside Xobas's round command tent. He wasn't Vastrothie, but Vastroth's General Mesfin had agreed to listen to Xobas's guidance because of his familiarity with the terrain and what was happening with Marzanna. It was an awkward arrangement at best.

"I'm here for Xobas," I told the tortoise boy guarding the tent.

"The commander is busy with General Mesfin," he replied, stomping his dual-ended spear into the snow. Narcyz would've fumed at that mistreatment of a spearhead.

"Even better."

I scampered toward the entrance, only to be met by the second, curved end of the spear. "Kuba, I know you're not deaf. Those ears of yours are better than ours, so let me be clear. Commander Xobas said he should not be bothered."

"That makes perfect sense," I said, moving my head out of range of his weapon. "Luckily, I don't plan to bother him."

Then I dashed past, ducking into the tent before the guard could stop me. *Being a jackal has* some *advantages.*

The moonlight vanished inside, and only a few candles near the end of their life lit the tent. Xobas was bent over the table alongside Mesfin, where those candles surrounded a group of wooden figurines. He looked up with a grimace.

"I told you no one…" His brow raised. "Oh, Kuba. Apologies. I didn't expect you so late. Do you bring word from Wacław?"

"They're in some mountain range to the northeast, but I didn't come for him."

Mesfin stood up straight with his hands locked behind him. He was even taller than Xobas, and compared to my jackal height, the dark-skinned veteran looked like a giant. A scary one at that. From the scars cutting over his nose and bald head to the built arms exposed by his sleeveless armor, the sight of him alone could make a zmora flee in terror. He'd tied seven violet stones into his long black beard—each an honor only the Vastrothie scions could grant for a great victory. If only his tortoise armor weren't so ridiculous.

"I hope you have something real to contribute," he said. "Płanetnik Eryk's scouting team has reported that two Horde armies are flanking us to the north and south. The Wyzra would protect us from the northern one during a normal summer, but it's frozen as hard as stone."

Ok, now this really sucks…

"Let me guess, you're trying to figure out a defense," I replied, approaching the table and plopping my front paws up onto it. That gave me a better sight of the wooden pieces—one for every army of both factions. "That's silly."

Mesfin punched the table. "What do you know of military strategy? How many battles have you won?"

He was right. I didn't know anything about strategy, and the figures might as well have been scattered randomly in front of me. They were confusing to me either way. What I did have an eye for, though, was a good prank, and this seemed as good a set-up as any.

"I got beat up a lot as a kid," I said. "Most of it was probably deserved, but I learned real quick that trying to fight when the other guys outnumbered me was dumb."

"Congratulations. It's good to know we aren't relying on you fighting on the front lines, then."

"Ouch." I feigned like he'd hit me in the face. "You're probably right. Wacław was always better with a spear or sword, but I could beat him when I was crafty. That's what we need to do here: Trick them into thinking it'll be an easy fight."

Xobas gave a slow nod. "What do you suggest?"

"Tell me," I said as I hopped down and began to dig through the snow. "How do you guys like mud?"

10

Otylia

How have these people survived?

JUST OVER A HUNDRED PEOPLE GATHERED in the shadow of a large cliff. It was one of the few places not covered in deep snow, with rocks blocking the worst of the blizzard's gusts, and they sat on various carts covered in cushions and fabrics.

All of them stared at me.

But that wasn't what unsettled me. Power emanated from the green shards woven into the gloves of the six closest to their elderly leader, Ira. Like the rest of the caravan, their faces resembled every tribe I'd seen and more, but these few lacked the ragged clothes of the others. Red embroidery of shapes and meandering lines trailed down their green coats, strapped shut along a diagonal seam across their torsos. They didn't have any *visible* weapons. I knew better.

"We are eternally grateful for your aid," Ira said loudly enough for everyone to hear, despite us sitting across from him. "In these trying times, it is heartening to see strangers willing to sacrifice for each other."

Wacław nodded beside me. I was annoyed with him for rushing off without me, but he'd been right. Morning had come quickly, stealing the strongest of my moon powers. That didn't mean I liked it.

"I'm glad we were near," he replied with a sweet smile. It was a striking contrast to his black veins and the demonic blood splattered over his coat. "Those upióry… Have you seen them before?"

An eerie silence spread over the rest of the caravan. Ira shifted on his worn cushion, similar to the one each of us sat on. "Too many times to count. They are why we are together, fleeing from the lands they've taken."

I studied the man. Instead of donning the finest clothes of the group and securing the best cart for himself, his possessions were remarkably basic for a leader. His gray coat matched that of the archers, save for green thread tying it shut. Even that had frayed edges and tears along the arms. The scarf tied around his neck, though, was immaculately kept, its designs the same as the shard-wearers' coats. *Religious or tribal?*

In-between bites of the cooked fish they'd given us, Mother extended an arm toward the others. "You must have skilled fighters or szeptuchy among you to have survived. These upióry seem far too dangerous for a band of refugees, and I am curious where you caught fresh fish in these frozen mountains."

I grinned. She'd used that tone many times when confronting Father. She knew something, but without her Bowmark on my neck anymore, she couldn't tell me silently.

"You have a keen eye," Ira said with a wry smile. "What did you say your name was?"

Mother took another bite before shooting Ira a fiery glare. "I didn't."

Wacław, oblivious to Mother's tactics, faked a cough. "Wherever the fish is from, I'm grateful for it. We've struggled to find much to hunt or scavenge, but perhaps we were looking in the wrong places."

He then spoke through our bond. *Why aren't you eating? Not everyone is suspicious.*

Then explain the shards pulsing with žityje and this foreign woman's perfect Krowikie.

Do their wisps say anything?

Ira replied to Wacław's pleasantries as I examined End's wisps closer. Most seemed normal at first for refugees, and visions flashed past of death and starvation. In each, that pain disappeared in a green light, followed by flames. My chest tightened, and when Ira's wisp showed me his ends, I shot to my feet.

"You're a żmij!" I snapped, light spear forming in my hand. My power was weakened away from the moon, but I was still a goddess capable of fighting a dragon.

My reaction caught Wacław mid-bite. Fish dropped from his mouth as he stumbled and stood, sliding Grudzień from his back. "What kind of trap is this?"

Ira just narrowed his eyes at me. "Ah, so my suspicions were true. When I sensed an immense amount of *żityje* nearby, it wasn't a płanetnik, but a goddess. I don't recognize you. It has been some time since I've involved myself enough to contact your kind, but I never forget a deity."

"What do you want with us?" I asked.

"To see your intentions." He looked from me to Wacław, a smile crossing his face. "Jawia is crumbling, and when the worst comes, so do its people. You could've tried to kill or rob us when you saw how defenseless we appeared to be. You did neither."

"Coincidence is often a lie with dragons," Mother said, standing slowly beside me. "They all want something."

Ira extended his arms to us. "So do you. Do not tell me you resist Marzanna's forces simply out of a selfless desire to protect Jawia or your tribes. Every person, mortal or not, has selfish reasons for their actions, and that does not make them evil."

"You, for example," he continued, "are hiding your identity. Selfish. The young goddess is protective of the few people she cares for because she's afraid of life without them. Selfish. Wacław came to our aid, but he's resisting the corruption in his soul, hoping good deeds can make right the sins he's certainly committed. Selfish!"

Mother flung open her arms. "So, you've seen our intentions. What does the almighty żmij ask of us next?"

"Do you see these people?" Ira asked. Smiling faces met him among the crowd, oddly happy considering their conditions. "They worship me because I saved them, and they follow me because I keep them safe. That was enough for some time. Now, things have changed." He motioned to the shard-wearers.

All six went to a different cart in the ring closest to us. A woman sat in each, and they spoke to the shard-wearers in various tongues before handing something to them.

Not something. Someone.

The shard-wearers turned back, carrying swaddled babies. Ira's smile grew as they approached. He rose and approached each at the edge of his cart, and as he spoke, he gently touched the children's faces. "Humanity, gods, and demons alike have driven many of my kind to Oblivion and the far reaches of Jawia. For so long, I despised mankind for this. My brothers often lived among them, but I could not. I stayed in these mountains, alone."

He turned back to us and leaned upon his birchwood cane. "You see, I am young for a żmij. I relied on my father's frightful tales, and when he perished to mortal trickery, I swore never to help them. This worked for countless years until mortals began appearing in my valley, wishing to flee their lands and find peace."

With each second that passed, his wrinkles disappeared until he looked no older than twenty-five with his hair and beard shifted to a light brown. He had a handsome face that was *too* perfect, like he'd washed away every blemish.

"These people showed me what it was to join together," he said. "They proved that humanity could do more than destroy. However, invaders soon came to take this land from them. I watched them suffer until I could wait no more. Joining the fray, I saved the last of them, and they became my first followers. Ever since, I have accepted all refugees who flee into my valley. I've protected them. Some, too, I have loved."

"Love?" I scoffed. "You have six wives, and these people look like they've been possessed."

One of the shard-wearers, a middle-aged woman, furrowed her brow. "No. Ira does not force us to stay or to worship him, but he has done more for us than any god or king. Why should we not love him?"

A dragon cult. Great…

Ira placed a hand over his heart, then both. "You may have your concerns, but I do not ask you to approve of my personal affairs."

Mother muttered under her breath before stomping toward him. "Get to the point or let us leave! We have far greater problems than a lustful dragon."

"We will discuss your futures, but first, indulge me. Who are you really?"

I rolled my eyes. "I am Otylia, goddess of endings. And I'll end *you* if this conversation goes on any longer."

Surprisingly, Ira bowed. "It is a pleasure, Lady Otylia. I respect a goddess willing to do more than sit in Prawia." He turned to Mother. "And you?"

"Dziewanna," Mother replied.

Ira's eyes widened. "Oh my. Not one goddess, but two! I recant on my wish for more Nawie to aid us. This will do plenty."

"Talk!" Mother and I said as one.

"Yes, I owe you more of an explanation."

He took a baby boy in his arms and approached us. At first, the child looked normal, with round cheeks and light brown hair down to his cheekbones, but his eyes were a luminescent green with three brown lines slicing through them like claw marks. His wisp pulsed vibrantly too, and I reached for it, hoping to foresee the boy's fate.

End pulled at my mind. The wisp shifted before me and became a group of dragons, grounded and surrounded by dark figures that slashed and stabbed at them. Pain, sharp and endless, poured through the vision until it shifted to show a single child falling from a dragon's grasp until he struck the ground. Then I snapped back to reality.

"Half-dragons haven't been seen for some time," Mother said, looking from the boy to Ira. "You must know my father's opinion of them."

Ira nodded. "Who could forget the god of thunder raining his fury down upon all dragon kin? Perun's aggression against żmije is a crucial element to my ask of you now. Nowhere is safe for my children among the Three Realms. Marzanna's demons will overrun us if we remain here, and the gods will punish me for mating with mortals if I seek shelter elsewhere. Guide us to your people and let us help you."

I didn't need to meet his gaze to know what he was thinking. Mother had a far harder heart.

"We won't protect you as you manipulate mortals!" she shouted, throwing out her arms before turning back to us. "It isn't love but sorcery that draws these people to him. Dragons are capable of entrapping entire cities to their will, and he'll do the same to all of Krowik if we let him."

Her expression begged for me to listen. Why? The Dziewanna I'd known would've never feared a lesser being.

"Is it true?" I asked Ira. "Did you manipulate them?"

He huffed, just a stride away now. "Why answer? What reason have you to believe me when Dziewanna opposes me so?"

Wacław suddenly snarled and punched Ira in the jaw. "You're doing it now! I've felt this before, but you're not as powerful as a Moonstone."

The dragon took the blow without a wince. His child cried out and the crowd rose to a roar, but Ira just clicked his tongue. "This one is no simple Naw."

"We should kill him," Wacław snapped. Ira had tried to manipulate him, and his anger washed over me.

"Wait," I said. He gripped Grudzień tight, and he would use it. But not unless I told him to.

During our argument, the shard-wearers had crept around the sides of the cart. The babies were still in their arms, but I doubted that would stop them from attacking.

"Ira probably deserves it," I said. "But what about the children? Do we kill them because their father is a domineering fool?"

Wacław's eyes softened. "No. We'll take them with us. Protect them. I would've been better off without Jacek, and they'll thrive away from Ira's control."

"You act as if you have a choice," Ira replied, signaling to his allies.

We tried to flee, but a magic wall stopped us at the cart's edge. The shard-wearers' chants echoed through the valley. All Ira's followers joined until their calls swallowed all other sound. We were surrounded, and as I readied my spear, wings sprouted from Ira's back. He cracked his neck, fangs growing from his teeth as deep green scales replaced clothes upon his torso. In a blink, he'd tripled in size.

"I offered you my aid," he roared as he took flight. His voice shook the air with fire bursting from his throat. "Instead, you have chosen to die."

11

Wacław

That could have gone much better.

IRA CLUTCHED ONE OF HIS HALF-DRAGON CHILDREN as he flapped his massive green-scaled wings. They sent gusts rushing over us, but I silenced the push and chased him into the air.

"Why try to control my mind if you wanted to be allies?" I shouted with Grudzień and my Thunderstone dagger hungry in my grasp. "I had pity for your children, but you are a monster."

"Look at yourself!" Ira breathed fire over me, but I dodged to the side. "Your veins mark your corruption."

"I can't fly," Otylia's voice said in my mind. *"We'll keep the priests distracted, but you need to—"*

Another blast of fire rolled over me, forcing me further into the sky. Good. This was my domain.

Stab him. Right?

"If that even works on a dragon."

Żityje flashed below as I dove at Ira. Silver light and green streaked through my vision, but I focused on his hide. Even dragon scales surely couldn't stop a Moonblade.

Ira swept away, but Grudzień found flesh. Barely.

The black sword's teeth skidded off his armor. A trickle of blood followed—little more than a flesh wound. I tried again with both blades, but they only sheered a set of scales free. The attack threw me off balance, and Ira snapped his tail as I recovered. It struck true, throwing me away as my ribs strained from the impact.

The baby continued its screaming in the nook of his arm, and the sound rang out from below too. Fighting a dragon would be hard enough. I had no desire to kill innocent children, though, no matter what beast they were.

Protect the children, I told Otylia.

"I'm just trying to survive! Mother can only use a bow we took."

The babies didn't attack us. This fool of a dragon did.

Ira reared back his head again to release his flames. This time, when I timed my dodge, he launched a second blast directly into my path. I was too slow.

Fire singed my skin, and I screamed as *żityje* worked too slowly. The winds slipped from my control for only a moment. It was enough. Ira rushed me with fire balling in his throat and his claws ready to tear me apart.

But before he struck, he released a mighty roar and arched his body back. He sent his flames skyward instead as a small object became visible in his stomach. An arrow, wedged between the beast's scales.

"His hide is too thick," Dziewanna called to me now that I'd fallen closer to the cart, one of the followers' bows firmly in her grasp. "Focus on his belly, but you'll have to be bold."

Otylia fought alongside her mother. Her glowing hands were extended before her, and a shard-wearer collapsed just strides away. Black and brown covered him as I sensed Otylia's enjoyment at controlling her forces of decay.

Four other shard-wearers still fought on, though, along with at least ten archers who sent arrows showering over the exposed women. I gritted my teeth, knowing there was little I could do. Only my control of the winds had given me any chance so far, and Ira alone could kill them quickly with a fireball from the air. It was up to me to figure out a way to kill him.

Unless…

I swooped up on the winds as Ira neared. Despite his size, he was quick, and his claws dragged down my back. The upióry had sapped my *żityje*, and as I sped away, I denied myself healing. Those four hearts had given me enough to fight, not enough to call a storm. If only a żmij were a typical opponent.

Ira kept up no matter how fast I flew. I needed to misdirect him and dive below, hoping for a lucky strike with Grudzień. No chance came.

His flames washed over me yet again, but I held Grudzień before me, using it and the winds to deflect the blast just around me. The heat alone was nearly enough to burn me again. It wasn't, though, and I countered directly at his maw.

Jagged teeth and breath reeking of smoke met me, but he hadn't expected the move. He'd heard Dziewanna's guidance too. *Be bold.* So I charged into the flames.

Ira's jaws closed around me as I slashed. My Moonblade found his gums, and a tooth fell free in a fountain of blood. My first real success. It drove me to strike again, but Ira roared.

Orange and red glowed around me. His jaw snapped shut, catching my entire sword-arm in his mouth as I felt searing heat over the same fingers that bore Marzanna's frostbite. My *żityje* waned just keeping myself from bleeding out. I was hundreds of feet in the air. Whatever I had left would need to catch me—if I could survive at all.

The heat grew, but Ira's jaws loosened. To release the flames, he needed to open his mouth, and the moment he did, I took one last stab with my dagger.

Heat greater than Dadźbóg's sun consumed me as I drove the Thunderstone blade into the top of Ira's mouth. I pushed against the pain until it was embedded up to the hilt. My other arm hung limply at my side. My mind slipped. My skin seared. But as I fell back, I tore the dagger free with all the power I could muster, dragging it across his mouth until I tumbled free.

The green dragon reared in agony. His cries echoed through the sky as he swiped his claws at me by instinct alone. They missed, and the child in his arms slipped into the open air.

I allowed all but the last of my *žityje* to heal my major wounds as I watched the child fall. My hand still felt aflame and black blood trailed behind me, but I needed that bit to catch both me and the little boy. Ira hadn't even realized he was gone. He was my enemy's son, but in his screaming face, all I saw was the little boy thrown out of his father's house at birth. I wouldn't let him die.

The battle still raged below. Dziewanna lay on the bottom of the cart, an arrow embedded in her shoulder, and Otylia's light was visibly dimmer. Sweat beaded on her brow. Yet she fought on regardless, sending a sweeping spell across a line of archers.

I'm coming down! I yelled through our bond.

She was too focused to reply. The ground was approaching fast either way, and I spun back toward the child, taking a deep breath. The winds circled me. They always became temperamental at the end of my *žityje* reserves, but enough of them answered. I just needed to stop before the ground.

"Catch us," I commanded them. "Catch the child!"

Cervenko's east and Dogoda's west winds rushed to him as another stayed with me. Familiar, weaker than the others, but I recognized Kyustendil's northwest quickly. *Good to see you again.*

Unfortunately, the demi-god slain by Jaryło had not completely recovered in such little time. I slowed but still hit the snow with a solid *thud*, enough to ironically knock the wind out of me.

The boy's fall was lighter. I took a relieved breath at him slowly dropping to the snow beside me. His green and brown-streaked eyes fixed on me, and he stopped crying… until his father ruined the moment.

"Stop this!" the dragon roared.

Blood still poured from Ira's mouth as he descended in a far sloppier pattern than he'd flown before. Around me, the sounds of battle ceased. The winds still whistled through the valley, but beyond them and the beating of Ira's wings, the silence hung heavy.

Rapid footsteps approached. "Wašek! Please tell me you're okay."

I groaned and fought to raise my head. Everything hurt. The wounds on my back would surely scar, and I could barely move my sword arm. I was alive, though. For that, I was grateful. "I would be better if your friend Kyustendil had been kinder, but I'm not dead at least. Please remind me not to do that again."

"Kyustendil probably found your fall funny in his odd way. C'mon." She helped me stand. "Looks like Ira's finally ready to be smart."

I staggered to the fallen baby and lifted him in my uninjured arm. Corpses surrounded us. A terrible sight for anyone, let alone a child. "We need to protect these children. He'll manipulate them, make them like him."

"We'll see. With you drained and Mother shot, we're hardly in a great position."

As we made our way back to the cart, Ira landed with his two remaining priests flanking him. The rest of his followers cowered among the waves of snow in the distance. Otylia climbed into the cart and whispered something to Dziewanna as I stopped beside it. Gods, my pain was terrible. Staring up at the dragon, though, I felt some victory in the damage I'd done to such an ancient beast.

"This will end with us all dead or maimed," Ira cried. "Enough of the blades and flames. I fled mankind to avoid such battles, not cause them."

"You attacked us!" I replied. "I helped you and now you try to kill me."

Dziewanna leaned up against the edge of the cart. It hurt to see her so frail, and I wished as much as Otylia that I could help her regain her power. "We do anything to ensure the safety of our children."

Ira nodded. "The goddess speaks the truth."

"What then?" Otylia said, clutching her mother. "You hoped to beat us into submission? How could that help your children?"

"If you will not help me, then you could expose us to Perun's allies. You are a threat to my children. I had no choice." He scowled at me, but his voice softened at the sight of his son in my arms. "Perhaps I was wrong, however. My little Vytis would be dead if it weren't for you showing him kindness despite your own weakness. Thank you, Wacław. My anger prevented me from saving the one thing I wanted to defend more than anything."

"Your children will not live out here," I replied. "Maybe you can keep them safe against the Horde and out of Perun's gaze, but that is no life. Nor can you be the father they deserve."

He released a column of fire into the air. "You cannot take them from me! I will show you mercy by allowing you to leave. Nothing more."

"I can't let them suffer!"

Dziewanna whispered again to Otylia, who nodded and stood. Even bloodied and exhausted, she stood strong, her black hair drifting behind her as she crossed the cart and approached the dragon. She held no weapons.

"Your family is your own," Otylia said. "Have your cult, but never go to the lands west of the Mangled Woods.

Ira glared down at her. "That is fair."

"No!" I shouted. "Would you leave siblings with Weles? Dziewanna fled to save you, and—"

"She can speak for herself," Dziewanna interrupted. An arrow was deep in her shoulder, but she stood anyway, glaring at me instead of the dragon. "I would fight to save all of my children for as long as it took, but these are not your blood. To protect your people after what you've done is just, and enough. Do not resist and doom them all when you may survive and ensure your people are free. I watched thousands die during my revolt against Perun because I was too thick-skulled to see that. The Three Realms will never be perfect, Wacław. A Naw should understand that more than most."

"I…" Words slipped away, so I bowed my head, thoroughly disarmed. "Yes, my goddess."

Otylia's eyes flashed white, and I saw the Threads of Life pulsing around us all. "A blood pact seals two sides to an oath. I can craft this pact between the both of you, eternal and unbreakable." She looked at me. "You are not to attack him again, Wašek. Can you swear that?"

Was I? The fight had happened so quickly. All I'd known was that Ira was a menace who'd controlled these people like Minna had done with Grudzień in Huebia. It was disgusting. Stopping his children from falling to that same manipulation would ensure they never became beasts like him, but what choice did we have? I'd injured him. Without *žityje*, I definitely couldn't kill him.

"I will," I replied with a disappointed sigh.

Otylia's gaze lingered on me, solemn, before she looked at Ira. "Will you honor our demand, allowing us to leave and keeping away from our tribe?"

Ira released a roar of rage and grief alike. "The gods strike me in the heart, and your demon skewers me with cursed blades! There is no honor in this fight, only misery."

"Misery caused by you alone," Dziewanna replied.

"I wish for no more death. Enough blood has spilled this morn."

Ira lowered his head. Blood trickled from his maw as he began to shrink, his scales retracting and his wings merging into his back. Moments later, he'd returned to his human form. A missing tooth left a gap when he spoke, and he lacked the smile he'd worn before.

"Thousands more will die before this war is over," I replied, moving alongside the cart and Otylia as Vytis turned his gaze from Ira. "I wish I could trust you to aid us."

Ira drew nearer. "The gods will betray you too, Naw. I will swear this oath for my son's sake, but I swear it to you alone, not to the goddess of false ends."

I gave him Vytis, then ran my dagger across my injured hand. It stung greatly. Even raising the arm set my shoulder ablaze. To survive, though, I needed to be stronger than my soul-form. Whatever pain I felt now was nothing compared to what lay ahead.

Part 2
The Deathless King

12

Otylia

If we can't face a normal żmij, what hope do we have against Czarnobóg?

THREADS BOUND ME.

Dark and light, colored and black as night, they entrapped my limbs, my torso amid the mists. I hung between the twisted trees of the Mangled Woods. Whispers drifted among the dead, gray trunks and leafless boughs.

"Save us, daughter of the woods."

"Redeem us, mistress of the moon."

"Remake us, ruler of the end."

An eclipsed moon hung high above, bleeding red across the empty sky. Each star among it should've been a living soul, but there were none. A void. It devoured everything like a ravenous beast, its hunger never satiated.

My own blood dripped down my naked form. Each Thread of Life sliced into my skin and drew more *żityje* from my veins and soul. I felt death after death, End's wisps flashing before me at each violent ending. A light Thread vanished with every fatality. Black replaced it, and joy faded to unending agony.

A man emerged from the reddened night. No, not a man. No man commanded the darkness like his right hand, ashes raining in his wake.

I spat fire. "I'll kill you!"

"Such vitriol is common among the young," Czarnobóg said, his voice far too smooth for a beast.

"And the ancient are prone to arrogance." Pain strained my voice and body, but I forced my gaze upon the beast. "You're no more than Jaryło! A petty coward, a fool!"

Czarnobóg opened his fanged mouth, and fire burst forth. It singed the trees and blackened the earth. But when it reached me, it did not burn my skin.

"Do not compare me to the gods who cursed the Three Realms!" he roared. The black and red mark on his pale chest flared at the outburst, and scales crept from his pauldron as he extended his hand. In it glowed a stone bursting with every color. "I will reforge the Alatyr Stone, mending what was broken at creation's birth. But first, they must come to an end."

I shuddered at the power emanating from the stone. "Alatyr won't listen to you. Rod created it for the gods."

"You have no understanding of the World Egg's greatest forces."

"I…" I didn't. Trapped before the dark dragon, I had no contention. I knew nothing. That didn't matter. I would fight and defeat his darkness, prevent the suffering I felt through the Threads.

That determination waned as he drew closer with the Alatyr Stone. All twelve Moonstones united within it, a power greater than anything I'd felt. It was suffocating, *intoxicating.*

"Child, you cannot stop what I have waited thousands of years to accomplish." He raised Alatyr before me. "You fear Death—I can smell it—but an eternity in Oblivion has only strengthened us. You can never kill the Deathless Sons."

Then he shoved Alatyr into my chest.

I awoke with a start, screaming at the pain of a thousand fires. Cold sweat clung my clothes to my skin. All was dark in our sleeping burrow, and I pulled my legs tight to my chest as I stared out the thin gap into the night.

Wacław was over me in second.

"Otylka, what's wrong?" Wacław asked. "You were restless…"

I just shook my head. It had been two nights since our fight with Ira, and despite my doubts about the dragon, Wacław had shaken off his rage against him. Mother's constant mix of anger and sorrow was hardly uplifting. Having Wacław be his caring self helped lessen my burden.

I rubbed my eyes and pulled myself free from my blankets. "I'm fine."

Being free from that nightmare was a gift anyway. Had it been just a dream, or had Czarnobóg been sending me a message? The suffering I'd felt…

Worry about it later.

Wacław furrowed his brow and led me into free air. I looked away. There was so much weighing on me that it felt petty. According to Kuba, Koschei's Horde had all but surrounded the Vastrothie army on their way to Dwie Rzeki. Mikołaj had sent reinforcements, but they were days away. Xobas believed the attack would come in the next day, making our arrival all the more important.

"We've been too slow," I thought aloud as Wacław stopped atop a hill. Our sight was clear here, but I dared not look northeast. Too much pain had come from the lands near Marzanna's palace.

"You're right." He stared west, over the eastern mountains of Perun's Crown, his hair brighter than gold in the moonlight with streaks of white speckled throughout. Without the dark veins, he would've been a fairly handsome man. With them, he resembled the sun drowned by a nightmare. "I'm sorry for that."

I crossed my arms and followed his gaze through the snowfall. "Where's Mother?"

"Somewhere west. We don't know exactly where we are, so she went to ensure we're headed the right direction and not right into Koschei the Deathless."

Deathless. Czarnobóg had used that same word. Why?

"You should've woken me."

Wacław shrugged, offering an apologetic smile. "You rarely seem to sleep lately. Figured I'd give you a chance to recover before we face the Horde. If one of us is going to be ready, it needs to be you."

I laid my head on his shoulder. "Don't talk like that."

He winced, still recovering from Ira's strikes despite me gifting him *žityje*. "Like I know exactly what each of us are? We need a goddess to win this, not a demon."

"You're more than a demon."

"Maybe, but does it matter? I can't protect everyone. I thought freeing Ira's children was right, but every person I try to care for is another distraction from the battle that's destroying the world."

"People will die, Wašek. Thousands more before this is over." I took a deep breath and spun around to face him. "We'll have to choose who we protect, because without the people we love, Jawia means nothing."

His head dropped. "And if we can't? Ira would've killed me if I hadn't saved Vytis. Czarnobóg—"

I kissed him to shut him up. Gratefully, he relented, taking my waist and leaning in until I eventually stepped back. "We need to leave as soon as Mother returns if we're going to help the Vastrothie," I told him.

He nodded before grinning. "You know we're only two nights from Noc Kupały, right?"

"So?"

"I dreamed of catching your flower crown for years as a child. We've jumped the fire, so this should've been the first year we're eligible." There was an unspoken ask in his words. Flower crowns on Noc Kupały were more than just childish games. For an eligible man to catch an eligible woman's wreath was the equivalent of an engagement... if the woman wanted it to be.

"I never sent a wreath after Mother died. After you left me."

He took my hand, and memories swirled on his wisp, as if End knew what Wacław wanted to show me. "I hoped anyway."

"Wašek, there are more important things than the solstice festival." I tried to step away, but he pulled me back softly.

"There's nothing more important to me than you." He kissed my hand, then released me. "I'll live the rest of my life regretting leaving you for those four years. Marzanna has caused so much suffering, but I'm glad this journey has brought me back to you."

I could only stand there, frozen in place, as he left to scout for Mother. His emotions were varied and complex, but I didn't need our bond to see what was happening. Huebia had changed him. He'd slaughtered at the Płanetnik's command, and he was fighting desperately to mend his errors. What he didn't understand was that I didn't think any less of him. Yes, he'd needed help to grasp his power and know who he was, but so had I. Wacław didn't need to prove anything to me. I loved his heart, his compassion for the weak and outcast. That was enough.

Why couldn't I find the right words to tell him that?

Maybe that was the problem. I crouched and studied the undergrowth. Wacław and my relationship had been suffering and sacrifice every step of the way, but the soft side of love was rare for us. Not that I was much good at it anyway.

"I think I know how to make you smile," I whispered after him.

Smoke clouded the night west of the mountains. The peaks had obscured much of it, but now, we had to search for clear patches just to breathe.

"It's strange to think I was here just a couple moons ago," Wacław said, staring at the ruins of Kynnytsia below with a hand squeezing tight his dagger's hilt. "Boz slaughtered so many people, but this… Should we look for survivors?"

"There likely are none," Mother replied. Despite her recovery, her eyes were sunken and her skin pale in the dim moonlight. "Marzanna and Czarnobóg's szeptuchy will have transformed those who didn't fight back into severed souls, upióry, and other demons."

Grief replaced Wacław's anger as he surveyed the charred forest and ashen buildings. "I wish I could've done more."

I took his hand as a silent comfort, but something else bothered me. "Czarnobóg has szeptuchy? He's not a god."

"Alatyr created him just as it did the gods," Mother said. "Most żmije are just dragons capable of shifting to humans, but Czarnobóg is a god in his own right."

"Great," I muttered.

She eyed me, sending a shiver down my spine. "It doesn't matter what he is. We must defeat him regardless and ensure he never returns."

"How do you do that to a god?" Wacław asked. "It was hard enough to keep Jaryło dead for a moon."

"I don't know, but Rod must." Mother sighed and shook her head. "It has been far too long since I stepped foot in Prawia."

"He'll know how to reconnect you to your force," I added.

"Perhaps. Rod has been distant to even Swaróg and Perun ever since they expelled Weles. After all these years, and with his obsession with balance, I am hardly the goddess he wishes to see."

We flew on in silence for some time. Wacław had been unusually quiet, and even when I squeezed his hand to draw his attention, he stared at the destruction below. Villages smoldered as we passed. The smoke grew thicker with each minute, as those further east had been mostly ash. The Horde had swept quickly through Astiwie lands after razing Kynnytsia, and we had a full view of both old conquest and new.

"They'll burn all of Jawia until nothing's left but ash and frost," Wacław said some hours later. Tears welled in his eyes, but there was more now. A hunger surging between us. For vengeance.

I touched his cheek, pulling his gaze to mine. "Then we'll march the dead to Marzanna's halls and siege her home until she wishes for Oblivion."

He gave only a solemn nod. I wished to say more, but moving figures below silenced me. A group of riders walked alongside each other, sweeping the woods in search of something. More filled the plains and valleys just east of the frozen Wyzra. Thousands of creatures, both human-like and misshapen, covered the landscape in a sea of darkness that stretched as far as I could see.

"I've never seen so many people in my life," Wacław gasped.

"They're not people," I replied, opening my vision to the Threads of Life. Most were frayed and black, like the many-mouthed skrzaki I'd found entrapping the demonic children in Huebia. "Only a few of them have any life left."

Mother ran her hand through the passing smoke. "We are obscured enough this high, but any chały or płanetniks could follow if they sense our *żityje*. Best we find a way around."

"There is none," I said. "Kuba told Wacław the Horde was surrounding them to the north of the Wyzra and into the southern hills."

Wacław released a sharp breath and drew Grudzień from his back. "Koschei's here. Cervenko showed me him in the east before, and I could never forget that feeling."

Mother pointed to the land north of the Wyzra, where the river curved toward Dwie Rzeki. "He rides with his chosen elites—some of the only living men left in the Horde—their stallions faster than any other tribes', but he will not attack himself. His demons and enslaved men will do the fighting for him. Palisades and mortal defenses won't last an hour."

"Wonderful," Wacław quipped.

But I felt the pull too. Whether it was simply through Wacław or not, I didn't know. Koschei's wisp likely floated among his army's, but there were too many to pick through. It shouldn't have mattered. As far as I was aware, Koschei was still *technically* alive. Where was his Thread?

"Ivan claimed he killed him," I said, remembering my kingly bear of a mentor from Nawia. "Is Koschei a demon?"

"Koschei isn't a demon, but I can't be certain what he is," Mother said. "Men can be stubborn no matter their form, however, and he figured out some way to ensure his soul endures no matter his body's suffering. Never trust sorcerers."

"Then how do we kill him?"

Mother wrinkled her brow. "I'd say, 'Gods know,' but we don't. Koschei has been a thorn in many of our feet over the centuries."

"Ivan said Baba Jaga gave him a horse fast enough to catch Koschei." I shook my head. "But that doesn't matter if he'll just come back."

Mother's concern shifted to a knowing grin. "My child, you misremember. Jaga did not aid Ivan. She lured him in with the promise of her mares, hoping to kill him like her many other victims. It was only because of a very insightful goddess that the creatures of the wood ensured his escape."

"So that's why Ivan helped me: He owed you."

"Not necessarily. He was a good man. There are few willing to act selflessly without personal gain." She glared down at the gathered Horde. "And many remain so tightly bound to their greed that it suffocates them even in death."

Wacław pursed his lips, running his fingers across the brim of his płanetnik hat. "Not all of them deserved this. Most were likely slain without raising a spear, turning demonic only when their body wasn't burned."

The Vastrothie camp came into sight before Mother could reply. Scattered tents filled the forests east of a small unwalled village, and lines of outward-pointed spears lined the edge of the two settlements. In spite of the snowy ground surrounding them, the camp's earth appeared oddly dry. Warriors ran about with torches lit from a hundred fires throughout the camp. Smoke billowed from them. It filled the sky and cast a heavy shadow over the Horde, who had surrounded the camp on three sides as they slowly marched to close the western flank too.

"You're good at heart too, Wacław," Mother said. "Just make sure you're not *too* good to do what will be necessary against mortals and your own ilk. Better Marzanna and Czarnobóg's minions die than your kin." She pulled an arrow from the quiver she'd taken from one of Ira's followers. She'd recovered quickly despite losing her connection to the wilds, and that gave me hope she could find it again. "We must act quickly before your allies are surrounded."

"You have an idea," I said, giving her a wry smile.

"I do, but only if your płanetnik is willing to let me borrow his winds."

I glanced at Wacław, but he already had his hat removed as he bowed. "It would be my honor."

Mother nocked the arrow and tested her bowstring. It wasn't her godly weapon, but it felt right to see her with a bow again. "Then quit the formalities and carry me toward the Deathless One. It's time to test this immortality of his."

13

Wacław

Well, she's definitely brave.

THE WINDS RUSHED BENEATH US as we charged toward where Dziewanna believed Koschei would be.

Surely the goddess had more of a plan than flying with my winds and shooting the immortal sorcerer in the head with a bronze arrow stolen from Ira's men, but if there was, she hadn't told me about it. That was… fine? My relationship with Dziewanna was hard enough with her being Otylia's long-lost mother. This whole her being a thousand-year-old goddess without powers thing only complicated matters. I wanted to be on her good side, though, so I played along.

Please let this be a good idea.

I pulled upon the clouds of smoke and storm, swirling them around us to conceal our rapid advance. No chały had rushed us yet, but Koschei knew I would come. It was only a matter of time before I faced opposition.

"Do you sense him now?" Dziewanna asked, flashing an eager glance over her shoulder. A deep green cape flapped behind her, and she almost danced with it through the gales, despite lacking the control I had over them.

I closed my eyes and let my demonic hunger guide me. The pulsing of *żityje* was vague at best, but Koschei held power more vibrant than the undead warriors and demons around him. The demon within craved it, needed it. If I could only—

"He's close," I stammered as I forced away that temptation. I was in control. Otylia took my hand, likely sensing my struggle, and the demonic urges faded.

"Where are you?" Dziewanna whispered.

Her history fascinated me, but there was something she hadn't told us. The Dziewanna of Dariusz's legends was a daring and challenging goddess, yes, but her urgency surprised me. Gods lived forever. Apparently, that didn't mean they were all patient.

As Otylia searched with End's Threads, I closed my eyes and sent the winds through the army far below. Koschei had seemed a menace when I'd seen him far to the east, but I hadn't understood the full extent of his army then. Neither had Otylia and Mokosz's other szeptuchy during their shared vision on the equinox. We'd been warned. This, though, was a force unlike any other. Koschei must've commanded many tens of thousands—mostly demons forced to obey the dark gods' calls. Even the united forces of Krowik and Vastroth, along with what remained of Simuk and Zurgow, wouldn't be enough. We needed more.

We needed Dziewanna.

"There," I said, opening my eyes with relief. Touching hundreds of dead, decaying creatures with the winds had me feeling sick. "Look toward the willows along the Wyzra's north bank. He rides the white horse."

Dziewanna huffed. "He's just like my insolent brother: riding a white horse, disgracing my holy willows… I half-expect him to betray Marzanna too. If only."

"What is your plan?" Otylia asked as I studied Koschei.

A tattered black coat hung over the sorcerer's shoulders and down the steed's side. Its arcing collar obscured much of his face, but I could never forget it after our previous encounter. Skin pulled so tightly to his face that it ripped in sections, exposing bone and torn muscle beneath. His eyes were as black as Thunderstone. They seemed from this distance like empty spheres molded from the same volcanic rock as the crooked, pointed crown upon his head. Cold. Lifeless. His elites rode beside him, their long cavalry spears and war-painted masks crafted of bone the closest thing to life about him.

While Koschei's demons mulled forward to encircle the Vastro-thie camp, he stood tall before leaning over to speak to a messenger. I worried at first that someone had spotted us, but he did not act as the messenger scampered away. We were clear, for now.

"I'll plant an arrow in his head," Dziewanna said, brow furrowed and focused, "and another in his heart… If he has one anymore."

"That's it?" Otylia asked. "Why can't I just hit him with a moonblast or Wacław with his lightning?"

Dziewanna gave her the wicked grin I'd seen from Otylia far too many times. "Koschei has survived this long because he is the most skilled sorcerer who ever lived. Gods are more powerful, yes, but he would sense and deflect a magical attack. A simple mortal arrow—*that* he doesn't expect. Besides, no power we wield will kill him for long. Better to waste arrows than *żityje* ahead of the battle."

She tested her bowstring again and stared down at Koschei. "I will loose each arrow quickly. Two for the sorcerer. One for each of his honor guard until my quiver runs dry. Wacław, use your winds to guide the shots, but I doubt I'll need much aid unless this ill-crafted bow fails me."

Then she let the first arrow fly.

The others followed before I could even think, her hand swiftly reaching into the quiver, nocking, and pulling the bowstring so quickly she became a blur. Each pierced the sky and sliced toward her targets. My storm had strengthened the gales, though, deflecting them enough.

One at a time, I focused on each arrow. Dziewanna had shot hard and true, so only a nudge was enough to put them back on target. The winds were mine for now with the chały grounded. I could only hope that control lasted long enough.

Dziewanna took a long breath behind me when she released the final arrow. Twenty loosed in mere seconds. Unfortunately, there were only eight winds.

I smiled as the first arrow found its mark, straight through Koschei's unarmored skull. The second was just a finger-length off. Flying wide of the sorcerer's heart, it plunged into his shoulder, but he was already sliding off his horse, his dark crown tumbling to the snow.

Is he actually dead? It couldn't have been that easy...

The other arrows arrived in quick succession. Most struck true with my help, but a few scattered into horses' hides or the snow. Nearly a dozen riders fell along with their master. A success, at least downing the Horde's general and many of his elite warriors, but Dziewanna showed no pleasure. She wrinkled her nose instead.

"That should ensure they attack before the encirclement is complete," she said, slinging her bow over her shoulder, "but he'll know we're here now."

My jaw dropped. "You *want* them to attack now? We're not ready!"

"Neither is the Horde. As long as the west remains an option for escape, your allies have a chance to survive."

"We need to land soon then," Otylia replied. "Dawn will come soon, and I don't want—"

Shrieks echoed through the plains. The winds rioted, fighting my grip as clouds rolled from the west. Not my storms, but Marzanna's blizzards.

I snatched Otylia's hand and bolted back toward our allies' camp as streams of black arose from the army. Familiar demons flapped their torn and mangled wings, their lightning sisters shooting into the air in blue-yellow bolts that sent thunder cracks rolling through the sky. Chały. More than I could even count.

Otylia slipped from my grasp in their tempest, forcing me to meet the first alone as my own lightning snapped around us. Imprecise, it offered some defense as I tried to focus on pushing through the chały's winds. My still blistered and burned arm ached with every movement. I had to fight on. The Vastrothie needed us. My friends needed us. And I needed them.

My tether to Otylia guided me through the swirling gray clouds. We were close, but Dziewanna's shout warned me that close wasn't enough.

A bolt shot before me. A female form emerged from its electric glow, her face ravenous and lightning dancing between her fingers. She wanted to duel on the gales.

I didn't play her game.

Grudzień slashed through her extended arm before I dove to the side and stabbed with my dagger. Surprise had allowed my initial strike, but the chała zipped away from the second. Lightning whipped across her hand. She eyed Dziewanna.

I anticipated the strike, launching Grudzień between the two and absorbing the resulting bolt with its blade. The chała shrieked. I echoed the call with a snarl, and we met in a torrent of lighting and wind. Mine struck as hers stung my already wounded soul-form. Each move was too fast to understand, but training and the winds' instincts guided my parries and attacks. The other chały were too near now. I sensed their swirling *žityje* as the first sunlight slipped over the horizon.

"Wašek, the sun!" Otylia said through our bond.

I know! I gritted my teeth and slashed with one final blow, taking the first chała's head clean off with Grudzień's teeth. Too late.

"We need to go, now."

I can't. There's too many. I deflected a bolt with my blades before pushing Dziewanna with the winds, hoping Otylia could carry her for a time. *I need your help, please!*

A calm came through our bond. *"You're smart enough to not play the martyr for once. Good. Can you fly me on the winds? I'll send Mother to the Vastrothie with the moonlight I have left."*

I fired lightning into another chała that had tried to catch me off guard. She dropped, a charred hole in her chest as another of her lightning sisters replaced her. *I can carry you. Just hurry.*

Bolts cut my limbs and chest as the chały surrounded me like the strzygi had. I'd proven in the Lake of Reflection that I could absorb a chała's lightning into my own power, but I hadn't succeeded in the move since. With this many chały, all I could do was defend.

They fought me for my own winds. It took more effort to wield my power than it did to spar each demon that shot into range, and the clouds obscured all but the closest of them. I would strike through the gray masses and find the chała gone in a flash, only for it to return with their own gales battering my back.

Otylia flew closer before releasing the moon's control over her. I tried to push in her direction but could only grant her the aid of Dogoda's wind. The few winds I had full control over were barely enough to keep me alive, so the kindly western granddaughter of Strzybóg would have to be enough.

Nothing about the storm was so kind. My defensive lightning and whirlwinds cracked through the lightning chały's ranks, but their blizzard rolled nearer. Hail clattered against me, barely a stinging distraction—for now. We needed to push free quickly, or the blizzard would overrun what control I still had over the storm.

The lightning chały shouted with glee as their winged sisters arrived. Black replaced the sky's shifts of light and deep grays. What little sunlight had begun to creep over us disappeared., leaving only flashes of lightning to reveal their horrific talons and jagged teeth.

Until white light pierced the storm.

Otylia surged through the rear of the chały's circle with her silver spear in one hand and moonlight swirling in the other. The moon had faded enough for her to lose flight, but she was still a goddess. Her presence alone sent the chały into shrieking panics.

"Take my hand," she commanded, reaching out to me.

"Why?"

She furrowed her brow. "Trust me."

So I sheathed my dagger and grabbed her hand. Lightning snapped between our fingers, my black veins along that arm glowing a bright blue as she held a hand before her.

"They'll recover," she said. "When they do, let them hit us with the lightning."

"What?"

She squeezed. "The last time you absorbed lightning, I was in danger. Our bond ignites something in your power, so do it again."

I shook my head. "No, Otylia. They'll—"

The chały regrouped from Otylia's arrival as one, swooping over us. Static cracked. I clutched both Otylia's hand and Grudzień as the lightning shot from them and struck in an array hotter than the greatest fires of Noc Kupały.

I focused on my power. The winds struggled, my storm fighting the oncoming blizzard, but lightning had already surged within me. Now, a new anger grew with the chały's attack. It had fueled my power in the Lake of Reflection, but their attack was many times greater than that single chała's. So was my response.

My vision turned an electric blue, lightning arcing from my skin and spreading down Grudzień's blade. The winds no longer fought. The blizzard no longer released its hail.

I was in command.

Żityje mended the worst of my wounded arm as I raised Grudzień above my head. Lightning snapped through the sky. Chały shrieked, charging as the Moonblade absorbed the blast in its colored lines. The demons slashed at Otylia, at me, but they found only pain.

I shouted with all my might. Lightning scattered from the sword in a rainbow of bolts. It snapped and swirled as if it was part wind, burning through each chała that dared approach. Still they came, but those who slipped through met Otylia's spells. Even without the strongest of the moon, she wielded *żityje* like a goddess unbound. Her skin pulsed white as my veins seared blue.

The sky erupted between our channeling. Clouds tore apart and reformed, my storm throwing back the blizzard as the chały who'd survived fled for their master. They would find him dead. It was a temporary victory, but as I flew alongside Otylia with thunder booming in my ears and power pounding my chest, I felt for the first time that we had a chance.

We lacked the numbers of the Horde. We lacked the food of the fields and life of the wilds. But we would rule the skies and the night, the storms and the moon. Until our last breaths, we would make the deathless fear Death himself.

14

Wacław

What chance do we have against such an army?

THE GROUND APPEARED TO SHIFT like a wave. Wedges of long spear cavalry charged the Vastrothie camp, followed by endless lines of demons both flying and grounded. Mounted archers followed their spear-wielding companions, loosing enough arrows to force me higher. No mortal force before could have compared to this.

They're coming, Kuba! I shouted through my mark as Otylia and I dove after Dziewanna, who'd safely dropped into the camp moments before. *We've kept the west open, but that's it.*

His response came as a yelp, *"Sure hope that means you're coming too."* *About to land. Hang in there.*

My flight had been faster than the cavalry, but not by much. The arrows had already fallen, and a few corpses lay on the bare earth. Most of the Vastrothie warriors formed ranks behind the anti-cavalry spikes. Their thin hide shields would be less effective than Krowik's wooden ones, but it would have to be enough.

"Xobas!" I shouted with the winds carrying my voice over the shouts of warriors and roar of the storm. "Where is Commander Xobas?"

A passing warrior looked at me in shock before pointing ahead and stumbling toward the front lines. They would need my help. First, I needed to understand Xobas's plan if I was going to be of tactical use.

Otylia wasn't so patient.

"Go find him," she said, stomping away. "I'll cover the warriors with the Mothermarked Daughters."

"Be safe!" I called after her. *Please.*

She was already gone, her silver spear shining in her grasp and her free hand pulsing with *žityje*. I shouldn't have been worried. Otylia was immortal. If she died, we had ways of bringing her back, but the rest of us weren't so lucky.

A voice yelled my name, pulling me from my thoughts as a dog-like shape rushed between two nearby tents. Kuba's light brown fur was matted and snow-covered, but he appeared unharmed.

"Glad to see you're okay." I laughed in relief. "Where's Xobas? Does he have a plan?"

He gave a jackal smile. "It's my plan, thank you very much, and I was coming to fetch you for him. C'mon, before we all die!"

At full sprint, I followed him through the cacophony of shouts and hailstorm of arrows, using the winds to deflect any that threatened us. Dziewanna was nowhere to be seen. I hoped she'd found somewhere safe to hide.

Smoke obscured much of my sight. The sound of approaching horses alerted me enough, and I clutched Grudzień as the riders broke through the haze. I loosened my grip at the sight of Xobas leading them.

"You're a sight for sore eyes, my friend," he said. Unlike the Vastrothie, he wore a sleeved tunic cut at the elbow with a leather vest to protect his chest. The horse tattoo and scar on his forearm seemed to burn in the light of the nearby fires.

I nodded up at him. "As are you. I'm glad we could make it in time for the battle."

Riding alongside Xobas, General Mesfin punched his chest and nodded his bald head. "Welcome, but there is no time for idle chat. Our strategy is in motion, and another płanetnik would be of great help." The violet stones in his beard reminded me of Ira's priests as he nodded toward a nearby figure, but despite our differences in opinions, I had gotten along well with him after Darixa had placed him in charge of the northern Vastrothie army.

"Aye," Eryk said as he emerged from the smoke with his grey robes torn and hair coated in ash. "Wacław and I can aid in the air. High Chief Mikołaj sent Strzybóg's Windmarked ahead as well, so we will have numbers against the remaining chały for once."

He and I grabbed forearms in greeting. My Eclipsemark pulsed on my fellow płanetnik's cheek, and I took heart knowing my alliance with him had paid off. Hopefully we could do the same for others.

"Then fly," Xobas said. "Mokosz's Mothermarked will follow young Kuba's plan and create a ditch and wall when the cavalry reach our lines. You'll like what comes after, but we need you to eliminate their horse archers."

Mesfin huffed. "Agreed. Our ranged units are too few. Down enough of them, and we may hold long enough to organize a retreat to the west."

"Then that's what we'll do," I replied with a glance at Eryk. "To the skies."

We rose to meet a group of six Windmarked szeptuchy above the swirling smoke. Holding short bows, they resembled Dziewanna's own stance minutes before, but none looked upon us with favor. They were the first of the Strzybóg's channelers I had met since gaining my powers. My stomach twisted knowing I was in some ways using their god's force without his permission.

"My name is Wacław," I yelled over the gales. "I'm here to help."

The one who appeared to be their leader approached. A tall, narrow-shouldered woman with dark blond hair, she wore light gray trousers and a flowing cape like the others. Each bore Strzybóg's mark of two crossed zig-zagging lines on their neck. "No introductions are necessary for one like you. The enemy's charge has begun. I trust you can help us counter it?"

"With your help, I hope so." I looked down at the cavalry, now bearing down upon the camp. We had less than a minute until they arrived. "Follow me."

I charged toward the north. The horse archers circled that way toward the western opening, shooting to their left as they rode, making them a quick threat to the escape route. There were more archers spread throughout the flanks, but our group was too small to split. A stray arrow or swarm of demons could kill my mortal allies too quickly to risk sending them alone.

With a signal to the others, I launched a first wave of windblasts with Eryk. The szeptuchy's arrows followed with their own channeling to guide their aim. The blasts and arrows struck together, sweeping across the rows of riders and the demons who'd taken ranks nearby.

It was nothing.

A swarm of Frostmarked replaced the ones we'd killed. Both living and undead horse archers pushed on, but their allied demons tore them down, devouring rider and mount alike. Zmory, upióry, multi-mouthed skrzaki, and other demons I'd never seen were a writhing mass of undeath. Hungry, desperate to feed, they didn't care who their allies were, just who they could devour next.

There was no time to pity them. Otylia had shown many demons were redeemable, but others were too far gone. There was nothing I could do to save them, so we put them out of their misery.

The Horde chargers reached the defensive line as we released our next wave of attacks. I winced, waiting for the pit Xobas had claimed would open, but still they rode on. Faster and faster, they lowered their spears and neared the final leap. Until they fell.

At first, the mounts just stumbled, their legs adjusting from the change from snow to bare earth around the camp. Except the ground wasn't solid.

Mud sucked in the horses' hooves, and when enough cavalry had reached the defensive line, it collapsed into a rift as the Vastrothie Mothermarked summoned a wall of earth around the camp. Hundreds of Frostmarked tumbled with their horses, wailing and screeching with their fall. Those behind tried to slow, to stop, but momentum carried them into the ditch. Those who managed to jump the few-strides-wide gap found only a growing wall that knocked them back into the pit.

Kuba, you're an absolute genius, I told him through my mark as I sent a bolt of lightning through a group of skrzaki that had taken flight on their hideous wings. The mouths scattered across their body laughed maniacally, deafening my already battered ears. Luckily, Kuba's reply in my head required no ears to understand.

"About time people admitted it. Can you say it again, just so I can remember the sound?"

I grunted and slashed Grudzień through a skrzak's chest. The resulting silence was as satisfying as the kill. *If we live through this, I'll tell you as many times as you like.*

The arrival of flying chały and strzygi only made stopping the horse archers more difficult. Otylia and I had thinned their ranks before the battle's true beginning, but there were still enough to draw my focus. A distraction I couldn't afford. The horse archers would soon complete the encirclement, trapping my friends and thousands of Vastrothie within the Horde's clutches.

I couldn't let that happen.

Lightning snapped behind me as I dove to call a whirlwind around the lead riders. So many had fallen, but the Horde advanced anyway. Everything below was decaying flesh and rancid blood, everything above storm and ever-advancing hail. How could I stop it? How could I save my friends?

A scream echoed behind me. Flames followed, a Windmarked szeptucha twisting and dropping through the storm clouds as her skin singed to the bone.

I dove after her, but a group of strzygi forced me aside. We traded blows as the szeptucha crashed toward the earth, too far for me or anyone else to help. Instincts commanded my muscles with each slash and block. I could only watch the szeptucha fall like a dying soul's star burning through the night sky, and when she met the earth as bones and ash, I prayed that Weles grant her a rare kindness in Nawia.

I never even learned her name, yet she died fighting beside me.

My breaths grew shallow. Images of Otylia and Kuba's deaths filled my head, followed by the faces of each innocent person I'd slain in Vastroth. Weakness. I'd failed to protect those I loved, and I'd failed to control my own mind. What use was power when I couldn't wield it to save my family, my friends, and those who needed me most?

The demon answered within me, *"Power is useless in a cage."*

15

Andrij

"NEMIZA!" THE VASTROTHIE WARRIORS SHOUTED over the roar of the cavalry's charge. "Calamity has come, and Calamity will inflict her wrath!"

I raised my spear and echoed Vastroth's new name for Otylia as she strode through our gathered ranks. We'd all been shaking in our boots with the massive horde advancing upon us, but a goddess at our side brought the men hope. It brought me hope too. With furs draped across her shoulders, deathstalker scorpion armor over her torso, and a shining spear of pure silver, Otylia appeared more like a monarch than Boz ever had. My king was dead. Now, I fought for her and for Dziewanna.

"Brace!" I commanded our spear line, returning my gaze to the mass of undead, but it came out as little more than a squeak. *What a commander…* So I yelled again, "Brace!"

Each man in that line wore warpaint in designs across their faces. I saw each as they nodded to me, some bearing Mokosz's Mothermark, others Otylia's Moonmark, and others still various symbols of protection from Vastroth. My own cheek bore Dziewanna's Bowmark.

Dziewanna had saved me in her final days before the equinox, and I whispered a prayer to her as I stared down the attacking beasts. Wild eyes of pure black and bloodied white met me. Gusts swept over us as Wacław and his allies fought the demons of the sky. But neither the winds nor a few powerful friends could stop the tide to come, not alone. Even Dziewanna was powerless now.

It was up to men like me to hold the line.

Our horn blowers waited until the horses were close enough for us to see their fogged breaths. I gritted my teeth, raising my shield and clutching my spear as another wave of arrows rained upon us.

Darkness fell with the missiles, clouds of storm and blizzard blocking what little light the ever-dulling sun had offered. My hope drifted with each *crack* against the shield. It seemed forever between the first and the last, and my arm began to ache from the impacts. I worried about my shield, but soon, the arrows stopped.

I returned to my braced position against the cavalry, biting my cheek not to tremble. The horns had blown. Where were the szeptuchy?

The thunderous advance grew as horses crossed onto the earth we'd cleared around our camp. Fire and hours of effort had done their job, and now all we needed was the Mothermarked to do theirs. It had surely been too long. Had something gone wrong or—

My breaths caught as the mounts stumbled. The ground dragged their hooves down before giving way completely. Their first line dropped into a ditch that hadn't been there a moment before, and dirt and stone rose between us as the rest of the chargers crashed to their doom.

Kuba, you genius of a fool.

I'd thought Xobas mad when he told me he'd agree to Kuba's plan. As the sounds of dying men and horses alike filled the air, though, I grinned. The Mothermarked had nearly killed themselves marching us through the mountains. This was all they could offer now, but their wall and ditch had given us a chance.

Two more blasts of the horn. I pushed away any doubt and stepped onto the raised back of the anti-cavalry spikes before our formation. Kuba's plan had worked. Now, it was my turn for a surprise.

"Ready the flames!" I yelled over the chaos muffled behind the wall.

The spearmen cheered, and the largest men raised their shields, creating a ramp for the torchbearers to reach the wall's peak—nearly two-men high. I watched with pride as a hundred fires appeared over our defensive circle.

That pride waned at the sight of a burning Windmarked szeptucha. Lightning had snapped constantly through the sky, but her scream drew all our gazes. Cloak set ablaze, she fell beyond the wall, turning our raucous anticipation to dread.

Dead Windmarked or not, I pulled the firebird feather from my pouch. Dziewanna's gift had burned the bandits at Małe Wzgórze. She lacked her power now, but her fury still burned. A single loss would not change our will to survive. The horn blew at my sign, and we shouted together as the men threw their torches into the army of darkness.

Burn in Dziewanna's flames.

I held my breath for each moment after. It was like a cavern opening in my stomach, knowing that if this failed, thousands would die. Narcyz would die.

No, the plan *would* succeed, and I forced myself to believe as we waited for the torches to fall over the alcohol-soaked ground. The Vastrothie had left Huebia with plenty to drink. They'd not responded well to my suggestion to burn it, but it had worked against those bandits moons ago. A dozen enemies or a hundred-thousand, numbers didn't matter. Fire burned all.

A chorus erupted from the other side of the wall. Pain? Burning? I took a shaky breath and looked up to the nearest torchbearer. "Well? Did it work?"

The man who'd climbed triumphantly moments before just stared down at me in disbelief. "It caught for a second, but there's a wi—"

A bolt of ice ripped through his throat. His eyes rolled back as he clutched at the weapon that had impaled him, but blood poured through his hands. He tried to speak regardless, to gurgle out a phrase. Nothing came, and he tumbled off the platform of shields, dead at our feet.

All around the camp, other torchbearers suffered the same fate. Ice joined the next foray of arrows as someone shouted for us to raise our shields. Only years of training saved me. My legs shook and my mind spun as I blocked an arrow that had been aimed right at my head. I'd failed. Fire would burn the demons, but I hadn't thought about Frostmarked channelers. They extinguished fire and struck us down from farther than any archer could.

A massive force struck the wall, sending dirt over us and into my eyes. I winced and tried to wipe it away with my sleeve as the smell of death hit my nose. I'd witnessed it before, but in these tight quarters, it choked me by the time I finally cleared my vision. We'd all rot soon if something didn't change.

"I really hate the sun," a familiar voice muttered behind me.

I turned back to see Otylia glaring up at the wall, now bearing a crack down its entirety. "You can't just call the moon back?"

She shook her head. "Not how it works, but I could really use flight right now. Climbing the shields to the wall's top would just make me everyone's target without doing much."

"We have to do something," I replied before reaching into my pouch for the feather again. "I think I can."

"A firebird feather."

"From Dziewanna," I said. "Its fire burned more than any mortal fire I've seen before. Maybe it can set the trap."

Another *boom* rocked the wall. Warriors shifted nervously around us, looking at Otylia as if she had a solution.

"You want to go up there?" she asked me. "Did you see what just happened to your torchbearers?"

I looked her dead in the eye. "They didn't have you to protect them."

She grimaced. "Fine, but only because that's Mother's firebird feather. Call your shields. I'd take the feather for you, but it'll be hard enough to protect you with all my *žityje* focused on defense."

"I wouldn't have asked otherwise." I signaled for the warriors to create the ramp again. "This fight is mortals' too. We can't act like the gods will save us without our help."

Otylia didn't reply, instead jumping onto the first level of shields and running ahead of me. I sighed and looked back toward our tent at the camp's center, where Narcyz lay unconscious. We'd see each other again, I promised myself. I just hoped it was in this life.

Atop the wall, ice bolts struck a shimmering silver shield Otylia had called before her. She held one hand out to maintain it as I reached her side. With the other, she seemed to be reaching out for the demons, her eyes flashing white.

Beyond her was Oblivion itself. A wave of thrashing, decaying beasts of every size beneath the raging sky. Each snap of lightning revealed the gaping maws in eager anticipation of their feast. Szeptuchy shot ice at us, our allies, and the wall itself in spikes and great boulders that shook me with each impact. Amid it all, snow and hail began to fall as the bitter winds swept through my coat and send the feather's flames drifting.

I stood high above, but I'd never felt smaller in my life. This was a battle of gods, of sorcery. I was just a man.

"Do it!" Otylia snapped, holding her ground. I could barely stand, yet she rose above the battle like a great force demanding to be heard.

I listened, but with the feather held before me, I realized I had no idea how to release the flames without losing Dziewanna's gift. Magic was strange. Wacław had spoken so much about *żityje*, but I'd never truly understood what it meant. That changed then. Something shifted in me, a burning in my chest growing with every breath.

A boulder of ice smashed into Otylia's shield, sending shards scattering over us and slicing my arms and face.

"Now, Andrij!" she pleaded. Sweat beaded on her brow, and the shield flickered. "Push your energy into it!"

I grabbed hold of that fire within me. My breaths were rapid, my heart pounding as my nightmares advanced upon the camp, and within it, my friends, the boy I'd fallen for. Narcyz always said he'd kill me if I died. So I released the energy boiling in my chest, sending it into the feather and pointing it toward the Horde.

"Burn!" I shouted.

Flames burst from the feather. Searing heat washed over me, and a force tried to throw me from my feet. I resisted, grabbing the feather with both hands and yelling with all my strength until the earth was fire and the sky nothing but smoke.

Then it stopped. My legs failed. I dropped to my knees, clutching the feather to my chest as another blow struck the wall below. Otylia repeated my name, but it was weak, distant. She grabbed hold of me, forced me to stand. I relented. My mind was gone, my lungs choked from death and ash, but despite her pull, I stared over the field of destruction I'd caused.

Demons screamed and burned. They struck at one another in anguish, some falling into the ditch and others fleeing into the tide of forces behind them. The Horde trampled friend and foe alike, but for the first time, they didn't threaten the camp. Or so I thought.

From the flames walked five szeptuchy with frost trailing at their coats' hems. Together, they linked hands and whispered to themselves. Otylia tried to launch a spell, but she was too late.

A battering ram of ice appeared before the Frostmarked. As large as a longhouse, it hovered in the sky before plunging toward us. Otylia's rushed spell struck it, but the ram only chipped. There was no time for her to try again or for us to flee as it crushed the wall below.

The ground disappeared in a torrent of stone. Stumbling, I threw myself back into our ranks, hoping I'd done enough. The smoke burned the sky for the entire fall, and as I hit a line of shields below, all I could do was pray Dziewanna would protect Narcyz as she had me. Her power had faded for now. That changed nothing. We needed the wilds to defeat winter, and I needed her strength to survive.

16

Otylia

I'm going to die surrounded by demons and sweaty men. It almost makes me wish for Jaryło's blade.

DIRT AND ASH FILLED MY MOUTH. Shouts hammered my ears as beasts leaped the chasm created by the Mothermarked. Monsters. I hated them.

The demons hurled into the anti-cavalry spikes, impaling themselves but fighting on with the weapons piercing through their flesh. Many flashed upióry fangs, and dark fumes poured out of diseased nezhits' mouths. Warriors collapsed with a single breath of the vapor. Their comrades tried to hold the line, but the upióry and zmory were faster.

I scowled and forced myself to stand. The Vastrothie lines were broken. Everything would turn to slaughter if I couldn't stop it, but the cursed sun burned above the clouds.

I raised an arm at the charging beasts. What little moonlight I could muster swirled around my hand, and I released a moonblast that threw the closest ones back into their own ranks. *Useless!* The same spell would've torn them apart at night. Instead, they devoured the corpses of their own before attacking the shocked warriors.

Get up, Andrij.

The Astiw had fallen beside me, but he was nowhere to be seen. I'd tried to protect him. The wall had just been so exposed, and my moonlit *pri* shield had faltered beneath the szeptuchy's barrage. *Stupid sunlight!*

Wacław pitied the worst of the demons. I didn't. End's force allowed me to help those with some fragment of life left in them, but these monstrosities pouring over the collapsed wall were too corrupted to save. I'd reached for the few Threads of Life among them, but there was no time for redemption in battle. The only mercy I could offer these tormented souls was death.

But none of that mattered if I got trapped in Nawia again.

Three horn blasts rang through the camp, and I followed the warriors as they retreated into a sloppy shield wall. The other sections of the Daughters' earthen barrier had held, but had cracks stretching down them. We'd be surrounded quickly. Andrij had killed hundreds of demons, maybe even a thousand, between Mother's firebird feather and his burning alcohol, but it wasn't enough. Nothing was. This camp was a death trap, and we'd walked right in.

Andrij's down! I told Wacław through our bond as the demons caught up. *Is the west open?* Warriors stabbed together, dropping back behind their shields before rising to strike again. A small *pri* shield protected me, and we slowly struck down the waves of unarmored attackers.

"I'm trying!" Wacław's frantic voice replied. *"There's just too many, and my żityje is fading. If we're going to get people out, we need to do it now in as big a charge as possible. Any longer and we're doomed."*

Then keep trying. I'll find Xobas.

The warriors cried out as I stepped out of the front line. Another warrior replaced me, but he wasn't the one they called Nemiza. They'd wonder how they could succeed if Calamity fled.

That was exactly the problem. We had no chance of victory. Our desperate defense had slain more demons than I'd ever seen, but it was barely a scratch against Koschei's forces. Mother had believed forcing them to attack early would help us. I had my doubts.

Once I pushed myself free from the ranks of Vastrothie warriors,

I shouted for Xobas. He'd be somewhere behind the lines, ordering the horn blowers to signal commands. I was no general, though, no warrior. I had no idea what the horns meant nor where he'd be. There was a rational, reasonable way to search, but I chose instead to run, screaming at the top of my lungs.

Don't panic, I told myself. *That'll just get more people killed.*

But the growing fear of the warriors was contagious. They knew their plans hadn't killed nearly enough of their enemies. They could see the endless wave of decay and death, and the only thing mortal men feared more than a strong woman was Death himself.

I reached the far northern edge of the camp as the rest of the wall crumbled. Any semblance of tactics disappeared in moments.

Men screamed and collapsed beneath upióry swarms that consumed their blood in vast amounts, growing larger and larger with each drained victim. Wilkołaks burst through the holes created by lower-order demons and joined the bloodsuckers. Their half-wolf, half-man forms flashed a harsh gray in the flashes of lightning. All claws and teeth, they tore apart what the upióry hadn't drained. I was all that stood in their way.

I tried to use my spells to help the Vastrothie re-form their lines, but it was no use. Out of formation, a single warrior struggled to stand his ground against lower-order demons like zmory, let alone bloodthirsty beasts larger than a bear and faster than a wolf. Zmory were frightening but fightable. A grown upiór alongside a werewolf was another story.

Retreat soon became my only choice. The northern flank had turned to a slaughter that made Bustelintin look like child's play. My stomach turned. Fear alone prevented me from vomiting, and I stumbled blindly through the camp with the smell of gore and sounds of suffering washing over me. End's wisps only amplified the agony, its visions of each death taking my mind as I struggled to control my power.

Calm! Ildes told me to be calm to control it.

How could I find my calm center when everyone was dying around me? Everything I tried only delayed more death, but I had to try *something*. Muttering spells in the old tongue at least kept the voices of the dying from driving me insane. I would help them. We could escape. We would—

I turned about, trying to figure out where I was, but smoke and nezhits' black vapors blocked all but a few strides around me. Was I still on the north side of the camp? The clouds blocked any view of the sun, and Wacław's battle had shifted so rapidly I couldn't tell if his lightning was still to the west. I couldn't even remember if I'd been calling for Xobas. The voices had just kept growing from whispers to screams, never relenting as I flung spells in every direction.

Living and undead, man and beast, they all appeared the same as they stumbled through the misty gray. Nightmares, all of them. I felt their pain, even that of the most corrupted. A terrifying, consuming hunger combined with eternal dread as the fragment of Wacław's demonic power flared within me. I'd taken it to save him in Huebia. Now, it tore me apart from the inside, and I fought desperately to live, to breathe, to be free of this prison of a battle.

A horse burst through the field of muck and blood. Xobas rode upon its back, crimson coating his armor and curved blade. "Otylia, are you hurt? The men said you disappeared."

"We need to leave!" I snarled.

"How? The west wall has fallen. The demons block our escape all the same."

I clenched my fists and released a shout that sent *žityje* shooting in an arc around me. "Send everyone at once. Wacław and I will open a hole. Then it'll take every single warrior to push through it."

He furrowed his brow, but I swung myself onto the back of his horse. "No questions," I said. "Go if you want to live."

Xobas pushed his horse into a canter, sending us storming through the uncoordinated battle faster than I could comprehend. He rode with direction, though, never slowing until we reached General Mesfin and the horn blowers. Then he patted my leg and nodded his head toward the right.

"I'll coordinate the charge. Go. Your mother is with Narcyz and the others that way. They'll need your help."

My legs carried me in the direction he pointed as four horn blasts echoed through the forest. Fear for Mother joined my other worries, and I hated myself for leaving her. Four years without her had been too long. No matter what, I refused to lose her again.

Stray demons had broken entirely through the warriors, forcing me to stab and moonblast my way toward Mother and the other camp followers. They had no way to defend themselves. The warriors had been their only hope, but now, it was up to me to lead them out.

Mother soon appeared amid the smoke. She stood atop a row of tipped, arrow-ridden carts with her bowstring pulled to her cheek and her cracked antlers slicing through the darkness.

"Mother!" I called as a pair of nezhits swarmed her.

Her only reply was to release the bowstring and nock a second arrow before the first had even struck. One nezhit fell. The other lunged at her with teeth bared, but her arrow shot straight through its open mouth with enough power to stick out the back of its head.

A round of weeps and sighs came from beneath Mother as I approached. People peeked out from the tent-like structure the carts had formed to protect against arrows and ice bolts. One of them was Kuba.

"We're definitely doomed, then," our jackal friend mumbled at the sight of me. "No way you'd be here if we weren't running."

I looked from him to Mother, who still stood guard. "We're running. Tell everyone to follow me."

His jackal tail drooped. "Narcyz is starting to move. He's asking for Andrij… Is he okay?"

"I don't know, and there's no time to search." I resisted the urge to look back at the turmoil. "Can Narcyz walk?"

"Kinda."

"Then throw him in a cart and get someone to pull. We're leaving."

I jumped up to Mother, *žityje* rushing through my fingers as another group of demons scrambled over destroyed tents and leafless trees. Mother released her arrows, but the trickle of attackers was growing. Soon, the flood would take all of us.

"Your friends trust you endlessly," Mother said once a break came. "As do the Vastrothie. Good. This morning will haunt them each night, so you'll need that trust the next time you command them to face the Horde." She lowered her bow and held a hand to my cheek. "My *mała dzika*, this war has only begun. I fear, however, that it may already be lost."

I tore myself from her grasp. "You taught me to fight! And that's exactly what I'm going to do."

"Fighting will only delay the inevitable," she whispered as I started leading the camp followers, mostly women, toward the west. "I've fought enough futile wars to know when one is lost."

"Then what do you want me to do?" I replied, arms raised. Demonic snarls drew ever closer, but so did the swarm of warriors pushing ahead of us.

She raised her bow and sent an arrow flying into the smoke, where End's dark wisp exposed a charging demon. "Take me to Prawia, to Perun. My father will free you from your oath once he sees the injustice in Jaryło's actions, and my husband will aid me now that I have awoken."

"Weles didn't care before."

We reached the western front before she could reply. Warriors raised their shields and pushed as others jabbed and swiped with their two-ended spears. It was the Horde's thinnest section, but more demons joined the fray with each moment.

Mother grimaced and shot into the armies ahead. "He denied you, but he's learned to fear me. So will Koschei when I'm finished."

There was no time to ask her how we'd gather the gods' forces behind us or even get to Prawia. The warriors wouldn't be enough. They needed me, and they needed Wacław.

Wašek, now's the time!

But he wasn't above us anymore. Instead, lightning snapped far to the east, where Andrij had burned the demons with Mother's feather. The chały's shrieks had quieted or were drowned out by the clashes on the ground. It was too difficult to tell, but I didn't need my ears to hear Wacław's foolish reply.

"I'm bringing Andrij out. Eryk and the others should be enough."

Leave the dead! I snapped. *The living need you.*

Shared frustration surged through our bond. *"So does my friend."*

So be it.

I yelled and rushed into the line of warriors. *Žityje* had become hard to track as a goddess, especially away from my moon, but I didn't care how much remained in that moment. Mother was right. These people worshipped me. They trusted me. Refilling my soul could come *after* I'd brought them to safety.

The air shimmered around me as I pushed onward with every spell I had. *Meti* threw the largest upióry aside. *Strit'i* sent moonlight slicing through the demons' decrepit forms. And once I'd cleared a path three shoulders wide, *byti* held the beasts in place.

"Go!" I commanded the Vastrothie. Every muscle in my body shook stilling so many demons at once. "Kill as many as you can on the way."

A figure dropped in a spray of lightning as what remained of our army pushed through the gap. Eryk, his Eclipsemark still pulsing on his cheek, lay dead. Wacław's first marked was gone.

I cursed, but with my focus used on the *byti* spell, End's voices stole my thoughts. The demons' deaths hurt me through his force. A spear to the side, another to the head. I cried out. Tears streamed down my cheeks, but I stood my ground, light pouring from my out-stretched fingers. I would not fall. I would not fail. Jaryło had believed me weak. Weles had thought me unready. The people who sacrificed in my name proved them wrong as they turned the cleared path into a river of black blood. Because of my allies, I was strong, and for them, I would fight until my last breath.

"Otylia!" someone shouted from above. "Otylia, you need to run!"

I shook my head, forcing myself from the daze End's voices and my rapidly draining *žityje* had pulled me into. "What happened?" I mumbled.

Mother took a long breath beside me as her fingers traced her bowstring. "Your allies are through. It's time to go."

Already?

It couldn't have been more than a minute, maybe two—far too little time for the couple thousand living Vastrothie to flee. But we stood alone in a circle of corpses. Thousands of demons glared at us, held in place by my spell. I could barely stand. My arms throbbed and my lungs burned. Empty, I could wield the spell no longer, but neither could I run.

I didn't need to.

Wacław descended with all the grace of a trained dancer. Never touching the ground, he extended a bloodied hand to me as the winds encircled us. "You've been holding your spell for almost an hour, my love, but we need to run. There's nothing left for us here."

An hour?

My lip trembled as I stared up at the boy who'd become a beast. What his dark veins didn't cover was painted in blood of crimson and black, and gore dripped from Grudzień in his off hand. He looked no different than the demons thirsting upon the blood of our fallen. Did that make him like them? A monster? A creature of the darkness? I tore my gaze from him to the demons, time slowing as hushed voices circled on End's wisps, waiting.

The force of endings let me see their ends and his alike. I'd seen destruction. I'd seen death. But at Wacław's core, I saw something else: love. For me and his friends, yes, but too for every single thing that bore a soul. Mortal, deity, demon, Naw... In one way or another, he cared for them all. That made him different. It had to. Whether Wacław was a monster or not didn't matter, because he fought desperately to protect the weakest and most lost, even when I thought it foolish.

I took his hand, my legs failing as the winds swept under Mother and me. A demon saving two goddesses. Most would've called it unbelievable moons before, but Wacław was right. If we were to have any chance, we needed the powers Nawie and redeemed demons.

I finally released the *byti* spell once we were out of the demons' reaches. A dull, heavy pain spread through my body as they finished the motions I'd frozen them in the middle of. Thousands of them lunged together, unable to stop, but I couldn't laugh at their silly flailing. The immense power I'd released had taken more than I could give. I needed to be ready. I needed to fight when the Horde chased down our allies, but keeping my eyes open was too much.

With my last bit of energy, I looked back at the burning camp. Ruin and death had taken it all, and the demons devoured the dead, searching for the *żityje* to fuel their miserable existences. A figure rode between them on a white horse.

"I'll kill you, Koschei," I whispered to myself. "You hurt my friends, and I'll make you regret it."

The exhaustion became too much, and Wacław caught me as I collapsed into sleep.

17

Wacław

I failed them. I failed her.

SMOKE HOVERED OVER OUR CAMP. Not the heavy, suffocating fumes of the battle, but a campfire's fickle puffs, which swung about with the wills of the winds. For now, it blew over me in annoying spurts. If only I had the will to raise the slightest of gales and bat it away.

I stared into the meager flames with Otylia asleep on her bedroll beside me, her head resting on my crossed legs. Heavy snow fell on my wide-brimmed hat and coat as Narcyz prodded the embers with a soggy stick. He winced with each thrust. Though he tried to hide it, I had spent enough time with the ironsmith's stubborn son to know when he was hiding his wounds. Kuba had already told me the full story anyway.

Back in Dwie Rzeki, we'd have called Narcyz a hero for saving that child and sacrificing himself to Koschei's cavalry, but his actions had gone all but unnoticed by the Vastrothie army just seeking to survive. He was surely beating himself up in spite of his bravery. What did saving one child mean when he'd lay unconscious during a battle where thousands of his brothers-in-arms died, when Andrij had nearly fallen? It meant everything to me. Narcyz bore my mark, and I was proud to be his friend, as many warriors would've protected themselves in his position.

"You should rest," I told him quietly.

He just huffed and threw the stick into the fire, then leaned back onto a fallen log. There were dozens of other campfires like this one scattered throughout the woods, but they were little more than orange flickers in the distance. Our entire group needed the isolation. Only Xobas had chosen to remain with the rest of the Vastrothie army.

Kuba lay nearby in a patch of melted snow with his head on his paws. He chuckled at Narcyz's silence. "We get it. You're tough, but staying awake ain't gonna fix Andrij."

I dropped my head. *I should've been faster.*

Andrij and Otylia had fallen with the Mothermarked wall, but he was only a mortal warrior. I'd watched Otylia fight her way through the demons with all the vigor I'd grown to expect from her. Andrij, though, had disappeared among the wave of attackers. If it hadn't been for him using the firebird feather to burn a small gap in the Horde's ranks, I would've thought him dead. It had seemed an eternity before I'd been able to break away from the battle in the sky and drag him out, and by then, he'd almost been dead. Unfortunately, choosing to save him over aiding my allies had come at a cost.

I removed my hat and traced the black bloodstain that still marked its interior. Eryk's blood. We'd been enemies when he'd lost that hat, but in the moons since, he'd become my first Eclipsemarked and first real hope that demons weren't all permanently lost. Now he was dead, slain by the chały and strzygi I'd left him to fight.

"It's not just Andrij," Narcyz muttered at Kuba, digging his heel into the melting slush. "Eryk was one of us. You, me, him. There were only three Eclipsemarked, and now one's dead. Could be us next. Just sucks."

Without knowing how to reply, I closed my eyes. The remnants of the fire flickered red across my eyelids like the anger pushing against my sorrow. I wanted badly to kill Koschei for the suffering he'd caused, but facing him again would just bring more pain. Narcyz was typically a brute. Hearing his worries only strengthened my own. How could I protect my friends when we faced entities capable of killing them in a single stroke? Would I keep having to choose between what I felt was right and what was strategic?

"I'm gonna search for the fern flower on the solstice," Kuba said after a long while.

Narcyz finally raised his gaze, his mouth crooked. "*You* think you can find the fern flower?"

"Yeah, I do."

"And how you plan to do that?"

"Well…" Kuba stood and pawed at the ground. "Jackals can smell good and hear good, so I figure if I smell the flower and hear the spirits around it, I'll probably find it."

Quick footsteps approached, and Ta's slim frame swept through the nearby trees to Kuba's side. She wore a long brown coat that trailed *into* the ground. It was high-collared and sleeveless, hiding Mokosz's Mothermark but revealing toned arms for a girl of only thirteen. When she spoke, her pace shifted as often as Kuba changed his mind. "Why ya' care about a flower? Some girl ya lookin' for?"

A whine escaped Kuba's throat. "I'm hoping Maja might be with Mikołaj's army. They didn't bring many camp followers into Solga, but this is different."

My heart sunk even deeper. "I'm sorry, Kuba." The rest didn't need saying. There was little likelihood Maja would have any interest in continuing their courting if she knew he was no longer human.

"Doesn't matter. I'll find the fern flower and get it to turn me back. The legends say it gives all kinds of powers if you resist the demons protecting it and everything. I only get one night to try."

Ta cocked her head. "That's one glass-built bet. I like it!"

I held a finger to my lips. "Otylia needs to sleep. Holding back the demons pushed her way too hard." She hadn't moved a muscle since she'd collapsed in my arms. Another cost of me saving Andrij.

"Sorry…" Ta said with a wince.

"So you're going alone," Narcyz said to Kuba. He spoke with intent, and I took some relief seeing him more like himself, if only for a moment.

"Have to, according to the legends," Kuba replied.

Narcyz huffed, then grabbed his chest with a grimace. "I'd say that's stupid, but all the other legends keep coming true."

I studied Kuba. He seemed confident of his choice, but enough of his ridiculous ideas had failed before. "When you step into the forest tomorrow night, you know there'll be no turning back, right? Everyone we know who has gone after the fern flower never returned."

"Yeah," Kuba said with a shrug, "but I'm not that drunkard Jon or Emil… or Kacper… or Mieszko… Okay! I get it. A lot of people have died going after it, but I have to try."

"Your funeral," Narcyz muttered. "Again."

Ta cocked her head, giving no care to the strands of unkept hair that draped over her face. "How ya know it'll actually work when you get it?"

Kuba just shrugged again. "Dunno. Figure something that can do whatever you wish could change me back."

"And you'll just be the first to find it? Sounds like an air-brained plan."

"Nah. Heroes find it in the legends, and they got all types of awesome powers and wealth." He grinned. "Might even be enough to build me my own longhouse!"

"Kuba, chief of the fools," Narcyz spat before throwing a loose twig into the fire. Sparks scattered over us, and I grimaced at the few that got past my guard and fell onto Otylia's face.

"Can you not make everything worse for once?" I snarled.

He reached into the snow at our feet and threw a handful of it over the fire. It sizzled over the logs as he stomped away, grumbling to himself, and in that moment before he disappeared, I could've sworn I saw a snap of light across his fist. It was gone in an instant, if I'd seen it at all. It was hard to trust my own mind after Huebia. Still, I could've sworn there had been a spark there.

Ta's attempts to save the fire pulled me from my thoughts, but the flames vanished anyway. All that remained were a few faint trails of smoke. The chill followed quickly, and I cursed Narcyz under my breath. Not for myself, but for Otylia, who needed the warmth to recover from holding Koschei's army still for nearly an hour.

I leaned down and kissed her temple. No movement still. She was stone cold, despite resting by the fire for a few hours, and I sensed little *żityje* in her soul. Dziewanna had insisted I not give her daughter the little I had left. My heart ached not being able to fix Otylia's pain, though, and the pain only grew when Dziewanna approached, glancing from the dead campfire to me.

"Kuba, Ta, can you give us some privacy?" she asked firmly. "This fire isn't doing much for your constitution anyway."

Kuba glanced at me as Ta scampered to her feet. I gave a forced smile and nodded in confirmation. His loyalty to me meant everything, but whatever Dziewanna had to say was for me to face alone. Going after Andrij instead of helping the army flee had been my choice. The consequences were mine too.

"Narcyz's work," I said, flinging my arm toward the smoldering embers as Dziewanna approached them.

She held her arms crossed. Her deep green dress was cut into rough slits below the waist—both purposeful and from the battle—revealing her hunter's trousers and a long knife sticking out of her boot. The blade had a well-crafted stone hilt, so I assumed she'd pulled it from one of the dead Vastrothie. Despite being tucked away, I got the feeling she wanted her counterpart to see it.

"Otylia told me that boy has the temper of a mare in heat," she replied with her toe kicking through the snow at the fire's edge. Head lowered, her cracked antlers appeared like razors in the moonlight. "We'll need that passion to survive this."

"We'll need more than that."

"That is true." She raised her gaze to Otylia in my lap, fury filling her gaze. "We'll also need you to not be too soft-hearted to realize that losing a single ally is better than abandoning those who need you. The Vastrothie lost warriors because you went back for Andrij, and your own marked płanetnik died without your cover."

I bit my cheek. "You're right, but it was only for a few minutes. I thought—"

"You thought you could be the hero and a friend, that your own emotions wouldn't cloud your judgement. They did! Without Otylia expending herself far more than she should have, the entire army could have been lost." She leapt over the fire with surprising speed, landing before me with her fists clenched at her sides. "Protecting Otylia matters more than anything else, Wacław. To abandon both her and thousands of desperate warriors and camp followers who *you* dragged from Vastroth was more than foolish. It put at risk the fate of every soul in the Three Realms."

My own fury burned in my chest. "I protected my friend, the messenger you saved moons ago! What's the point of fighting if we lose everyone we love? I thought I cared about saving everyone in my tribe and beyond, but I was wrong. I didn't fight my way to Nawia, through Vastroth, and to Marzanna's palace because I'm afraid of losing people who've despised me my entire life. I did it because I love Otylia, because I want to keep my friends and family safe."

I gritted my teeth. I'd tried to hold back my anger, but I'd done what I thought was right in the moment. Andrij had needed me.

Dziewanna crouched before me. This close, the scars beneath her skin were obvious, and the pain in her expression was all too familiar. "You don't think I know what it's like to be hated? I lost my place in Prawia because I fought my father. I spent centuries married to a man I did not choose, serving Jaryło each spring so that *he* could have the glory among mortals for slaying Marzanna. Fighting blindly with my emotions left me broken, alone, and without worshippers. You are good to protect your friends, but in war, you have allies, not friends. Keep alive those you need most or your efforts will crumble like my own did against Perun."

"You said before that parents do anything to protect their children," I replied. "How is this any different?"

She ran her fingers along Otylia's cheek. "Perhaps you're right. Otylia is our strongest asset, but she is far more than that for you and I. You must decide, then, what you are willing to sacrifice to keep her alive. The same for each of your friends. It is harsh, but the line deciding that choice will be different for each of them."

"What would you give for her?"

"I gave everything, and I would give more if I could." Dziewanna stood and took a long breath, looking to the moon. "Nothing in the Three Realms matters to me without her. It could all burn, but as long as she and I are together and free, we can rebuild what was lost."

18

Andrij

It's all ash.

Gray filled my vision. Shadows moved behind the veil, but they were vague forms at best. I'd tried a hundred times to wipe away whatever rubble that must've messed with my eyes. Nothing had changed.

Pain shot across my side as I tried to sit up on the bedroll Wacław had set me on. Without sight, it was hard to know my surroundings, but the feel of the woolen blankets calmed my panic as I listened to the wind whistle through the trees. The sound was dampened, so I assumed Wacław had found me a tent after he'd flown me to the rest of the group after the battle. It had all happened so fast...

Footsteps crunched through heavy snow outside—Narcyz's, based on the weight and his grumbling. We were far from the remnants of the army. Their voices were only audible if there was an exuberant shout, but after the slaughter we'd just endured, there was little joy to be had.

"He'll get himself killed," Narcyz mumbled as his shadow became visible. "I won't go to Nawia to save him this time. Not that idiot."

I chuckled, then gasped at the resulting pain, spurring him to rush to my side.

"You're awake!" he said in a far softer voice than he used with the others. "Sure as iron thought you were a goner when you didn't come back with Otylia."

"You should be resting too."

A rustling, then a drumming. His fingers against his leg? "Maybe. Just couldn't stay still after I missed the battle. I should've helped instead of lying there while everyone else fought."

I shook my head, which was a mistake. Even my neck was stiff, and the motion had me dizzy. "We both know that would've been a bad idea. You can barely walk, let alone fight thousands of demons."

"Better than letting you fight alone." His voice cracked, and he paced as much as he could in the small space. "Couldn't even find a healer. All the herbs are dead or covered in a load of godsforsaken snow! Maybe it don't matter. We'll all die anyway when we lose."

"I treasure your optimism."

"My what?"

I grinned. "Your positive spirit. It was sarcasm."

Whatever expression he gave was too subtle for me to tell, but the snow crunched beside me, signaling he'd knelt there. He reeked of sweat after traveling for so long. "How am I supposed to be positive? All of them just died out there, Andrjusha. That was almost us."

"We have good friends." I raised a shaky hand to where I thought his cheek was. Thin, scattered patches of stubble covered it from his time recovering. He hated when I pointed out his inability to grow a full beard, but it was cute. "We can't stop Marzanna, so we have to do what we can to help them do it. Dziewanna and Otylia will find a way."

He scoffed, but didn't pull away. "Dziewanna doesn't even have her powers."

"Her feather!"

I tried to push myself up to search for it, but the pain sent me collapsing back to the bedroll. Each breath sent fire through my lungs. I heaved and coughed as Narcyz took me in his arms, my ears deaf to his appeals. There was nothing he could do to help. The fall had done its damage, and I would at least need time to heal—if I even could.

He pressed the firebird feather into my hand. "What's wrong with you?" he asked when I managed to stop writhing. "Why do your eyes look all weird?"

I closed them and took short, sharp breaths between each forced word. "The fall. I can't see more than shadows."

Silence. Not even a breath from him. It held for a long time, so I focused on the creaking of the trees beneath the weight of the oncoming blizzard. Wacław had told Narcyz through his Eclipsemark that the blizzards disrupted his power, and that only made me more nervous. He and Otylia were our greatest weapons. We had szeptuchy, but before the battle, there had been only a handful of Mother-marked ones from Vastroth and the Windmarked ones Mikołaj had sent ahead. How many had survived?

Maybe Narcyz is right. We're outmatched.

Narcyz shifted until he lay beside me, half-on the narrow bedroll. He tried to roll to his side at first, but then yelped and settled on his back like me. "What you smirking at?" he asked.

I hadn't realized I'd been smirking, but at his comment, I laughed. It didn't matter that it hurt. My heart needed the bit of joy. "I missed you."

"Shut up."

"You don't need to ask me twice."

We lay there for a while, quiet again. His breaths, though, were quick and shaky. If he were Wacław, I wouldn't have been surprised by his worry, but Narcyz never panicked like this. I shifted closer to him until our elbows touched, then scooted a little more.

"We'll face it together," I whispered. "I promise. Once we're healed, we'll face them with all the fury of wildfire and speed of lightning."

19

Wacław

How do we move on from this?

SCREAMS PIERCED THE DAWN AIR as I weaved my way through the scattered remnants of the Vastrothie army. Healers treated the wounded and cared for the dying, but they were few. The lack of available herbs with the snowfall only made matters worse. Men and woman alike died in agony, no medicine to numb the pain.

I kept my head low, so the brim of my hat protected my face from the whipping wind that had come with Marzanna's most recent blizzard. In truth, it was more than that. I couldn't meet the gazes of the Vastrothie warriors and camp followers. They had suffered in their homeland because of me, and now many more had died when I'd left to save Andrij. Even if they didn't know that, Dziewanna's words weighed heavy on my shoulders.

How many of them would I give for my friends, for Otylia?

My heart gave one answer and my mind another. Protecting those I loved was more important than anything to me, but did it matter when they would die without allies? War was about strategy and numbers. I wished it could be simpler, that I could face Koschei myself and end this with a duel between the two of us. Unfortunately, nothing was simple anymore.

The faces I did see through the camps were solemn. Men wept and sat in the snow, as many of their belongings had been left in the desperate retreat. Women stared emptily at their repair projects, and their hands shook when they managed the heart to push onward. Today was supposed to be the summer solstice—a day of annual celebration for Krowik and many tribes—but not a chin was high. Not a mug of oskoła was raised. The fires of Noc Kupały were smothered in frost, cold and dead like the enemies we faced.

And the winds… I raised my arm to greet them, but no answer came. Marzanna's magic was too powerful amid her blizzards. This one, though, was the greatest yet, taking any connection I had to my power. I felt exposed, mortal.

The central camp covered the middle of a valley full of dense trees. In Krowikie fashion, Xobas gathered with eight other commanders beneath the branches of an oak. Father had always said Perun provided guidance beneath his tree, but the oak looked as dead as all the others.

A knot filled my stomach as I approached my old mentor with a nod. Xobas returned the gesture, but he was no better than the rest. Dark circles shadowed his eyes. A new wound had also joined the old scar and tattoo along his forearm, still ripe with drying blood. Some would've thought him too prideful to have it mended, but I knew him too well. He knew how badly the army suffered. A scrape wasn't enough for him to take the healers away from the men and women surrounding his camp.

One of the Vastrothie commanders was speaking, so I kept my silence, opting to stay near the edge of the circle.

"How can we trust this foreigner any longer?" the man barked at General Mesfin. "Xobas led us here at the whims of the Krowikie, one who is a demon! He promised us aid from Krowik and the eastern clans, but instead, we are left to the slaughter."

A few others murmured in agreement until another man stepped forward. Dressed in the same tortoise armor as the others, he had long braided black hair that had a single violet stone at its end, representing a great victory recognized by Vastroth's former scions.

"We should return to our lands. This war is lost. The longer we stay here, the less of us who will live to defend Vastroth when the Winter Witch attacks again."

"We have orders from Queen Darixa to aid Krowik until the war is over," Mesfin replied with his arms crossed. Despite the chill, sweat beaded across his bald head. "Fleeing now would make this entire march mean nothing."

The commander with the braided hair scoffed. "The queen is a child. She answers to the Great Mother, and *she* would understand that losing a thousand men is a reason to pull back. That number doubles if you count the wounded who can't fight anytime soon."

Two thousand casualties? I sucked in a sharp breath. That was nearly half the Vastrothie army dead or injured in a single battle.

"I will step aside," Xobas replied. "The clans will arrive soon with the Krowikie, and I promised the young Simukie marzban that I would lead his warriors. It is your right to choose your generals."

Mesfin nodded. "I appreciate your help in recent weeks. You are not to blame for our losses, but if this satisfies the dissenters, then it's enough."

The first commander who'd complained voiced his agreement, but the braided-hair one just clenched his fists. "This changes nothing! Our men are dead, and the rest of us will follow if we stay here."

"Wacław," Mesfin said with a questioning glance in my direction. "What do you say?"

I surveyed the commanders, ending with Xobas. He was the one with experience leading armies, not me. My input had helped lead to the clans' loss at Kynnytsia, and now I'd done the same with the Vastrothie. "I don't know."

" 'Not knowing' isn't an option," the braided-hair one replied. "Doing nothing in war is death."

"Then at least wait for my brother. Mikołaj will have warriors and hopefully a strategy. Once he arrives, I need to leave anyway."

Mesfin raised his brow. "You what? We would have been completely surrounded without you and that moon goddess of yours."

"Otylia," I corrected.

"Yes, her. The two of you kept this many of us alive. Morale is already low enough, and it would crumble if you left."

I averted my gaze. Xobas gave me the same shocked look as the others, but we had no choice. Answers to Dziewanna's power—and hopefully how to kill Koschei—lay in Prawia. Staying with the armies would save lives. It would lose the war.

"I will explain further," Dziewanna said from behind me, making me jump in shock. The commanders all took a step back as she stopped at my side. That same fury from the night before filled her eyes. "Marzanna and Czarnobóg have drained me of my power. Without it, I am of little use to you, and I believe I am the only one who can stop them. I must go to Prawia with Otylia and Wacław. Perhaps there we will learn how to slay Koschei as well."

"How long will you be gone?" Mesfin asked. "The Krowikie and clans will not be enough to stop the Horde when they attack again. We will have to fortify and stop their scouts at most."

Dziewanna shook her head and stepped into the middle of the circle. None dared to look away as she looked at each of them, then responded to Mesfin, "I cannot say. It is unheard of for a goddess to become disconnected from the force she wields, and there is strife between the gods. We will act with haste, but you must protect Dwie Rzeki until we return. Otherwise, Jawia is lost."

"The world?" Mesfin's eyes widened further. "What of Anvora, Solga, and the lands further south?"

I wondered the same thing silently. What did one village mean for the entire living realm when there were cities far larger than our own capital?

Dziewanna sighed. "There are forces in even this realm that mortals should never know. You trust my mother and my daughter, so trust me too when I say that if Dwie Rzeki falls into the Horde's hands, all the Three Realms will suffer." She spun toward the dissenting commanders with the knife from her boot suddenly in her grasp. As she approached, she held its blade to her throat. "Marzanna and Czarnobóg will spare no one. Not a goddess. Not a dragon. And not a commander too cowardly to do his duty."

Then she stormed away, and the commanders scrambled to let her by. No one dared stand in Dziewanna's path. Powers or not, Otylia was right. The wild goddess was a force to be reckoned with. We'd need that when we faced Jaryło and Perun in Prawia.

"So that's it?" Mesfin huffed at me. "We're left to fend for ourselves until you return to save the day?"

Xobas stepped to my side, laying a hand on my shoulder. "I'd hoped you'd stay longer."

"We'll stay until Otylia has recovered," I replied with guilt twisting away in my stomach. This wasn't my choice, but that didn't make it feel any better. "I'm sorry, but she and Dziewanna will need me in Prawia."

"Understood." Xobas pulled me into a tight hug that caught me by surprise. My father had never shown me true care like that, and it took a moment before I could hug Xobas back. I needed it more than I wanted to admit.

"Now go and prepare," he said when he released me with a slap on the back. "Bring our friends. A shield wall means nothing when you stand alone."

I gave him a smile and made my way back to our group's camp. Despite the pain and guilt, I had a mission—a purpose. So much of my life before the equinox had been consumed by my search for it, but my goals were clear now. I met the gaze of each Vastrothie, for I would fight for them. I brushed my fingers against the bark of each trunk along my path, for I would help Dziewanna breathe life back into them. I clutched the Mothermark amulet hanging from my neck—returned to me when Darixa had become queen—for I would protect Mom and all those I loved. And I traced the joined Moonmark and Eclipsemark upon my forearm, for I would never leave Otylia again.

This realm had despised me, betrayed me, exiled me, but I swore to myself I would save it. Gods be damned. I would save Jawia, no matter what stood in my way.

20

Wacław

I never thought I'd be so happy to see him.

A TALL, BUILT YOUNG MAN RODE a chestnut horse at the front of an army that stretched into the forests behind. High Chief Mikołaj of Krowik had his mother's light brown hair and our father's pride. Furs covered the shoulders of his coat, leading down his woolen cape as he raised his chin at the gathered Vastrothie.

"My allies from the south," he said loud enough for all to hear. "Where is my accursed half-brother? Your scouts said he survived the battle, thank Perun."

I smirked at his attempt to care whether I lived or died. "I'm here, Miko," I said, approaching my half-brother with a touch on the brim of my płanetnik hat. "Or should I say, 'my chief'?"

He dismounted, handing off his horse to a Krowikie warrior before approaching me with a cocky grin. "High chief, thank you very much."

"You're welcome. It was my plan that gave you the position, after all."

"Yes, Narcyz informed me." He stopped before me and grabbed my forearm in greeting. It was a gesture of respect he'd never given me before. Had he truly changed, or did he just fear what I could do to him now? "Your exile is over, by the way. It was hard to contest Mieczysław's anger after the show you put on back home, but I think you and your woman being our only hope to survive changes things."

I gripped his arm hard enough to make him wince. "*Otylia* grew up with us, Miko. We both know she'd rip your guts out if she heard you couldn't even say her name."

Another rider dismounted nearby, and I smiled at Zakir as Sosna, the red fox Otylia had called in Bustelintin, leapt from the back of his horse and rushed to me. Zakir kept his head low. "She may do so when she hears what has happened. Where is she?"

"Resting," I replied, giving Sosna the attention she so badly wanted. "She used a lot of *żityje* to help the Vastrothie escape the Horde and hasn't woken since."

He whispered to himself before raising his voice. "We must talk."

"Zakir's right," a soft voice said from above. Sabina drifted from the branches, her nymph wings fluttering weakly, barely catching her when she touched the ground. Slashes still covered them from her battles in Vastroth, and without the moon, she couldn't use Otylia's power to fly either. She stuttered, trying to find her words until a golden eagle swooped to her side.

"It's about Ara," Vlatka said. The witch who'd returned with us from Nawia was trapped in an animal form like Kuba, but she'd taken the transformation much better than him.

A pit formed in my stomach. "What happened?"

Zakir's face was gaunt as he looked at Mikołaj. "High Chief, Xobas will lead my warriors from here."

"I will take High Chief Mikołaj and High Priestess Zhaleh to him," General Mesfin said, approaching from the crowd. "Our commanders must discuss how to proceed."

Zhaleh waited nearby, not dismounting or even looking my direction. Zurgowie green crossed her cheeks and long cloak, and the sun symbol of her people's god, Otlezd, patterned her tunic. I gave a nod in her direction despite her hostility. The usually aggressive high priestess was somehow even less compromising than Rasa before her, but she was an ally. I hoped her unwillingness to speak was just a temporary mood. Knowing her, though, I doubted she would be forthright about aiding the rest of the alliance.

Politics could wait. I guided Zakir and Sabina toward our camp nearly at a sprint. If something had happened to Ara, why hadn't we heard sooner? She and Sabina both could've contacted Otylia through her Moonmark. Unless…

"Please tell me she's alive," I said, glancing back at them.

"I… I think so," Sabina replied. "Just let Zakir talk when we get there. I don't want to mess up the details."

So on we ran until we reached the extinguished fire that marked our group's camp. Neither Narcyz nor Andrij had woken from their hastily made tent yet, and last I'd seen her, Dziewanna had gone into the burrow I'd dug for Otylia.

Kuba noticed us from beside the fire, rushing toward the new arrivals with a yap. "You made it!"

"Where are the others?" Vlatka asked. "It has been some time since I have seen Dziewanna, and she will definitely want to hear what we have to say."

"Otylia cannot be woken as far as I can tell," I said, "and Dziewanna is tending to her."

Sabina gasped at my mention of Dziewanna. She ran her fingers shakily across her high cheekbones. "She's actually here? I thought I might never see her again…"

"I am here, my little Sabinka," Dziewanna said, rising from the burrow with a smile only matched by the one she'd had when she saw Otylia. "I was furious to hear that Weles and Jaryło killed Ivan and Kyustendil, but it was a relief when Otylia told me you were alive and her first szeptucha. A fitting role for a loyal friend." She smiled at Vlatka, who flew onto the goddess's shoulder. "And if it is not my favorite witch. Wings suit you."

"They are witchy, are they not?" Vlatka quipped.

Sabina dropped to her knees. "I tried to convince Master Weles to—"

"Rise," Dziewanna replied. "You're not at fault for my husband's errors. Men become no less stubborn after a thousand years."

Narcyz pushed his head through the tent flap behind them. "What's all the—Oh! It's the nymph and the potion guy."

"Alchemist…" Zakir muttered.

"No way that's a real word," Kuba quipped back.

Dziewanna raised her hand sharply. "Enough childish banter. Bring Andrij if he is well enough, and let us listen to what our new arrivals have to say. It doesn't take much to fluster Sabina, but I know that look. Speak, young one."

As Narcyz helped Andrij limp out of the tent and onto one of the logs, Sabina wrung her hands and looked at Zakir for help. "Well… I… Maybe he…"

"Ara has been taken," Zakir said flatly.

Send me to Oblivion.

"By who?" I asked, moving to pace before realizing I had a fox wrapped around my leg. "She was in the middle of the clan encampment. How could she have been taken?"

Zakir grabbed a stick from the base of a nearby tree and began drawing in the snow. "I do not know. She was practicing her channeling, then returned to our tent. This was there when I arrived."

When he finished the drawing, Dziewanna cursed and lashed out at the air. "That idiot!"

I had to twist my body to see around the gathered group, but my own curses followed when I saw what he'd drawn.

"Jaryło's Springmark," I whispered before raising my voice. "You didn't recognize it, Sabina?"

She blushed. "I did, but I was with the Krowikie until we reunited with the clan a day ago. Otylia must have been focused or already unconscious by the time I tried to contact her."

"Why would he take Ara?" Narcyz asked. "That blood pact thing wasn't enough?"

"She's collateral for the wedding," Andrij said, but something seemed off about him. He looked at no one directly, his gaze seeming distant.

Dziewanna grimaced as she held a fist over her heart. "He saw the same flaw in the pact that we did. *He* cannot harm any of Otylia's loved ones, just as *she* cannot harm him, but that does not stop others from doing so based on their wishes."

I traced my Thunderstone dagger's hilt. "You're saying he knows I intend to kill him?"

"Doesn't take a genius to know that," Narcyz replied.

Kuba laughed. "Definitely not if you figured it out."

"Kuba," I warned. "We have an undead army led by an immortal sorcery, a goddess who needs to find her power in Prawia, a blood pact to break, and now a friend taken hostage. The last thing we need is to be fighting among ourselves. There's something else too…" I swallowed, the weight of what I was about to say making my stomach do flips. "Last night, Dziewanna and I were discussing Nawie, demons, and severed souls. We think that the Horde has grown this large because Marzanna and Czarnobóg are bringing back their dead enemies in whatever form, like we saw with the Frostmarked guards I'd killed in Huebia."

"Otylia told me Marzanna demanded a sacrifice for each Frostmarked you killed," Dziewanna said. "Manipulating souls and bodies alike requires immense amounts of *żityje*. The sacrifices she did not turn into demons likely fed her power to transform others into these severed souls."

Narcyz ground his boot into the snow. "You're saying we'll be fighting our own people when they attack again?"

"Likely so. It explains how the Horde's numbers have swelled despite fighting their way across Jawia." Dziewanna turned to me, her brow furrowed. "Have you informed the commanders?"

"Not yet. They deserve to know, but we needed to discuss this as a group first."

Andrij shifted uncomfortably, gripping his knees with his hands. "We can't ask warriors to fight their brothers-in-arms without telling them they're doing so."

Sosna yawned and released me, allowing me to pace. "Those aren't the men they used to be. I've seen the Threads of Life through Otylia's power. Many demons still have some part of them left that can be saved from the corruption, but these severed souls… They're gone."

"Unsuprising," Vlatka said. "Czarnobóg's power is the most cruel of the gods.

"Andrij is right," Dziewanna replied. "There are some forces that mortals cannot know, but this they must. Let them know what Marzanna and Czarnobóg have done to their kin and let them fight with the fury that follows. That desire for vengeance may just save them."

With her hands pressed to her chest, Sabina rounded me to Dziewanna's side. She shrunk before the goddess and bowed her head when she spoke. "It could cause them to be reckless too. We don't want more of the living to die."

Dziewanna pushed up on Sabina's chin and gave a sorrowful smile. "Many more will die to hopelessness if we do not give them the fire they need to burn away my sister's winter."

"Then we'll give it," I said. "They deserve the truth anyway, and we can't expect them to trust us while we're away if we can't tell them what they face. Jaryło took Ara to Prawia, but we were going there anyway. Let us beat him at his own game."

"You're not going alone this time," Narcyz said.

Andrij pushed himself to his feet, clutching his stomach but standing as straight as he could. He stared at me with distant eyes. "I'm coming too. We all have become friends in such a short time, and Dziewanna, you saved me when I thought I was doomed."

"Both of you need to recover," I replied as I approached them. "Having you with us would be an honor, but the journey may not be easy."

Narcyz scoffed and rose to meet me. "I'll be ready whenever Otylia is. Wouldn't be much of a warrior if I let a witch recover faster than me."

I took his arm, then Andrij's. "Then I'll be happy to bring you. I'd give you a hug, but I don't think your ribs would appreciate it."

"I'd rather swim the Smorodina's flames."

Sabina took Dziewanna's hand. "I'm coming too… If that's okay? You and Otylia are everything to me. My abilities are still new, but—"

"All whom my daughter trusts may come," Dziewanna said.

I looked back toward our sleeping burrow. "We'll be opposing Perun, Weles, and Jaryło combined in Prawia. We're no match for them in a fight, but I would rather have every ally we can in case the worst occurs."

Dziewanna gave me a sharp nod. "Answers to your Naw soul may lie there too. There are secrets even I do not know." She bent down, pushing her fingers through the snow and whispering in the old tongue. Nothing happened, and she bared her teeth in frustration. "For alliances bound like this, I would normally offer a symbol of our allegiances to one another, but my force still refuses to answer. Are there any others who you will want to bring? We should have someone remain with the army to send messages if needed."

"Give me your mark," Zakir said, almost too quietly to hear. "Ara says a marzban should not leave his people."

Footsteps approached from the path to the other camps, and Xobas spoke as he appeared beside the tent. "He should not. But he also shouldn't swear allegiance to any deity. It is not the Simuk way."

"Then who should we message?" I asked.

Xobas smiled as he approached and gave me the Simukie greeting, pressing two fingers to his nose before extending them toward me. "You've been like a son to me ever since your father commanded me to train you. Jacek was blind to who you are. I am not." He held out his forearm without the horse tattoo. "I will take your mark instead."

I stepped back. "Xobas, I… I can't…" Tears welled in my eyes at the gesture. Taking my mark would make Xobas even more of an outsider among his people, who believed only in their sacred connection to their horses. He'd sacrificed so much for me already, almost dying outside Kynnytsia to help me complete my journey. I had looked to him for guidance for years. Now, he wished to swear loyalty to me just a day after my first mark had died because of me.

He grabbed my shoulders with a firm grip, and when I tried to pull free, he only held on harder. "This is my choice, Wacław. We've both faced exile from our people and been forced to prove our worth. You're as much my clan, my family, as any I've had. I've seen your worst, but I've seen your best too. I will be your voice here."

"Eryk died because I couldn't protect him," I said. "He trusted me too."

"Dying is part of war. We wouldn't sing about the survivors if it wasn't."

It took all my strength not to say no. A mark was about more than sending messages. It involved control, loyalty, and I'd never demanded that of Xobas. He'd fought for me when he hadn't needed to, but if the demon were to take hold of me again, he would suffer under its wrath. About war, though, he was right. Death was inevitable. Perhaps my mark could help protect him and the men he led.

I took his arm in my grasp, drawing upon my lightning. "This will hurt."

He just huffed, so I pushed further upon my power. The winds remained silent beneath Marzanna's blizzard, but lightning snapped at my fingers anyway. It surged within me now. At my beckoning, it crossed to Xobas with a *crack*, burning my Eclipsemark into his skin. He didn't even flinch.

When it was finished, I pulled away, taking a deep breath from the expended *żityje*. I was low, but some things were worth using it for. It's not like I could use it on much else during the blizzard anyway.

"You don't owe me anything, Xobas," I said as he rubbed the pulsing red mark.

"I have found my second chance because of you," he replied,

"but this isn't about a debt. Now, come. Your Krowikie friends prepare for the solstice festival."

"We're at war," Narcyz said, crossing his arms and then immediately regretting pressing his ribs.

Dziewanna chuckled. "Joy is more important in trying times than any other, especially on the days when magic fills Jawia more than any other. Go, dance and jump the flames with some pretty girl—or boy—if you wish. Mother knows if it'll be your last chance to experience Noc Kupały."

"There is a girl with the Krowikie looking for you too, Kuba," Vlatka added. "I told her what happened. Seems like she's still excited to see you."

I let myself smile at that. Kuba had been close to wedding Maja before we'd left on our journey after the equinox, and now he had the chance to see her again. "See, she still loves you."

But Kuba only backed away, fear filling his jackal face. He whimpered and paced before finally blurting out, "She can't see me like this! Not like this!"

"You can go after the fern flower if you want," I said in the gentlest voice I could manage. "Just go see her first. Don't you think she deserves that?"

"She deserves a man, not a dog!"

He took off into the woods before I could reply, darting through the trees with a speed I couldn't match. I lost sight of him quickly in the thick snowfall, and I stopped beside a spruce, using its thick branches to cover me. Kuba had made his choice. The fern flower was a dangerous journey he would face alone. Part of me wished I could've convinced him not to go, but what would I have done in his situation? The magic of Noc Kupały offered him the chance to become human again. Could he really pass that up?

Call for me if you need help, I told him through my mark. *Legends or not, I won't lose you again.*

By the time I trudged through the snow and back to our camp, only Dziewanna, Narcyz, and Andrij remained. Narcyz was halfway down the trail, looking back at Andrij, who held out the firebird feather to Dziewanna.

"You saved me with one of the last days of your power," he said. "Take your feather back as my promise to serve you when you regain your force."

Dziewanna took the still flaming feather and examined it in the snowfall. It neither faltered in the winds nor dampened against the frost, and a smile crossed her face. "Thank you, Andrij. I wish I could say I saved your life out of pure selflessness, but I am glad that you have done more than just deliver a message that began my daughter's journey. When the time comes, I will make you my szeptun, as I no longer have my szeptucha. Keep the feather for now. Maybe you will have the chance to burn Jaryło with it before I do."

With that, Andrij bowed, took the feather, and hobbled toward the main camp. Narcyz gave him a kiss before guiding him with interlocked arms. I both smiled and ached at that. They would likely jump the fire tonight, declaring their relationship to the tribe and the gods. Whatever had happened to Andrij's vision, though, I feared was permanent.

Dziewanna glanced over her shoulder at me. Curiosity filled her eyes. "You may come out now, Wacław."

I stepped out from behind the tree I'd been hiding behind. "I should've known better than to think you wouldn't notice me."

"Even without the force of the wilds, I am the goddess of the hunt, and you are not as stealthy as you believe." She studied me from head to toe as I approached. "Otylia should finally wake with the aid of the moon, though not yet recovered. You should join the others until then. They look to you for guidance, and one does not need divination to see that you could use the distraction."

"I look that bad?" I asked, dropping onto the nearest log.

"Yes."

My head dropped, and I hadn't the strength to lift it. "Eryk died yesterday along with a thousand Vastrothie, and Otylia is unconscious because I saved Andrij instead. You said it yourself: This is my fault. Now Jaryło has taken Ara, I don't know how to break his blood pact with Otylia, we still have no way to kill Koschei, and my mom is sitting in Dwie Rzeki, waiting for me to return or for a messenger to inform her of my death."

She slowly sat down beside me. The smell of deep forest moss came with her, and my fear of her vanished as she laid her hand on my shoulder. "I was harsh with you earlier because you needed to hear it. Gentle teaching is not my way, but it needs to be said that I see your pain. More will come, but it is not disgraceful to mourn. Take the time with Otylia. I have other duties I must attend to."

"Such as?"

"Every goddess has her secrets."

Then she left, straying away from the camp and toward the Wyzra to the north. Surely she was hiding something, but I had no choice but to trust her. She was Otylia's mother, our only hope at stopping Marzanna. Still, a thought itched at the back of my mind.

Does she know the truth about the Nawie?

It was hard to know how much time passed as I sat on that log. Between the clouds obscuring the sun and the winds stinging my face, it seemed an endless misery. Doubts and regrets haunted me, and I feared returning to Otylia and admitting my choice had forced her to push herself so far. What love we had was stronger than that. Some part of me knew that. If only my mind allowed me to believe it.

Drums and cheering came from the main camp the closer that night came. The Noc Kupały festival was the most important of the year, a night of celebration, joy, and love. It was my first year as an eligible man. I should've been wading into the river to catch a beautiful girl's wreath and then jump the fire with her. Instead, I sat on a cold, wet log. Sober, joyless, hopeless. At least the rest of my friends and the army could find some happiness amid the struggle.

I whispered a prayer to no god in particular, asking for guidance and for them to protect Kuba. It was ironic that though it was impossible to deny the gods' existence now, I believed in their ability to change things less than ever. They did nothing as Jawia crumbled. Still, I needed the old repetition of praying like Mom had taught me. Before I stood, I prayed to the Great Mother for her too.

The warmth of the sleeping burrow pulled me in as night began to fall. Little Sosna was curled up beside Otylia, her whimpers echoing through the space. At least the fox would never fail her.

I knelt beside them and patted Sosna's head before kissing Otylia's forehead. She was deathly pale, but Dziewanna had assured me she wasn't suffering from Marzanna's Curse again. Even her *žityje* wasn't drained. Her body had just succumbed to the most intense channeling she'd ever used before, and it would take time for her to recover physically. Apparently, even gods needed to train their bodies to handle the pure power of the forces they wielded.

As I repositioned our bags to allow me to lie next to her, something slipped out of the top of Otylia's. I held the circular object up in the light slipping through the burrow's entrance. Then my heart broke.

It was a solstice flower wreath, woven with needles from the few living trees instead of the usual blossoms of summer. Otylia had never worn one. I'd always wished to catch hers, and now, with it in my hands, I wept out of joy and grief. Somehow, she'd found time to make my dream come true while we traveled through Marzanna's horror. What had I done in return?

"I love you," I whispered to her through my tears. "And I miss you so much."

The chill drifted away as I put the wreath back into her bag and slid next to her, wrapping my arm around her waist. The scar on her cheek released a dull glow at my touch. I took heart in that as I nuzzled my face into the crook of her neck and allowed my own worries to fade. I focused on the three freckles dotting her cheek and the smell of her snow dampened hair. Her soft breaths carried my thoughts away until only she filled them, and I stared at the shared marks on our forearms for a long time.

"Wake with your moon, Otylka. I'm sorry for all I've done and all I'll fail to do."

21

Kuba

This was a stupid idea.

KROWIKIE DRUMS ECHOED through the forest near the Wyzra River as I searched for the fern flower. Strange, ridiculous ideas were kind of my thing, but wandering at dusk had me regretting my choice. Once, I'd ignored the legends talking about the summer solstice as the peak of magic in Jawia. The Three Realms were closest during Noc Kupały. So were the demons.

The blizzard blocked my sight beyond a few strides. Each shadow made me flinch and spin, anticipating an attack. None came, but that didn't stop my heart from racing.

"It's fine," I told myself. "There's no creepy demons hiding in the woods. Besides, they probably know Wacław, right?"

Didn't help. I was deep in unfamiliar woods with no visibility, food, or way back to camp.

Wait… Where's the drums?

I looked back the way I came, but it was silent. The festival drums never stopped during Noc Kupały. Maybe the Horde had shown up all of a sudden, but there'd have been some sounds of combat. I definitely hadn't gone *that* far from camp either, unless I went into a daze like that one time when I'd drank far too much oskoła.

No, that wasn't it. It was too hard to get drunk without hands, and I remembered the path I'd taken. Except it wasn't there when I looked for my pawprints. Just a blanket of snow for as far as I could see. That wasn't very far, but still, it wasn't snowing enough to cover my prints completely in seconds. Something was fishy. Luckily, fishiness would probably mean magic. As long as it was the fern flower's magic and not some weird spirit out to suck my soul or something, it would be fine.

That's what I told myself at least.

Night eventually took over the forest. It was hard to tell when exactly with a giant mass of gray smothering the sky, but it was obvious enough when I couldn't see because of both the snow and the darkness. For once, being a jackal was actually useful. I heard everything that could be heard and smelled the super weird scent from ahead. It was in the direction I'd thought the Wyzra was, so I kept heading toward it.

Why is this so familiar? I wondered as I stuck my nose to the ground and sniffed my way along what seemed to be a trail of some sort. Deer, rabbits, and even wolves had become familiar to me during my couple moons in this body, but this wasn't like them or any other animal I'd smelled. It was stinky, like a damp cloth left out long enough for Mother to get mad. It didn't take long for me to discover why.

A man came into sight. Or at least it looked like a man. He wore only a sopping wet tunic that stretched to his gnarly knees. Enough hair covered them that he could've been a wilkołak like Wacław had described Bidaês as, but this one didn't growl or anything. He just stood there, swaying back and forth.

"You drunk?" I asked from what felt like a safe distance.

The man raised his head, exposing his empty eye sockets that his winding brown hair curled into. His skin sunk into his cheeks, and a gash tore open one side of his mouth to expose teeth and sinew. "The flower," he moaned.

I checked around him, but there didn't seem to be any other lurking spirits, at least that I could hear or smell. "Not drunk, then. Yeah,

I'm looking for the fern flower. Seen it anywhere?"

"It is a curse and a gift both."

Bad omen. Old priest Dariusz would've told me to listen and run, but I wasn't backing down now. "My mother calls me the same thing. 'Jakub,' she always says. 'You're a real pain, even if you're the greatest thing that's ever happened to me.' "

The spirit thing hobbled forward, and I backed up just as far. "Whoa there, buddy. Not to be rude, but your stench is really bad, and I'd hate to ruin the fur I spent all morning grooming."

"You do not understand what you shall encounter, boy," the spirit continued. He raised a wobbly hand to his right. "Many pursue the flower. Many die trying. Others falter in its grasp."

"You mean with it in their grasp?"

"No."

I looked toward where he pointed. It looked like the rest of the woods, but what did I know? "It's that way, then?"

He just stood there, unmoving. I paced back and forth, but still nothing.

"All right, then. Guess I go that way."

Down a gully and through what looked like an abandoned farm field, I plodded along through the storm. The chill had become familiar, but I still longed for warmth when I passed the farmhouse. Maybe just for a few minutes? I could at least get out of the wind and free my fur of the frost caking it.

Something pulled at the back of my mind as I rounded the house's side. It was a memory of the fern flower's tale and the trials a searcher faced. Some were aggressive spirits, but others were tricks. This seemed safe enough, though. It was just an old farmhouse.

Tufts of thatching were missing from the sloped sides of the roof that stretched all the way to the ground on either side of the wooden door. Chips flaked off the wooden boards too, but it was common with age. My family's house had decayed too without Dad's effort. He was always too busy drinking or hitting someone he wasn't supposed to, Mother and me included. Piotr the Iron Fist, they called him. It had definitely felt like iron…

The door crept open as I got closer. It was dark inside, but the holes in the roof allowed a few small rings of light near the center of the room's dirt floor. A thin object slithered across the edge of one.

NOPE!

I scampered back as fast as I could. "Bad snake. Bad snake!"

Hissing answered. Not the little hiss of the catchable grass snake that newlyweds liked to put under their bed for some "good luck," but a chorus that said to get out or get bit. I didn't need any extra warning. When the first of the brightly colored serpents appeared in the doorway, I sprinted with all my jackal speed back into the field, continuing in the direction the spirit had pointed me.

The hissing followed for longer than was comforting, but it disappeared as I entered a part of the woods where leaves actually covered the trees. Snow was lighter here with the dense canopy. It was darker too without the moonlight, and all I saw was my fogged breaths as I stopped to listen for threats. There were none I could hear.

"Don't go in creepy houses," I huffed. "Got it."

Once my heart stopped pounding, I pushed deeper into the leafy forest. Underbrush joined the life soon, and the snow on my coat began to melt as the air warmed. Vines and thorny plants made each step difficult in the dark. Smells of prey just waiting to be caught met my nose too, and it took all the focus I had to keep moving forward. This wasn't about a quick catch. I needed my body back if I wanted to woo Maja again. I needed my life back in general too. Being a jackal just felt wrong.

"Kuba..." a sweet voice whispered, tearing me from my thoughts. A familiar voice.

"Maja?"

Excitement and fear gripped me. I so badly wanted to see her, but not like this. It had been moons since I'd left on the equinox as a man who'd only just jumped the fire. So much had changed since then. I would tell her about our journeys, likely over-emphasizing my own role to impress her, but she couldn't be with a jackal.

I walked on as her voice continued, growing louder with each step I took. It didn't matter that I traveled the opposite direction. Still, she followed, and my heart warred with itself. This was the only way. I needed the fern flower to prove myself to her.

The underbrush grew thicker with each step. Or maybe my will-power faded. Either way, the forest seemed to be pulling me back to her, the ground shifting beneath my paws to force my direction. My jackal instincts took over my mortal ones, and I sprinted on in hopes of escaping her voice. It had filled my dreams every night since we'd left. I could wait a few more hours. I could resist...

The vines and thorns gave way to a grove, ringed by oaks and maples. Moonlight illuminated a woman in the middle of it. My woman.

"Maja..." My voice trembled.

This couldn't be some spirit or trick. It was truly Maja, with her round cheeks blushed pink and a wreath of purple flowers adorning her braided hair. A sleeved brown dress hugged her body, draping just over her shoulders.

She smiled softly, and I missed the press of her soft lips against mine. The stolen moments we'd had away from our parents' judging gazes. "Kuba, why do you flee?" she asked with a tear streaking down her cheek. "Don't you want to jump the fire with me?"

"I do," I replied, taking a step toward her. "It's just complicated."

"Come to me. Let me see you again."

"But I'm a beast."

Her feet drifted across the earth as she drew closer. "You are the hero who saved Wacław and Otylia. They would be dead if you hadn't sacrificed yourself to kill Marzanna's witch."

"How... How do you know about that?"

"Who in the tribe doesn't know of Kuba the witch slayer? Some even claim you defeated the witch of the Mangled Woods herself." Maja reached out for me from the light. "Come from the shadows, my love."

I followed her gentle command, moving into the moonlight and raising my paw to catch her hand. "See? This is why I need to find the fern flower. You can't marry a jackal."

Something burned in her eyes. "You are not worthy of the flower."

I tried to pull away, but she snatched me as her skin seemed to rise from her body like steam. What remained was a shifting, shadowy nothingness that devoured the moonlight, her fingers turning to talons that raked across my front legs. Fangs flashed in her teeth as she lunged for my throat.

A *whoosh* whipped through the air until a force struck the demon. I tumbled with her into a pile, flailing with all four limbs as I tried to claw my way free of her death grip. Black blood covered the ground around us, and when I finally succeeded, I looked down to see an arrow sticking through her head. Its head glinted a dark bronze, unlike our tribe's iron ones.

"Uh, hello?" I called out to my savior.

Sticks cracked to the side, but the darkness and snow obscured my sight. All I saw was the shadow of a tall, slim figure, a quiver strapped to their back and a bow gripped in their hand as they swiftly navigated the foliage. I considered making chase, but the pain in my legs warned me not to.

"Thanks!" I said again before muttering to myself. "Whoever you are…"

At my feet, the demon dissolved, its body becoming nothing more than strips of dark vapor. Good riddance. The spirit or demon or whatever it was had imitated Maja to manipulate me. It deserved that arrow.

Vines grew around the rim of the grove as I moved to cross it. They left a single path open, and that made me hesitate at first. How could I tell what was another trap and what was the right way? The first spirit had seemed to point me the right direction, but what if he'd sent me down a doomed path?

I looked back, but the vines covered where I'd stood moments before. There was no escape. The fern flower called me forward, so forward I would go.

"Come on, Kuba," I muttered to myself. "Let's find this stupid flower and get out of here."

22

Otylia

Leave me alone!

END'S VISIONS PIERCED MY DREAMS.

I swam in time's colorful current for what felt like an eternity, falling into visions whenever a wisp met my path. No matter what I told End, it wouldn't listen.

First, I saw joy.

Narcyz gripped Andrij's hand as they fought even to stand. Their pain was terrible. It struck me in the chest as they eyed the bonfire the Krowikie had lit in the camp's center, but there was something else stronger. Excitement. Memories flooded Narcyz's mind—each about Andrij.

"Let's jump," he said.

Andrij shook his head. There was something off about his eyes, but End's visions were blurry and indistinct, making it impossible to tell what. "We can barely move and you want to jump *that?*"

"We got one chance. Might be dead by next year, and I want to do it with you."

Cheers erupted around the camp as another couple jumped, the flames dancing along the bottom of the woman's skirt and the man's trousers. Andrij stepped closer amid the noise and nearly shouted in Narcyz's ear, "What are you saying?"

"You're really gonna make me say it?" Narcyz grumbled. "Fine! I'm fond of you, Andrjusha. I don't know what we'll make of this, but I'd rather jump the fire with you than die cold in my bed at night."

I scoffed. *What a romantic.* Was I really any different?

Andrij glanced around. "And you aren't worried what they'll think about us?"

"I never should've cared," Narcyz replied, then pulled Andrij along. "C'mon. It's getting late, and I want to down way too much oskoła before this night's over."

"Deal," Andrij replied, half-running, half-shuffling toward where a few other pairs had lined up.

Ahead of them, the girls giggled and played with the wreaths on their men's heads. It signaled he'd found hers and wished to marry her. A silly tradition, but my heart ached remembering the wreath I'd made. Wacław had so badly wanted to catch mine. What had happened instead, or was this vision in the future?

I grinned watching them go, despite my pain. Narcyz had always been an idiotic brute, but he'd faced as many trials as any of us since the equinox. Even he deserved to be happy. Why not with someone as loyal as Andrij?

The vision began to fade as the two stumbled their way toward the bonfire and leaped. They didn't get as high as the others, but neither winced at the heat before they collapsed together on the other side. Their laughter echoed through the camp. All had turned to watch the two men jump, contrary to our tribe's tradition, but any scorn was kept to whispers as Narcyz took Andrij's face in his hands.

"We'll face this together," he said.

"And win," Andrij replied.

Then they shared a long kiss, and the vision slipped away as I shared a moment of their happiness. It had seemed so easy. They had their doubts, but their joy together was undeniable. Wacław had foreseen it once Andrij joined the group. Others had said the same about my relationship with him too, but we were far from easy. I loved him. That didn't mean there weren't scars left behind from the pain we'd caused each other. How could we address it when the Three Realms seemed to need us every waking moment?

End pulled me again, forcing away my thoughts as a group of spiraling wisps met me. Indigo, gold, black, red, and light blue, they swept past a trio. One shone with bright light, another grayer and dim, and the final seemed to combine and split into eight fragments before striking at the first group. I fell to the earth when they all embraced me.

My bare feet splashed into a knee-deep riverbed. Wide like the Krowik, it bent and cut through a narrow gap between two forests, where hundreds of indigo and yellow Kupalo-da-Miawka flowers bloomed. But the river was not what mattered.

Two women, one bright and one dim like their wisps, stood before a massive bound man. Each of the women wore kokoshnik crowns with the sun positioned at opposite ends of its cycle. Their dresses carried colors of their time of day, dawn and dusk, as I realized who they were. The Zorza sisters—Poranna of the morning and Wieczorna of the evening. They were the guardians of the gates that Dadźbóg's sun and my moon used to pass from Nawia into Jawia and back. That meant the man between them could only be one god.

"Simargł…" I whispered with memories of Father's story circling my mind. The god of unbridled fire. The gods had tricked his twin children, Kostroma and Kupalo, into falling in love. When they found the truth and killed themselves, Simargł revolted until the gods chained him to the north star to be guarded by the Zorza sisters. Noc Kupały was supposed to be a celebration of the love between Simargł's children. The legend made the bonfire and wreath catching feel much more sickening.

Then why was he here?

I moved closer as a woman dressed in black spoke from the shore. "Simargł," she said in a sharp tone. "Why do you look away from your wife?"

Wife? Of course it was Kupalnitsa. The gods had admitted guilt after ruining their children's lives, so they must've granted the goddess of night a single meeting a year with her husband. But why was End showing me this?

"He remains ashamed of defying the gods," Poranna replied. "Why would he not be?"

Simargł doubled the height of the women, but despite the immense power radiating from him, he kept his bearded chin dug into his bare chest.

More was said, but I didn't hear it. Instead, I focused on the people rushing from the forest behind Kupalnitsa.

A woman in a slit riding dress poured *żityje* from her hands. Moons ago, I would've scoffed at the indecency of her deep neckline and exposed arms, but she wielded her beauty like men did a sword. That elegance faded when she turned to reveal her skinless back. The dress split around it, like she wanted mortals to see what she truly was. Not just Kostroma, goddess of fertility and water, but the first miawka demon.

The river shifted around me at her call. The goddesses of dawn and dusk called shields of light to protect against whatever strike she planned, but Kupalnitsa split them with a burst of darkness. Kostroma's water blasts spiraled from the river and struck her father's bindings through that gap.

I covered my eyes at the burst of *żityje* that followed the collision, but Simargł's binds held. The fire god himself gave no expression until the second twin neared with gold pulsing from his skin.

Kupalo grinned as the flowers bearing his and his sister's names swirled around him. The god of summer, peace, and joy now bore dark splotches of corruption. He didn't have the elegant clothes of Kostroma, but there was a smoothness to his movements she lacked. Baring fangs like that of the upióry, he released a golden blast that snapped across the clearing like lightning.

It didn't hit.

The winds rushed from every direction as a gray-haired man in flowing robes met Kupalo's spell and flung it overhead like it were nothing. He blew into a horn and rose above the battle, the clouds swirling around him. Surely this was Strzybóg, god of the winds. Kostroma glared at him, and the entire river shuddered with her power.

Chaos followed. Each god flung *żityje* across the narrow clearing and over the river, shattering trees as the noise grew deafening. I'd never seen so many gods at once. It was impossible to comprehend, and End's wisps zipped around me as if even they didn't know how to understand it. That was before the ice goddess appeared.

My hairs rose the moment she stepped foot among the Kupalo-da-Miawkas. Marzanna in the flesh.

Gods help us.

Ice crept across the river as Marzanna strode onward with a sickle in one hand and crackling *żityje* in the other. Symbols of black cut across her pure white dress, joining with her dark hair that rose with each spell she cast. She called spires of ice that rose among her shower of icicles and a blizzard that clashed with Strzybóg's winds. At her heels came Minna—Vida—the undying szeptucha we'd faced in Huebia.

The Zorza sisters looked on in fear. Strzybóg fought to the side, distracted by Kostroma's growing rage, leaving them outnumbered and outmatched. Their light managed to occasionally hit one of their opponents, but they were slipping back into the frozen river. Marzanna took advantage the moment Wieczorna's shield faltered.

An ice spear shot from the ground, straight through Wieczorna's chest. She screamed for only a blink before her dusk light vanished completely.

Poranna tried to hold on by herself, but her situation was hopeless. She called for Strzybóg and for Dadźbóg in the sky. The former was occupied with Kostroma, who'd taken flight with a spiraling pool of water, and the latter was in Nawia until day. Dawn was alone, and when Strzybóg fell from the sky, Kostroma digging her demonic fangs into his neck, the last Zorza knew it was over.

Golden light flashed through the night as Kupalo rushed toward Simargł. Poranna instantly became an afterthought compared to the power that exuded from the now freed fire god. He flexed his muscles and extended his arms, wings sprouting from his back as fire burst from his throat.

Simargł was free. The god whom legends claimed would burn Jawia to ash. The god who despised all the reigning lords of Prawia for betraying his children.

That freedom lasted but a moment. Ice burst across the space, entrapping each member of Simargł's family as Marzanna stood among them and licked the crimson blood of gods from her sickle. The vision started to fade again as she looked each in the eye. I wondered about her plan. I wondered what chaos she could cause with both the black dragon and flaming god in her grasp.

But in the final glimpse I had of the vision, Vida drew a dagger of ice. Marzanna's back was turned to her szeptucha. She didn't see the strike coming, and the last thing I saw was Vida plunging the dagger into her mistress's spine.

Warmth and comfort met me when I awoke, but I kicked out anyway. Shock washed away everything else. I lay there, clutching myself as I remembered each moment of the fight between gods. Was worse to come? What had happened to Simargł? To Marzanna?

I would surely learn soon enough. Prawia held the answers to Mother's force and likely Wacław's soul. Why wouldn't it also teach us more about the gods we faced, and those we could ally with—if any would actually bother to help?

My eyes burst open at something licking my face. A wet nose and a bundle of fur met me. "Sosna?" I asked with a surprised laugh.

"She's been by your side since the Krowikie arrived," Wacław said from behind me. That explained the hug I felt around my waist.

I turned to meet him. This close, he reeked of smoke and sweat, but I tolerated it for the sake of his warmth. "Ara is here?" The discomfort through our bond gave me the answer before he could speak. I pushed myself up, no longer caring about warmth. "I haven't heard from her in days. What happened? She should be here if Sosna is. How long have I been out?"

Wacław, gods bless him, did his best to try and lay me back down, but I fought my exhaustion. Ara was one of my few true friends. If she was hurt…

"Just tell me, Wašek."

He sighed and sat up, pulling in his legs. "It's Noc Kupały. The others are out celebrating, or in Kuba's case, going after the fern flower. Ara… We think Jaryło took her in case you try to trick him."

Now that I was awake, I could hear constant drumming and cheering in the distance. It was definitely night, and my soul welcomed the pull of the moon. Ara's kidnapping devoured any joy that came with that. "I'm going to kill that idiot."

"Yeah, that's exactly why he did it."

Sosna nudged her head under my arm with a yap until she lay half on my lap. I was coiled as tight as Weles's snakes, but I couldn't reject her. "We have to get her back."

Hesitant, he touched my arm. *Good, some old part of him is still there.* "We will, but Prawia was already going to be difficult before. Your blood pact—" My growl at the mention of the pact cut him off. "Right… We have to figure out a way to beat Jaryło either with the gods' help or a blade to his heart. Not that killing him will actually fix this, since he'll just come back."

I groaned. Everything felt terrible. Did channeling that much without training affect me like a hangover? Not that I'd ever had one of those with szeptuchy being banned from drinking, but the headache and urge to vomit sure matched Ara's descriptions. "You used to be the positive one."

"I'm *positive* we'll get through this." He intertwined his fingers with mine, that small smile tugging at his frost-cracked lips. "No more going on my own or acting without you. We do this together, every step of the way."

"Mother already yelled at you for me. Didn't she?"

"Maybe."

I furrowed my brow, but that only ignited my headache to another level. "I forgive you for trying to save Andrij. I don't forgive you for this terrible headache."

Softly, he held his fingers to my temples and rubbed. It dulled the pain a little, and I leaned into it, shutting my eyes. "This help?"

"It does, but I'm still mad."

He chuckled. "I'd be concerned if you weren't. Anger is your natural state. Rod would be upset at you throwing off the balance of the Three Realms otherwise." Then he paused, his fingers stopping their circular motions for a moment before continuing. "You're not the only one who suffered because of what I did."

I opened my eyes to see the tears welling in his. "What happened?" I said as softly as I could manage, which was no kinder than an ironsmith's hammer.

"Eryk..." Wacław sat back on his heels, head dropped. "The chały and skrzaki overwhelmed him without my help. He died, along with probably dozens of other warriors who were killed before you held back the demons. I should've been there. I just saw Andrij go down, and I knew Narcyz—"

"Oh shush." I grabbed him and pulled him close, cradling his head against my chest. Oh, how other girls were frolicking and making love on the solstice night. For once, I longed for that simplicity. "You saved Andrij's life. End just showed me a vision of those two jumping the fire together tonight. That's because of you."

Some of his tension released at that. "It was still my responsibility to protect my marked and help the army escape."

"You're one Naw. You can only do so much."

"That army..." He sniffled. "Do you really think we can defeat them, even with Dziewanna? You're a goddess too, but there are so many of them that you nearly killed yourself trying to hold them still."

I shuddered, remembering the battle. There was nothing worse than the screams and pangs of death I felt through my force as thousands of Vastrothie fled or died. Even as an immortal, I'd feared for my life. Who wouldn't against the tide of undead we'd faced?

"I don't know," I replied after a moment. "Mother believes she can, and I trust her. There's just this feeling in my gut that says it'll have to be me somehow. End keeps showing me destruction, and I think it might be Jawia's ending."

Wacław pulled back with worry in his gaze. "What do you see?"

I shook my head. "I don't understand it. I'm bound in the Mangled Woods, and I feel an endless number of deaths. Czarnobóg arrives with the completed Alatyr Stone, talking about how the Deathless Sons must rebuild the Three Realms to 'mend what was broken at creation's birth.'"

"Deathless Sons? Like Koschei?"

"Or Czarnobóg himself. I don't know." My whole body burned remembering the dreams and the dark dragon's power. "I shout at him, but every time, he shoves Alatyr into my chest as all twelve Moonstones release their power. Then I wake up."

Wacław's expression grew stern. "This is End warning you about something. It has to be."

Tell him everything, a voice said in the back of my head. The thought made me want to coil upon myself and build a wall around my heart, but it was right. Fighting alone had only gotten me hurt. I needed to trust my friends. I needed to trust him—with all of it.

"Wašek, I owe you the truth," I said, taking Mother's amulet in my hand. For once, I didn't squeeze too hard.

"You don't owe me anything." He reached for my free hand, but I dug it into the snow.

"Just let me say this, okay?"

He nodded, lips pursed.

"Follow me," I said, grabbing my bag and heading out of the burrow. "I've been in here too long."

My muscles complained as I pulled myself into free air. Whipping snow stung my cheeks and nose, but I didn't care. End's dreams had released me. Even the horrors we faced were better than experiencing distant nightmares I couldn't change.

We passed an extinguished fire in silence, its coals already smothered by the blizzard. Celebrations rang out in the distance regardless, and an orange hue revealed the Krowikie bonfire. I grinned knowing Narcyz and Andrij would jump it together if they hadn't already. Time was odd with End's visions, but I was glad it had showed me their joy. Someone deserved it on Noc Kupały.

Sosna trotted at our heels as we entered the forest. Unfazed by the snow, she bit at each flake in excitement, then whined when it melted in her mouth. She was Mother's creature, yet she remained loyal to me even as Mother lost her connection to the wilds. I'd been an entire realm away, but still she'd kept by Wacław and Ara's sides until we reunited. What had I done to deserve that? Sure, she was just a fox. That didn't make her devotion to me mean any less.

Just as dutiful, Wacław kept quiet, straying only half-a-stride behind. Close enough to let me take lead, but not far enough to be away from my side. *He's too gentle for this. Why did you curse him, Sudiczki? His fate should've been as light as his heart.*

Whispers seemed to drift through the woods as I stopped beneath a tree and sat with my back to its trunk. An alder, like the one at Mother's altar outside Dwie Rzeki. Some bit of home.

Only my thin cloak kept my butt dry, and I finally tugged up my hood to protect my face from the wind. Wacław stared down at me, shuffling through the snow in an awkward wait to be invited to sit. He'd become bolder since the Płanetnik's control. Some part of him would always be that boy, though.

"Remember when we sat beneath Mother's alder tree in the swamp?" I asked.

A smile passed over his face, then disappeared. "Of course. You'd just told me I was a demon, and despite you saving me from the utopiec, I was sure you'd stab me for taking Marzanna's mark."

"I wanted to."

"I have no doubt." He finally plopped down next to me, hiding a wince. We'd all taken damage in the battle, but I worried we didn't have enough time to recover. Ara needed us in Prawia, and we needed answers. "I was also shocked you were speaking to me after four years of distant glares. The wild witch. The girl I'd been fond of as a child. The only person I was forbidden to speak to. It was a lot on top of controlling the winds for the first time and nearly being killed by two demons."

I blushed against my will. Of course I'd had similar feelings for him when we were younger, but our separation had happened when we were twelve. It had hardly been an age for romance. "It's hard to comprehend how much things changed that day," I replied. "I'd hated you for so long, but when I realized what you are… I don't know. It took a lot for me to change my mind during our journey to the Mangled Woods."

"No surprise there."

"I've been thinking a lot about fate—about our fates." I cringed at how that came out and set my head back against the tree. *I really am terrible at this.*

Wacław shifted uncomfortably. "You mentioned the Sudiczki in Huebia. Something about you becoming my queen?"

"Yes… That was odd to say at the time."

"Nothing about any of our lives since the equinox has been normal. Besides, I liked the thought."

Part of me squirmed, remembering Mother's call for me to be untamable, but Wacław hadn't tried to change that. He made me want to come back to him. No coercion or control needed. "That was the first Sudiczka's fate for me," I said without acknowledging his attempted flirtation. "We were bound at birth. You were supposed to become king of the tribes north of Perun's Crown, and I would be your queen. Immortal rulers."

"Oh…" He sank lower against the tree. Despite his hat dipping over his face, he let it hang as he pondered for a minute. His voice was rough when he spoke. "So our relationship wasn't our choice?"

I forced myself to break the tension, taking his hand and squeezing hard. "Anyone can be bound. That doesn't mean we had to love each other. Besides, Destiny said our parents changed our fates when they took us from our homes."

"That makes sense. My corruption came from Father betraying his first words to me, but does that mean I could've been a king instead of this monster? What would I have become as a Naw without a demon taking my second soul?"

"You're not a monster, but I don't know what would've happened. Maybe you would've been corrupted later. We haven't found a Naw without a demonic soul."

He looked at me, his eyes wide. "What if there are some? What if we're not doomed to corruption?"

I held up our joined hands. "You've shown there's hope for Na-wie, even without a mortal soul. But I don't know what would've happened to you. Destiny said that fates change, but not completely. We still ended up together after all. Maybe we'll still be queen and king."

"I wonder if that was the first Sudiczka's fate for me too."

"Probably, but I wonder what the others said for you." I snatched his hat and placed it on my head, smirking. "Did the second foresee your power? Did the hag make your fate to be a demon? Destiny said—" I caught myself.

Wacław's smile disappeared as his dread pushed through our bond. His heart raced, and he gripped his knees before him. "You said during the Trials of Love and Loss that my corruption would kill me and then you. Did the Sudiczki say the same for me?"

I took a long breath, removing the hat and running my fingers along its brim. "Destiny told me that corruption would be my end, but I assumed that it was your corruption. It might not kill you, and it might not be *your* corruption that kills me. That dream of Czar-nobóg—"

"I won't let him kill you!" he interjected. "Whatever I do, I won't let him take you. He can't complete Alatyr as long as I have Grudzień anyway. You said even eleven Moonstones aren't enough."

"They aren't."

He took my face in his hands. They shook with his voice. "Then he cannot win as long as we live. Even if we lose, we flee with our friends and family to somewhere where he and Marzanna can never find us. They can rule Jawia, but they cannot mold it to their wishes without Alatyr."

I huffed and lowered my gaze. "You don't mean that. When this all started, I said I was doing this for just Mother and the wilds, but you were fighting to protect everyone—even those who hated you."

"You're right, but the last few moons have shown me I can't save everyone."

I looked at him again and forced myself to grin. "I love you be-cause you'll try anyway. Whether it's the manipulated son of a żmij or a Frostmarked Naw looking for help, you'll risk yourself to help those who need you. I need your heart, because I'm not like that. People are threats to me until they prove otherwise. The only reason I care about our tribe is because I see them through your eyes, the loyalty and hate you have for them."

"You're too hard on yourself," he replied with a kiss on my forehead.

You don't know the final piece. I resisted the need to tell him about my pact with Death, but he deserved the truth. "There's one more thing I didn't tell you."

Wacław just laughed. "I already know."

"You do?"

He reached for my bag, pulling out the makeshift flower wreath I'd made. A scraggly thing of needles and vines. I wasn't proud of its appearance, and the joy on Wacław's face only strengthened my guilt as he placed it on my head. "It fell out of your bag when I came to visit you. Otylka, you didn't have to do this."

Conflicted, I turned my cheek as a stray tear broke free. I should've been happy with him, but I needed to tell him about Death's deal soon. *In the morning,* I promised myself. *I'll tell him then.*

Worry replaced his glee. His fingers lightly traced my cheekbone, intercepting the tear's descent. "I'm sorry. I know you hate the solstice."

"No." I forced my gaze back to him. This *was* good. Us. The trials of the future would meet us in the morning, but Noc Kupały was a night of magic, love. I'd denied myself its excitement ever since Mother's death. She was back now, though, and we needed an escape from the world's pain. I needed it.

"Please stop believing you don't care about people," he whispered. "The way you helped Sabina and those trapped by Weles in Nawia was amazing. Then you redeemed demons and freed strangers in Vastroth. You do care, but it's okay to be wary of strangers. It just makes me feel all the more special that I had to earn your trust."

"Multiple times," I laughed.

He echoed it. "Right? Who cares what the Sudiczki or godsforsaken Jaryło have to say? Bound by fate or not, I'll never stop loving you until my immortal soul vanishes into Oblivion, and I'll never stop fighting to earn that love from you."

You deserve to be happy, I told myself as I took his waist and kissed him. *Listen to him, not your doubts.*

"Wašek Lubiewicz," I breathed when we parted, our noses still touching. "I'll give you a choice: I can throw this wreath in the Wyzra and make you break through the ice to get it, or you can take it now, pledging to be my king of endings. My force shows me them, and you will make them come true for our enemies."

He kissed me without reply. I let him, then pull him down so he lay on the cloak and I knelt over him. "Choose," I said with my wreath in hand. "Or the crown goes where even Marzanna would freeze."

"I choose you, now."

"Then the wreath is yours."

I placed it upon his head, giggling like a child at the way his scattered hair stuck through its vines. Our bond revealed his joy. Despite the silliness, I felt how much this meant to him, and when he pulled me down to him at the alder's base, I didn't resist.

23

Kuba

If I was a magical flower found only one night a year in the middle of a creepy forest, where would I be?

IT WAS WEIRD ENOUGH when Mother told me to put myself in someone else's shoes. As if they'd fit. Thinking like a plant was a whole different problem.

My jackal paws crunched the underbrush along the path the spirits had led me down. Apparently nature spirits didn't own a sickle or anything else to cut the thorny stuff, and gashes covered my already wounded legs. It was fine. This was all fine. Nothing wrong about being a person in a jackal body trying to find a magic flower. Was a magical flower even a plant? Maybe that's why I couldn't find it…

I really am losing my mind. Not sure if that's new or not.

Whispers started again as I entered another grove, ready for more trickery. No, just one whisper. It came from the right, but the forest grew more dense there. Denser? Words were never my specialty. The underbrush got even thornier, the trees closer, and the hooting of owls started as I inched closer.

"Nah, definitely a trap. No way *that's* not going to kill me."

But the magical forest decided it didn't like my mistrust. Right when I turned around, vines and thorns pulled back, leaving a completely open trail straight toward a red glow at the base of an oak tree, or at least a tree that looked like an oak. You could never tell in a magical forest. The closer I got, the more that glow started to look like the shape of a flower—the pretty knee-high type that girls liked in spring.

"See, now I definitely think it's a trap," I said to the forest. "Those vines could just grab me the second I go in there."

The forest gave no reply. Of course it didn't. It was a forest, and I was a talking jackal.

"Fine…"

I crept toward the edge of the woods, that whisper and the two incredibly annoying owls getting louder with each step. Made me wish for Ara's bow. Maybe we could've had some good meat for the first time in forever then too. We'd never eaten owl back in Dwie Rzeki. Dad said it was bad luck, and Mother thought it tasted 'as good as a half-baked spider.' Always wondered what a full-baked spider tasted like, but neither of them had been all that interested in that either.

There was no movement when I stepped onto the trail, but I kept on guard. I was so close now. Sure, I would've died if the mysterious archer hadn't put an arrow in the demon in the last grove. That didn't matter when I was strides away from returning to my human body and then seeing Maja again.

As I reached the trail's end, a breeze carried mists around the fern flower's tree. I stepped into the space before it until the mass of gray covered everything so heavily that someone with actual hands couldn't have seen them in front of their face. Gods, I really missed hands. The fern flower was still faintly visible through the mist, so I just kept walking.

Then came the shadows.

Figures circled me, their voices drowning out the fern flower's whisper. Each was familiar.

"He was always an idiot," Narcyz's said. "Probably has an animal brain anyway."

Laughter replied—my friends' laughter.

"Wacław's better off without him," Otylia replied.

Narcyz huffed. "I dunno. Kuba sure makes Wacław look like a lot less of a klutz in comparison."

"All he ever did was make things worse," Wacław confirmed. "We should've left him with Weles."

So many followed that their sources were impossible to track.

"I doubt Maja even misses him."

"A real warrior could've blocked Yuliya's ice bolt."

"He's nothing but a distraction."

"Look at his plan against the Horde. Did he really think mud would stop thousands of undead?"

My progress stopped. Hearing my friends' mockery was too much on top of my pain. Had they really said those things? I knew I wasn't the most liked boy in the village, but my own friends abandoning me when all I'd done was try to help? I'd died for Wacław and Otylia. I'd taken this jackal form so I could return to Jawia and help them fight the Horde. My plan against the Horde *had* worked, even if we hadn't won the battle.

"Just give up," the voices said together. "You're not good enough for this. The fern flower deserves better."

What if they were right? Besides jumping in front of Yuliya's ice and killing her at the same time, had I really helped the group at all? Maja could've found another man. She probably hadn't even cried when she'd heard I died. Dad definitely hadn't.

But Wacław's voice pulled me from my doubts. Would he ever have considered leaving me in Nawia?

"No," I said. "You wouldn't."

Wacław's shadow seemed to stare down at me, that funny płanetnik hat swooping around his head.

"Narcyz I get," I said to him, "but you'd never leave me. Not when I was getting beat by some brute or when I nearly broke my arm swinging off a tree. You kept with me no matter what. Even when Jacek 'bout killed you for helping me put that gunk in Mikołaj's mug."

I dug my claws into the earth and pushed forward. *This isn't real. If he isn't, then the others aren't either.*

My realization didn't make the shadows or their voices disappear, but the glow brightened. I was close now. I had to be. All I had to do was ignore the spirits' attempts to manipulate me into doubting myself. Acting as arrogant as Narcyz for a few minutes couldn't be that hard, but my confidence disappeared when I broke free of the mists, standing just two strides from the fern flower. Dad blocked the way.

"Look at ye," he slurred before taking a swig of oskoła from a cracked horn. Some of it dribbled down his wrinkled, unshaven chin and onto his torn tunic. Mother had tried to stitch as many of them as she could, but Dad's habit of destroying his clothes was faster than she was willing to mend. "Good fer nothing dog! Jumped the fire and became eh dog. Not even eh man!"

"I killed a szeptucha!" I snapped back at him. "What have you ever done?"

He held out the horn toward me, spilling its contents over the ground between us. "I saw Jacek's wars, killed brothers for 'im. That's all loyalty gets ye! Enough nightmares to make drowning in oskoła a better fate."

"A loyal dad would've actually been there."

"Da. Maybe one would've, but ye turned out better than if I'd been there."

I growled and dug in my paws, ready to pounce. "Didn't matter. I'm still not good enough for you. Now get out of the way so I can take the fern flower!"

He gave a single laugh. "Ye would never attack me. Yer too much of a coward."

Watch me.

I lunged at him, biting at the arm that held his horn, but found only vapor. His form disappeared as I passed through. That left me skidding into the tree, just barely avoiding stepping on the flower.

"Is that it?" I asked, hopeful.

Yet again, the forest had no decency to reply, so I approached the flower to touch it with my nose. It smelled wondrously sweet, like Lubena's desserts for Wacław's birthday when no one else celebrated. Possibilities seemed to pulse within it until my nose struck.

Blinding light shot every direction. Red and gold, it swirled with a bright dust that covered the forest and my fur. The trees shifted from behind the oak, and I gasped as a massive figure of bark and roots emerged from the woods. It had deep green eyes and a mask of flowers whose thorns spiraled to the sides like a ram's horns. Each of its steps shook the earth as it circled the tree. It stared at me, never looking away until it stopped before me and bowed its head.

"Jakub Piotryk of Krowik," its voice rumbled.

"Eh," I interrupted. "Only Mother calls me Jakub. I like Kuba better."

The creature raised a hand in front of itself and bowed. "Kuba, then. None of the fern flower's protectors expected you, of all people, to succeed against the temptations of these woods."

I had some help… I just smiled at the tall bark thing. "You're a leszy, right? My friend Wacław told me about another one of you he met. Maybe you know him?"

The leszy threw its…*his*… head back and laughed so deeply that leaves fell from the trees. "Not all spirits of a kind know of each other, boy. However, if you speak of the one that fell to Marzanna's call, I know of the one you speak. He betrayed the forest by aiding winter's temptations of your friend." He knelt on one knee and tilted his head to the side. "This is not about the płanetnik. It is not because of him that you have found the fern flower."

"I came to get my body back," I replied meekly. It was hard not to be threatened by a creature that large, even if he seemed friendly.

"Indeed."

The leszy shut his eyes. Around him, the ground shifted, and his form shrunk, roots and bark returning to the ground as skin took shape around his body. It was one of the weirdest things I'd ever seen, but considering he was hopefully about to give me what I wanted, I stayed still besides some impatient paw taps on the ground. Luckily, it wasn't long before he resembled a human. He'd kept the mask of flowers and thorns, but the rest of him just looked like a short old man in scraggly brown and green robes. He held a wooden staff with all kinds of markings across it that I didn't recognize.

"The form we take is about more than ourselves," he said in a much frailer voice. "It influences how we relate to those around us, and I believe this is your reason."

"It is."

He hobbled toward the fern flower and bent over to run his fingers over the streaks of gold on its petals. "Then the spirits of the fern flower have an offer for you. You may either take the flower and enjoy its many gifts, seeking great treasures and power beyond your imagination, or we may transform you back into your soul's original body in this life as a reward for your search, thus protecting the flower's magic for many solstices to come."

I stared at the flower with its magic pulsing so strongly I felt it beat with my heart. "Why wouldn't I take it and transform myself? Isn't it better to have all of its power?"

"Many would say so." He stood and approached, staring me in the eye. "All great power comes with just as great of a cost, however, and I do not wish for you to suffer when you could receive exactly what you came for. Unless your true reasons differ from those you have spoken?"

"I…" I didn't know. For my entire journey through the woods, I'd thought all that mattered was getting back into my body, but the power I felt in that flower was incredible. It could make me important like Wacław and Otylia. I wouldn't be just some man with a pointy stick. I'd be the one who found the fern flower.

I turned to the leszy. "What's the cost?"

"Ah, so there is more?"

"Maybe I'm just considering my options?"

He huffed and crossed his arms, tucking his hands up his opposing sleeves. "Very well. The fern flower's power is known to feed the vices of its owner until they are consumed by pride, vengeance, laziness, or lust. Much can be accomplished with its power, which is why it is so difficult to find. Know that the trials you have faced tonight would be only a fraction of what you face with the fern flower in hand, especially as your life shall be extended beyond any mortal's." Then he gazed up at the trees around us and those two stupid owls that had come back. "Jawia's magic is a complex thing, influenced by gods, their forces, and many other factors mortals cannot comprehend. The fern flower is one, and without it to protect the wild magic at the edge of this realm, this place will falter until you perish."

The disappointment in his eye told me enough about what decision he wanted me to take, but did his opinion matter? He was a spirit of a strange place. Would Maja care? The fern flower could help me beat Marzanna and Czarnobóg, making me a hero. Or it could kill me. What a fun choice…

I went with my gut.

"Just change me back," I stammered, part of me resisting the decision.

"Are you certain of this? You likely will never be accepted back into this place that you are now choosing to protect. You may never see the fruits of your sacrifice."

I took a long breath. Dad would laugh at me for not taking the flower, but he was a drunken idiot. I didn't need to make him proud. I needed to be better than him, like my real friends saw me. "I'm sure."

"Then Kuba Piotryk," he said, holding the fern flower's petal with one hand and my shoulder with the other. "Return to your human form, and go forth as the champion of the fern flower, protector of the magic realm."

The swirls of gold and red whipped around me, then vanished. I coughed as dirt filled my mouth and eyes, and when I finally cleared it away, the lively forest was gone. A blizzard's harsh winds found me instead. It stung my unprotected neck and cheeks, forcing me to shiver.

I shot my hands up to my face. Smooth. Then my hair, still not well combed but straight enough. My old tunic, trousers, and cloak covered my body like they had when I'd died, but luckily the blood stain was missing. I was *me*. Not a jackal. Not a soul traveling Jawia or Nawia. Just a mortal with a great looking face and the best jokes east of the Krowik River.

A glow pulled me from my thoughts. Dull beneath the snow at my feet, it pulsed over and over.

So I dropped to my knees and dug with my bare hands. It hurt, but it felt good to even have hands. I'd never take standing up straight or being able to grab things for granted again. When my fingers broke through the snow and touched the glowing object, I smiled at the realization of what I'd grab first.

The fern flower emerged in my palm, floating under its own power. "I don't get it," I said to the world.

Even now, the forest didn't reply. It didn't need to. I had my body back, and apparently I'd earned the fern flower by rejecting it in some backwards test. Gods, I felt alive for the first time since my actual death.

Drums sounded in the distance.

"I need to find Maja!"

I took off at a sprint, darting between the trees and shrubs. Some scraped at my calves, but I ran on through the pain. The girl I loved, yes *loved*, was waiting for me. I'd made her wait too long already without admitting how I really felt. This was my chance, and I sure as Oblivion wasn't going to waste it.

24

Wacław

THE MORNING GUSTS BLEW Otylia's night black hair over her face as our group gathered in the darkness. She and I stood together, our hands intertwined. Last night had been a rare respite. I wanted nothing more than to stay with her longer, but between Kuba's return to his mortal body and the sun's delay, there was too much to discuss. Kuba had run off to have his time with Maja. Soon, though, we'd have to figure out what the fern flower could do.

"Dadźbóg is never late," Dziewanna said, pacing across the circle as Andrij worked to start a fire with the firebird feather. She'd held a stern expression ever since she'd called for us to gather, but a smirk broke through whenever her gaze fell upon Otylia and me. I worried how much she knew.

More important than my relationship, though, was the fact Dziewanna was right. It should have been mid-morning, but instead of dawn's light, we were stuck with only the moon above. On the longest days of the year, that was more than concerning.

"He's been lousy since spring," Narcyz replied from alongside Andrij on one of the logs. He hunched over himself with his arms crossed, either from the chill, his injuries, or both. "It's his job to heat Jawia, right? So what's he been doing?"

Dziewanna exchanged looks with Otylia. "What I have feared for some time—falling to my sister's seductions."

I huffed. "Marzanna's hardly seductive."

"Yet you fell to her whispers too." I blushed as she narrowed her eyes. "It was in a different fashion to Swaróg's youngest son, but you have seen the power in her temptations. Dadźbóg has always been jealous of Perun and Weles. His brothers rule Prawia and Nawia while he must travel with the sun, trapped where it is."

"But I don't follow the moon." Otylia said.

"True, but much of your force's strength does. Dadźbóg is the same. Since he has far less *attachment* to Jawia than you," Dziewanna continued with a wink, "he has no trouble splitting his time between the realms."

Otylia tensed at her mother's prodding. *"She's going to antagonize both of us about this,"* she said through our bond. *"Mother never lets a good chance at wry joking pass her by."*

I think she's actually happy we're together, I replied.

Vlatka, who'd been perched in a nearby tree, swooped down and landed on Otylia's shoulder, spurring her to curse the eagle's weight. "This is about more than just seduction, then," the witch said. "In all my years, I have never seen the sun stray from its pattern. The morning gate must not have opened."

"Oh gods," Otylia muttered. She glanced at me and tensed further. "My force shows me endings in my dreams, but it's hard to know when things happen—or if they're even certain to. When I was unconscious from the battle, I saw the god Simargł escape with the help of his family and Marzanna."

"The force of endings is powerful," Dziewanna replied. "Don't doubt it."

Narcyz scoffed, teeth bared at Otylia. "Were you too busy with Wacław to tell us the godsforsaken *sun* wasn't coming back?"

"Don't test me!" Otylia snapped back. She released my hand as light burst from her fingertips, swirling around her in silvery wisps.

"Fighting ourselves will not win this," Xobas interrupted. My Eclipsemark pulsed a deep red on his exposed arm, and a pang of guilt hit me at the sight.

"He's right," I added, stepping to Otylia's side and softly laying a hand on her back. "Every step along this journey, we've had reasons to distrust each other. A few of us started together as rivals, others friends or mentors, and more still as enemies. A lot of that has changed, but we don't need to all be best friends to be allies."

Narcyz stamped his boot into the snow. "Good speech, but we need to know this stuff. Anything else you want to tell us?"

A flash of panic spread through my bond with Otylia. She looked at Dziewanna, and some unspoken conversation caused her to drop her shoulders. "There is."

"Well?" Narcyz pushed.

I gave him a warning look. "Narcyz, back off. If Otylia has a secret, then it's for a good—"

"No," Otylia said, turning to me with fear in her eyes. "There's more that I wanted to tell you last night."

You don't have to do this, I told her silently.

"I'm sorry. I should've told you before."

She looked back toward the group as she took one of my hands. Both her worries and mine dulled at the touch, but they swelled again when she spoke. "Most of you know that I fought Czarnobóg during the Trial of Death. He defeated me, and when I fled, I ended up somewhere in the veil between the Three Realms and Oblivion. Wacław was there, dying."

"After Kynnytsia," Andrij said. "That poisoned arrow nearly killed him."

Otylia nodded. "Whatever you all did to keep him alive gave me time to get to him, but Death wanted his soul. I wouldn't let him have it." She wrinkled her nose and stared at her boots. "To save Wacław, I gave Death a single promise that I'd fulfill at his request in my immortal life."

I released her hand. "You did what?" Staggering back, I tried to remember what had happened at Oblivion's edge. There was a gap where I'd lost consciousness completely. Had she truly given Death himself a promise to save me? "Otylka…"

"Oh, child," Vlatka whispered, wrapping her wing around Otylia's head. "Oh dear child."

"Don't patronize me!" Otylia shouted. Vlatka launched herself onto a branch as Otylia clenched her fists by her sides, flaring the moonlight emanating from her skin. "I know what I've done, but I didn't realize how much power I'd have at the time."

Sabina held a hand over her mouth. "You're the goddess of endings. What... What could he ask you to end?"

"Everything," Dziewanna answered, oddly calm. She gave Otylia a knowing look. "Many a spirit has tricked our kind into such promises. Otylia is not alone in this. Unfortunately, Death's force feeds our two greatest enemies. They will without a doubt use this against us."

She already knew, I realized then. Otylia was usually more sensitive to her mother's comments than others, but she hadn't reacted at all to this. What else did Dziewanna know?

"Then why hasn't he done it?" Narcyz asked. "Otylia could probably kill all of us if she wanted to."

"Death wouldn't waste such a promise on mortals and Nawie," Dziewanna said. "We also don't know his final goal."

My head spun at all of this, but I forced myself from my shock enough to speak. "Don't we? If his force is connected to Marzanna and Czarnobóg, won't he want them to succeed?"

Dziewanna rounded the fire and stopped before Otylia. "Gods are embodiments of our forces. We channel them like szeptuchy channel us, but they are spirits independent of us. They have their own hidden wills to shape the Three Realms to suit their force. This gives us some insight into what they want, but Death, for example, could forego killing now if the feast is greater for him later." She fixed Otylia's stray hairs, then placed a kiss on her brow. "Otylia is likely not yet strong enough to achieve his goals. Soon, that will change."

"You were mad at Wacław for taking a Frostmark but then gave Death a promise?" Narcyz laughed. "We're so doomed."

I stepped forward, hand clenched before me. "I said back off!"

Lightning cracked across Narcyz's arm. He screamed and fell

back into the snow, his cockiness replaced by fear in an instant as Andrij rushed to his side.

"You idiot!" Narcyz snapped, gripping his wounded arm.

Weapons greeted me wherever I looked. Even Otylia held her light spear. "Wacław, drop the lightning," she demanded, grabbing my arm.

The rush of anger abated, and I grunted as I complied. My hand was still extended before me as if I'd intended to choke him. A few snaps of lightning cracked between my fingers before disappearing.

Narcyz hauled himself to his feet and brushed off the snow. A smirk replaced his frown. "Ha! Glad to see you have some guts now. Just don't do that again."

"Shut it," Otylia snapped. "Nothing about this is funny."

I finally lowered my hand, taking a deep breath. My muscles were locked tight, and the rage's sudden disappearance at Otylia's touch had left a burning across my skin. "What just happened? Narcyz…"

Vlatka studied me. "Do you believe you truly have your demon under control?"

"I thought I did." My legs wobbled at the possibility I might lose control again. *Please tell me I just lost my temper…*

"Your eyes flashed black," Otylia replied flatly, still holding my arm. "What did you feel?"

"Anger. It came so quickly…" I tried to pull away out of fear of hurting her, but she only gripped harder. "I am sorry, Narcyz. You didn't deserve that."

He shrugged, but Andrij frowned. "We're your friends. It doesn't matter how angry you are. You could've killed him!"

I hung my head as Otylia nodded. "The demon's weaker, but you still need to control it. Whatever part of it that's in me flared with yours too. I'll use that as a sign next time."

Dziewanna stepped closer. "Even I don't know the origin of Nawie, but you are known to surrender to your demonic souls eventually. With the last part of your mortal soul in Otylia, Wacław, you must stay close to her."

"What if Death let me live because he knew I'd help Otylia complete his demand?" I said through shaky breaths. "If he knew I'd break down away from her, then he knew he'd have both of our powers for the pact."

"It's a thought," Dziewanna replied, "but the pact itself would have been enough for him."

"Nothing is going to get any easier, is it?"

"Nope," Narcyz huffed as he tossed a few split logs on the fire. The pain was obvious on his face, but he appeared content to ignore his injuries instead of letting them mend.

"I must return to the generals," Xobas said, arms crossed. "No more fighting among ourselves. Last thing we need is more trouble."

As he left, Kuba passed him, grinning. That boyish smile I'd become so familiar with over our years of friendship was back, along with his ridiculously unblemished face and sharp jaw. If it weren't for his personality, Kuba would've found himself surrounded by girls on Noc Kupały each year. Instead, he'd found Maja. She was a girl willing to tolerate his jokes and calm him down just enough to make him reasonable. Exactly what he needed.

"Xobas looks like he saw a zmora," Kuba said, chewing on the stem of some dead grass that I hoped wasn't poisonous. "What'd Otylia do this time?"

She punched his arm hard enough to spur a yelp. "Even the fern flower can't make you any less of a fool. Amazing."

Kuba held up the red and gold-streaked flower he'd shown us the night before. Radiant, I sensed the immense power held within, but Kuba had been too excited about seeing Maja to discuss what it could do besides change him out of his jackal form.

Remembering the conversation, I released Otylia's hand and rounded the fire, sending a breeze over it to give the tinder a breath of air. "You missed Otylia telling us that she made a pact with Death to save my life after the Battle of Kynnytsia."

"Oh, so just light and fluffy stuff then." He grinned. "What? Not even a chuckle? I get it. This stuff sucks, but what's a deal with Death when we've already got two gods and a blood pact with Jaryło to handle? We're in over our heads no matter what we do, so might as well enjoy it."

"You sure you didn't smoke that flower first?" Narcyz asked. "Because you sound dumb as iron."

Kuba stuck the flower behind his ear. "Sure didn't. The flower's supposed to make me rich, understand animals, and all other types of stuff, but besides hearing what the birds have to say, I haven't figured it out."

"Sorry to interrupt," Andrij said, still seated on the log with his gaze toward the fire, "but how are we going to reach Prawia, break Jaryło's pact, and then defeat Death. We can hardly survive against Koschei."

"Yeah, good point. Sounds like you guys have your work cut out for you."

I raised my brow. "You're not coming with us?"

"Should I be?" Kuba held out his arms and spun slowly. "Look at me. I'm just a guy who can throw some javelins. I just got my life back! You think I'm going to leave Maja and SAVE THE WORLD?" He laughed. "Of course I'm coming with you. Sorry, I suck at keeping a straight face."

Otylia punched his shoulder again.

"Ow! What was that for?"

She grinned. "Just felt like it. Andrij is right. We don't have a plan, but we should focus right now on Prawia and Jaryło, then Koschei. My deal with Death will haunt me eventually, but I have no idea when he'll call in the favor. Until then, we keep going."

"Luckily," Dziewanna said with a tap on her broken antler crown. "You have among you a goddess who was born in Prawia. There is a secret among the gods that must not leave this circle, and I will not hesitate to kill those who spread it."

"What about Xobas?" I asked.

Dziewanna put her hands on her hips, wrinkling her nose like her daughter. "Xobas may know if you trust him, Otylia. You know him well."

"Even I'm curious," Vlatka said with her eagle head perked. "You told me much about Nawia, but never Prawia."

"It is the realm of the gods and is protected for a reason," Dziewanna said. "Neither the moon nor sun travel there through the gates, and there is no Way of Souls for the dead to travel to it any longer. There is only one way to access Prawia—the Hearts of Jawia."

Otylia nodded. "Like how we used the Heart of Nawia to get here."

"Because that worked *so well*," Kuba quipped.

Dziewanna chuckled and patted Kuba on the head, as if he were still a jackal. "My mother likely interfered with where you landed in Jawia, hoping for you to free her worshippers. The Hearts of Jawia are more direct."

"Hearts?" Otylia asked. "There's more than one?"

"There is a Heart for every god who resides in Prawia. Like traveling the branches of a tree, each Heart connects us to the forces we wield, also allowing us to reach our section of Prawia."

"Which means you have one," I said, my heart suddenly racing. This was our chance. If there was an easy way into the realm of the gods, then we could spend our effort focusing on what happened afterward. "Where is it?"

A sorrowful smile flicked across her face. "Well, that is the problem."

Otylia took her mother's hands. "You were exiled for rebelling against Perun and Swaróg. Weren't you?"

"Yes."

"So your Heart, wherever it is, wouldn't work?" I asked.

"It would not, but my Heart was likely destroyed anyway." She smiled at Otylia. "You did a wonderful job protecting it for years."

Otylia's jaw dropped. "The altar… I thought it was just a place for sacrifices. I tried to save the tree, but—"

Dziewanna pulled her close, holding Otylia's head to her chest. "It is my fault that I never told you the true power in that alder tree, but you could not have saved it against Marzanna's rising disease."

"Then how do we get to Prawia?" I asked with a kick of the snow.

"Maybe just fly up for a long time," Narcyz replied.

Kuba giggled. "Now you're sounding like me."

"That would not be a good decision," Dziewanna said. "My own Heart will not work, but my mother and father's should—if either allows me to use theirs. Father's Heart is hidden somewhere in the mountains, but Mother's resides in the place you call Mokosz's Grove in Dwie Rzeki, not far from Jaryło's."

"Jaryło's?" I asked.

She smirked. "Yes. The place you call Perun's Oak is falsely named."

Kuba cocked his head to the side, looking just as lost as he was in his jackal form. "I wasn't really that into the gods before all this, but I thought at least Perun's Oak was actually… you know… *Perun's.*"

"Jaryło has never liked the truth, has he?" Otylia said with a scoff. "But why are so many Hearts near Dwie Rzeki? Doesn't that make the gods vulnerable?"

"Hardly," Dziewanna replied. "Mortals pose no threat to a Heart of Jawia. Even if they attempted to destroy it, then the god could transfer its power somewhere else. The only real threat is another god, so hiding our Hearts near each other was meant to ensure Mother could help us protect each other. Jaryło, in his typical arrogant nature, decided to hide his in plain sight. Marzanna knew this, which is why she is marching her Horde toward Dwie Rzeki to destroy his Heart."

Vlatka fluttered, her feathers puffing aggressively. "Then why did she target you first? You wanted to protect her!"

"Because I was trapped, and she needed another god's power to recover past the equinox."

"Why don't we just destroy Jaryło's tree, then?" I asked. "If Marzanna could infect your alder, then Otylia and I combined should be able to do *something* to limit Jaryło's power and get rid of Marzanna's reason to attack."

Dziewanna stepped away from Otylia, staring into the fire with her arms crossed. She pondered for a moment, then looked back at me. "She will conquer until all who worship Jaryło, Perun, and Swaróg are dead, and Czarnobóg's rage only feeds more into that. Destroying Jaryło's heart would inhibit his abilities. It would also give Marzanna exactly what she wants while turning every other god against us. None would tolerate the destruction of another's Heart of Jawia."

Otylia raised her brow. "They tolerated yours."

"I am an exile, and I am aware my greeting in Prawia will not be a warm one. As Perun's blood son and Weles's adopted one, Jaryło is heir to not only Jawia, but all of the Three Realms. It will be hard enough to convince the gods of his betrayal without destroying his Heart first."

"Then we go home," Narcyz said bluntly.

My heart skipped a beat at that realization. Mokosz's Grove was just behind the longhouse in Dwie Rzeki. I'd be able to see Mom and my half-siblings, if only for a moment. So much had happened in recent moons, but with a couple days to rest, it had dawned on me how much I missed Mom's care and little Nevenka's rambunctiousness.

When I pulled myself from my thoughts, I met Otylia's gaze. She looked at me with all the fierceness I'd become familiar with over the years. Dziewanna had given her a way forward, and nothing would stop her now.

"We go home," she confirmed. "Then we expose the betrayer."

25

Otylia

I'd be fine if the sun never came again.

WE SPENT THE BETTER PART of the next two days helping the armies prepare to defend against the Horde while we were gone. Or we at least thought it had been that long. With Dadźbóg trapped in Nawia, the only way to tell time was the waning of the moon.

Two days was longer than I'd hoped for, but in truth, we needed the time. Narcyz and Andrij's injuries were only beginning to heal. Wacław was still caught in guilt's grip, building makeshift walls and trenches with the winds to make up for the deaths he blamed himself for. And I was far weaker after my recovery than I let the others see.

Anxiety had gotten the better of me by the time we were ready to go. I'd made decisions, and now that the consequences were coming due, I wasn't ready. Ascension had granted me power, but channeling too much had knocked me unconscious for over a day. We couldn't afford that. Mother needed me to help her face the gods and regain her connection to the force of the wilds. Wacław needed me to keep his demonic soul under control. Everyone else needed me to keep them alive as they fought. Only the constant moon above gave me any hope that we'd succeed.

Wacław knew something was wrong. He'd asked in his caring,

gentle way, but nothing he said could change that pressure. It was mine to bear. But he was Wacław, so he tried to comfort me to an almost annoying degree.

That feeling grew as we took flight with the rest of our group. I'd argued that I should carry at least a few of us, but Wacław had insisted I save my strength for Prawia. He was trying to help. I knew that. A knot just twisted inside my chest whenever he did anything for me that I was capable of doing myself. Recovering or not, I wouldn't sit back and let him do everything for me. It had started with Noc Kupały, but I worried which part of the solstice had made him so determined: my recovery or our time alone in the woods.

As if hearing my thoughts, Wacław drifted closer, slipping through a scattered cloud to reach my side. His light blue wisp kept close to him instead of dancing closer like usual.

"You're mad at me for not letting you fly," he said through our bond.

Maybe, I replied, clenching and unclenching my fists. Had I been that transparent?

"If you'd rather have space, then I can go." He hesitated, then continued. *"Even Dziewanna said it's best for you to rest while you can."*

I spun sharply toward him. Flying with his winds was odd enough, but being parallel to the ground messed with my head enough to make me dizzy as I turned. He gently caught my arm when I over rotated.

"Let go!" I snapped aloud, yanking myself free. His cheeks grew bright red as he backed off. "I don't need your help every moment, okay? What happened on the solstice happened, but just because I gave you my wreath doesn't mean I'm some helpless woman who needs her man to do things for her!"

His blush deepened as I noticed the rest of the group out of the corner of my eye. The dark clouds had obscured sight of them a few moments before, but they were definitely close enough to have heard my outburst. Wonderful.

"I don't... I'm not..." Wacław mumbled before dropping his head. The moon cast a ring around the rim of his płanetnik hat, but left his face in shadow. "I'm sorry. You'd just been unconscious, and after your admission about Death, I didn't want you to have to sacrifice anymore. Especially not for me."

The regret hit instantly, but he was gone before I could reply, his hat tugged down further. Of course nothing could be easy.

Fluttering wings approached. I hid my sorrow as Sabina and Ta took Wacław's place beside me. Sabina's slashed nymph wings had recovered well, but the attacks in Vastroth had left gruesome scars down them. For once, though, she appeared more confident than Ta, who kept looking at the ground far below.

"He won't drop us, right?" Ta asked. "Would hate to die because you and him got into a fight a thousand feet off the ground."

"I'm not mad at him," I replied, shaking my head at myself more than her. "It's everything else in these stupid realms."

"You hoped Lady Dziewanna would be able to fix things too?" Sabina asked with a sigh. "Kyustendil and I had planned so many things we'd do once we found her and her power."

More heartache. The god of the northwest wind had been one of the most unusual people I'd ever met, but things were far less exciting without him. "I miss him too. Kyustendil was a fool, but a brave one to go against Weles in his own realm."

Sabina smiled sweetly—one far too kind for the cruel state we found ourselves in. "You fought him in his own realm too. Your own father!" She'd almost squeaked the end.

"I wish he wasn't. Weles broke my body, and I'd probably still be trapped there if Wacław hadn't given me his *żitje*."

"Woulda thought a god would have more than a stone brain," Ta muttered.

Sabina chuckled before her expression turned serious. "Do you think I'll find someone to care about me like Wacław does about you?"

Now my chest felt ready to burst. Was I wrong to resist his attempts to care for me? Was there some middle ground? "Nymphs live a long time," I said, half-in-thought. "You'll find someone when this is over. Either a mortal who strays too far from home or another nymph who'll see how strong you are."

She giggled. "Me? Strong?"

"You're the only reason I was able to kill that mother chała in Huebia." I raised my hand and weaved a little woodland nymph with the moonlight. "Even before you took my mark or met me, you followed my mother behind Weles's back. That takes strength."

"A strength all three of you share," Mother said, suddenly swooping through my creation. "Or should I say four?" She glanced at the golden eagle drifting closer. "Yes, Vlatka. Just because it's dark doesn't mean I cannot see you."

"I would never try to hide from you," the witch replied.

"Then you misremember our first interactions. When I heard a powerful witch had died, I searched you out, but you saw me as Weles's wife." Mother chuckled. "I couldn't blame you. Every year that passes seems to carry my name away more. Little did you know at the time that we were more alike than different."

Vlatka veered closer before landing on Mother's back, spurring another laugh from her. "Witches and gods tend not to get along well. Most of your ilk like to control who wields sorcery."

"I am hardly like most gods."

"And neither is your daughter." Vlatka looked at me with one of her eagle eyes. "I didn't know what I saw in her at first, but I am glad to see she inherited more from you than Weles."

I raised my brow. "She made *sure* of that."

Mother smiled back in a forgiving way. "Oh hush. You would have enjoyed living in the everchanging landscape of Nawia, but you have seen Weles's control now." She bit her cheek and paused. "Dariusz had his own influence on you, however. I can be stubborn, but your distrust of others is certainly from him."

"Didn't you try to overthrow Perun or something?" Ta quipped.

"I had to trust many people to attempt that. Not enough."

A voice peeped in response, but it was hardly loud enough to hear over the wind. Mother noticed and turned to Sabina, throwing Vlatka off her back in the process. The eagle extended her wings as Mother spoke. "You have no reason to fear, Sabina. After you helped save Otylia from Nawia, I owe you more than you could ever know."

That only made Sabina's eyes widen more. "I… I…" She looked at me, so I twirled my hand, ushering her to speak. "I was wondering what your plan is with Master Weles. He is your husband still, right?"

It was hard to tell mother's reaction in the dim light, but my force gave me better vision than most in the darkness. She seemed to pale, her eyes darting toward me. "We are alike again, my daughter. Perun and Weles forced my marriage upon me, and now they attempt the same with you. For a time, I did learn to love him, but his seductions were lies. At least our marriage bore something good in you."

"Mother, tell me you won't go back to him!" I insisted, the knot in my chest suddenly exploding. "He imprisoned and almost killed me. He traps nymphs like Sabina every day and treats them like slaves!"

"I know."

I grabbed her hand. "Then why go back to him? If I can defy them, so can you."

She squeezed hard as tears filled her eyes. "I have given everything so that you can be free. If I have to suffer for a while longer to ensure you do not have to wed Jaryło, then that is what I will do."

"Not an option."

"Sometimes there are no good options."

Fire burned in my heart. I refused to let her suffer Weles any longer—not for me. "You taught me to fight, Mother. So fight! Once we show all the gods how Jaryło betrayed us, they'll turn on Weles and Perun for trying to gift him Jawia."

"If only there were a fraction of your bravery in them," she whispered, pressing our hands to my chest. "Follow your heart, my *mała dzika*. Do not worry about me."

I tore myself from her grasp. "What happened to you? The Dziewanna I served would never have given up a second chance at freedom."

"I haven't given up."

Vlatka cleared her throat. "Perhaps there is a middle way—"

"No," I muttered, crossing my arms and turning my head toward my other shoulder. "Weles wants to control us. Either we stop him or let him win. There's no other way."

Then I dropped away, desperate to be alone. I couldn't believe Mother was giving up. She'd always fought to the end before, but now that I had rescued her, she'd lost her will? I refused to accept it. Whether *she* wanted to or not, I'd do whatever it took to free her from Weles.

Villages along the Wyzra passed by quickly below the clouds. I preferred it down here, even if it wasn't as safe from Marzanna's scouts. Jawia stretched for every direction, and it was comforting to see how small human settlements were compared to the vast tracts of forests and plains that were Mother's. Winter and night ruled them for now. If we succeeded, then life could return to the wilds at least, and only then could mortals be saved. Without the wilds, the tribes were nothing.

The clouds soon split above to reveal Narcyz leading the rest of the group. Andrij clutched his hand, needing the guidance after our battle with the Horde. He'd tried to hide it, but that cloudy look in his eyes was too obvious to miss. Andrij had lost his vision because I'd failed to protect him on that wall. I'd left him to die. Wacław hadn't. Which of us was right? Or was there nothing truly right in war?

Tell me we can do this, I said to Wacław through our bond without drawing closer. My heart longed to, but my stubbornness won. *Tell me we can best Jaryło and get Ara back.*

No reply came for a long time. I felt him tense at my message, probably expecting aggression instead of my need for reassurance. Eventually, though, he glanced at me over his shoulder and pushed up on his hat to reveal the slightest smile crossing his otherwise stoic face. *"Together, we could wrestle Prawia from the gods and take their place on its throne. We could descend to Nawia and do the same there. No one could ever stop us. I'll just do my best not to get in your way as you show Jaryło he messed with the wrong goddess."*

I failed to resist my own grin in response. *Thank you, Wašek... For all of it.*

"Don't thank me yet. I certainly could still mess this up."

I meant for caring about me, even when I don't want it. That stubbornness pushed against me, but I let myself continue. *I didn't mean it about the wreath.*

He chuckled. *"Loving you means enduring your wrath every now and then. I knew that when I confessed my feelings."*

At least I haven't tried to kill you.

He winced, drawing Narcyz from his conversation with Andrij. The brute jabbed Wacław in the arm just hard enough for the pain to hit me through our bond, but I was glad to see they'd become friends. Wacław had felt as alone as me for years. He deserved a group to support him, like the one I'd found over recent moons. My group had a gaping hole without Ara, but I'd fix that. Send me to Oblivion, I'd get her back.

"You do remember you actually took my mortal soul, right?" he quipped. *"I'm pretty sure that's the equivalent of killing me."*

I raised my brow. *But don't you see? You tried. I succeeded. Take that as a warning.*

"Like I need another with you."

You're a man. You forget easily.

He spun on the winds and plopped his hat onto Kuba's head before slowly moving toward me. " *'A man never forgets the blade in his heart, for it's the one that makes him bleed most.' Xobas told me that a couple years ago ahead of the solstice when I'd been nervous."*

My father said something similar but less violent.

"Dariusz will probably be violent once he hears you gave me your wreath. I didn't exactly leave him with the best impression last time."

I tapped our shared mark on my forearm. *The demon doesn't control you anymore. Show Father who you are, and I'll show him how I've changed too. I didn't think I'd care about his approval, but after meeting Weles, I actually miss him.*

His expression soured. *"The feeling isn't mutual. He hid a lot from you—and me."*

So did Mother.

"That's not the same."

Isn't it?

I remembered back to the days of Father's stern gazes and my adventures through the forests with Mother. Simpler times. Even with Mother back now, I wished I'd clung to each moment. Life could never be that way again.

"Some days," I said, taking Wacław's hand and whispering in his ear over the wind gusts, "I wish I'd never known the truth. Maybe we could've been happy together in the village once we figured out our problems."

"I would be lying if I said I didn't dream of the same," he replied.

"But you would've still been a Naw. The demon would've taken over, and I couldn't have stopped it." I raised our joined hands to his heart. "These moons have been both the worst of my life and the best. That's because of you. This journey brought us back together, so as stupid as it sounds, I'm glad for it too."

He gave a soft smile. "It's not finished yet."

26

Wacław

I've missed home.

THE CLOSER WE GOT TO DWIE RZEKI, the more impatient I became. So much depended on our success in Prawia, but those responsibilities were a distant thought compared to my chance to see Mother and my little half-sister Nevenka again. It may have been petty to focus so heavily on such a small personal concern.

Our descent felt horrifically slow. Technically, I controlled the speed, but many in our group were still unfamiliar with flying. Narcyz had already vomited once, and the last thing we needed was for someone to think we were attacking because strange substances were raining from the sky.

We estimated it to be early evening by the time we landed in front of Mom's house. Compared to the usual bustle of the summer labor, it was quiet. Tanek was in his pasture, though, having been cared for by Ara while I was gone, and I assumed Zakir had ensured he'd been brought back after Ara's disappearance.

The chestnut horse rushed over to the fence line at the sight of me, huffing with each breath. I had no grain or treats for him, but he didn't complain as I blew into his nose in greeting and rubbed his neck. "Have you been protecting Mom?"

His only reply was a careless swing of his head that knocked me out of the way and caused him to sprint across the pasture in his shock. Kuba laughed and hopped onto the fence beside me, watching him go.

"Horses are dumb sometimes."

I grinned and pushed him into the pasture. "So are you."

"Hey!" he exclaimed, barely catching himself as the door to the house swung open. A gasp followed.

"Wašek, is that you?" Mom asked, the light from within haloing her bright blonde hair. "This godsforsaken darkness makes it impossible to see anything now."

I pushed myself over the pasture with the winds, landing before her at full speed and wrapping her in a hug. "It's me, *Matka.*"

She returned the embrace and pulled my head down to her. "Are you safe?" she whispered. "I've worried about you every day since you left, and when Ara told me the demon controlled you…"

"Otylia quieted its pull. A lot has happened since I left, but she's helped me figure a lot out."

Footsteps approached, and Mom smiled as Otylia, Kuba, and Dziewanna neared. "It feels like it's been an eternity since I've seen each of you. And Kuba, how—"

"Worry not," Kuba quipped with his arms out like some kind of performer. "The rumors of my death were… well… completely correct, but I'm back thanks to Wacław and the fern flower."

Otylia rolled her eyes. "Guess I didn't Ascend and literally lead you out of Nawia or anything."

"Yeah… Yeah, she was there too."

Tears streamed down Mom's face as she hugged him. "Once dead or not. I am so happy to see you back home." She quickly turned to Otylia and grabbed her too before she had a chance to flee. "You too, Otylia! Wašek had himself worried into fits about you. That wonderful szeptucha of yours, Sabina, told us all about your Ascension. My gods! I should be bowing."

As Mom dropped to her knees, Otylia caught her. "Lubena, you of all people shouldn't bow to me. Not after all you've done to care for me."

"Well, Wacław's friends were few and far between, and I always loved seeing you two together." Her bright eyes said she wanted to ask further, but that now wasn't the time. Instead, she examined Dziewanna, her confusion turning to awe. "It's really you, isn't it?"

Dziewanna beamed. "It is. I'm sorry I had to leave, but I have heard all the stories of what has happened since that time. Seems you had a great part to play in ensuring our children reunited." I blushed as Otylia glared up at her mother, but Dziewanna gave her no heed. "I hope you can forgive me for not telling you the truth."

Mom bowed her head anyway. "I am honored to have called you a friend during your time here. To imagine I knew a goddess… It stuns me."

"Imagine how I felt," Otylia replied.

"Not much has ever phased you, but that is a surprise greater than most." She touched Otylia's cheek. "You have the beauty of a goddess; though, I'm sure Wacław tells you that every day."

I rubbed my temples. "Not now, Mom."

Gratefully, Narcyz trudge toward us, looking as frustrated as ever. "Hard to tell what day it is anymore. Otylia's got her moon stuck up there."

"Yes…" Mom stared up at the moon, now barely a sliver as it approached the end of Czerwiec, the sixth moon of the year. "I was curious about that as well."

"The gods are fighting," Otylia replied. "We need to get to Prawia to fix it and find a way to kill an immortal sorcerer." We both knew she was leaving out her pact with Jaryło, but I did not want to discuss that with Mom. There was enough to worry about without dealing with *more* relationship questions.

Mom's shoulders slumped. "So I assume you will be leaving immediately then?"

Otylia and I exchanged glances, but Dziewanna replied for us, "We have traveled a long way today. Wacław especially will need to rest after carrying us so far, and there are many conversations that must be had." Not so gently, she pushed both of us toward the house. "Stay with Lubena for some time. I will take the rest into the village, and we can speak with Dariusz once you are done here."

Then she left with the others, ignoring Otylia's silent plea to save her from relationship talk. No aid came, and Mom ushered us inside, where she already had soup cooking over the stove. Calm came with the familiar smell. A sense that everything would be all right. It didn't matter how ridiculous the feeling was, and I let myself relax as I sat alongside Otylia at our small wooden table.

As Mom poured a bowl for each of us, I surveyed the home I'd barely stepped in for moons. My bed was still made in the corner across from Mom's. A couple of tunics and pairs of trousers were folded beneath it, as if she were waiting for my return.

She was, I realized. *She's probably never stopped worrying.*

All my calm faded at that thought. Mountains of guilt replaced it. Otylia must've noticed, since she took my hand, holding tight. I forgot sometimes that we could feel everything the other did, as it had almost become normal unless either of us was experiencing a particularly strong emotion. That bond was a gift and a curse. In times like this, though, I treasured the unspoken connection between us.

"Sorry we didn't send word ahead of time," I said as Mom placed the clay bowls before us. "With the armies joining us in the east, anyone bearing either of our marks was gone before we could send word of our plan."

Mom gave a solemn smile. "You never need to warn me if you're coming, as long as more demons aren't following close behind this time."

Images of her dead body flashed through my mind involuntarily, not helping my guilt. "How have you felt since Bidaês's attack? The Moonstone healed you, but—"

"I'm fine, Wašek, really." She reached across the table and took my free hand. The tug at the edge of her lips indicated she knew Otylia held the other. "I want to hear about you. About *both* of you."

I sighed. "Well, it would be lying to say it's been easy. We barely escaped Nawia, even with the help of a group of nymphs and trapped people who were willing to help Otylia. Then, when we thought we were on our way home, we found ourselves trapped in Vastroth."

"That is where you lost yourself to the demon?"

I pulled my hand free and sipped some of the soup. It was delightfully warm, and after moons of travel, a meal at home was a welcomed comfort. Not enough to numb the painful memories. "The things I did there…" My voice cracked. "I killed a lot of people, Mom. Frostmarked, yes, but innocent people too. And I… I liked it, or at least the demon did. It made me feel powerful until Otylia woke me up and I realized what I'd done. All the damage I had caused."

For a minute, I just stared down at the bowl, my spoon trapped in it as I lacked the strength to eat. How could I ever make right so many deaths?

"It's hard not to hate what I've become," I whispered through tears. "Accepting I'm a Naw has made me stronger as a person, but I can never fix what happened in Huebia."

"Some burdens we must bear our entire lives," Mom replied softly. "What have you done for the families of those you killed?"

I took a long breath. "I don't know who they were."

"Is there anyone you know who does?"

"General Mesfin might've heard," Otylia said. "Or the Daughters. We could ask them when we return from Prawia."

Mom's voice grew more confident at that. "There may be no way to mend your errors, but you can at least offer closure to those families. An apology is the least they deserve."

Something shifted inside me. Positive or negative, I didn't know, but the thought of confronting the families of those I'd slain was enough to make me want to hide forever. They were right, though. Fleeing the pain I'd caused would only allow my guilt to grow.

"Then I'll do it," I said. "Once we're finished in Prawia, I'll return to Huebia and admit my wrongs."

"Few men would do the same." Mom's head dropped. "Your father never apologized for the slaughter he caused in his wars to unify the tribe. Many resented him for it."

"I doubt they'll forgive me."

"Maybe not, but you'll have given them the chance to confront you face-to-face."

"We've all done terrible things on this journey," Otylia said, forcing me to meet her gaze. "But we're doing what we can to make it better. That's what's different between us and Marzanna."

Mom gave a solemn smile. "I am glad to see you won't be alone through it either."

"He won't ever be," Otylia said with her chin raised. Her nervousness met me through our bond, but she showed none of it on the outside. "Lubena, I gave your son a wreath on the solstice. You know the traditions."

"Oh my goodness!" Mom pushed aside her stool and rounded the table to hug her. "This is wonderful news after such sorrow. My little Wašek, pledged to the woman I prayed to Mokosz he'd wed!"

My cheeks burned. "Mom! That is the last thing we have to worry about when the world is literally falling apart."

She waved me off. "Oh, hush!" She'd not cried during my story about Vastroth, but tears welled in her eyes now. "Every mother dreams of this day. I hadn't thought it would come like this, but I couldn't be happier for you both."

Too many stories about her own relationship with Father followed, mostly revolving around her regret for allowing him to treat her as secondary. Otylia sat stiffly through all of it. When she did look my way, though, she gave an almost girlish smile, and my heart rushed at the realization that she was actually happy about this. The girl who'd spent all her youth claiming she'd never wed was happy she'd given me her wreath.

Mom then asked a hundred questions about how our relationship had evolved. I replied to most, recalling everything from our interactions on the equinox to our first kiss and our struggles throughout, but I left out anything too embarrassing. She was my mom. Though she cared about all of it, she certainly didn't need to know all of it.

When that was finished, she asked the question that forced Otylia's discomfort to return, "Does Dariusz know?"

"Not yet," Otylia replied, wrinkling her nose.

Mom picked up the bowls and placed them on a shelf nearby,

chuckling. "That should be fun for you both. Since you are only stay-ing the night, you should run along and deal with his fury then."

We hugged her with goodbyes and headed back into the darkness. Both of us hesitated before walking toward the village. Mom had been happy, but Dariusz would not be. Our only hope was that Dziewanna may have calmed him first.

27

Otylia

Father is going to kill me.

THE GUARDS AT DWIE RZEKI'S EASTERN GATE were more alert than during peacetime, but they let us through quickly with our group's advance warning. Both eyed Wacław distrustfully. Had his last visit been that bad?

There was no time to linger on that thought, as Father's house was just inside the gate. I prayed that Mother would still be there. Despite Wacław's admission of his demonic attacks, Lubena had taken the conversation well. I'd actually *enjoyed* talking with her about our relationship, especially compared to the daunting topics surrounding the rest of our journey. Father wouldn't be so easy. Mother could divert some of his attention, but I didn't know whether she'd ignite his temper or cool it. She'd had quite the habit of making him angry.

"Let me do the talking," I told Wacław as we started down the trail toward the house. His arm had been around my waist, but I pushed him off with a bit too much force.

"Frightened of the old priest?" he asked with a laugh. "It's not like he can shatter your bones, unlike your actual father."

I grimaced. "Please don't mention Weles. Especially not around my parents."

A torch lit the entrance to our three-room house. Larger than all in the village except the longhouse, its thatched roof didn't slope directly toward the ground, instead breaking over the room on either side of the main one. It made the house appear like a series of interlocked hills that Wacław and I may or may not have run up as children. Those memories made me smirk, but its looming presence reminded me of the figure who lurked within.

"Your mother was excited for us," I said. "I still can't believe she literally prayed to my grandmother that we'd end up together, but this will not go that well. Father will try to hurt you, and Mother may just make it worse."

"I thought she approved?"

I huffed, stopping outside the door. "That's the problem. Getting Mother and Father to agree is like asking the moon and sun to meet in the same realm."

He took my cheek softly in his hand. I leaned into it, badly needing the support. Why was this worse than battling demons? They were my family, but it felt as if I was about to face trial. "Dadźbóg is trapped in Nawia," he whispered. "Your moon has filled the sky for days. Perhaps even Dariusz and Dziewanna can get along for once."

Then he kissed me, and I cursed him for it. It would be so much easier if I didn't love him, if my time alone with him didn't make my soul feel complete for those few rare moments. But no, he had to have a heart of gold and eyes bright enough to make me wish for the day's sky. Even those demonic veins couldn't ruin him. *Gods, is this what I start sounding like when I'm missing Ara?*

"You'll do great," he said as he parted.

"Just don't say anything that'll make him hate you more."

I pushed open the door to reveal Father slouched over the wooden table in the room's center. His head was in his hands, and Mother stood across from him, arms crossed as the bone amulets hanging from the ceiling swayed from the winds that followed our entry. Father's many statuettes of the gods lined the walls. All of them seemed to judge me, and I scowled at the one for Jaryło in the corner.

"You dare bring that fiend back into my house?" he shouted through his hands, then shot to his feet. The door remained open behind us, and his rage froze me along with the chill. "Well, girl?"

"Dariusz!" Mother snapped, the care she'd shown me replaced by a fire greater than Father's. "Our daughter has returned home after being killed by her uncle and Ascending as a goddess. You will show her more respect."

Father shook his head. His long, graying hair lay over his robed shoulder. It was well-kept as always, a stark contrast to Mother and my gnarled locks from our time in the wilds. "Swaróg will not be pleased when he hears of this. He protected you, Otylia, by bringing your mother to me, and you repay him by granting your wreath to a demon? Obscene!"

So much for revealing that part softly.

I looked at Mother, but her mouthed "sorry" fixed nothing. She'd revealed information that was mine to share. There was no saving the conversation now, and Wacław decided to make matters worse.

"I saved her from the gods!" he snarled, the demon rearing its head until I snatched his hand, forcing it to retreat. His breaths remained heavy and his grip was hard enough to hurt. I held on anyway as his voice turned to an exasperated mutter. "Despise me all you want, High Priest, but I'm not the one trying to force Otylia to wed a god she hates. I'm not the one who slit her throat."

"You certainly tried," Father spat in reply. "It appears the demon is not as finished as Dziewanna claims."

I stepped forward, insistent. "It doesn't control him anymore, Father. I helped him silence it, and I saved other demons too. Ask Mokosz. Ask the people of Vastroth who we freed from the Frostmarked. Ask your *wife* who he nearly died protecting during the rescue."

"She tells the truth," Mother added. She neared Father and touched his arm lightly, but he yanked it free. "Wacław is a Naw, not a demon. The corruption inside him is not his fault, but Jacek's. Do not blame the son for his Father's errors."

Father's spine curled like a beast ready to strike, but he hesitated, studying me. "The goddess of endings. Your moon haunts us now as we starve and freeze. Have you ever wondered if you are part of Marzanna's plan? Of Czarnobóg's? Using a volatile girl to Ascend and fall in love with a monster who could help her destroy Jawia? That would make the dark dragon's task much easier as your gifts to Death rain upon Marzanna's realm."

I glared at Mother. "Is there anything you didn't tell him?"

"Your fate is yours alone to reveal," she replied.

Could even that convince him? I glanced at Wacław, wrinkling my nose. Father wouldn't like the Sudiczki tying my destiny to his, but maybe he would accept it. "The first Sudiczka bound us," I admitted. "She claimed we would become queen and king, but that isn't why I gave Wacław my wreath on the solstice."

"No." Father stepped closer, going toe-to-toe with Wacław. I worried either of them would strike, but Wacław held himself back in spite of the anger I felt through our connection. "You think you love him, but who do you love? The boy that left you to pander to his disgrace of a father? The demon who tried to kill you at Marzanna's command? Or the supplicant who only controls his anger because you hold the last mortal fragment of his soul in you?"

"Enough!"

Light flashed through the room along with a blast that threw Father back onto the table. Statuettes and bone talismans alike shattered and covered the floor with shards. I stomped forward, glaring down at him with moonlight bursting from my fingertips. "I tried to be nice, but you taught me otherwise. Wacław isn't perfect. Neither am I. Everyone in the Three Realms is determined to control me, use me, or kill me, and the only reason Wacław ever stopped protecting me was because I took his mortal soul. Me! *I* was the one who made the deal with Death. *I* was the one who made the blood pact with Jaryło that put us in this situation. So if you need someone to blame, Father, then blame me."

I backed away. "But in the end, it doesn't matter. I'm done pandering to gods and men who only care about their egos and precious titles. Swaróg told you to protect me, so you can either help us or get out of the way."

Father stared at me in horror, then looked at Mother for aid. She did nothing but scoff. "You claim to love me, Dariusz, but then chastised me whenever I tried to teach Otylia about the world. What you have done to protect us is honorable. That does not make you without fault."

"My love…" He clambered off the table and fell onto his knees before her. "All I wanted was for her to be strong and safe. A demon…" He shook his head. "Forgive me. I have grown desperate with Swaróg's distance. It seems the only deities that dare face this threat are the ones before me, and I defy them. What a priest I am!"

Mother grabbed him and pulled him to his feet. "Get up! If you want to be useful, then ride to the Krowikie armies and tell them the gods are on their side. Preach for your wife and daughter! Give them all the lies of a priest when their morale breaks."

"I do not deal in lies!"

"People need hope," Wacław replied. "We build stories of our heroes with a grain of truth, but a field doesn't grow unless the soil is tilled and watered. Give them the promise that they will be victorious upon our return."

Father took a sharp breath. "And if you don't return?"

"Then it won't matter," I replied. "They'll die anyway."

He turned away, pacing to the altar for Swaróg at the far end of the room. The statuette portrayed an elderly bearded man with a mighty hammer that bore his Forgemark. I'd believed him to be the eldest god before I'd met Rod, but I still wasn't sure who or what Rod really was. Eldest or not, Swaróg had been silent ever since he'd helped Mother escape Weles during her pregnancy. I was grateful for that aid. Why did he do nothing now?

"I do not understand his absence." Father placed his hand on the altar, head bowed. "Swaróg and Perun spoke on the holy days, but they send neither fire nor thunder to strike down winter now. Why do they scorn us?"

Mother stepped to his side. It was the most hesitant I'd ever seen her, and she stopped before slowly resting a hand on his back. "They await your daughter. Unless she shows them the truth, they will believe Jaryło's deceit, naming him heir to Jawia and forcing Otylia to wed him. Whatever happens in the coming days will alter the future of the Three Realms, but it will also determine her fate. It is your choice to let her leave with the belief you care more about the gods than the woman you raised, or to accept that she has grown strong enough to choose her own path."

Then she crossed the room to us, gave me a smile and a hand on the cheek, and stepped into the darkness. The cold seemed to return without her. I'd forgotten it amid the argument, and I shivered until Wacław calmed the winds. Another example of why Father was wrong about him. Wacław *was* dangerous—only to anyone who dared to hurt me.

"Weles will never be my father," I said, finding the calm I'd lost. "That's you."

I turned to follow Mother, but as my foot hit the threshold, Father called out. "Wait!"

"What?" I muttered. I wanted to ignore him, but another hope held me there.

Father rushed into my room to the right, throwing aside the linen covering it before returning with a pot in hand. In it bloomed a black hellebore flower. Remarkably, it was alive, though a few fallen petals littered the pot's soil. "I tried to keep it from dying for you," he said with his eyes pleading. "Without your channeling, it was difficult with the frost, but I know how much it meant to you."

I offered a sorrowful smile. "Thank you, Father." There was more I should've said, but I couldn't. That flower had been my last bit of mother, as black hellebores had covered the forest after her death. Wacław had given me that particular flower, but that only added to the sentiment it held. Father rarely showed his love. This didn't change all his fury and judgement. It was his way of proving he cared, though, so I took it as that. "But the flower was to remind me of Mother. I have her now."

I held my hand to the petals and sent my moonlit *żityje* into them.

"Plant it somewhere where the moon never leaves during this long night. People need someone to believe in. Your gods won't answer, so it might as well be me."

Wacław joined me as I headed toward the village center and Perun's Oak—*Jaryło's* Oak. Knowing I'd revered that tree for my whole life made me want to vomit. Was there anything about him that wasn't crafted by lies?

The rest of the group was already there, relaxing together as if we weren't about to face a foe just as fearsome as the Horde itself. Mother stood among them with a knife dangling between her fingers. As Narcyz and Kuba swapped stories far too loudly, she tossed the blade and caught it by the hilt before giving me a grin.

"Dariusz does not see beyond his old ways. You are on the right path, my *mała dzika.*"

"The village is quiet," I said, ignoring her attempt to discuss our familial dispute. "I know many of the women went to provide support for the warriors, but where are the children and elderly?" Snow or shine, they would often gather around the village center for gossip and trade.

"Demons come out at night," Kuba said as he and Narcyz played some type of game with sticks and stones in the snow. He made his move in the game before looking up at me. "The sky is black. The men are gone to fight. You really think mothers want their kids outside to get eaten by some monster?"

Narcyz scoffed. "Most of it's just stories."

"I can't tell what's a story and what's true anymore," Sabina replied. She sat at the base of the oak with her legs pulled in tight along with her wings. "Jawia is so different than what I expected."

"You're a magical nymph," Andrij replied. "I was standing guard outside the Narrow Pass before all of this. It was boring and safe as long as I didn't anger King Boz."

"Real easy," Narcyz muttered. "Right Wacław? Wacław?"

Beside me, Wacław was staring longingly at the longhouse. He shook himself from his daze at Narcyz's insistence. "Sorry, I got lost in my thoughts."

"You good?"

Wacław shook his head and drew the Thunderstone dagger. Its black blade seemed to absorb what little light the moon gave us. "It's been a long time since I was fine. This stupid dagger took the life I knew, and for some reason, I'm still carrying it with me."

"You could always bury it in Jaryło's chest again," Kuba snickered. "Just for fun."

Mother glanced his direction. "Did that work last time?"

"No…"

"Then why are you wasting your breath suggesting it now?" She pointed at him with an open hand. "The spirits protecting the fern flower decided that you are worthy of its power, so prove it."

"You still haven't shown us what the flower can do," Vlatka said from the branches above.

He shrugged. "It gave me my life back. That's all I really care about right now."

"C'mon!" Ta exclaimed, stomping toward him and trying to rip the flower from his grasp, only for him to pull it out of reach at the last second. "You've gotta be at least a little curious."

"Dunno. It makes my arm all tingly when I focus on it, and there's a couple squirrels nearby chatting about how much Narcyz stinks."

Narcyz clenched his fists. "That new face of yours hasn't been punched in yet! Want to change that?"

Mother rolled her eyes and stepped between them. "Wield it well, and that flower could be of great use in Prawia. You have already discovered that you can hear animals with it, but you should be able to understand spirits, sense valuable or powerful artifacts, and tell if someone is lying to you."

"Ooh!" Kuba exclaimed. "I wanna try that one. Wacław, tell me a lie."

I rubbed my temples in a failed attempt to hold off the coming headache. "Kuba, that's not how it works."

"Oh, right…"

"Besides," Wacław said, finally tearing his gaze from the longhouse. "We grew up together. Try it on someone whose secrets you don't know."

Kuba grinned at Sabina. *Oh no…*

He hopped in her direction, playfully waving the flower as he looked her up and down. "Sabina, have you ever been fond of a nymph boy or someone else while you were in Nawia?"

"I… I don't want to talk about it." I hadn't thought it possible for her to pull her legs in closer, but she did, looking at Kuba with distrust.

"I guess that's true? How am I—"

"Drop it, Kuba," I demanded, digging my heel into the snow. My light pulsed unintentionally with my frustration, but abated as he backed off with his hands raised.

"All right, all right. Sorry to offend."

Ta crossed her arms, head cocked. "This is silly. You don't really know me, so try it on me instead."

At her offering, Kuba's eyes widened like a pup seeing fresh meat. "How long have you been a szeptucha?"

"Just over a year," she replied without a moment to think.

I nodded. "She's only thirteen."

"Interesting…" Kuba tapped his chin. "And have you told us everything you know about Mokosz?"

Ta shrugged. "What's there to know? Otylia's her granddaughter, and I'm just some kid with her mark on my neck."

"Hmm." Kuba mulled to himself. "Don't feel anything different, so I think *she* thinks it's true. Any other secrets you've kept?"

"I don't know…"

"AHAH!" Kuba shouted. Despite the glares in reply, he stomped over to us and pointed directly at Ta's nose, which was definitely not the best choice. "Liar!"

Ta kicked him in the shin. "We've all got secrets."

Kuba nodded his head in an exaggerated fashion as he limped away and gave Wacław a smile that screamed for help. "I've done my part. Flower works. I'll be way over there if you need me." He scrambled to the far side of the village center.

"Sorry about him," I said to Ta. "He deserved that kick."

She smirked. "I know he did. Felt good."

"So it works," Mother said, pacing as she stared up at the moon. "That may be helpful, but I fear I have failed to foresee my sister's plan with this endless night."

"Is torturing the people of Jawia not enough?" Wacław replied.

"What does Marzanna not have that we do?" Mother asked. She extended her arms as if she were a priest awaiting an answer. "One of you should see this too."

"People who aren't dead?" Narcyz said.

"Friendship?" Sabina added.

I shook my head and stepped toward Mother, following her gaze to my moon. "You're talking about Dadźbóg. We have a way to Prawia through Mokosz's Heart of Jawia, but Marzanna doesn't. Dadźbóg can help her through his Heart."

"Yes." Mother cursed and spun away with her fists clenched. "I should have seen this sooner."

"Will Marzanna face us there?" Wacław asked. I didn't need our bond to hear the fear in his voice.

"She would be foolish to attack herself so soon, but that does not mean she will not send another." After a moment, Mother dropped her head. "We are not prepared to face another faction in Prawia."

Wacław rounded the oak to my side. "What choice do we have? Marzanna wants us focused on the Horde, but everything points us to Prawia. Your wild force, Jaryło's blood pact, and whatever the key is to finally killing Koschei—none of it can be addressed here." He took my hand and raised his chin. "We've had a long few moons. All of us need to rest and prepare for what comes tomorrow. One last night. Then we face the gods—no matter whose side they're on."

Mother looked from him to me, her cracked crown of antlers almost glowing in the moonlight that split through the branches and bones hanging from Jaryło's Oak. "May we live to see the next sun."

Part 3
The First Realm

28

Ara

If these are the gods, no wonder the demons are so bad.

"MOTHER SAYS THAT YOUR COMPANIONS have nearly arrived," Jaryło said with his hands behind his back. He held his chin high, making it all the more tempting to slit his exposed throat.

If only I'd had a knife.

Without hearing a reply, he spun on his heel to face me from across a long wooden table. I'd gathered from over a week spent trapped in Prawia that things worked differently there than in the real world. Candles emerged from floating flowers throughout the large room, but light came from everywhere and nowhere. Rows of grain stalks, flowering trees, and plants formed barriers between rooms and what I guessed were buildings, but there were never any ceilings. At least, in Jaryło's palace there weren't. I hadn't been allowed any-where else, so I didn't know much more about this strange realm.

The palace's lord was just as strange. Under the guise of Juri dur-ing his time traveling with our group to the Mangled Woods, Jaryło had pretended to be some eccentric monster hunter. He still wore his silver blade strapped to his back, its length left almost completely uncovered by a gold and red cape that draped from his left shoulder. The sword contrasted sharply with his elegant tunic—embroidered with winding designs upon the trim—and his crown of grain and poppy petals. I wondered where the Moonblades were, if not with him.

"Why take me?" I asked for the hundredth time, shifting so that the viny binds entrapping my arms behind my chair's back stopped digging into my wrists. "Otylia was coming anyway. All you're doing is pissing her off, and we both know what she's like when she's angry."

He grinned. "Indeed. She becomes irrational, and that is what I need. The more foolish she acts in front of the other gods, the less her word will mean when she wishes to defy our blood pact." His crooked smile only widened as he leaned on the table traced a line with his finger. "Though, it will not be difficult with her bringing a demonic Naw with her."

"How do you know so much about where they are?" I asked. "Didn't your marked leave with the Krowikie army?"

He stood straight again and rounded the table toward me. "Both Weles and Perun consider me their heir, granting me an immense amount of resources to use as I please."

I repeated that to Otylia as a warning, but based on the fact I'd heard no reply since Jaryło took me, I doubted my messages were reaching her. Zakir had to have told her I'd been taken by now. I just hoped this wasn't as much of a trap as it sounded like.

"If you're so important," I said, sneering at him, "then why are you here, talking to me?"

"Because today is the beginning of a new era, and you have a part to play in its arrival."

"Yeah, right. Like I'd ever help you."

Jaryło stopped behind my chair, and the sound of a dagger sliding from its sheath split the otherwise silent room. I tensed, but didn't move. He wanted me to fear him. Otylia would want me to stay strong, so I forced myself not to draw upon her force. Jaryło would just overpower me anyway.

The dagger was cold against my hand, but after an initial brush against the metal, my fingers found the hilt instead. "Listen to me carefully," Jaryło whispered. "In a few minutes, my servants will arrive to kill you. Escape before then and you may just live."

"You're the one who captured me," I replied. "What is this? A trick?"

He turned away, his footsteps fading toward the interwoven wheat stalks that formed the doors of his palace. "It is your only chance to save your little mortal life, Ara. I suggest you take it."

Then he left. Like I said, strange.

There was no time to decide whether I was running straight into another trap. Jaryło was often a liar, but I had no doubt he would actually send his goons if I didn't do what he said. So I cut. It was difficult to slice at the magical vines without sight. After a few minutes of rapidly wriggling the knife in a direction that felt was right, though, the resistance gave way, and my hands were free.

I jumped to my feet, rubbing my sore wrists and examining my options for escape. There were four: the door behind my chair that Jaryło had taken, the one across from it where Jaryło had entered, and another on either side of the room. Jaryło's servants—masses of grain stalks, vines, leaves, and flowers—had led me through the one to the right to enter here in the first place. Behind it was a smattering of strange rooms I'd only half-seen through the foliage walls. None of those had resembled an exit.

That meant the door on my left was the only option. Jaryło likely knew that, but doubts would only slow me down. A creak came from the door behind me as I started walking. Then came the shouts.

"Stop!" the servant shouted in rough, forced Krowikie.

I didn't yield, bursting through the side door and into a narrow hall. A smaller door was along the opposite wall just strides away, but a glance through the plants revealed a bedroom. I needed out! So I ran down the hall and ducked down a side passage as the door I'd left through opened. The servants lumbered after me. They were slower than my running pace, though, and I could track their location based on their equivalent of footsteps. Their legs didn't quite move up and down. Instead, the vines loosened and tightened over the ground, almost pulling them along with a sound that reminded me of Kuba slurping his soup.

The passageway led me toward what appeared to be outside. It was impossible to tell with the weird light that allowed no shadows to exist, but the trees were larger ahead, as if forming an exterior wall. I ran toward it with all the pent-up energy I had from my time trapped by Jaryło. Lush chambers or not, I'd have rather been anywhere else than stuck with that traitor.

When I threw open the double doors at the hall's end, I realized I'd been both right and very wrong at the same time. The trees marked an end to the maze of wooden floors and lush, yet natural decorations. They also encircled another trap of its own.

My bare feet struck dirt as I stumbled into an enclosed garden. Not what I wanted. Yes, it was outside, but in a palace with no roof, what wasn't?

A dirt path wound through patches of various kinds of plants. Cabbage, apples, rye, and barley formed an outer ring, while blooming flowers filled the center. It was all well cultivated, and I imagined Otylia's sneer at the taming of the wild plants. I had no such luxury.

I followed the path across the gardens and into another hall. Across it, an open, circular room displayed at least a hundred swords on stands and mounted on the wall. Each was crafted in ways unlike any I'd seen, with colors and etchings covering their blades of every shape. Twelve wooden altar-like tables formed a semi-circle at the room's center. A hilt protruded from six of them, their blades seemingly driven into the altar. I recognized the fourth one.

"Kwiecień…" I gasped. This was where he kept the Moonblades—inside a temple to war.

More shouting came down the hall to my left. I ignored it, focusing instead on the Moonblades. *How angry would he be if I borrowed one?*

It was a silly, childish thought. I was being pursued by spirits from the realm of the gods. This was a god's palace, and there would surely be security around the Moonblades to prevent someone as foolish as me from taking them. But what if there wasn't?

"This is so stupid," I muttered to myself as I sprinted for

Kwiecień. Not only was it the blade I recognized, but it was the closest, giving me the best chance to escape. I was risky, not a complete idiot.

The sword hummed as I stopped before the altar and grabbed hold of Kwiecień's hilt. A longsword, it was built to be held with either one or two hands, so I managed to get a solid grip on it and pull with all my strength. Nothing. Not a budge or a creak. The only sound was a whimper, and that came from pathetic mortal me, trying to pull a god's blade from a magical altar.

I turned to flee, but two of Jaryło's servants blocked the entryway. Their eyes were slits, their arms ending in thorns that prepared to strike at me as they rushed forward.

I threw Jaryło's knife at the first, embedding it in its throat. It didn't even stumble. "Alunam!" I cursed with the name of the Zurgowie dark god. At this point, he could've been a reference to Czarnobóg or even Jaryło. It didn't matter. It just felt right to curse in my native tongue.

The servant with the knife in its throat swiped as it drew close, but I dodged toward the wall, grabbing for the closest sword. A massive thick blade of gray stone, it nearly tore my shoulders from their sockets as it slipped from its case and clonked onto the wooden floor. I'd have laughed about the indent in Jaryło's palace if the servants weren't upon me.

They attacked from either side, faster with their arms than their legs. I was slower with the cumbersome blade and cried out as thorns ripped through my torso. The pain gave me a last burst of strength. With a scream worthy of the wild goddess herself, I spun and swept the sword behind me. It struck the first servant in the equivalent of its stomach before slicing right through to do the same thing to the second.

Then it slipped from my hand.

Momentum carried the sword straight into the wall of plants and beyond. The monstrosity didn't even slow as it sent the blades mounted above crashing down, then continued on through the room behind it and into the next wall. Then the next. And then... *Is that outside?*

I imagined what the other gods must've thought at the sight of a ridiculously large stone sword flying across their peaceful realm at the speed of a hawk. The thought made me laugh to myself, but the sound of more servants approaching took that joy. Luckily, I now had a way out of the palace. Spirit or not, they couldn't catch me now.

Sharp pain jabbed at my stomach as I reached down, grabbing a shorter blade with a pointed notch on its end like an angular hook. Odd, but it would do. I gripped its hilt with one hand and my wounded stomach with the other. Then, I ran without worry about pain or blood. I would escape. Otylia would come. And then we'd make Jaryło suffer together.

Except when I emerged into the world of the gods beyond Jaryło's palace, I realized how terribly lost I was.

The palace wall gave way to a field of waving grain, lined with more flowers and other crops. This, at first, seemed normal, but the sky was very *not normal*. Sprawling masses of earth floated above and in each direction. Winding wooden bridges connected them to a massive object in the distance that resembled the trunk of a tree. With the grain blocking much of my sight, I couldn't see what was on the other floating islands, but if this was Jaryło's palace, perhaps the entire island was his. Other gods likely had the same. That would make getting off Jaryło's island no easier than escaping his palace.

I still had no idea what escaping meant, but that tree looked like my best chance. Otylia had mentioned the Krowikie beliefs around the World Tree that connected their Three Realms. Could this be it?

Something rustled in the foliage nearby.

Well, it's the best I've got.

I sprinted into the field, hoping to find the edge of Jaryło's island and the bridge toward the World Tree. It was a maze—one haunted by spirits that had orders to kill me. Their faces appeared on and off through the grain. Some resembled the woodland servants from the palace, but others were made of the crops themselves. What should've been just a patch of grain would suddenly morph into a monster grabbing at my heels as I ran. They made me turn so many times, I couldn't tell anymore if I was heading away from the palace or toward it. There was no time to tell. All I could do was run and swing at anything that came close. Unfortunately, I wasn't amazing with a sword.

Vines wrapped around my calf as the edge of the island became visible. I struck out at my attacker, but while I could shoot a deer at a hundred strides, my slashes were more like random flailing than a real defense. The attacks sent me sprawling towards the island's cliff edge. There was nothing to grab, no way to prevent the fall to come, but more vines extended, wrapping around my waist as I hung over the edge with only the tips of my toes still on the ground.

"This is not your realm, child," the creature said in an oddly soft voice. It emerged from vegetation as its vines turned me back to face it, and it wasn't a servant. Nor was she a creature at all.

The middle-aged woman who'd caught me had skin and hair matching the golden colors of the grain around her. Strands of the stalks seemed to wrap around her body to form a dress that's fluffy layers were lined with grain heads. With a narrow, pointed face, she appeared dainty. There was strength in her gaze, though, and the obvious power she'd used to catch me threw any other assumptions of weakness aside.

"You're right," I replied. "That's why I was seeing myself out."

She chuckled. "You must be the girl Jaryło's servants were whispering about. Ara?"

"Now that you know my name, can you let me down?" I glanced over my shoulder at the endless drop. More islands were scattered below, some with structures built upon them and others as bare as Vastroth's desert.

The vines retreated, setting me on the ground before retreating into the earth at the woman's feet. She stepped forward with her hands clasped before her and her chin held downward. "How did you escape Jaryło? It seemed as if he had a purpose for you, and he does not take well to those who disobey him."

"He tied me to a chair and then gave me a knife." I couldn't find a reason to lie. This woman had just saved me, and she was perfectly capable of pushing me to my death if she didn't believe me. "Then he sent his servants after me. I don't know if this is some type of game or what."

"Then it is true…" she ran her fingers over the heads of grain nearby, thinking for a moment. "You are connected to Weles's daughter—the goddess to become Jaryło's wife."

I raised my brow. "Do you plan on telling me who you are?"

She held out her arms to touch the stalks on either side of her. "Marzyana of the grain, not to be confused with my wintery cousin. If you intend to escape, I believe I may be able to help, but it will not be simple. The elder gods have their servants closely watching the branches to the World Tree."

"Nothing in my life is simple lately. Lead the way."

29

Wacław

They didn't want me in Jawia. They didn't want me in Nawia. And they surely won't want me in Prawia.

I WAS MORE NERVOUS THAN I ADMITTED to the rest of the group as we met at the village center the following morning. For those of us from Dwie Rzeki, our families had gathered to wish us luck. Well, at least Mom and my little half-sister Nevenka did for me. Natasza and her other children just watched from a distance. I'd never liked Father's *other* wife, but a twinge of regret took hold of me knowing I had left my siblings fatherless, alone with the witch of a woman who'd thrown me out of the longhouse as a child.

It was almost dark around that same longhouse. This new moon marked the end of the Czerwiec moon and the beginning of the Lipiec one—the seventh of the year. Mom and I normally toiled in the fields during the summer heat, but it was dreadfully cold now. Our lack of a sun only made it worse than before.

"Be safe, Wašek," Mom said with a hug that told me she never wanted to let go. The feeling was mutual, but we'd waited long enough. Prawia awaited us.

I pulled out the Mothermark amulet she'd given me moons before. "I'll always have you with me."

"You didn't promise," she replied with a furrowed brow, countered by a grin.

"I would if I could."

Beside her, Nevenka waved for me to come closer, so I crouched to her level. "Waci," she said. "Will you tell Mokosz I've been good? Mother says your opinion doesn't matter since you have rat blood, but Otylia likes you. Maybe she can tell her?"

"Rat blood?" I asked. "I promise you that I don't have rat blood."

She cocked her head. "Then why you have all those marks on your face?"

"You know what?" I asked, plopping my hat onto her head. "Maybe you should ask Otylia yourself. I think she'd *love* that."

"Really?"

"Hurry! We'll have to go soon."

Nevenka ran off with all the speed of the winds as I rose. Mom met me with a kiss on the forehead. "Pleas to the Great Mother aside, all I ask is that you keep Otylia with you. Both of you are better that way."

Otylia spoke with her father across the village center, near Perun's—*Jaryło's*—Oak, until Nevenka rushed up and began rambling. I wondered how Dariusz had taken the news that he'd been preaching at the wrong god's Heart of Jawia. Perhaps it didn't matter in the end. Jaryło had betrayed us, but Perun had so far sat back and allowed Jawia to fall, no matter how much priests and warriors prayed to him.

The oak didn't hold my gaze, but Otylia did. Wearing a fur-lined cloak over her white and black-embroidered dress from the Drowning of Marzanna festival, she had the presence of a chieftess. Moon amulets hung from her white leather headband and over her ears, and necklaces of colored stones shone with the light radiating from her skin. Tradition dictated she braid her hair or wear a headscarf, but she left hers free to drape over the silver fox pelt at her shoulders. Gray makeup shadowed her eyes. When she noticed my staring, they became bright emeralds, beautiful and dangerous.

"I won't leave her," I said, unable to hold back my smile. "That I can promise."

Mom brushed off my festival tunic. It was the most formal attire I had, but it failed to compare to Otylia's own. Knowing her appearance was because of her engagement to Jaryło hurt. Of course she didn't actually plan to marry him, but the boyish longing in my chest reminded me of all the years I'd wished to be with her on the solstice, only to be rejected by every girl I spoke to. That wish had come true in time. Maybe she'd dress that way for me one day.

"That's the same way you looked at her every festival," Mom said with a laugh. "Oh, how you would protest and claim you weren't fond of her, but a mother knows!" Squeezing my arm, she sniffled and forced a smile. "Now go and ruin a god's wedding so you can have your own when this is finished."

"*Matka!*" I exclaimed before joining the others near the back trail leading to Mokosz's Grove. Something stopped me, though. I glanced back over my shoulder at Mom and the village that I'd never left for sixteen years. So much had changed. It would never return to the way it had once been for me, but if we succeeded, at least everyone else could have a normal life.

Otylia was still crouched before Nevenka. She actually seemed to be enjoying the girl's frantic joy.

Coming? I asked her silently.

"*Do I have to?*"

I raised my brow. *Cold feet?*

"*Jest again and I'll trap yours for eternity. Your sister is just telling me all about the ideas she has for flowers in your hair when we wed.*"

You said "when."

She whispered something to Nevenka, then shot me a glare. "*Don't get so excited. A blood pact still outweighs a flower wreath when it comes to engagements.*"

Kuba interrupted me before I could reply. He wore a similar, but simpler, tunic to mine with five javelins strapped to his back. They looked like nothing more than sharp sticks, but one had killed Yuliya when Otylia and I had struggled. Not everything needed to be complex.

"I forget you two can do that talking in your heads thing," he quipped, hands on his hips. "Really feels uncomfortable to watch."

"Usually we're more subtle," I replied.

He patted me on the shoulder. "Yeah, right…"

"Are we prepared?" Dziewanna called, particularly in Otylia's direction.

Otylia rushed to us, her cheeks red from the chill as she returned my hat. "Sorry. Wacław sent a child to distract me."

I shrugged. "It worked, didn't it?"

Dziewanna wrinkled her nose at me, her tone sharpening. "You do realize we are moments away from stepping into the realm of the gods, right? What happens from this moment on will determine both Otylia's fate and the entire fate of the Three Realms, so I expect you to quit the childish games. You and her are mere weeks away from completing your seventeenth year. Act like a man who jumped the fire, not a boy."

"Yes, my lady," I croaked. The fire in her voice was enough to make me sweat despite the cold. Though I'd needed the laughter to distract me, she was right, and my stomach did flips as we entered Mokosz's Grove.

Narcyz smirked at me as he walked, but Andrij's firm grip upon his arm prevented any further jests. How many mortals had ever stepped foot in Prawia? Nawie? Nymphs? We were a band of misfits who barely belonged on Jawia, let alone the realm of the gods. I'd feared what I would find when I descended into Nawia, but I had been going to rescue Otylia then. This was something else entirely. I could defeat demons, nymphs, szeptuchy, and Nawie alike. Against gods, I was just a pawn, barely able to beat Jaryło at his weakest and completely useless when Weles had attacked Otylia. Could I uphold my promise to protect her? My friends?

They could all die at Jaryło's hand. I doubted the other gods would even flinch at mortal deaths. Otylia and Dziewanna were the only ones who couldn't die, but they could be forced into serving others for eternity.

I shuddered.

"Otylia, join me by the altar," Dziewanna said, stopping before the wooden statue of Mokosz in the center of the clearing. The statue depicted the Great Mother with open arms, and I hoped that spirit extended to our entry to Prawia. "Everyone else stay back."

As Dziewanna and Otylia placed their hands upon the statue, I surveyed the grove. This was only the third time I'd ever stepped foot here—and the first time I wasn't sneaking in—as it was considered a holy place only for the Mothermarked diviners to conduct their rituals. Otylia and the others had foreseen the Horde's arrival on the equinox. We just hadn't realized it yet.

Clouds rolled overheard as the goddesses whispered. A blizzard was coming. I could feel it on the winds, and I mourned the suffering it would cause Mom, Nevenka, and the rest of the tribe. They had exiled me once, but this past day, I had been welcomed back by those who mattered. Except for Dariusz. Convincing both Otylia's adoptive father and blood father to accept our relationship would be difficult. The question was whether it would be harder than fighting the gods.

A hum soon crossed the grove, ending the chatter among our group. All turned to the statue, but none of us dared approach until Dziewanna spoke.

"My mother has granted us access to Prawia through her Heart," she said. "Come quickly, as every moment she keeps the connection open, it wastes more of the *żityje* she uses to keep this realm alive." Then she stepped into the statue.

Unlike in Nawia, where the Heart's trunk almost formed a door, the Heart did not move at Dziewanna's arrival. Instead, she simply stepped into the embrace of the Great Mother and disappeared in a blink.

"Uh…" Narcyz mumbled, rubbing the back of his neck. "Was that supposed to happen?"

I just pushed him on. "Go, before Dziewanna shoots us all for not listening."

Otylia waited as each of us approached the statue and disappeared in turn. My heart beat faster and faster, so I kept my gaze on her to calm myself. When my turn came, she took my hand.

"Don't worry. We'll have Mokosz and Mother on our side."

I took a deep breath and studied her face, adorned with all the markings of a bride. "I've never been more afraid."

Without replying, she pulled me forward to the statue. The world went dark when we passed between Mokosz's arms. Then bright light washed over us, blinding as we entered the realm of the gods together.

30

Otylia

I'm not ready to be a wife… anyone's.

THAT THOUGHT ROOTED ITSELF IN MY MIND as Wacław clutched my hand hard enough to wring a boar's neck. His worry was obvious, even without our bond. Many men could hide their emotions, but my poor Wašek wore his heart on his face even more than his sleeve. And his face looked like a deer who'd just spotted a hunter.

I loved him more than my terribly unromantic words let on. Someday I'd complete my promise to wed him through the flower wreath tradition. That day wasn't now, but having him by my side, even as a nervous wreck, helped calm my own anxieties.

Prawia didn't.

I blinked away the spots dotting my vision as we stumbled through Mokosz's Heart onto solid stone ground. It was rough and uneven beneath my boots. A familiar feeling, it reminded me of the caverns I'd traversed with Kiin to reach the Hidden Waters beneath Huebia. Sorrow came with the memory of the Daughters of the Earth's fallen leader, so I pushed it away. I had enough ahead of me without mourning what had come before. There would be plenty of opportunities to regret my failures later in my immortal life. Besides, there was the wonderfully strange realm of Prawia to confront or explore.

Light hit every part of the gardens around us, banishing shadow as ripe fruits and vegetables overflowed their beds and lured Kuba to them. The stone path we'd entered on wound its way through them, and sheep wandered across it in a lazy fashion. They covered everywhere the gardens didn't between us and a wooded hill with windows carved into its side, but even that couldn't keep my attention for long.

"How are they not falling?" Wacław asked, gawking at the floating islands above. Mother had warned me about the branches of the World Tree that connected it at Prawia's center to each god's isle. Mokosz's was among the highest, but enough islands still filled the sky for it to be awe-inspiring.

Mother grinned back at him. "Do not expect Prawia to follow the rules you understand from your realm. The World Tree alone is enough to hold each god's home aloft."

"You had one once?" I asked.

Mother's smile disappeared. "Yes, I did."

I wondered what had become of it, but the sheep's parting pulled me from my thoughts as the Great Mother strode between them. She was queen among gods. The earth and flora wove its way into her dress of golden browns and greens, tied along the front with threads of actual gold. Her crown arced like the sun's path. It matched her dress, and the embroidered spiraling designs on its surface glowed with every step she took.

"So it is finally time," she said with her back straight and her hand resting upon the head of one of the sheep that had followed her.

"I wish it wasn't," I muttered. Why was I so stiff? Mokosz had been one of my patrons during my time as a szeptucha, and she'd risked Weles's fury to aid me in Nawia. If anywhere was safe in Prawia, it was here with her.

She patted the sheep once more before moving through our group. A head taller than me—and taller than our previous meetings—she towered over all but Wacław and Mother. When she stopped before me, she held her hands to her heart. "There are bindings wound so tightly they cannot be broken and others that can be untied with the correct patience and diligence. Let us hope your blood pact with Jaryło is the latter for all of our sakes."

"She only did it to protect our friends," Wacław said, "and those who helped her escape Nawia."

Mokosz gave him a motherly glare. It wasn't directed at me, but a shiver still ran down my spine. "Do not give me that questioning look, Wacław. I know what you are better than even you, but I also know what you surrendered for Otylia to Ascend. Do not lose the love that pushed you to accept that decision. It is the only force standing between the two of you and the darkness that threatens us all."

"That darkness includes Jaryło," I replied without hesitation.

"Your strength of will never ceases to surprise me." She held my cheek, sorrow filling her eyes. "My son's errors are great, and he deserves punishment for them, as my daughter did for her own betrayal."

Mother huffed and crossed her arms. "I sought to reduce Father's control over the Three Realms and the rest of us. Jaryło released the dark dragon after millennia of imprisonment. We are *not* the same."

I'd never compared her appearance to Mokosz's before, but in her frustration, I saw that she'd inherited her mother's thin nose and wide brows—traits I shared with them too. That gave me some solidarity with the women who I was only now starting to see as family. If only they would get along.

"Dziewka, my dear," Mokosz said. "You and Jaryło possess the same stubborn will that you have passed on to your daughter. It is both a powerful weapon and a great threat to the strongest of gods. Perun and Weles have been too blind to see Jaryło's flaws, but they will see yours and Otylia's clearly."

Mother closed in on Mokosz until there was no space between them. If we'd still been in the chilled grip of Jawia, her fogged breaths would've covered the three of us. "Stubborn will is the only way we convince them to disown him."

"Those are strong words." Mokosz sighed and turned away. "Let us speak more within my home. It is not right for me to leave guests standing in my gardens, especially on an occasion as auspicious as this."

"This wedding is hardly in our favor," Mother said as I walked between arguing goddesses, our group trailing behind.

The sheep parted for us, and I felt as small as them with my grandmother and mother on either side of me. They debated my fate, yet I had no plan to alter it myself. Even if Wacław could kill Jaryło and somehow separate him from his Moonstones, the blood pact would not be broken. We needed something stronger.

A wry smile crossed Mokosz's face. "Is it not? Come now, you were raised as a princess among these branches. What is a gathering of the gods if not an opportunity for each of us to seek alliances, exploit rivalries, and position ourselves for the era to come?"

"Then you have a plan?" I asked, not getting my hopes up too much.

"Nothing is for certain. You have worked yourself into quite the difficult situation." She glanced at Mother, her glare fading for a moment. "Before we can address Otylia's ills, we must mend your severed bond with the force of the wilds. Do not be surprised. I know much, and it was not hard to understand what Marzanna had done when my szeptuchy reported you fighting with nothing more than a bow against Koschei's army."

Mokosz held up a hand with her palm facing her. Colored wisps dashed between her fingers, similar to End's. But I knew these from years of experience. This was the flow of time in her grasp, moving like a river as it twisted around itself and pushed onward in whatever direction it pleased. I opened my vision to my own wisps to see if they changed around her. A violet one spiraled around her skirt and up to her hand with a constant glow greater than any I'd seen from gods, Nawie, or mortals. What secrets did it hold?

Jaryło's showed Mother's suffering, I thought with a shudder. *What pain would come with knowledge of the Great Mother's end?*

"Topics such as this also should not be spoken in open air," Mokosz said as the wisps continued around her hand. "Let us say that time works its wonders in restoring the balance of the Three Realms, and sometimes, that cycle is longer than even the years many gods have seen." Her gaze fell upon Mother at the end.

The hill at the island's center loomed over us now. Golden and violet spirits in womanly forms carried yarn, shears, and baskets full of their pickings to and from the open doorways into the hillside. Wild grasses covered the slopes, and more of the spirits sat with large looms, weaving with the sheep's wool. Each spirit we passed bowed at us before continuing in silence.

Then we entered the hill.

My connection with Wacław revealed both of our worries. So much depended on Mokosz's help, and it didn't help that the mere appearance of this realm was enough to unsettle me. It was beautiful in its own way, but nothing felt normal. Each word Mokosz spoke only made it feel less so.

The tunnels within the hill were nothing like those in the Vastro-thie city of Sheresy. Instead of dark halls and narrow turns, light emanated from everything as we passed through open spaces decorated with furs and statues depicting women at work—even female warriors. I wished Ara could've seen them. She hadn't been proud of much when it came to her former Zurgowie clan, but she'd bragged often that their women weren't held back from battle. Once we rescued her from Jaryło, I promised myself she'd get the chance.

We soon reached a rounded room filled with short, wide chairs lined with sheep's wool and arranged in a semi-circle. Mokosz sat opposite of the entrance as I studied the series of murals that covered every part of the stone wall. Starting over Mokosz's left shoulder, they depicted a baby girl growing into adulthood. Her wedding came a third of the way through the room, then her pregnancy and motherhood. Images of work and seasons were scattered between the life events, and in the final painting over Mokosz's right shoulder, the woman rose from her funeral pyre as a raven. Smoke curled to form her wings. Her family watched as she flew into the distance, free until her descent to Nawia.

"I hope you do not take offense to the paintings," Mokosz said sweetly. "For the patron of wives and motherhood, it is difficult to have a daughter and granddaughter so opposed to those practices."

"I never opposed them," Mother replied, standing uncomfortably in the center of the room. "I simply did not support you and Father forcing me to wed against my will. Whether it was Weles or those you suggested before him, my say did not matter."

Mokosz sat up straighter with her hands in her lap. Her tone sharpened. "You were a princess of Prawia. We could not let you chase after mortal men, and when you revolted, we were left with no choice."

Mortal men? Mother had never spoken about her romantic interests before her marriage to Weles. Based on her suddenly flushed face, I wasn't sure I ever wanted to.

The room seemed to chill as she clenched her fists and stared at the ground. "Centuries later, you still refuse to say his name? Ivan was a great man, Mother, and every time his soul returned to Jawia, he proved both of you wrong."

"Wait, what?" I blurted out, rushing to Mother and snatching her arm. "Ivan was your lover?"

She gritted her teeth. "It was complicated. But in one of his previous lives, yes, I loved the soul you knew by that name."

"He protected me in Nawia." My gut wrenched at my last sight of the bear-turned-king who'd organized the effort to free me. "Weles killed him…"

"I know." She paced to one of the images and traced its strokes. In it, the woman ran hand-in-hand through a stream with her daughter. "I like to think a bond connected us through the cycle of his soul's lives. He was always loyal when I asked anything of him, down to the last request: to keep you safe when Weles found you."

Tears ran down her cheeks as her open hand closed over the woman's face. "Why portray me in these murals, Mother? Why show a life I never lived?"

I hadn't noticed it before, but as I spun to look at each image, I realized Mother was right. The woman bore a close resemblance to her. Her daughter, too, had my black hair and green eyes, and I swore I could remember that exact moment in the stream with her. Father's furious calls would echo through the woods, but they'd meant nothing when we were together.

Now my own tears came. I cursed, turning away from the others and dreading that my makeup would smear.

Wacław caught me in his gentle embrace. "I'm sorry you lost her," he whispered.

"I painted this room myself while I was pregnant with you," Mokosz replied to Mother, crossing her legs properly. "It was never meant to show what you had to be, but my gift of divination revealed portions of your life far before they occurred. While Otylia sees endings, I see possibilities and processes, the middle of the story without the beginning or completion. I knew you would fall in love, have a daughter with hair as black as her night and eyes as green as the depths of your wilds, and become a strong, independent woman."

"You wished for a life I would never have," Mother replied.

Mokosz lowered her head. "Every mother wishes many things for their child that they cannot give. I have failed at many parts of motherhood with Marzanna, Jaryło, and you, but I do not regret wishing. Nor do I regret who you have grown to be." She looked at the rest of the group. "May I have a moment to speak to my daughter and granddaughter alone? There are aspects of a god's power that mortals cannot know, no matter how trustworthy you all may be."

Silence hung over us for a time, but the others began filing out as Mother stood with her shoulders hunched. Wacław moved to leave with them until Mokosz raised her hand. "You may stay, Wacław. Considering your bond with Otylia, little is secret to you anyway."

He winced at that, averting his gaze from me as he thanked her. Why hadn't I trusted him with the truth of my promise to Death sooner? I shook away my regret. He knew now, so all I could do was move forward.

Wacław and I took seats near Mokosz. Mother refused, instead rounding the room, inspecting each mural as if secrets lay within. It was hard to imagine what she'd been like hundreds of years ago. What had she thought of Jawia after being raised in a realm like this?

"How can a god drain another's force?" I finally asked after what seemed an eternity of tense silence.

Mokosz's expression lightened. "It is reassuring to see that this journey has not changed your determination. To answer your question, however, I do not know. Demons and Nawie are capable of draining the *žityje* of others, but gods are not supposed to be capable of such acts. We already know Czarnobóg's soul is corrupted. Marzanna's is likely the same."

"That is not enough," Mother replied. "They did not only drain my *žityje*. They severed my connection to the wilds, stole all my power."

"Not all of it. You remain immortal, and if you wished it, you would likely be able to channel like any witch, as Otylia did after the Trial of Isolation until she Ascended. Our forces guide how our spells manifest. They do not grant or remove our ability to use them."

Mother shrugged. "That would require more *žityje* than I have managed to muster in the weeks since Otylia woke me. Few worship me now, and without my only szeptucha, I have nearly no sacrifices with which to replenish my strength."

"How does she get her force back?" I asked Mokosz. "Worshippers or not, Mother needs to bond with the wilds again if they're to survive."

Mokosz held her fingers to her lips, pondering as she stared up at the stone dome ceiling. Narrow glass windows arced up its slope. Light came from everywhere here, even indoors, but she seemed brighter than all else in that moment. All gold and regality. "For that, we must appeal to Rod. Only he has knowledge of our forces' source, and only he would know how to restore the connection Marzanna and Czarnobóg have stolen."

At the mention of Rod, Mother spun on her heel and returned to the room's center with her hands locked behind her. "I would not call Rod my greatest advocate, but you're right. I only wish there were a more discreet way to reach him than climbing the World Tree. We need to appear strong in front of the others."

"I disagree," Mokosz said.

Mother scoffed. "Of course you do."

"Now, now. I am only trying to help." Mokosz stood and carefully approached Mother, then took her hand. "I am not the only one with szeptuchy among the clans. Perun and Weles already know that you have lost your force, and we can use that to our advantage. Discretion will ensure they do not know you have *regained* your strength. Let them believe they have you and Otylia under their thumbs until the moment is right."

I squirmed in my seat. "So you want me to play along?"

"For now, yes. We all know you do not want this marriage, so all you need to do is tone down your anger, then release it when we are ready." She looked from me to Mother. "This does not mean you are to do nothing. Your moonlight illusions can provide you and her cover while you visit Rod. He will want to speak with both of you."

"And the blood pact?"

Mokosz's smile shifted from motherly to sinister. "Such a pact can only be broken if both sides agree. That leaves us a single option: make Jaryło agree."

Wacław wriggled his chin. "That's it? How do we make him agree when we're giving him everything he wants?"

"By taking everything he believes he has." Mokosz stepped away from Mother and extended her hand to Wacław. "That is where you will be important. Come with me. We have much to discuss while Dziewanna and Otylia visit the eldest among us."

My chest tightened. "You want us to go now? We just got here, and I barely know anything about this realm."

"Then we are both lucky your mother is quite the guide."

31

Otylia

How is this realm even possible?

THE SQUAWKS AND CHIRPS OF HUNDREDS OF BIRDS met me as Mother and I stepped onto the branch of the World Tree that connected to Mokosz's island. Eagles, hawks, and smaller nightjars and ravens passed between the islands with bits of parchment tied to their legs. Others nestled in the World Tree's branches far above or below. A golden eagle circled among them, keeping a single eye on us as she watched for danger with the other.

Mother had resisted Vlatka's insistence at first, but this was one of the first times being trapped in an eagle's body was advantageous. She blended in with the other birds, hopefully giving us enough warning if we were spotted.

I took a deep breath and added a few details to the illusions covering Mother and me. Silver mists swirled around us to give us a vague resemblance to the Great Mother's spirit servants. Normally, the sorcery behind my moonlight illusions gave itself away upon close inspection, but we were mimicking spirits whose forms were indistinct. It was the skill I'd practiced the least. All things considered, I was pretty proud of the result.

Keeping the illusions stable was difficult with the uneven terrain.

Instead of a typical wooden bridge, the branch resembled a massive version of an actual tree's limb, knots and all. A few spirits walked with us or toward us. The Threads of Life showed odd, indistinct lines connecting them to Mokosz, but the Threads revealed that others were clearly sent by other gods. We passed one whose body consisted of deep gray vapor and eagle-like wings that stretched far to either side. Another had the wooden torso of a leszy with moss and water dripping from its limbs, but its serpent head and cattle horns revealed clearly who it served.

The disguise must have worked, since both Perun and Weles's spirits passed without so much as a glance in our direction. Granted, it was difficult to see what direction a spirit was looking.

Mother adjusted the basket of wool she carried. I instead had a bag slung over my shoulder, full of fruits from Mokosz's garden. She'd assured me that the other gods brought offerings to Rod out of gratitude for the forces they wielded, so it would not look out of the ordinary for us to climb the World Tree to his abode. Still, I was nervous of the consequences if we were caught.

"Keep looking forward," Mother whispered from ahead. "The kind smile may be an illusion, but they'll know something is off if you continue gawking at everything."

"It's hard not to."

"Then you understand why so many lust to rule this realm."

It was unspoken, but I knew that included her. At least it had. The scale of centuries still stretched my mind. Even that long couldn't change Mother completely, though. A spark still burned within her, and I understood it now. Prawia was too amazing of a realm to be ruled by manipulators and betrayers. But that wouldn't change anytime soon.

Vlatka swooped over us as we neared the World Tree's twisting trunk. It had the bark of an oak, but no leaves hung from the branches. I wondered if they ever did, or if Prawia reflected the death consuming Jawia below.

"All clear above," our eagle friend said as she came too close for comfort. "Just take the right staircase. Some more of Weles's servants are coming down the other side."

"Thank you," Mother replied. "Now fly off before you draw too much attention."

She did, but I caught movement out of the corner of my eye. Just a blur, the figure disappeared into the World Tree. Had they actually noticed us? I shook my head. Paranoia would get us nowhere. We had to keep moving.

The branch led into a cavern within the World Tree's trunk. An uneven ceiling full of vines stretched above us, and altars of varied shapes and types formed a circle along the trunk's inner edge. Scattered servants approached each and placed various objects upon them. Stone and dark-wooden altars alike bore Mokosz's Mother-mark, but there were others I didn't recognize.

"Simargł's palace was once across the World Tree from here," Mother whispered, nodding to a symbol showing a winged dog breathing fire. "It's nothing but ash now."

"What are the servants doing at the altars?" I asked as one of Mokosz's spirits set down a bushel of wool, which then dissolved into dust.

Mother smiled. "Gifts from the gods. These objects you see are manifestations of the *żityje* each god gives back to their worshippers. Sometimes it resembles the gift's area, such as a woman's weaving for wool, but often it is more indistinct. This blessing likely is one of Mother's attempts to aid all living animals against Marzanna's winter."

"I don't have spirits. Does that mean I'm not helping?"

"Quite the opposite. Those like Mother with many spirits are often more indirect with their involvement, nudging Jawia in a direction over years instead of using their strength in great bursts." Mother sighed. "It makes sense for her power to be dispersed through all women and the earth. Others are simply too apathetic to devote their attention to mortal woes."

There were two spiraling staircases lined with colorful ribbons of crystal on either side of the tree. We followed Vlatka's directions and headed right. Well timed too, since three of Weles's spirits stepped out of the opposite staircase the moment we ducked into ours. The crystal didn't block all view of us, but I hope it obscured us enough to make it to the next level. I held my breath as we hurried. Luckily, they didn't move to follow.

Mother glanced back at me reassuringly. "You acted immune to others' pain for many years, Otylia, but you aren't like the other gods. Someday, you will have some servants to tend to your wishes in Prawia. That doesn't mean you should ever stop fighting."

We soon reached the next level. Armored spirits guarded the space with fire shooting from the gaps between their iron plates. They carried hammers, swords, and even melted metal to Swaróg's Forgemark altars as frolicking, wispy spirits of young couples danced and brought flower wreaths and wedding veils to Łada's Starmark ones. I'd once thought them to be the eldest deities—the ones who birthed Perun, Weles, and Dadźbóg. Rod had proved me wrong.

"If Swaróg and Łada live here," I whispered to Mother, "then where is Perun's island?" He should've been on the same level as Mokosz, but I hadn't seen any of his servants yet.

She scoffed and leaned closer. "He is king of Prawia. Whoever holds domain over the realm takes the highest branch, and Father has dwelled there ever since Swaróg gave way to him. So much as his servants try, even they cannot reach Rod." She pointed out one of the openings to the spiraling eagles. "Perun is always watching what happens below. Can't have the minor goddess rebelling now, can he? Oh, I meant minor 'gods' of course."

None of the spirits seemed interested in us here, and there was some type of discussion around the branch toward what must've been Swaróg's island. A shifting spirit of smoke and another in a flaming wolf-like form were advancing on the branch. The metal guards swung long hammers with massive golden heads. The aggression forced back the wolf. But the smoke spirits just charged faster.

More of Swaróg's spirits descended on the brawl. Łada's took on more aggressive stances too, surrounding the aggressors as Mother threw down her basket of wool and pulled me up the next staircase.

"What was *that?*" I asked, glancing over my shoulder to try to catch a glimpse of what would come next.

But she was ghastly pale. The green fire in her eyes was gone, and her grip on my arm only intensified. Whatever it was had been bad if she'd sacrificed any attempt to blend in. Not much frightened Dziewanna, so my stomach was doing flips by the time we reached Perun's level.

"Do not ask questions," she hissed, releasing me. "Walk and keep your eyes forward."

My nerves were frayed as we stepped beyond the crystals' protection. Our illusions wavered. Poor timing, as a dozen person-sized eagles greeted us here. They sat among the branches of an oak planted in the center of the World Tree. It resembled the one at Dwie Rzeki's center, but that one had been a lie all along. We were the ones living the lie now, and I felt each of their eyes watch us approach the final set of stairs.

Instead of two, only one spiraling staircase led to Rod's isle above. Mother had been tight-lipped about it, but if Rod was anything like our meeting during my Ascension, I expected riddles and more questions than answers.

The stairs themselves didn't appear to lead to the creator god. Sky blue mixed with streaks of navy, flakes chipped off the stairs with each step. There were neither crystal ribbons nor railing of any kind to line its edge. We just climbed, exposed and wearing fading illusions, toward the vine-covered ceiling above the oak. I held my breath. It was probably a poor decision, but I needed to keep my focus to hold up what part of the illusions remained. Why did my force even work here? There was no moon in this realm. Was there even an end?

I stared at the branch leading to Perun's island in hopes of seeing some remnants of the skirmish below. There were few gods who could've had servants like that. Dadźbóg might've been swayed by Marzanna, so perhaps he was using his position in Prawia to attack Swaróg. Maybe. But I wasn't convinced. Something else was going on beyond the preparations for the wedding and our own schemes.

Another frightening thought took my mind. I'd seen visions of Simargł's return on the Solstice. Could the servants below have been his? He had fought Marzanna then, but the god of destructive fire was hardly an ally. Swaróg had imprisoned him in the north star for a reason.

The World Tree narrowed around us as we reached the top of the stairs and passed into the level above. Any thoughts of Simargł, Jaryło, or Marzanna vanished. This was the peak of the Three Realms, where few had every stepped foot before.

It was empty.

The gentle warmth of Prawia gave way to a temperature that could only be described as moderate. What color had existed on the stairs dissolved into strands of gray. The eternal brightness faded too, leaving us in the dim light of an overcast autumn day, and I dropped our illusions as the slightest breeze tugged at my unbraided hair. Here, at the top of everything godly, mortal, and dead, was nothing but a void.

Mother moved toward the only texture in the nothingness. A branch like those below led onward to an island that was both as bright as the summer sun and dark as Oblivion's edge. It appeared neither too far a walk nor too close to be easily studied from the World Tree.

I couldn't follow her. I imagined roots stretching from the trunk and holding me in place, climbing down my throat and choking me. In the face of the one who'd created everything, I wasn't in awe. I was *terrified*. This wasn't Marzanna. This wasn't even Czarnobóg. Rod had granted me my force; he'd formed the Three Realms from the World Egg before Swaróg ever swung his hammer against the Alatyr Stone. He was infinite. He was beyond understanding. And he was our only hope for Mother to regain her connection to the wild force.

"Mother…" I croaked. "Mother, what is this place?"

"The place where it all began," she said over her shoulder. Even she, the brilliant, powerful goddess I'd worshipped all my life, looked so mortal here. It was wrong. It had to be.

"This isn't Prawia. Everything is different here."

Mother continued on her way, giving a half-hearted wave for me to follow. "Everything is always different in Prawia. Whatever you think is normal does not exist here."

With her urging, I pushed toward the branch. My feet dragged and my breaths were shallow, but I trusted Mother. She'd faced Rod more than me. It was her power on the line, not mine. All I had to do was remain at her side for support, maybe get some information from Rod about the endings I'd seen, and then leave. Simple. Or it would've been if we were speaking to anyone else.

I risked a look over the edge of the branch as we walked, Mother's hand squeezing mine. The other islands and branches seemed puny below. We surely hadn't climbed that far from Perun's level, but I could barely see his giant eagles, and the mountain that rose from the center of his isle looked like an ant hill compared to the heights of Rod's own island. Except nothing truly stood so high ahead of us. There was only a small square building made of the same flaking blue-gray stone as the stairs.

The air shifted when we neared the branch's end, and Mother stopped before a figure formed from nearly translucent vapors.

"Who seeks to address the creator while he rests?" the vapor asked in a monotone voice, unidentifiable as male or female.

Shockingly, Mother bowed her head. "Dziewanna of the wilds."

The figure did not reply, and I swallowed at the realization it was waiting for me. "Otylia of the endings and moon," I finally said.

Another pause. This time, it shifted again, taking on a shape that somewhat resembled a torso and head. Then it turned and floated toward the solitary building. I looked to Mother for guidance, and she nodded before following it with her hands locked behind her. That familiar determination had returned to her eyes. It gave me confidence that my initial fear hadn't been unreasonable, but that we could face what lay ahead.

A wooden door bearing Rod's Wheelmark appeared to be the building's only entry. It wasn't tall like those in Weles's palace or wide like those in Mokosz's. No, it was a door like the entry to any villager's house, and the mark etched upon it even had cuts from points where the chisel carving it had slipped.

I stared at that Wheelmark, repeating Rod's words to me when I'd first bonded with the force of endings. "For though all things in the Three Realms are a cycle, there must be an end for them to begin anew."

A wheel never stopped turning. Would Jawia?

The spirit never touched the door, but it crept open with a slight creak. "He will see you now."

Mother led the way inside, where six stone columns of streaked blue and navy offered rare color to the otherwise dull space. Rod sat upon a throne beyond them. It was a middling gray, like much else, but he wore white robes trimmed in gold and red. His face was aged and his cheeks more rounded than square. At our entrance, he stood with a grin, stroking his beard.

"I have waited for this day for many years," he said in a deep voice that echoed beyond the confines of the room. "The child of the wilderness has come to begin the cycle once again. The Deathless Sons have risen, and so they shall fall. How far, the Sudiczki do not speak of. Yet with each breath they speak of the unbridled mare, the silver fox, and the scarlet eclipse."

Rod held out his arms. "Come, sit, and let us discuss the end."

32

Wacław

A monster among gods. Do they fear me or just what I represent?

ONCE OTYLIA HAD LEFT MOKOSZ'S ISLAND with Dziewanna, the rest of us finally settled in the sitting room. None of us knew what the Great Mother had planned. She'd implied it would be up to the me to uproot Jaryło's perceived strength, but how were we supposed to do that when we were in a realm ruled by his father?

"It has been many years since the last Naw stepped foot on my island," Mokosz said once we were all quiet. Well, most of us. Kuba still mumbled to himself about a quip Narcyz had made.

"Why are there more of us now?" I asked. "A Simukie one betrayed me, and another is leading a group of strzygi in the Horde."

Mokosz studied me, her gaze enough for me to wriggle self-consciously. "A fine question. Nawie have always been present in one form or another due to your extended lifespans, but your generation has shown a remarkable number appear. Perhaps it was because of the strength of demons during eclipses that occurred around many of your births."

I shook my head. "That can't be it. My corruption was caused by Father rejecting me at birth, regardless of the blood moon."

"Those two factors may not be as connected as you believe." She held out her hands palm up, then raised the right. "On one hand, special births are more common during eclipses, which have become more common in recent years. On the other, demonic influence has grown along with the number of Nawie exhibiting demonic second souls. There are also those who instead have spirits inhabiting their second souls. Both the number of Nawie and the portion of those corrupted by demons may be increasing together."

"May?" Narcyz asked. "Aren't you supposed to be the mother of everything?"

Mokosz chuckled like Xobas had when I made a silly mistake during training. "Unfortunately, Ascension did not grant me omniscience. Or shall I say fortunately? My divination has its limits, and even it often shows me more than I wish to see. Visions show me the rise of Nawie, but I do not know why there have been more eclipses or those born beneath eclipses."

That didn't sit well with me. If even Mokosz didn't know why there were more of us, then who did?

"What are we?" I asked. "Sure, we're born with an empty second soul until a demon or spirit inhabits it, but why? There must be a reason *someone* created mortals who could channel these things."

"Wise insight, Wacław," Mokosz replied. "However, mortals existed before I was born, and as far as I am aware, Nawie were among them even then. If Nawie were deliberately created, then there are few who could know why. Rod or Swaróg would be the most likely options. We must also consider that Nawie may have not been created by any god."

She drummed her fingers along the arm of her chair, then took a sharp breath. "Regardless of your kind's past, it is the present that matters. My son is prideful and vain. He displays his Alatyr shards as Moonblades among the rest of his swords, collected from great warriors throughout history. If he were to be relieved of his control over those shards, then he would have a far weaker bargaining position. He is also quite vulnerable without them because of the curse that dampens his force while Marzanna lives. This is the same for her, yet it appears her draining Dziewanna's power may have dampened the curse's effect."

"So we just take 'em?" Narcyz asked with a grin. "What kind of idiot is he?"

"Jaryło is no fool, despite how he acts. The altars each blade is embedded within are imbued with sorcerous protections to ensure no one can simply steal them. They can only be released with a drop of his blood."

Andrij crossed his legs, his veiled eyes staring blankly toward the center of our circle. "Then what do you need us for? We'd be the first people Jaryło expects to attack him."

"I am counting on that expectation," Mokosz replied with a grin. "Every god in this realm expects something out of each of you— goddess, Naw, nymph, or mortal—and our only hope to prevent Jaryło's plan from succeeding is to convince them they were right. Fall into his trap, then exploit their complacency once he believes you are beaten."

"So you want us to lose?" I asked. "What does that gain us?"

"I hardly *want* you to lose, but as long as Jaryło has Lipiec—this Moon's blade—you will hardly stand a chance, even while you bear Grudzień yourself. Between that Moonblade and your Thunderstone dagger, however, you will be able to draw enough blood to be sufficient to open the altars."

I shifted uncomfortably. If the plan was to lose, then Jaryło would ensure it was a painful one. "How much do we need? And how do I collect it without him noticing?"

Mokosz raised her brow. "Come now, Wacław. Are you not one who wields the winds? I am sure between you and these friends you have gathered, you can find a way to divert enough of his blood into a container."

A challenge. I saw it in her eyes, much like her daughter and granddaughter. It was surprising coming from a goddess who'd appeared so gentle, but I appreciated her cunning. We needed it if there was any chance of this working. Luckily, as I glanced around the room at our allies, a plan began to form in my mind. "Then it'll be done."

Kuba laughed obnoxiously and stretched out his legs. "Yeah? How?"

"There will be plenty of time for you to discuss the specifics," Mokosz interrupted, "but Perun will soon call for me."

"Gotta learn somehow," Ta replied.

Mokosz nodded, then continued, "Following your interruption, Jaryło will detain those who attack him with the permission of Perun, Swaróg, and Weles. You will be stripped of your weapons and placed under guard, so you must retrieve them before you escape."

"And how are we supposed to do that?" Narcyz asked.

"Through a friend who spends much of her time on Jaryło's island without his knowledge. Marzyana may share a similar name to our enemy, but she is a minor goddess of the grain and is very much an ally. With her aid, you will free yourselves from Jaryło's dungeon and reach his palace, where you will use the vial to take the Alatyr shards. What happens from that point onward is up to you and the rest of the gods."

Kuba raised his hands in an exasperated fashion. "Wacław's a Naw, but Jaryło will kill the rest of us if we get in his way."

With a huff, Mokosz stood and walked slowly toward the entrance. "You will need enough allies to retrieve the Moonblades and escape. Allow Wacław and the szeptuchy among you to take the brunt of his strikes. Besides, this is about perception, and it is in our favor for you to prove how powerful mortals can truly be."

Then she left, her long dress sweeping behind her and leaving me in another moment of awe. It was easy to forget we were speaking with gods who'd lived for hundreds of years. Reflection, though, reminded me how strange this all was. We were plotting with a goddess who had decided to trust half the Alatyr shards with mortals and a Naw.

"Who will go?" Sabina said, hugging herself as if she were badly chilled. Except Prawia felt like a paradise compared to the eternal tundra we'd left.

"There are seven Moonblades," Andrij replied, "so all six of us should go, plus Vlatka, but I doubt she could carry one in her beak."

Ta huffed. "Not you. Can't stab a god without eyes." She winced as Narcyz's glare met her. "I meant—"

"We got it," Narcyz muttered.

"We're a person short without him," I said, "but Ta is right. Andrij, you can't put yourself in danger like this. The ally Mokosz mentioned can take one of the blades, and some of us can carry two if needed."

Sabina squeaked. "This sounds… risky… at best."

"If we're going to succeed, we need to forget our doubts," I replied sternly. "We need to work together at every moment, or Jaryło will make us suffer. Do you trust me?"

"Of course. We may want to consider our approach, though."

"I have an idea, but are you all willing to risk your lives for this?"

Narcyz nodded and stood, arms crossed. "The Horde will kill us anyway if we don't try. Might as well go out trying to make a god bleed."

Ta snickered. "This'll be fun."

"No, it won't be," I said, returning to my seat. "But we're not here for fun. While we handle Jaryło, there will be more pressure on Otylia. I hate leaving her behind, but she needs to keep Jaryło distracted."

Andrij held his fist over his heart. "I will do what I can to help her while I'm here. I haven't been all that honest about my vision, but—"

"C'mon," Kuba scoffed. "We all know you can't see more than a one-eyed drunkard."

I shot him a glare. "Poorly stated, but he's right. We've noticed you've been acting oddly since the battle. Whatever you can do, we'll take. I value your loyalty in that."

"Enough mushiness," Ta said, popping to her feet. "How we gonna get Jaryło's blood?"

"The same way we bested him twice before. Make him think he's won."

33

Otylia

The end of what?

THERE HAD BEEN NO VISIBLE PLACE TO SIT, but moments after Rod told us to do so, twisting vines and roots formed a chair as wisps of a thousand colors weaved a second. The rainbow fell to a deep gray when the wisps stopped moving, emitting a dull glow.

Mother and I needed no explanation as to whose seat was whose. We took them silently under Rod's studious gaze. He didn't sit until we were comfortable, and even then, he sat on the edge of his throne with a grin never fading from his face.

"When I offered you the force of endings," he began, "I did not expect you to become intertwined with fate so quickly. It was my error, in truth. You have never been one to be passive, and once engaged, your force never ceases to root itself in every fragment of reality. Endings are everywhere. I promised you this, yet I did not understand my promise at that time. Forgive me."

I looked at Mother, but her expression revealed nothing. How was I supposed to respond to that? Rod had given me my force upon my Ascension. Now he wanted to apologize for it?

"I don't," I said, instantly regretting the words. "I don't forgive you for giving me this force, because I doubt I'd be better off without it. End showed me the way to Mother through others' memories. It allowed me to save demons and free Wacław from his demonic soul."

He thought for a moment, then took a long breath and sat back. "They call you 'Nemiza' in Vastroth now. You are the goddess who returned their sacrificed children and punished their enemies. Often, mortals amaze me with their ability to be accidentally right, as they are when they gave you a name whose meaning is calamity. There is no better word to describe the impact your birth and Ascension have inflicted upon the Three Realms."

I scowled. "I'm not the one releasing Czarnobóg and wiping out life on Jawia!"

"That is true, yet you have bound yourself to the Deathless Sons so tightly that fate itself bends at your word." He took the end of his long beard in his grasp, squeezing. "You owe Death a promise. You owe Jaryło marriage. And you intertwine your soul with Wacław's, pledging him the same marriage you offered Jaryło a mere moon before. The gods gather to crown Jawia's next king and queen. They plan for peace between Perun and Weles for the first time in millennia. You threaten not only that pact but the very existence of the Three Realms as they are."

My temper drowned in his words. I dropped my shoulders and averted my gaze. "What will Death ask of me?"

"You granted him a single wish, so he will select the kill that will be his greatest victory."

Mother sucked in a sharp breath. "No, she won't do it."

"Such things as this are not connected to one's will." Rod looked at me and then her again. "The pact is made, and failing to honor it would have far greater consequences."

"Rod, this is—"

I shot to my feet, fists clenched at my side. "What are you two talking about? This is my consequence to bear, so tell me it instead of talking around me like I'm a child."

Rod gave me a solemn smile. It hurt more than them ignoring

me, as it was the look of a father whose daughter had just claimed she was old enough to take on the world. "Death will ask for my immortal life. No number of mortals could match the weight of my soul to him, as there will always be mortals, but there will only ever be one creator."

I collapsed back into my chair. It seemed to spin around me as I tried to comprehend the consequences of my decision. In my desperation to save Wacław, had I really traded his life for the god that had created the Three Realms?

"But I can't kill you," I mumbled. "Even if Death commanded it, you are far more powerful than me."

"Not alone, true," Rod replied. "However, his servant is coming, and your control over endings is his only way to bring finality to my life."

When I raised my head, I saw Father in him. Judgement. Disappointment. I'd selfishly clung to love without knowing what I promised, and now all the Three Realms would suffer. "I won't do it. I'll never help Czarnobóg, no matter how much pain I have to endure."

"Death is not so kind to inflict pain on you alone. Do you remember the world I showed you the moment you Ascended? Flames and ash. Life on the brink. This is what Jaryło has wrought by helping Marzanna sever the barrier between the Three Realms and Oblivion. The dark dragon has come, and soon all those corrupted like him shall follow." He leaned forward, his already elderly face seeming to age another decade in the motion. "As the master of balance and the inevitable cycle, I cannot stop it. You, however, are the goddess of endings, allied with your mother and capable of redeeming Nawie and demons alike. My death will bring chaos on its own accord. Should you choose to sacrifice yourself and those you love to appease Death, then the result would be far worse."

"I believed I was the only one who could defeat Marzanna," Mother said, his head sunken and her voice hoarse. "But it's her."

"Perhaps," Rod replied. "The balance of the Three Realms is fragile, and so are its fates. You have always been your sister's opposite, even before her corruption. You may be the one to face her, but you are bound so tightly with Otylia that neither I nor Destiny can see what will come. I know only that I cannot mend it."

I shook my head. "This is my choice to bear. I made the pact with Death. You don't get to just kill yourself for me."

Rod suddenly slammed his fist into the throne's arm, cracking its stone. "Foolish child! Do you not understand? I crafted the Three Realms with the World Egg. They are my life's work—a far longer life than even Swaróg or your mother could grasp—and I shall not let it falter because of the whims of a young goddess's heart. That life has granted me much, but I am old, my power dispersed with each gift I grant the gods and spirits of my realms. If it must end, then let it be to prevent the destruction of all I have done, ensuring the cycle comes to an end and the Three Realms can forever move forward."

"Now, if that is finished," he said, waiting for a nod, which I reluctantly gave, "then there is the matter of your mother's connection to the force of the wilds."

Mother stood and then swiftly knelt on both knees. Her submission would've shocked me if I hadn't already been thoroughly jolted by the fact I'd be the cause of the eldest god's death.

"I discovered Jaryło's deception too late," Mother said. "It was my responsibility to kill Marzanna, no matter what allies she brought to her aid. I failed. But I ask now for a chance to prove I deserve to wield the wild force. For the sake of my daughter and for all nature in the Three Realms, let me unleash my fury against Czarnobóg. Let me give Marzanna one final opportunity to free herself from her corruption."

"Perhaps you should teach your daughter such respect." Rod sat back again and gave a wry smile. "Dziewanna, do you remember when you first Ascended?"

"Of course."

"You came to me asking for a force powerful enough for you to prove yourself to Perun. You wished to match your father's power more than anything, and then you promptly attempted to overthrow his rule of Prawia."

Mother swallowed but kept her gaze upon Rod. "I did. My opinion of his rule has not changed since then."

"Do you wish to rule one or all of the Three Realms?"

"I dare not lie to you."

He smirked. "For the sake of brevity, I would like to hear you say your intentions."

Mother tilted up her chin at that. "As a child, I lusted for Prawia's throne like a prince does for his father's armies. That's changed. I belong not among the gods, but the mortals and creatures of Jawia. The wilds are more than my force. They are my heart and soul, and I wish to protect them from both mankind and the corruption that threatens their existence. You are the bearer of balance in your realms. That is what I desire for Jawia—to rule as its protector, ensuring mortals live but do not overrun nature and its unbridled power."

Her shame was gone. Instead, she'd spoken with intent and a passion I'd seen often in her as a child. This was the wild queen I'd worshipped and served. Not the goddess who knelt, but the one who stated her goal, then chased it with all the power of wildfire.

"So many seek to rule Jawia," Rod said, studying her. "Perun and Weles's wars have only just become distant memories, but their ambitions return along with Jaryło's. Czarnobóg and Marzanna both wish to control not only the Three Realms, but each other as well. Now it appears as well that Simargł has escaped the cage Swaróg made for him all those years ago. Yes, many would contest your claim."

"I do not want war, Rod, just to end the one my siblings have started."

Rod stood slowly and held out his arms. The room seemed to fade as an orb of swirling green and brown filled the space between us. A familiar awe filled me at the sight of it—the same that I'd felt during my Ascension.

"The force of the wilds," I said without thinking.

"Indeed," Rod replied with a smile. "Still as fervent as the moment your mother took up its mantle centuries ago."

"How did she sever my bond with it?" Mother asked as she reached for the orb. It responded instantly, drifted along the back of her hand like a cat rubbing its cheek against its master.

"Marzanna is corrupted, but corruption alone only allows for the draining of another being's *żityje*, not the complete breaking of a god's bond with their force. Only a being of pure darkness is capable of such a thing." Rod's joy faded. "Czarnóg is beyond my creation. I never foresaw the gods shattering Alatyr when I gifted it to them, so I was as unprepared as Swaróg when it struck Jawia, bringing Czarnóg and the other demonic beings into my precious realms. Luckily, I can at least reforge the bond he broke."

He held his hands open in front of his mouth and blew, sending the wild orb into Mother's grasp. Roots and leaves twisted their way up her arm until they formed into her skin and left only wisps floating behind. Mother smiled watching the process, but her expression shifted when flames erupted in her palm.

Heat washed over me as the fire replaced the roots. It consumed her arms and grew further, setting her clothes aflame and sending smoke spiraling around her. At first, I lunged to help, but the heat sent me reeling as she raised her arms with the fire balling in her hands.

Then it went out.

Smoke billowed around Mother as she approached me. Her old dress had burned away completely, replaced by a white one with vibrant red flowering plants cascading up the skirt's sides. Similar embroidery flowed from her shoulders and collar down the center of her torso to meet a burgundy belt that matched the stripes along the dress's hem and sleeves. The reds shifted with her steps. Like fire, they never stayed still, and her bright green eyes burned with them as wisps formed a cape of spring leaves down her back.

"You look like a queen," I stammered, gawking at the pure confidence she held now that she'd regained her force. Her antlered crown restored itself too, as if to confirm my statement.

She tilted her head back and took in a long breath. "It feels as if I had lived an eternity away from the wild's embrace."

I grinned and touched the embroiders upon her sleeves. "The fire is new."

"Wildfire has always been a part of my force, but it was never that prominent before."

"Every force has different manifestations," Rod said, stepping closer with an approving look. "This is why there are some gods that can draw from similar or overlapping forces. Czarnobóg and Marzanna are both Death's chosen deities in differing forms, but both the wilds and endings have only one goddess each. It appears this time, the wild force wished your flames to be more prominent. Listen to its will. Even I cannot match the understanding the forces have over their domains."

Mother clenched a fist before her and drew a spiral of fire from it. She seemed pleased. "I will. Thank you, Rod. You have gifted us much despite what we must take."

He bowed. "It is an honor to see each of you grow and learn from the forces that choose you. Death will take my soul when the time comes for Otylia to kill me, but though this life for me comes to an end, my soul will certainly not be gone forever. Czarnobóg returned after millennia. So too will I." He raised an arm toward the door, his wide sleeves sweeping away the smoke and bringing my mind back to the room we'd never left. "It is time for you to return. This wedding, no matter how it ends, will take time. I shall not use more of yours."

We exchanged farewells and headed toward the door, but as Mother stepped outside, I stopped and spun back toward Rod. "Wait, Wacław wants to know how you created the Nawie."

"You assume I created them?" he asked with his brows raised. "Curious."

"You didn't?"

He stroked his beard as he paced, visibly nervous for the first time. "Not willingly. My own force, that of balance, often inhibits me, but it can also act on its own. There must be the cycle of life and death to retain balance. Demons threaten this, so it created Nawie with one living soul and one dead one to combat them. Nawie were to become inhabited by a spirit or demon, then use that power to travel between the realm of the dead and that of the living to protect the Way of Souls and eliminate the unredeemable demons—not those who died in unnatural ways, but those who chose to live in cruel and unnatural ones. I foresaw the inevitable that Balance did not. When granted the opportunity, demons took advantage of mortals' mistreatment of Nawie to corrupt them through the second soul."

My heart lightened. "So Wacław isn't some monster?"

"No. If anything, he was meant to destroy them."

I bowed slowly and deeply. "Thank you, Rod. You have given me more than I deserve, and I will fight every day to make up for my error with Death."

"You will do me proud." He turned toward his throne, and his final words to me echoed through the room for what felt like an eternity. "Remember that your life is long, and that it is best cherished with more than fighting."

34

Wacław

Can we actually outmaneuver the gods in their own realm?

I LAY ON MY PLUSH BED WITHIN MOKOSZ'S PALACE for a long time, staring up at the ivy creeping through the slits in the domed stone ceiling. Ever bright, it was impossible to tell how much time had passed. It was ironic, in a way. Jawia endured endless darkness while the gods enjoyed enough light to cast out even the smallest of shadows.

How long would it be until Otylia and Dziewanna returned? Otylia's emotional bond to me had broken after some time, and I assumed it had to do with her entry into Rod's palace—or whatever he had up at the World Tree's peak. Lacking that connection made me feel isolated. I hated it.

Mokosz and Dziewanna seemed to trust Rod, but I knew next to nothing about him. Before Otylia's Ascension, I'd thought Swaróg to be the eldest god who created the Three Realms. There was another instead. Cryptic, according to Otylia, Rod was supposed to represent the cycle of the realms and the balance between opposing forces. Did that devotion to balance make him unable to act against Czarnobóg and Marzanna? Or was he like Perun and Weles, refusing to get involved until they could settle their disputes by forcing Otylia to marry Jaryło?

I tilted my head to the side, studying the unsheathed Moonblade and Thunderstone dagger resting on my nightstand. Beyond, a view of Prawia's sky met me through the open balcony door and two windows alongside it, their bright copper shutters glinting in the bright light. That same light reflected off the colored streaks on Grudzień's blade. It created a thin rainbow that should've been impossible, but if even light didn't work the same here, I assumed much was different.

This realm is strange, but at least I have a blade to protect me.

I worried for Kuba, Andrij, and Narcyz—and Ara too, wherever Jaryło had her trapped. None of them had weapons or magic capable of killing a god. Hopefully, it didn't come to that with the gods other than Jaryło, but we needed to be prepared.

An idea came to mind, so I swung my legs over the side of the bed and plucked my dagger off the nightstand. It felt as if years had passed since I'd pierced my skin with it to appease Marzanna. Her Frostmark was gone from my palm with Otylia's Moonmark now on my arm, but phantom pain remained. So did the regret.

An earthen brown rug edged with symbols in the old tongue ran from the balcony to the narrow entry door, softening my footfalls as I pondered my next move. There was no rug outside, and quick steps reached the doorway just as I did.

"Oh!" Kuba exclaimed, nearly jumping out of his boots. I glanced down. Well, he would've if he weren't running around a goddess's palace barefoot. "Scared me there, Wacław."

I chuckled. "What's got you in a hurry? I was actually planning to come see you."

His eyes widened as he noticed the unsheathed dagger, as I'd been staring at its black blade. "Hopefully not to use that thing on me."

"Actually, I intended to give it to you."

"You what?" He laughed nervously and stepped away.

I sheathed the dagger and held it out to him handle first. "You're in a realm surrounded by gods and their servants with only a few wooden javelins to protect you. I have Grudzień now. The dagger was useful as a back-up weapon, but you need it as your first if you're going to help protect Otylia."

"More like I need it to protect me from *her*." He gave a wry smile but snatched the dagger, tossing it in the air, bobbling it, and then dropping it in quick succession. "I meant to do that."

"Right…"

Smirking, he drew the dagger and gave it a few practice swooshes down the wide hall, toward the rooms where the rest of our group was staying. "It's lighter than I thought it'd be. Like, I know it's a dagger, but it feels like I'm swinging a leaf."

"It's permanently sharp too, and more importantly, perfectly capable of piercing Jaryło's heart."

"Think we'll actually have to kill him again?" Kuba said with a lunge. The attack hadn't been directed at me, but I caught his arm anyway and kicked his leg out from under him. As the dagger clattered out of his grasp, I caught it with the winds the moment its tip touched the floor. It took focus to leave it balanced there. A couple moons before, I would've lacked the control, but the winds stayed steady under my command. If only they weren't so quiet with Strzybóg's apparent death.

"Careful with that thing," I said. "Just because it can kill a god doesn't mean it can't kill a mortal, and plenty of people and gods alike would be happy to take it off your hands."

"They'll have to kill me first." He reached down for the dagger, but I flung it into my grasp. "I get it, you have the winds!"

I returned it to him. "I'm giving this to you both for your sake and Otylia's. She's more powerful than any of us, but you need to watch her back. Everyone here is either a god or a servant of one."

With a raised brow, he sheathed the blade and stuck it into his leather belt. "She's really got you worried. Not used to seeing you like this."

"The world is literally on my shoulders," I replied, leaning against the wall and shutting my eyes. "Otylia is probably the one who can end this war, but it's my job to protect her. It just seems like she's the one saving me all the time. Her pact with Death. The destruction I caused in Huebia…" I flexed my hands at my sides as memories flashed before me. "What if I'm getting in the way?"

"We'd all be dead if you hadn't kept our escape route open during the battle."

I shook my head. "Then I left my position to help Andrij. Eryk died, and Otylia had to expend way too much *żityje* to stop the Horde from overrunning the rest of you."

"Enough of that," he said, throwing his arm over my shoulder and pulling me off the wall. "It's in large part because of you that I'm not still stuck in Nawia. Every single one of us is here because we trust you and Otylia. Sure, we fight in the group, but we need both of you. And Otylia *definitely* needs you."

"Thanks, Kuba," I said with a forced smile. "Are you worried about Maja? I appreciate you coming, but—"

He wagged a finger as we walked down the hall. "Don't start. I knew what I was getting into… kinda. You're saving the Three Realms, and I'm sure not going to miss that. Maja understood. Through tears, sure, but she was just happy I'm alive. We need to keep everyone that way."

"We'll do what we can."

We reached a curving staircase that headed down to the first floor of the palace. Multi-floor buildings were rare in Krowik, but between the massive Glasstone Tower in Huebia and Mokosz's palace, it was becoming oddly familiar. Even the Dwie Rzeki longhouse felt small compared to the endless sprawling rooms here.

A tension built in my chest as I started down the stairs. *She's back.*

With a quick spin, I freed myself from Kuba's hold and took off at a sprint, hopping down multiple steps at a time. Kuba called after me, but he didn't have the winds at his back. His footsteps were almost too distant to hear by the time I skidded to a stop at the palace entrance. Two spirits approached from the gardens. I knew better, and I smiled as Otylia ran up the steps to me, dropping her illusion the second she stepped within the palace's protection.

"We need to talk in private," she whispered, snatching my hand and yanking me in the direction of the room we'd gathered in before. "Now."

Kuba huffed and puffed into the room just as we reached the next hall. "Where you going?" he asked.

"We'll tell you later," Otylia snapped back, leaving him with Dziewanna, who now wore a white dress trimmed in elegant red embroidery.

So on we walked, or more ran. Otylia pulled me at a pace that made me realize how it must've felt to be Kuba. When we reached the sitting room, she threw the doors closed and then dropped to her knees not more than a stride from the doorway. Her eyes were red with tears.

"Wašek, I've ruined everything."

I knelt beside her and took her in my arms, cradling her head against my chest. "What's wrong? Tell me everything."

"Rod…" She shuddered. "He said Death would demand I help Czarnobóg kill him in return for the favor I owe. It's either that, or Death takes everyone I love, and the Three Realms fall to Czarnobóg."

I opened my mouth to reply, but words didn't come. My mind spun just trying to comprehend what she'd said. The death of the creator god couldn't be good, and if he was the one who gave the rest of the gods their forces, what did that mean for the future?

She laid her head against my chest, tears running down my tunic. "I thought I was doing the right thing. I just couldn't lose you."

"I'm sorry," I whispered. "This wouldn't have happened if I didn't fall for Death's trick to take the last of my *žityje*."

"You're *not* taking the blame for this!" she snapped as she pulled back. Her eyes were ablaze, and her gripped tightened. "You thought you needed to save me, and I thought the same for you. Death tricked us both, but I was the one who promised him anything." She sniffled and shook her head. "I just didn't think this was possible."

I held her hands in mine, doing my best not to shudder. "How is Czarnobóg coming? Is it with Dadźbóg's help?"

She just shook her head again before wiping the tears from her eyes. "Rod didn't say. But he's not our only problem either. Simargł is here too, probably to take revenge for Swaróg imprisoning him for centuries."

"So we have not one but two gods who the legends say will end the world. Wonderful." I sat back, lightheaded, then chuckled. "Maybe if we turn Simargł against Czarnobóg they'll destroy each other first."

"That actually might work."

I huffed. "It was a joke. You really think working with the god of fiery destruction is a good idea?"

Suddenly torn from her sorrow, Otylia jumped to her feet and paced. She wrinkled her nose as she finally settled behind Mokosz's chair. "Remember the vision I had when I was unconscious? Marzanna helped free Simargł, then tried to give him her Frostmark, but I swear I saw Vida trying to stop her. What if she succeeded?"

"Then Simargł escaped and is definitely here for his own reasons."

"Right." Excitement pushed into her voice, a welcomed release from the tension in our joined souls. "And he wants nothing more than to punish Perun, Strzybóg, and Swaróg for forcing Kupalo and Kostroma to wed, not knowing they were twins. We can use that."

"He probably hates Marzanna for betraying him too," I added, but this idea didn't sit well with me. There were enough dangerous forces on Jawia without adding another capable of destroying everything. "How is this any different than Ira, though? I highly doubt Simargł has purely good intentions once he's got his revenge."

Otylia winced. "Having a żmij could've saved us against the Horde."

"He manipulated people!"

"And I traded away the eldest god's life for the boy I love. You could argue I'm the evil one." She crossed her arms and circled back toward me. "We've all done terrible things for what we think are good reasons. Ira was selfish and so was I, but we fought him instead of using him against the Horde. We have the chance with Simargł to not do the same."

I stepped away. "You're willing to unleash Simargł just for a chance he'll work with us? What if he burns Jawia instead? Ash or snow. Does it really matter which if everyone we love is dead?"

She caught my arm before I could get too far, narrowing her eyes up at me. "Marzanna released him. Now, we either make him our enemy or our ally. We have enough enemies already."

"Allying him won't fix Rod, and it'll only ensure Perun *definitely* wants us dead."

Before I could reply, the door swung open, and Dziewanna swept into the room with a curious look. "Are you having the discussion I assume you are?"

Otylia released me and turned away as her dread returned through our connection. "We talked about Rod, yes."

"And?" Dziewanna eyed me, then her. "I know you're hiding something."

"Simargł," Otylia replied. "What if we helped him get revenge, then turned him against Czarnobóg and Marzanna? Maybe he could stop us when I try to complete my promise to Death?"

"Ah, yes. That explains the horror on Wacław's face."

I threw myself into the nearest chair. Exhaustion fought frustration, and my reply came out as little more than a mumble. "What good are we if we work with him?"

"Alive," Dziewanna said.

Otylia's jaw dropped. "You agree with me?"

"What other choice do we have?" Dziewanna circled the room again, examining herself in the murals. "The Three Realms are never what we want them to be. To succeed, we'll need to sacrifice what we hope for in return for what we need."

"I thought getting your force back would be enough," I said.

"Perhaps it would've been if Simargł had not decided to send his servants ahead of his arrival." The goddess stopped beside Otylia and smirked. "Together, we are powerful, but Simargł is among the first generation of gods. His presence alone could change alliances and start wars. Tell me, will this alter my mother's plan for you and the other Nawie?"

"It shouldn't," I replied. "The three of us intend to ambush Jaryło when he meets with Otylia for the first time. We'll lose, but all we need is a few drops of his blood to unlock the altars that hold whatever Moonblades he's not wielding at the time. Once we're in his palace's dungeon, we'll escape and steal the blades. Losing them should give us enough leverage to convince him to release Otylia from their bond."

Dziewanna's smile disappeared. "Neither Jaryło nor Perun will take your theft lightly. We risk another war among the gods."

"No," Otylia said. "The war has already come, and Jaryło started it the moment he helped Marzanna release Czarnobóg. All we're doing is putting an end to his schemes."

"When will Simargł arrive?" I asked. "And Czarnobóg?"

"Weddings are not short affairs among the gods," Dziewanna said. She wrinkled her nose, mirroring Otylia as she thought for a moment. "I anticipate Simargł will make his appearance closer to the ceremony itself in order to draw attention. Czarnobóg—and Marzanna, if she wishes to show her face—will likely try the same. They will want to strike when the gods are gathered and tensions are high. Ironically, Simargł played into their hands, even with his defiance of Marzanna's mark."

I pondered that, then stood. "We shouldn't reveal that we stole the Moonblades until just before then. Jaryło will know we did it, but he'll have no proof until we confront him about releasing Czarnobóg in front of all the other gods."

Dziewanna looked at Otylia. "It sounds like you will have quite the exciting wedding. I am jealous. If I hadn't been so nervous, I could have slept through Weles and mine."

Otylia's glare was enough to cut iron, and even Dziewanna took a step back as Otylia ground her heel into the ground. "No amount of humor will fix this, Mother."

"Nor will anger among us. There is no sun here, but we all have been awake for far longer than you are used to. Rest. This process will take many more days than we wish it to, and you both will need all your strength."

With a kiss on her daughter's forehead, Dziewanna left with her cape of leaves rustling behind.

Otylia stared at the door for a long time, as if anticipating another intrusion. Her eyes were sunken and her black hair hung over her face, and she just stood there, motionless. My heart broke knowing the part I'd played in getting her—us—to this point. Sorrow threatened to drown me in the void that the demon inhabited in my soul. It never came next to Otylia. No more than five strides from her, though, I felt alone, useless, and beneath the sorrow, fury burned.

"We'll make Czarnobóg pay when he shows up," I said, barely keeping the demon's growl from my voice. "We'll figure out a way to save Rod after we break your blood pact with Jaryło."

She slowly looked my way, and pain struck my hand as she clenched her fists hard enough to dig her nails into her skin. "The last thing Rod told me was that you and the other Nawie were created to destroy monsters, not become them. Don't listen to the demon, Wašek. It doesn't matter how angry you are. We're facing powers greater than us, and *we* are the ones that have to pay for that."

Leaving me without even a breath in my lungs, she followed Dziewanna out of the room. I didn't, and instead collapsed back into my chair.

I wasn't meant to be corrupted.

That thought lingered in my head as I thought over the events of the last day. Had it been only a day? Time was impossible to follow here, but my body's exhaustion told me it had been far too long since I'd slept. Though Dziewanna was right about our need for rest, I knew that if I closed my eyes, I would wake one day closer to the horror to come. I had lived almost seventeen years without unconscious sleep. Dreams were strange, and part of me still feared them. I'd been isolated before, but there had been a simplicity to living the night alone in my soul form. What had been my physical body was gone now. This soul form was all I had left.

I looked toward the door, my heart growing lighter for a moment. *No, I have them too.* Everyone I loved was relying on me.

The demon stirred within me as I pushed myself to my feet, but I took a long breath and silenced it. If I'd truly been created to fight the demons of the Three Realms, then I could defeat my own.

35

Wacław

Why won't he make his move?

WE WAITED DAYS FOR JARYŁO to show his face. Each agonizing moment that passed was another that our allies in Jawia fought the Horde without us, so I took the time to train Kuba how to wield a Moonblade. Besides that, all we could do was wait in Mokosz's palace until Perun and his son declared the wedding preparations ready, and I was certain they were taking their time for a reason.

"I'm going to cut him from navel to throat if you don't do it first," Otylia muttered through gritted teeth as she paced across the palace foyer. A servant had come earlier to announce Jaryło's arrival, but that had been hours ago.

I caught her hand and spun her toward me with a smile, forced through my own nerves. "I'll do my best. All you have to do is glare at him and look beautiful doing it. I am jealous that he gets your attention, though."

Kuba faked a gag, but Mokosz had dressed Otylia well for the arrangement. This would involve only her and Jaryło's closest relatives meeting in Mokosz's gardens, but all things considered, that included most of the powerful gods. I was certain she'd outshine any of them with moonlight glowing silver off her skin and creating an aura over her dress of glimmering silver. Despite my response, though, she still nervously fiddled with the moon amulets hanging from her headband and over her ears.

"Aim below his stomach," Narcyz replied with a tight grip on his spear and shield. "Don't want to deal with little Jaryłos in the future."

"I'd rather have my fingers cut off one-by-one than give him a child," Otylia snapped, her glare sending Narcyz reeling.

"I didn't mean with you!" Narcyz said.

Kuba chuckled. "What, you going to bed him instead, or are you too busy with—"

Narcyz raised its spear until the tip hovered just before Kuba's nose. "Finish that thought and I'll make you wish you had that jackal face back."

"Narcyz…" Andrij warned from a wooden bench among the foliage lining the far wall. "We're all tense and could use a laugh."

"He's right," I said. "We're all tense, but you shouldn't be in danger. Leave the fighting to me. As long as Ta and Sabina can use their channeling to hold Jaryło still, I'll be able to get the blood."

Ta loudly tapped her foot until Otylia waved for her to speak. "Are you *sure* I can't take a whack at him too? I'd really like to hit him with one of my throwing blades."

"Join the line," Narcyz replied.

At that moment, Mokosz entered the room through the double doors at the rear of the foyer. Her earthen attire allowed Otylia to take the attention, but she held herself with confidence as she eyed Ta. "You are my szeptucha, and I will need you by Otylia's side in the battles ahead. Unbridled courage can also be folly."

Sabina nodded. "We are chosen to serve, not get in the way."

Ta mumbled a reply to herself, then gave Mokosz a bow and circled away.

"How much longer?" Otylia asked Mokosz. "And where is Mother? She went to the gardens a while ago and hasn't come back."

"She knows as well as I the responsibility a mother has to host the groom's family," Mokosz said with a gentle smile. "That is why I have joined you as well. My servants have informed me of Jaryło's arrival, and as this is my palace, I must pretend that he is welcomed."

Otylia tensed instantly and attempted to pull her hand to her chest, where she likely intended to grip Dziewanna's Bowmark necklace, but I held firm.

"We're all here," I whispered. "You don't need to hold the amulet to pray to Dziewanna. She's waiting out there for you."

She wrinkled her nose. "So is *he.*"

"Pretend my hand is him as we walk."

Mokosz's wispy servants pulled open the doors, and she led the rest of us out into the bright gardens beyond. Our friends flanked us on every side as Sabina and Ta tucked into the gardens to prepare their ambush. I twitched, ready to grab Grudzień when needed, but Otylia's death grip struck me first. It was rare that I needed a reminder of how strong she was. The vice she tightened around my hand was plenty enough, and I had to avoid wincing as the reason for her anger appeared.

"Ah, dear sister," the golden god's voice carried through the gardens. The words came slathered with charisma and pride, but I could've sworn the overflowing greenery retracted as he neared. "It is wonderful to see you again."

Jaryło went to hug Dziewanna, his cape drifting behind him in the wind to expose an elegant gold and white tunic. If I hadn't hated him, I would've been jealous. He was arrogant in every movement he made, but he looked good doing it. From his flawless skin to his stark white smile and muscular build that only the most experienced warriors could match, I imagined most women would've fawned over him. Otylia… Otylia looked at him like he was a pile of dung.

Gods, I loved her.

"Is it wonderful?" Dziewanna asked with her arms folded. "I thought you preferred me gone, as you left me to die."

Without her to return his hug, Jaryło huffed and dropped his arms. "If only I could have faced both Marzanna and Czarnobóg by myself. It truly is a shame that you lost your connection to the force of the wilds as well. At least you have your daughter left."

So he doesn't know about their visit to Rod. Maybe something could go right for once.

Jaryło and his sister exchanged wry grins as he pushed past her with a small army of wooden and crop-like servants in his wake. A single blade hung at his side. *Silver or Moonblade?* It was impossible to tell with it sheathed, but he noticed my look.

"It is unfortunate that you have not thrown the demon aside," he quipped to Otylia before extending his hand toward her. "My bride-to-be, it is a pleasure to have you in the realm of the gods. This is where you belong, not in that hovel among mortals."

I waited for the szeptuchy to strike, fighting my will to stab Jaryło then and there. He would take the trio of vials strapped to my belt beneath my cloak if I was too obvious about dripping the blood within it.

"I prefer Jawia," Otylia replied.

Jaryło gave an exaggerated sigh. "Yes, I have seen as such. There will be plenty of time for me to convince you otherwise." His gaze fell upon Grudzień at my back. "I see you are as skilled at stealing my twin's Moonstones as you are at stealing mine. Perhaps I should add it to my collection and bring us one step closer to sealing Czarnobóg away once again."

I ran my fingers along the wide brim of my hat. "End this forced marriage and maybe I'll let you have it."

"Adorable," he said, turning back to Otylia. "Even now, he believes he has a chance with you."

A commotion came from among Jaryło's servants before she could reply. They parted as two servants resembling smaller versions of leszy dragged two girls toward their master. Blood covered the path behind them, and I gritted my teeth when Ta raised her beaten face toward us.

Jaryło glanced down at them, then back at Otylia. "Oh dear, is this your doing? I surely hope your szeptucha and my mother's were not acting under your orders."

"No," Otylia replied. "They were supposed to be in my escort, not hiding in the gardens."

"Then you won't mind if I punish them for it." He raised a hand swiftly, and Sabina cried out as his servants grabbed hold of her wings.

I'd had enough.

Grudzień swept free from its sheath with the speed of lightning. But it found only metal, sending sparks cascading over us as Jaryło spun away with the red blade of the Lipiec moon in his grasp.

"Silly demon," he cackled. "I knew this was *your* doing, and though I cannot harm Otylia's friends through our blood pact, that changes when they threaten my life."

I snarled and lunged, exchanging strikes. Another scream echoed behind me as we fought, and I caught a glimpse of Narcyz and Kuba rushing to help the szeptuchy. As the servants fought back, the entire gardens turned to chaos.

"You may have bested me when I was weakened and distracted," Jaryło said as he parried my blow and countered. "You will have no such luck this time."

He was right. I tried my best with Grudzień, but spears, not swords, had been my primary weapon during Xobas's training. I could use the winds to speed up my movements against most opponents. Jaryło was a master of the blade, though, and my windblasts were weakened with Strzybóg dead. Sweat already clung to my skin as he forced me to retreat through the garden. He breathed as calmly as someone resting.

Frustration took hold with each blocked jab. Jaryło began to succeed with nicks across my arms. *Žityje* healed them, but they were small victories that made me hesitate, distracted by the pain and worry that he could hit again.

The shouting from the path only grew louder as we continued our dance through the gardens, isolated from the rest of the skirmish. This was personal to us both. I saw the greed in his eyes. He wanted me dead after all I'd done to him, and that feeling was mutual.

I pulled on my lightning.

Red and blue arcs snapped at my fingertips. I rolled aside, letting Jaryło believe he could unleash a powerful strike and allowing him to fall off balance. Then I shot back to my feet with a blast arcing from my hand.

But he was ready, spinning to meet the bolt with a golden shield that formed from a bracer upon his forearm. "My father is the god of thunder," he shouted over my gales. "You believe you can best me with your own lightning?"

The winds spiraled around me with my growing fury. They ripped shrubs and stones from the gardens and blocked nearly all view beyond our sparring ring. A large oak ringed with chest-high boulders separated us now, and we circled it, waiting for the other to act.

"You did this!" I snarled. "You caused Jawia's demise because you can't admit you're the reason for Marzanna's corruption."

"And if I did? Does it matter? I am Perun's eldest son, adopted ward of Weles. I am the heir to Jawia, and you are simply a Naw who doesn't know when to stop!"

The demon stirred in my chest. It didn't command me as it did before, but its power was there, waiting for me to unleash it. To do so was irrational, stupid. Our plan had failed, and any attempt to draw Jaryło's blood now would likely lead to my death. The thrill of battle rushing through my veins said otherwise. I needed to beat him, to prove him wrong. Just a little of that power could make all the difference...

In a flash, I unleashed a portion of that rage, trying to control it unlike I had in Huebia. All the debris I'd collected launched at Jaryło. He barely raised his shield to deflect it, but pieces got through. He felt pain, and that distraction was enough.

Lightning snapped at my feet as I sprinted at him. I added bolts to the rubble, striking him from every direction before swinging Grudzień at his hip when he moved the shield to block the blasts. I badly needed the power I'd wielded with Otylia's hand in mine, but I was alone. My friends seemed realms away from this patch of garden.

The moment Grudzień touched Jaryło's body, a blast shook the entire island. Static cracked across my skin as it threw me back into the stonework lining the gardens. My bones broke like twigs. My breaths were ragged. Blood seeped around me as I forced my *żityje* to mend my body.

Otylia? I asked through our bond. *Otylia, are you all right?*

"I've been trying to call for you!" she exclaimed. *"Come back before this gets worse."*

I winced, clutching my broken ribs as they stitched back together. Jaryło watched me from atop the stone rim around the tree with a smirk. "Sparring time is over. It is time for the gods to handle what must be done."

Then he dashed off faster than I'd ever seen someone run.

My heart grew heavy. The cage holding the demon within me held, but a bit had slipped out in that moment—more than should've. I took as many long breaths as it took to find my calm, ensuring it remained silent beyond its ever-present hunger. Quiet but never gone. Beyond just using the demon, I'd wasted much of my *žityje* in the fight. For what?

I raised Grudzień, examining its black blade streaked in color. One particular color caught my eye.

Bright crimson blood covered the longest two teeth on the jagged blade. Only a few drops, but I laughed to myself as I scrambled for the clay vials and held them beneath the blood. It would have to be enough. I prayed to Dziewanna, Mokosz, Otylia, and every friendly spirit that inhabited the Three Realms that it was.

"Where are you, Wašek?" Otylia asked. *"Hurry!"*

I'm coming, I replied, tucking away the vials. *And I've got the blood of a god.*

36

Otylia

So he finally shows up…

MY EARS RANG AS I SHUDDERED and pushed myself up to my knees. The rest of my friends lay beside me along the low wall of the gardens. All were hurt, but none looked severely wounded.

Ahead, the gardens met me, cleared in a ring around a built man of middling height as servants struck by his blast dissolved into dust. His deep-set eyes pulsed an electric blue that coursed down his exposed arms to an ax that he'd slammed into the stone moments before.

The king of the gods had arrived.

"What outrageous behavior is this?" Perun's voice boomed. He stomped through the opening his lightning strike had created. Both our friends and the gods' servants had been thrown by the blast, but he cared for neither, his gaze remaining fixed upon me.

"Jaryło was torturing my friends," I replied with the little confidence I could muster. *Žityje* healed my wounds, but the stones lining the gardens had torn my sleeves and skirts in multiple places. This was not how I'd wanted to appear before the thunder god.

As if on cue, Jaryło burst through the shrubbery and to his father's side. He seemed unharmed except for twigs and bits of stone that marred his perfect hair. "Sorry for the delay. I had to put a Naw in his place."

"Is this accusation true, my son?" Perun said, crossing his massive arms. Even Jaryło looked like a child compared to him, and I quickly decided it was best not to get on his bad side.

Jaryło scoffed. "Her and Mother's szeptuchy were attempting to ambush me. As my blood pact with Otylia ensures I cannot kill her friends, I commanded my servants to do so."

"Then you are lucky the płanetnik stopped you! You should know better than to believe that servants made of your own essence could escape the restrictions of your blood pact."

Of his own essence?

I glanced at the servants who remained—Mokosz, Jaryło, and Perun's new arrivals alike. They'd seemed to be acting independently before, but were they just manifestations of a god's power?

I pushed that thought away as Weles arrived, flanked by his wooden and snake servants who bore his cattle horns. My blood father was a stark contrast to his rival. The half-brothers shared their gray beards and defined cheeks, but while Perun stood tall, Weles hunched and leaned on a birchwood cane. His simple earthen robes billowed around him as if he were swaddled in blankets. But the lord of Nawia was no child. I'd experienced his wrath firsthand and wouldn't let him get the better of me again.

"Nice of you to show up," I spat at him. My muscles ached as I rose with as much dignity as I could muster. "Not that you'd bother to protect your daughter anyway."

Where was Mother? I'd barely had an idea how to handle this if things had gone according to plan, let alone if it had all fallen apart. We'd counted on Jaryło imprisoning my friends, but even that was up in the air now.

"Our last meeting in Nawia ended on unfortunate footing," Weles replied with a solemn look. "It seems that matters have their way of righting themselves, however, and you are here to wed Jaryło nonetheless."

When Weles advanced, both his and Perun's servants swiftly

formed ranks between the two. Massive eagles glared at tree servants who swung their bullish heads. *They're not as united in this marriage as we thought.* There was an opening there, but my mind spun with how quickly things had fallen apart. I couldn't counter Weles or find a witty jab at Jaryło. So I just stood there, gritting my teeth and clenching my fists at my sides.

Hurry up, Wašek.

"The płanetnik and his co-conspirators must be imprisoned for their treachery!" Jaryło exclaimed through my silence. "They have betrayed the traditions of this wedding, seeking to gain from my focus on Otylia."

He whined like an infant to his mother, but I held back my smirk. Perun was also the god of justice. What would he consider just punishment for our attack?

Perun looked from Jaryło to me as the shrubbery rustled again. Wacław appeared, head bowed as he set down his sword. "Do not worry. I am done fighting."

The god frowned, and lightning cracked at the end of his ax. "This marriage was intended to end the war between Weles and myself, forging a new bond between our children to rule Jawia. It seems some among us do not desire that unity." He turned on his heel toward Mokosz. She held her composure far better than me, despite taking the same blast. "My love, do you harbor dissidents within your palace? Tell me. There must be an explanation for this."

"The only possible explanation is the most obvious one," Weles replied with a stamp of his staff. "Otylia seeks to undermine the blood pact through the płanetnik boy."

Mokosz clasped her hands before her as she stepped over the debris and to her husband. "Is it any shock that the girl opposes this marriage? Did you not learn from our experience with your own daughter?" She looked to the side, where Mother circled the servants toward me, never taking her eyes off the gods. "I aided you against her revolution, but forcing her to wed sparked her rage. Do you truly believe unity can come from another?"

"The girl will learn," Perun replied.

"She may." Mokosz looked at me, giving the slightest of nods before turning back to Perun. "I have stated my opinion, but the pact has been sealed in blood. This attack only furthers the dark dragon's attempts to sow discord among us. We should detain Wacław and Otylia's other allies until the wedding has completed, as I fear further punishment would only further enrage our young bride."

Fire burned in my chest, but I took her signal for what it was. We needed to pretend we were weak… for now. Once Wacław had Jaryło's Alatyr shards, Mother could reveal her reforged bond and we could strike. *I can last until then,* I told myself. At least I hoped so.

Perun huffed, running a hand quickly through his beard. "You give prudent advice as always, dear. Very well. Jaryło, they have wronged you, so you will detain them until the wedding has completed. We cannot have them interrupting again."

"No!" I shouted, giving them the show they wanted. Sabina grabbed at my arm out of genuine shock as I rushed to them and fell to my knees. *Let them see a girl, not the goddess of endings.* "I need them. Please!"

"Tend to her," Perun ordered Mokosz. He stepped around me and waved for his servants to follow. "Then we shall conduct the formalities and be done with this."

I raised my gaze to Weles. "Father, he is your rival. Don't let him do this!"

But he slowly shook his head. "Perun speaks sense for once. Let us do what we must for the Three Realms, and then you will discover in time that this was right for you as well." Then he passed me too, leading the serpents and leszy-like servants into the palace.

Jaryło lingered.

"Whatever you plan will not work," he whispered, leaning in close. I wished I could hate his breath, but it was sweet like nectar. "This wedding will happen, and I will become king of Jawia. What becomes of you after depends upon your actions from this point forward. You can rule freely at my side or find yourself wasting away until your precious moon becomes nothing but a faint memory. Choose wisely."

He backed away with a hand on his sword's hilt and spoke with a raised voice. "Grab the traitors. Store their weapons, and put Grudzień with the other Moonblades. I want the Alatyr shards together when I complete my collection."

Wacław met my gaze as Jaryło marched into the palace. *"I would say to be strong,"* he said through our bond, *"but you're the last person who needs a reminder."*

The servants took his arms and grabbed Grudzień from the ground. I swallowed and tried to smile back at him, but it came out as a grimace. *No matter what he does, don't listen to the demon.*

"It's stronger away from you. I won't lose control again, but it pushes me to attack."

Remember who you are.

"I promise." A wry smile crossed his face as they dragged him away, but I felt the pain he tried to hide. *"As long as you promise not to get married without me."*

I wouldn't dare.

Mother tugged my sleeve. "Come. You two can talk from halfway across Prawia. You don't need to be gawking at each other to do it."

I checked on each of my friends as the servants took hold of them. Perun's lightning strike had released a ridiculous amount of *żityje*, but it had been directed toward the direction Jaryło and Wacław had run off in. I'd felt Wacław's ribs break. The rest of the group had been luckier, which was crucial considering only he and I could heal ourselves with our *żityje*.

"Are you sure you are well enough to continue?" Sabina whispered, slowing me in the foyer. "Your dress—"

"Is just fabric," I interrupted. "Besides, a little moonlight can fix a lot. Stay safe."

As the servants dragged off my friends, I took a deep breath and weaved my moonlight over the splits in my dress. This work was far simpler than copying Mokosz's servants, but even it would falter beneath close inspection. Ara said she'd been working on her illusions since she'd left Huebia. The power was mine. That didn't stop me from wondering if she could teach me to use it more effectively—yet another reason why I needed her back.

Mother pulled me along once I was done. "This is not finished. You will have to endure days of this before the wedding, as Jaryło will seek to parade you before every god and spirit of Prawia."

"Even Simargł?"

"If we're lucky."

We headed through a series of halls to Mokosz's dining room. The gods were already seated at the diamond-shaped table made of intricately crafted violet stone that filled the room's center. Compared to the welcoming rounded edges of the room, covered in ivy and foliage like the rest of the palace, the table's sharp corners felt formal and uninviting. The dozens of servants standing near the doors didn't help matters.

The men rose at our entrance, but they stood for Mokosz, not me, as she led us into the room. She bowed her head as if there hadn't been a battle in her gardens, then joined Perun on his side of the table. Mother took my hand as she left.

"I must join Weles, but do not worry. I will be right next to you."

I nodded slowly and walked by her side, feeling the eyes of the gods and their servants. I kept my own gaze down as we sat, and a deathly silence hung over us until the doors opened. Mokosz's wispy servants swept around us. They carried wooden plates and brought the wonderful aroma of beef, poultry, and stews that made my stomach rumble. I'd been too stressed to eat much in recent days, but food seemed the perfect distraction from the frustrating conversations that were sure to come.

Unfortunately, the silence ended with the meal's arrival. Perun leaned on his elbow and stared across the table at Weles. "This beef cannot match that of the cattle you stole from me, but Mokosz has never failed to provide a meal worthy of a king."

"Is that why you have grown old and fat?" Weles muttered.

I choked on the red wine that had come with my meal, spurring a warning glance from Mokosz. *Maybe he's more like me than I thought.*

Perun didn't find it so funny. He slammed his fist into the table hard enough to crack its wood and rattle every plate and cup. "We invited you to Prawia out of a desire for peace!" he yelled.

"You are a god of war," Weles replied with a wry smile. "What do you know of peace?"

"Fathers, please," Jaryło said quietly. It was the meekest sound I'd ever heard from him, but it faded quickly. "Your blood pact has kept the both of you from destroying Jawia again. This marriage ensures neither you nor Marzanna can do so ever again."

Arguments ensued, and I watched with glee. The array of meats and vegetables spread before me were as delicious as their anger. These were the gods who sought to control me. Any divide among them would make uprooting their plans easier, and any attention on them was less attention on me.

I was nearly finished eating by the time Mokosz set her hand on the table, sending a gentle vibration through it. The gods silenced at once. Perun's face was bright red and spittle marred Weles's beard, but they didn't dare challenge her.

"That is enough," Mokosz said in a simple, calm tone. Her glare exposed her rage, but she spoke barely louder than a whisper. "Each of us has our own desires, but we are meeting today to plan how we will introduce the couple to the realms. Both gods and spirits will wish to see them ahead of the wedding, particularly due to Jaryło's aspirations to rule over Jawia."

Weles leaned forward to listen before snatching his cane when she finished. He spun it in his hand, vines creeping across its surface as he thought. "We must welcome my allies from Nawia. Otylia is my daughter, and I will not have this wedding be entirely controlled by Prawia."

"The plans have been made," Perun said, crossing his arms.

Jaryło held out open arms. "Invite the nymphs and spirits. We should be open to all those from the highest and lowest realms as well. Best we not alienate them and give Marzanna and Czarnobóg the chance to take advantage."

"I agree," I said. There would be few opportunities for me to speak my mind honestly, so I had to take advantage. The more people who were present, the more who would hear of Jaryło's betrayal.

Weles smiled at me. "I am pleased to hear your support on this, my daughter."

The kings of the opposing realms continued to lay out their demands for some time. These turned mundane, so I looked into End's wisps and watched each god's drift through the space. Perun's thundercloud gray one seemed to spark with his contained frustration. He gestured sharply as he spoke about the importance of Jaryło's position compared to mine during the wedding, and the wisp followed his hands. It came closer with each motion, giving me a bad idea.

I reached into my force, willing for the wisp to cross the extra stride to me. What secrets could Perun's endings hold? Could they give some answer to why he'd not stopped Marzanna sooner?

The wisp neared my potential reach, but I had no way to slyly touch it. I knew I shouldn't. Falling into a vision would leave me dazed for a few moments. My curiosity was stronger, as this could be my only chance to reach into Perun's endings without him knowing. I had to take it.

My wine was empty, but I grabbed the cup anyway and raised it in an exaggerated motion. It likely looked ridiculous. They were distracted though, and no one even looked my direction as my fingers brushed the edge of the wisp. End pulled at my mind. Once, it would've torn me away without giving me a choice, but I held the power as I pretended to drink and set the cup down, the wisp following dutifully. Only then did I allow my force to take me into the vision.

I tumbled through images of lightning, fire, and mountains that rose from nothing. What control I had over End was gone. It tore me deeper and deeper until I crashed into the hard ground.

Ash filled my mouth as I pushed myself up. There was little to see, as smoke covered what appeared to be a smoldering forest. It drifted in each gust of wind, and soon, Perun became visible at the base of a great oak. He knelt, leaning on his ax as golden apples sparked on the ground around him. His cape was ripped, and blood trickled down his arms. Each of his ragged breaths shook the air as footsteps approached from behind us.

"I gave you everything," Perun said with his head bowed, "and this is what I receive in return?"

A younger version of Mother stopped beside me, an arrow nocked in her beautifully carved bow. A bear pelt draped over her head and down her back. She reflected its scowl, and flames flickered at the end of her fingers.

"You took Ivan!" she screamed, pulling back the bowstring. "You took everything!"

Perun stood, but left the ax stuck in the ash. When he turned, I gasped at the burns covering half his face, exposing bone and sinew beneath his skin. "So you took the world."

Her breaths were heavy, ragged. The bow swayed with each as she glared at her father, but its point never drifted from his head.

Then she shot.

Fire streaked behind that arrow as it rushed toward Perun. The thunder god just stood and watched with his shoulders hunched. There was acceptance in his eyes, a defeat that was hard to imagine compared to the mighty god who'd unleashed his thunderblast outside Mokosz's palace.

But the arrow didn't strike—*him*. A creature rushed from the shadows, covered in decaying skin and flashing teeth worthy of a wolf. It was strides from Perun's flank when Mother's flaming arrow embedded itself in the beast's skull.

"I have gone too far, Father," she huffed. Tears streamed down her cheeks, but she still stood like a trained archer, another arrow pulled from her quiver in a heartbeat after releasing the first. "Punish me all you like when this is finished, but help me fix this!"

"Prawia will never be your home again."

"I know."

"Then surrender any claim to the Three Realms, and I will aid you in destroying the forces you have unleashed."

She bowed her head. "I surrender my claims, but know that Jaryło will make you regret not having me."

Perun ripped his ax free from the ash, then grabbed a golden apple from the oak's base. "Jaryło has not destroyed Jawia for his own gain."

37

Wacław

How do we outmaneuver a god that powerful?

MY BODY STILL ACHED FROM PERUN'S THUNDERBLAST hours after the battle, but that wasn't my concern as I paced in Jaryło's prison of interwoven plants.

His servants of grain and vines had dragged my friends into another cell not long after I'd been thrown in my own. Based on the sound of Ta's muffled protests and Narcyz's curses, they were nearby. I needed to find them before searching for the Moonblades.

But how?

The servants had of course stolen Grudzień, and there was no door to windblast open, as the grain forming the walls had simply shifted aside to allow them to throw me in. Lightning could work. Unfortunately, I'd used way too much *żiłyje* in my fight with Jaryło. Expending more of it before I'd even reached the Moonblades was too risky, and I doubted he'd let his prison burn so easily.

No, there had to be another way. *I'll find a way to you,* I told Kuba and Narcyz through my mark. *But this is different than I expected.*

"What?" Narcyz quipped back. *"You didn't expect a dungeon of impossibly thick grain? I'm so surprised."*

I ignored his taunting. There was no time for arguments. Jaryło would use every moment to control Otylia., so without another apparent way to escape, I dug into the stirring emotions in my chest and threw lightning at the wall in my friends' direction.

Blue bolts shot from my grasp and charred the surface. I grinned at the sensation of power rushing through my veins, but beyond that initial burning, it pushed no deeper into the wall. I channeled for another few seconds before stepping back, sweating, yet no closer to escape. For all my effort, I hadn't even created a tiny hole. The demon's growing hunger for *żityje* mocked my failure.

I took a long breath, then punched the wall. Instead of blocking the strike like stone, the grain shifted to catch my fist, and it only tightened when I tried to yank myself free.

Great. Now I can't even move.

If that wasn't enough, new stalks wrapped themselves around the charred bit to replace the damage I'd managed to inflict. The entire wall continued to move for some time. The rustling resembled the familiar sound of grain waving in the wind, but it wasn't a reminder of home. It felt sinister, and all I could do was wait with my hand trapped within.

Then it stopped.

Silence fell over the dungeon. All the shifting grain remained still, which had me even more nervous.

Another rustle came from behind the wall before me. Whatever made the noise had plenty more *żityje* than the servants, and it sent my demonic senses into a frenzy. I needed to feed once we got out. The hunger would only grow.

I considered calling out to the being, whether it be a god, a szeptucha, or a spirit. This was Jaryło's palace, though, so it was likely just another guard he'd sent to ensure I stayed put. I'd earned a special place in his head if his fury had been any indication. Did he consider me a threat to his plans, or just competition with Otylia? I scoffed at the thought of him believing he could ever convince Otylia this marriage was in her best interest.

Żityje suddenly rushed from the being and into the wall. The grain stalks twisted and fought, then slowly released me, retreating to form an opening in the wall. Two women stood on the other side.

"What did you do to end up here?" Ara asked with a smirk. Her huntress clothes were ripped along the sleeves, and she wielded a sword that angled back suddenly at its tip.

"Ara?" I blabbered in shock. "How did you escape?"

She patted the shoulder of the woman beside her, whose dull golden dress was woven out of the same wheat as the room. Like with me, the vines reached toward her, but she gave a graceful wave. Instead of rearing back, they seemed almost soothed, their stalks curling into themselves as if falling asleep.

"This is Marzyana, goddess of the grain," Ara said, "but we'll have time for introductions later. Jaryło won't like us killing his guards, and I really don't want to be trapped here again."

Marzyana and I exchanged nods as I stepped free and gave her my thanks. The hall was made of the same materials, its wooden floor only marred by the ash left behind by dead servants. "Where are the others?" I asked.

Marzyana's already bright face lit up even more. "You are referring to the nymph, eagle, and mortals, one whom shouted so loudly that my ears are still ringing?"

I nodded. "That's Narcyz."

"Wonderful!" she exclaimed, hands to her heart. "We brought them out first, because I could not allow youth to suffer such conditions. Their weapons were stored nearby and have been returned to them. Shall we escape now?"

I bit my cheek and checked on the vials on my belt. The servants hadn't considered them a threat, but would they be enough? "I need to find Jaryło's Moonblades first."

The goddess cocked her head, her hands locked before her like a little girl confused at her mother's words. "I do not understand."

"The Alatyr shards, Moonstones. Jaryło stores them as swords, and I need to steal them. It's the whole reason we purposely let him throw us in here." I glanced at Ara. "How'd you find us anyway?"

"Enough questions." Ara ran down the hall to an area that seemed no different than the others. "Let's talk in here."

Marzyana followed, placing her hand on the wall alongside Ara and opening it like she'd done to my cell. Inside, our friends crowded inside a small room, and Vlatka squawked at the sight of us from her perch on Sabina's head. Ta spun at the noise and raised one of her throwing blades. "Oh, it's you…"

"Nice plan, Wacław," Narcyz muttered. "Fight Jaryło while the rest of us get hit by Perun."

"It was prudent at the time," Vlatka replied.

I pulled out one of the vials. "I never wanted you to get hurt. The distraction wasn't what I expected either, but it worked in the end."

"You actually got it?" Sabina's translucent wings fluttered. "Gods, maybe there is still hope."

I gave what I hoped was a reassuring smile. "There is as long as we find those blades."

Ara coughed and swung her sword over her shoulder. "Seems I might be of use then."

"I was wondering where you got that thing. Why didn't you tell Otylia through her mark?"

"Well, her Moonmark…" She dropped her head, the sword slipping to her side. Then she pulled down her coat's collar to reveal where her mark should've been as a szeptucha. A dull downward crescent still lingered, but over it was Jaryło's Springmark. Black tendrils spiraled from it up her neck and down her collarbone. "I don't know what Jaryło did to me, but I haven't been able to channel ever since I woke in this realm."

A shiver ran down my spine as I stepped back. "That looks like—"

"Your demonic veins, yeah."

Marzyana stepped forward, wincing. "I have lived on Jaryło's island for some time, as I lack the worshippers to maintain much strength on my own. Apparently, I was not as cautious as I believed. Mokosz discovered my presence and promised to not expose me if I aided Otylia in her opposition to the wedding. It was not long after that Jaryło arrived with this one." She smiled shyly at Ara. "I had noticed the master of spring acting strangely some time before, but only when I saw her Springmark did I realize he had been corrupted."

"Otylia…" I clenched my fists and held in a snarl. "I left her with him." My voice trembled, and though I reminded myself that both Mokosz and Dziewanna were watching over her, I'd experienced both Perun and Weles's powers. If Jaryło could sway even one of them to fight by his side, he could easily defeat the goddesses. Nothing I could do would stop him then.

"The Moonblades can still stop him," Ara replied. "I know the way to them."

Marzyana's worried expression deepened. "Jaryło's servants will be waiting. Though I have some power over the elements here, it is still his palace."

"You're not alone," Narcyz replied, stomping his spear into the dirt.

Kuba raised the Thunderstone dagger. "Yeah! A bunch of mortals with sticks and daggers will definitely help."

Ta rolled her eyes. "Keep behind us, dirt brain."

"That's enough bickering," I said. "We need everyone here to help if we're going to survive this."

Ara shook her head. "Getting yourselves trapped in Jaryło's palace was quite the plan. This won't be easy."

"Since when has anything?" I pulled down my płanetnik hat. "Keep each other in sight. No one gets left behind. Not in a place like this."

Ara groaned. "This is a mistake."

Marzyana suddenly held her finger to her lips. Footsteps came from outside the room, followed by muttering and a shuddering of the grain stalks. "We must continue on," she whispered. "Let us go now."

When I nodded, she opened the far wall, and Ara pointed her to the right. These palaces were massive. I hoped as we navigated the halls that its size would keep the servants from finding us. Their voices were muffled through the grain, but the desperation of their search was obvious. Jaryło badly wanted to keep us here. All the more reason to escape.

We soon reached a staircase heading up onto what Ara said was the main floor. Apparently there was no roof to the actual palace, and that alone was enough to bring a smile to my face. The servants would use Jaryło's power over the palace. That meant little when I could soar above their tendrils.

Marzyana led us up the stairs, each of our footfalls echoing off the wood. I used the winds to lift us just enough to prevent our feet from striking the ground, but it was too late. The walls shifted rapidly as voices shouted from above.

"Run for the wall opposite the stairs," Ara whispered. "We'll dive through a few rooms and hopefully beat them to the swords."

We made for the top of the stairs as quickly as our wounded friends could manage. The stalks grew closer with each step, and by the time we lunged onto the main floor, they snatched at our heels. Six servants waited for us there too, but Ara and Narcyz cut the first two down as I released a windblast that swept the others aside. The way was clear. Except Sabina and Kuba's screams echoed behind us.

Roots and stalks entrapped their limbs. They fought and spun, only drawing their binds tighter, and Marzyana gave them a panicked look, one hand extended toward the now open wall and another toward the stairs. "I cannot hold them both at once."

"Focus on freeing them," I replied as I kicked a servant in the head before it could rise. "We'll hold them back."

"You do realize I have no training with a sword," Ara said. She took my side, slashing and stabbing at the advancing squad. More joined them with each passing moment as the palace's vines pulled them along and added to their bulk.

"Xobas always said combat is a wonderful time to learn," I replied, flipping over a few of the servants, then driving down onto the nearest's head. Its wooden neck cracked, and I dropped into a roll, the others' attention now fixed upon me. "I recommend stabbing them in the back."

Vlatka swooped overhead and unleashed flames from her beak. They burned a path through the servants before charring the wall. "Or burn them from above."

Ara smirked and copied my advice, spinning around the servants and slicing. Two more fell in quick succession as I kept them distracted.

The final pair flanked me now. A familiar song hung in the air as they advanced, their vines suddenly splitting open at their chests. They lumbered to a stop until Ta threw her circular blades through their heads. The vines creaked as they tumbled to the dirt.

"Let's go!" Ara demanded. "More will come."

"And Jaryło will certainly know you have escaped," Marzyana added. "He will be displeased."

We passed into the next room, a garnished bedroom full of more plush bedding, rugs, and drapery than I'd ever seen. Three nearly identical rooms followed. None were occupied, but the sounds of moving stalks drew nearer. I grew impatient with every moment we had to wait for Marzyana to open each passage. To make matters worse, Otylia's emotions pushed through our bond. A sudden rush of confusion, then anger, adding to my anxiety. I hated being away from her. She was more powerful than me, but things were so much easier by her side.

We're almost to the Moonblades, I told her in hopes of reassuring both of us. *We've found Ara too… Or more she found us. Jaryło corrupted her Moonmark somehow, so she couldn't message you.*

"She's with you? And what do you mean, corrupted?"

She is, and I'm not sure. Sorry, I don't have much time, but we'll talk more when we get back.

There was a pause, then Otylia's voice came as little more than a whisper. *"Tell Ara I need her back."*

"Otylia says she needs you back," I repeated to Ara as Marzyana opened yet another passage. "She's been worried sick."

"That means a lot," Ara said, "considering she never worries about anyone but you and Dziewanna."

"Vastroth changed that for her."

She eyed me. "Yeah, I've noticed. It changed both of you."

What did she mean by that? I knew *something* about me had changed since the Płanetnik's control, but Ara had known me for years. What had she seen that Otylia and Kuba weren't willing to say?

I didn't get the chance to ask, because the wall opened again, and we stepped into a garden. Enclosed on each side by trees bearing flowers and fruit, it smelled wonderfully sweet. Mokosz's gardens had been lush and overflowing. These were confined, trimmed back to form a controlled design that wound its way from crops along the outside to flowers and other plants I didn't recognize through the center. We followed the dirt path until it ended at a doorway.

"The Moonblades are in the room across the hall," Ara said, stopping us away from the opening. "We need to wait for an opening. It's an easy spot for them to trap us and one of the only rooms with a ceiling. I escaped before by ripping a hole in the wall with a super heavy sword. Once we've got the Moonblades, Marzyana should be able to open a path out, or at least to a room where we can fly."

"Why not use that sword again?" Narcyz asked.

"It's long gone. Something must've been magical about it, because it just kept going when it slipped out of my hands."

Ta giggled, her gaze seemingly elsewhere. "It probably went on and sliced a servant clean in half."

"Hopefully, it was one of Jaryło's," Kuba replied with his own ridiculous grin.

"Or it's going on forever, flying to the end of the Three Realms," Vlatka quipped, perching herself on my shoulder. Going higher for too long would draw attention from the other gods. As long as we were inside the walls, we would be harder to track.

Marzyana's hazel eyes darted from one sister to the other. Then she sat back against the wall, tongue stuck in her cheek. "Mortals are never what I expect them to be."

Kuba shrugged. "We don't really get each other either. Technically, Wacław and Sabina aren't even mortals."

"Do you return when you die?" Marzyana asked, looking at me.

"No."

"Then you are not immortal. Immortality is a way of life you cannot understand, no matter how long you live." Marzyana glanced around the corner with her hand pressed to the grain stalks. "The way is clear. Are you prepared?"

I took a sharp breath. "Not really, but what choice do we have?"

"There are always choices."

"If only we had any good ones."

We burst into the hallway beyond, where a round chamber lay strides before us. The semi-circle of altars Ara had described arced through its center with seven hilts sticking from their wooden surfaces. Over half the shards of Alatyr in a single room. Jaryło was arrogant, and he believed his power could protect this place. That would be his undoing.

Unfortunately, either he or his servants had foreseen our route, as no less than twenty of the creatures ambushed us the moment we stepped into the chamber. Stalks and wooden claws slashed from every direction. I had no counter without my blade. All I could do was duck and roll, windblasting enough to give myself space to reach the twelfth altar and Grudzień within it.

My friends were somewhere behind, so it was down to me to drip the blood and hope there was enough to free all the blades. Grudzień came first, but freeing my own blade wasn't enough to convince Jaryło to stand down. We needed more.

I snapped lightning across my hands, sending a bolt through the closest servant's chest and directly into the one behind. More lumbered toward me. The vines pulling them along were slower than a person's run, though, so I had time to pull one of the blood vials and pour a single drop onto the altar as Narcyz and Kuba took up defensive positions nearby.

Please work...

Nothing seemed to change. The blood soaked into the wood, but Grudzień remained planted within the altar, as Mokosz had warned the swords could not be pulled free by force. Then, after a few excruciating moments, the sword pulsed. I took it as my sign.

Vial held tight in one hand, I yanked Grudzień free with the other. It slid easily from the altar, and I smiled in relief at the familiar grip of the jagged blade of the twelfth moon. Kwiecień had been a magnificent sword and had saved Mom's life. Something about Grudzień felt different. I had fought Marzanna's allies and myself to take it, and its darkness split by streaks of light reflected how I felt about my soul in recent moons. That light would grow. For now, though, I needed the blade to do what it did best—slice.

I burst upward on the winds with a spin, sending Grudzień clean through the necks of the surrounding servants. They dissolved, and I landed in the clearing I'd made before bolting to the next Moonblade.

Październik, the tenth moon, was the last of Jaryło's time of the year. Its sword was gray, like the late autumn sky, with old tongue symbols of white and black visible near the blade's hilt. Two servants guarded it, but they fell swiftly to Grudzień's toothed edge, giving me the space I needed to work.

My friends noticed the switch and moved to guard my flanks. That gave me time to sheathe Grudzień before pouring the drops of blood again. I hated leaving myself unarmed in the process, but though I was skilled with the winds, they weren't all that good at precision with small objects. There were few precious droplets in the vials. I couldn't afford to lose any, so I poured as carefully as possible before pulling Październik free the moment the altar pulsed.

That's two.

Another wave of Jaryło's servants rushed into the room with their vines and stalks forming a barrier over the entrance. I needed to move faster.

"Ara, take Październik," I said, handing it to her since she was closer to anyone else, then beginning the process on the violet blade of Wrzesień. She stared at the sword with a look of befuddlement across her face. I groaned. "Drop the other one! Only the Moonblades matter now."

She did so just in time to deflect an incoming blow. Most blades would've only parried the strike, but the Moonstone core of Październik sliced through the servant's claws without her even needing to counter.

"All right," she said as she moved in tandem with Marzyana to cover me again. "I get why you like these things."

Wrzesień came free quickly, but doing so used what remained of the first vial. I bit my cheek. We wouldn't have enough for all the Moonblades at this rate. "We might have a problem."

"*Might?*" Narcyz quipped from across the room, wincing as he took a strike from a servant. Ta raised a dirt barrier before him and Sabina, and I took some relief knowing at least she was safe for now.

But that left Ta exposed herself.

Marzyana diverted many of the vines reaching for the Mother-marked szeptucha, but Ta had been caught near the entrance when I'd retreated. She'd apparently run out of blades, and with her channeling focused on protecting the others, she wasn't watching her back. The servants' vines snatched her legs when she tried to break away.

"Ta, catch!" I threw Wrzesień to meet her, guiding it into her grasp with my winds.

Her terror turned to glee as she caught the blade and cut down her attackers. "I could get used to this!"

The tide turned as I moved onto the next altar. Instead of swarming like a pack of wolves, the servants cowered as Ta and Ara cut down their allies. And when I gave Marzyana the orange sickle-shaped blade of Sierpień soon after, they turned to flee, leaving the wispy remains of their comrades to fill the room.

"Just giving them to the girls?" Kuba grunted after tearing through a serpent with his dagger. The others disappeared into the mass of stalks and vines blocking the entrance, and he grinned despite the blood trickling from a few cuts along his arms. "I promise I can use a shiny sword too."

"Give me a moment," I mumbled back.

Our lack of enemies gave me time to examine the blood in the remaining vial. It looked like if I was careful, I could free the three remaining Moonblades with the last drops. Kwiecień, Maj, and Czerwiec remained, as Jaryło had apparently kept Lipiec with him to ensure he could recover if slain during this moon.

Narcyz held out his arms at me. "What are you waiting for, Jaryło to show up?"

"Sorry," I said, shaking myself free from my thoughts and wandering over to Kwiecień.

"I believe it would be prudent to escape with haste," Marzyana replied. She held Sierpień like one would a dead mouse left on the threshold by a cat.

"We can't leave any, so please don't rush me."

I rested my hand on Kwiecień's golden pommel. Memories came with it. Grudzień had become my blade, but Kwiecień had saved Mom's life. It didn't matter that any Moonstone could've during its moon. Kwiecień had allowed me to wield its *żityje*. That was enough.

I freed both it and the neighboring deep green blade of Maj with ease. Both Kuba and Narcyz eyed me greedily, so I handed them Maj and Kwiecień respectively.

"What's left?" Narcyz asked.

I turned to the final sword: the white blade of Czerwiec. All that remained of Jaryło's blood was the tiniest portion lining the bottom of the vial. "I don't know if there's enough blood left," I replied, raising the vial and holding it over the altar and tapping it to force out the blood.

The wait was excruciating. Either Jaryło or his servants could return at any time, but we needed to take as many of his Alatyr stones as possible. Not even the gods knew when we'd get another chance.

Luckily, my patience paid off, as the tiniest of drops splattered onto the altar. Czerwiec hummed. It was quieter than the reaction of the other altars, but when I grabbed hold of its hilt, the sword pulled free. I took a sigh of relief before handing the blade to Sabina. Her grip on it was loose, untrained, but training would take time we didn't have.

"Time to go," I said, turning to Marzyana. "Can you get us out of here before Jaryło shows up?"

The goddess swept toward the back of the room's curved wall, placing a hand gently upon it. She whispered something, and the wood peeled back to reveal whatever room lay beyond. "Follow, master of the storm, and let us reveal spring's wicked ways."

38

Otylia

She destroyed Jawia...

I SNAPPED OUT OF MY VISION with a start. Mother raised a brow in my direction, but I couldn't find a reply. End had shown me the truth she'd been too afraid to reveal. Now, it felt like I met a stranger's gaze.

"Are you well?" Mokosz asked from across the diamond table. I'd forgotten her existence for a moment, all of Prawia fading with my realization about the goddess I had worshipped.

"I'm not," I said flatly.

Weles sighed and traced a crack running along the left horn that stuck from his head. "I do not understand why you are so opposed to wearing the braid of an unmarried woman. It is for a few days at most until the wedding."

I cocked my head. *How long was I in that vision?* The last time Weles had demanded I braid my hair was when I was in Nawia, but no one here had even mentioned it when the vision had begun.

"Fine, whatever," I muttered. That was a hill I'd have died on minutes before, but how I wore my hair was a stupid worry when I'd seen my mother ending the world in flames. I stood, accidentally pushing back my chair with a horrific grinding noise. "But I must be excused."

"You cannot leave now," Weles insisted. "There is much still to discuss."

"I'm sure you can make the decisions without me. You've made the rest that way."

Without even a glance at any of them, I hurried out of the room, my head spinning. Mokosz's servants tried to help me toward my chambers, but I pushed them away. The last thing I wanted was to be around anyone else. Not after the horror I'd seen.

I stumbled halfway up the curved staircase and had to catch myself to avoid smacking my head. Sitting only made the dizziness worse. It got to my stomach too, so I forced myself onward before I hurled in the middle of the upstairs hall. Mokosz wanted me to appear weak, but I feared running off while Wacław stole the Alatyr Moonblades would be suspicious. Did it matter? Jaryło would know either way. Whether he could prove it to Perun and Weles, though, I didn't know.

Wacław's message came soon after I collapsed onto my blood altar in the corner of our room, crafted from silvery moonlight. It was the first good news I'd heard in too long—Ara was alive and with him—but his comment about Jaryło corrupting her Moonmark was yet another worry. Had Jaryło become corrupted like Marzanna?

I lifted the blood-filled bowl to my lips, refilling my *żityje* with the offerings of animals, crops, and whatever else my new worshippers could give. The process hadn't become easier moons after my Ascension, and I had to force myself not to gag. It gave me a chance to clear my thoughts, though, before I dropped face first onto the bed and wished I was anywhere else.

Why couldn't I just be excited to reunite with Ara? There were just too many problems swirling in my mind. Death would soon demand I fulfill my oath and kill Rod. My lover was a Naw who still struggled to contain the demon's rage when he was away from me. Jaryło and both his real and adoptive fathers would be difficult to convince to end the blood pact. And now End's vision made me doubt Mother's past.

"Was it power, Mother?" I asked the empty space beside me. "Or did you actually believe all the destruction would be worth ending Perun's reign?"

Not knowing hurt, but I feared the answer just as much. Could she have lost all her worshippers because she'd inflicted as much pain as Simargł or Marzanna? Neither Father nor anyone else spoke about her that way. They'd just pretended Dziewanna didn't exist at all, besides "helping" Jaryło kill Marzanna on the spring equinox. Had Mother and Father hidden the truth to protect me, or did mortals not know what she'd done?

I had to ask her. I knew it. But as I rolled over and stared up at the domed ceiling above, I couldn't will myself to return.

After, I promised myself. *After we're done with Prawia, I'll ask. Jaryło is the focus until then.*

That brought some relief with it, but not enough. The true relief came when I finally heard from Wacław again after another half-hour.

"We did it!" he exclaimed through our bond. *"We have all his Moonblades except for Lipiec."*

I took a deep breath and leaned back against the warm stone headboard. At least something had gone right. Jaryło kept Lipiec with him as it was this moon's Alatyr shard, so that wasn't a surprise. Losing six of spring and summer's Moonblades would give Jaryło more than a headache.

Tell me you're out of there now.

"Almost. Ara was with a grain goddess, Marzyana, who's helping us avoid the island's defenses, but we're both running out of žityje after all the fighting." He paused, and when his voice returned, I felt him tense. *"Did Jaryło look like he knew what we were doing?"*

I don't know. I left after I saw a vision about my mother and Perun.

Pain flashed across my shoulder, followed by the familiar feeling of the Płanetnik's hunger. *"Well, his servants seem to have figured out where we're going, and Perun's too. There are eagles everywhere…"*

A single *thud* came from outside. I sprang up, summoning my silver spear and preparing to channel. *I think he's here.*

The door crashed off its hinges and fell to the floor. Lipiec's red hue covered Jaryło as he stomped in with Perun and Weles at his sides.

"Did you think I wouldn't know?" he snapped. A dark streak cut across his eye for only a moment as the entire room shook. "Your friend Ara remains trapped in my palace, bearing my *altered* mark, and I sensed the moment she went to help Wacław."

No wonder why Ara hadn't responded. If Jaryło had done something to her Moonmark... I needed to check on the others.

Sabina, are you okay? I asked through my Moonmark, waiting only to sense her presence on the other end of the message. *Jaryło has me trapped. I don't know what happened to my mother and Mokosz, but you need to alert the others.*

On the outside, I grinned at Jaryło through my shock. "Then you know Wacław took your Alatyr shards." There was no use hiding it if Perun and Weles already knew. They had me cornered, alone.

"Yes. Quite a trick, I admit, using my dungeon as a way into the palace, but as Wacław has taken what I desire most, I must now do the same to him."

I stamped my spear into the ground, sending a ringing through the room. The gods' wisps flinched at the motion, and I took some heart that I could ignite some fear in even the most powerful deities.

"I wish we hadn't left you!" Sabina finally responded. *"I'm on my way with Ta and Vlatka; though, I don't know where the boys went."*

Find Mother first. Perun and Weles are too powerful.

Jaryło edged closer, rounding the table in the room's center while his fathers stayed near the door. "We both know the terms of our blood pact. You cannot hurt me, Otylia."

"I know."

Then I did something very stupid.

Spear extended, I charged in hopes of catching him by surprise. He raised Lipiec out of instinct to block the strike. But I wasn't trying to hit. When the spear's tip neared his chest, I dismissed it, instead pushing myself into the path of his blade.

My vision blurred the moment Lipiec cracked against my skull. Excruciating pain washed over me like it had the first time Jaryło killed me on the top of that hill in the Mangled Woods. It wasn't the bluntness of a fall, the stinging of a cut, or the burning of frostbite. It was the sharp agony of Death. I'd met him once and fallen to his power once, and now, as my body grew distant and Lipiec drew my *žityje* into its blade, I knew I would meet him again.

Is this what you wanted? I asked him with my last thoughts. *To revel in my death?*

39

Wacław

Otylia?

MY HEART STOPPED AT THE SUDDEN WAVE of pain that rushed through our connection. Perun's eagle servants swarmed me, but I couldn't raise my blades to counter. Otylia's pain disappeared as quickly as it had come, a feeling I'd only experienced once before.

I can't lose her… Not again.

The last I'd heard from Otylia, she'd warned me that Jaryło had discovered our plan. He couldn't hurt her, but had Weles or Perun killed her as punishment for her betrayal? A sudden fire burned me free of my fear at that thought.

I spun with Grudzień sweeping at the eagles. Their talons raked across my limbs, but while *żityje* healed my wounds, the Moonblade cut them to ash with ease. Little of my life force remained after I'd used so much to escape the palace, but I didn't care. These beasts were fragments of the gods who'd betrayed Otylia. They would suffer for it.

Storm clouds gathered as I dove through the servants' ranks, freeing my friends from their grip. My winds lifted all but Sabina and Ta—who could fly themselves—but Weles's leszy-like creatures and Jaryło's servants joined the eagles by climbing towers of vines rising from the island. Far too many. It was bad enough to be caught in enemy territory, and the land literally fighting us only made it worse.

But the air was mine. *Žityje* drained quickly from my soul, so I pushed the others further up, toward Mokosz's island. That allowed the servants to surround me instead. Exactly what I wanted, and when my friends reached the edge of Mokosz's island, I shouted with all the pain burning in my chest.

Lightning exploded from my limbs and blades. Screams followed, the bolts shooting from servant to servant until only charred bits remained of them.

The blast had only eliminated the closest of the servants, but it gave me the space I needed to flee. My *žityje* was failing, the winds barely holding me aloft. I needed every advantage I could get. The demon within me yearned for blood, though, not to run. My foes offered no hearts for me to consume, but revenge was revenge.

Jaryło doesn't need his servants to be a threat, I told the demon. *We need to kill* him.

I pushed upward with all the energy I had left. Controlling the demon felt good, but it had left its mark. My flight was on the slightest breeze, not the gales that I needed to burst to safety, allowing Perun's eagles to close in again with lightning cracking in their maws and thunder rolling with each flap of their wings. They had all the strength of Perun pulsing within them. But I held one of the most powerful blades in all the Three Realms. A shard of Alatyr, coursing with the forces that created the gods themselves.

I held Grudzień before me when the eagles released Perun's lightning. Static cracked around me, but the Moonblade could only protect part of my body. The rest of the bolts slipped through. Pain followed, but I dug into it, reaching into my anger and my *need* to protect Otylia. I couldn't fail her. I needed her connection, and on the other side, I felt a tug that turned to a taut line.

She's here.

My veins suddenly seared blue, the eagle's lightning surging into my *žityje* as it had at the start of our battle against the Horde and in the Lake of Reflection. Otylia held the key to my power. I needed our bond more than anything, and though I had no idea how she was responding to my reach, I didn't care at that moment. A piece of her godly soul rested in me, and what remained of my mortal one was in her. I wouldn't let her suffer.

With a series of slashes at the nearest servants, I burst upward with not the winds but lightning itself bursting from my fingers. The only force keeping me going was my bond with Otylia. I clung to it, pulling toward her as if I were climbing the Thread binding us instead of flying.

But even that power was limited. My *žityje* faded as I neared the edge of Mokosz's islands, my friends waiting with weapons ready. I wouldn't make it.

My lightning failed with a snap, sending me spiraling into the eagles' grasps until a new gust pushed me upward. Not controlled by me, it was chilled but gentle. I struggled to keep my eyes open. All I managed to see was a flash of violet, and then the *whoosh* of an arrow passed by my head. The eagles' calls faded soon after.

The winds deposited my slumped form onto firm ground. Narcyz tried to pull me up, but I barely had the energy to keep awake, let alone continue to fight.

"Come on!" he demanded. "You literally just pushed us through a hundred servants. You can walk to the palace!"

"Otylia…" I mumbled, digging my fingers into the dirt and pushing myself to my knees. "Jaryło killed her. I feel it."

His eyes widened. "Then *let's go!*"

The wispy forms of Mokosz's servants approached, but our enemies did the same. Eagles circled above as wooden and grain-stalked beasts crawled onto the island behind us. Were there more waiting ahead in the gardens? The trio of gods had brought a small army to their aid, and I was in no shape to face them.

Apparently, I had no choice in the matter, as the wispy servants grabbed hold of me, pulling me to my feet and dragging me along. My friends fought back with their Moonblades, but they were badly outnumbered. Mokosz's servants, too, appeared more transparent. They fell quickly when they tried to slow our attackers' advances, but bought us time to retreat. I worried more enemy servants would be waiting. With Otylia inside the palace, though, we had no choice but to push into the gardens.

Flames met us there. Washing overhead in waves that left a smoky haze behind, they burned our enemies and opened a path ahead. I forced my legs to hold me as I looked for their source, gasping when I did.

"The firebird feather can do *that?*" I huffed at Andrij, who emerged from the brush with Narcyz at his side and a bow of deep green and red in his grasp. Flames spiraling up his arms. His eyes remained murky, but there was a vigor to them that was missing before.

He reached into his quiver, and the flames curled up the arrow as he nocked it. Then he shot into the next group of servants, the arrow exploding and turning them to nothing more than ash. "Not the firebird," he said with a grin in my direction. "Its goddess."

"Could use your lightning too!" Narcyz shouted, raising his large rounded shield and blocking a dive from a giant eagle before giving it a jab with Kwiecień. "But *no*, demons' marks don't give you powers."

"Dziewanna?" I asked as I staggered behind Andrij and the line of Moonblade wielders. "She made you a szeptucha?"

Andrij pulled at his collar to reveal Dziewanna's Bowmark before nocking another arrow. The fire was hasty, though, and the whole arrow dissolved midair. "Szeptun, yes, but I'm still new at this. She only made me one when she realized all of this was falling apart."

"Where is she?" I asked rapidly. "Where is Otylia?"

He winced, then shot again. "We have a lot to talk about. Best we get inside. Dziewanna and Mokosz are clearing a path to the palace, so we should be fine if these eagles don't cut us off."

"I got 'em," a voice replied from behind the haze.

Ta emerged at full sprint, swinging Wrzesień's purple blade and chanting in the old tongue. A pillar of rock rose before her, and she leapt upon it, straight into the eagles' paths.

"Kid's got guts," Narcyz said as he helped me head through the garden maze.

"Sorry my mark's not much help," I said.

He scoffed. "Saved me from Mieczysław, didn't it? I've just got to figure out how to do that again."

I gave a wry smile. "It probably doesn't help when I'm drained."

"Do that less often, then."

"Why hadn't I thought of that?"

An eagle dropped before us, lightning readied in its beak. "Don't know," Narcyz replied, "but now would be a great time for you to figure something out." He stabbed at the eagle, but it dove aside.

"Flank it," he demanded, hopping to the other side.

I did as he said, then raised Grudzień in hopes of blocking the lightning. But the bolt wasn't directed at me. Luckily, Narcyz was quick, and he dodged out of the way just before the bolt left the eagle's jaw. It skimmed the edge of his shield, though, and left behind a singed section.

"You owe me a new shield," Narcyz muttered as he circled the eagle.

"Paint an Eclipsemark and you have a deal," I quipped, keeping opposite of him with my shuffled steps. The thrill of battle brought the demon's energy through me. I kept it at bay, but it was right that this was where I needed it to be strong. Weakness would mean my friends' deaths. They needed me.

When the eagle spun to send another bolt, this time at me, Narcyz took advantage. I slashed to distract the beast, and he ducked, thrusting Kwiecień's golden blade through the underbelly of the giant eagle. The lightning faded from its beak as it dissolved.

I dropped to one knee, leaning on my sword. Each breath took all my energy. "Good work."

"C'mon." He offered me a hand. "We're not done yet."

I groaned, but took the offer. Yet another friend risking their life for me. Narcyz had once been my rival, so seeing him wielding a Moonblade by my side was a shock. If it hadn't been moments after I'd sensed Otylia's potential death and seen Andrij channeling Dziewanna's fire, I would've been amazed. Instead, I was numb, agony and rage dulled to a single thought in my *żityje*-drained mind.

Keep going.

So I ran. Slowly and without the winds, but I ran nonetheless. Every stumble reminded me how frail it was to be mortal. The full strength of my Nawie powers were still so new, yet I felt as if I'd never lived without them. How could I ever have been without the winds and storms at my command? How could I have ever been anything but Death's blade, able to defeat my foes at will and devour their hearts for *żityje?* In truth, I was still the boy who'd jumped the fire on the equinox, but I'd learned I would do anything for Otylia, for Mom, and for my friends. Power had changed what I was. With the demon caged in my soul, I reminded myself it wouldn't change who I was.

The gardens seemed to go on forever, their wonderful aromas a harsh contrast to the clatter of battle around me. It lacked the horrific smells of death, as the servants dissolved to nothing, but that only added to the terror. False safety against creatures channeling gods could mean death.

Gratefully, few servants got in our way. Those that did offered little resistance, as Narcyz, Kuba, and I dispatched the strong but slow beasts of Weles and Jaryło with relative ease. My friends grinned with each swing, and I recognized the unique sensation of wielding a god's sword. Every boy grew up watching warriors swing swords and hearing them talk about gods' mighty weapons. Even channeling couldn't match the giddy feeling of holding a Moonblade, then defeating your enemies with a single blow.

We finally reached the central gardens that stretched toward the palace entrance. They had been covered in debris from Perun's lightning strike and my fight with Jaryło hours before, but now they looked pristine.

Besides the ragged goddess standing atop a fountain.

"Get inside!" Dziewanna yelled down at us as she balanced precariously upon the shoulders of the stone mother figure carved beneath her. She shot with a bow carved with symbols resembling antlers, horses, foxes, and bears. Flames crackled down its string. Like Andrij's, her arrows burned as they flew. She shot far quicker than him, though, loosing what should've been a full quiver before I had the chance to take a breath.

Ara led the way with Marzyana at her side. The grain goddess was drained, using only her Moonblade, and her lack of training with a sword showed. While Narcyz blocked and countered with precision, she took wide two-handed swipes that hit mostly air, but her unpredictable strikes at least helped keep the servants at a distance.

I glanced back over my shoulder as Kuba helped me limp through the palace doors. Dziewanna was already on the retreat. We'd made it, but that gave me no relief.

"Where's Otylia?" I demanded of Andrij once everyone was inside, looking from him to Dziewanna. "I felt—"

"Hold the door with anyone who can still fight," Dziewanna ordered him before making for the hall toward our chambers. "Come, Wacław. Otylia lives, but just barely."

A knot released in my chest. *She's alive.* I nearly collapsed in relief, forcing Narcyz to catch me.

Ara looked torn, taking a half step after Dziewanna before turning back toward the door. "Otylia would want you there too," I told her once I'd recovered my wits.

"They need my help," she said.

"Not with that mark on your neck they don't," Dziewanna replied. "We have plenty of allies to fend off these servants, so come. I am not giving you a choice."

We winded through the palace halls before heading up the stairs toward our sleeping chambers. Dziewanna threw my arm over her shoulder to haul me up as my legs dragged. It was agony feeling so useless when I needed to get to Otylia, but the goddess didn't look at me like a burden, instead holding pity in her eyes. That only deepened the dread in my chest.

When I stepped into Otylia's room, my stomach turned at the sight of blood covering the rug in the center. Mokosz's servants were in the middle of rolling it up, but that alone had already told the story before I even saw Otylia. She lay with her eyes shut and her hands folded over her chest. The position of a corpse, not how she slept, and Sabina sat by her side, red-faced and crying as she held a bowl in her hands.

I rushed to Otylia so quickly that I tripped, catching myself on the bed's side. She didn't move, and though I'd sensed *something* of her ever since I pulled the eagles' lightning into me, the Thread connecting us didn't seem to draw tight as it did when we were near. If anything, it was far looser than it had been near the island's edge.

Otylia's hand was warm as I clutched it. Gauze covered her head like Kuba, but it wrapped around almost the entirety of the left side of her face. Blood seeped through, and a fire ran through me knowing Jaryło had done this. He'd tried to kill her after putting her through Oblivion in recent moons. I'd make him suffer for it.

"Where is he?" I shouted as I turned back to face Dziewanna. My face burned. My arms trembled. I didn't care how drained I was. I would beat Jaryło with my fists if I had to after what he'd done. "Where is Jaryło?"

That same fire reflected in Dziewanna's gaze. "Gone, likely suffering for breaking the blood pact he forged with Otylia. Perun and Weles's servants had helped him take control of the palace, but then they retreated outside when the gods disappeared."

Ara joined me at the bedside, weeping and holding her cheek to Otylia's chest. "I can't go without you again," she whispered, then gritted her teeth. "Why would he do this? He told her breaking a blood pact was worse than death."

"He's a liar," Sabina said, barely peeking out from her tightly held legs. "Lady Dziewanna, you always called him a schemer like Master Weles. What if the pact was not so serious?"

Dziewanna crossed her arms. "We would not have come all this way if that were the case. Perun and Weles honored their pact not to directly seek to control Jawia for hundreds of years because they feared the consequences. No, he would not have done this on purpose, which means Otylia did."

"I don't understand," I said.

Mokosz stepped into the room behind her daughter, holding her hands behind her back. She appeared unharmed, but any gentleness in her expression was gone. "Otylia was cornered by three of the most powerful gods in the realms," she said. "Jaryło had discovered our plan, so Otylia realized there was little she could do to stop him except to ensure *he* broke the blood pact. From how it appeared when we arrived, she had likely feigned an attack against him, only to dive into the path of his blade when he attempted to parry. A Moonblade does more than wound one's body. It absorbs the target's *żityje*, and Otylia had all but none left when we found her."

She nodded toward Otylia's shimmering silver blood altar in the corner. "It is a mercy she established an altar here, allowing Sabina to help her drink the offerings her worshippers have given. Her recovery will take time. Such a blow would have killed her instantly had Jaryło put more than a parry's effort into it."

"She tricked him into freeing her from the pact..." I cursed, gripping my head. This wasn't how any of it was supposed to go. "Why did I feel her soul outside more than now?"

"The process of a god's death is an odd phenomenon for a mortal—or even a Naw—to consider." She looked from me to Ara and then to Sabina. "It is not a topic I should discuss, but if Dziewanna wishes to speak upon it, she may when I am finished. I will say, however, that Otylia lingers on the edge of life, so her soul remains for now, seeking to replenish her strength from bonds she holds within the Three Realms. This is why you sense her, Wacław."

I touched Otylia's cheek, a pang hitting my chest as I remembered her first death. There couldn't be a second. "Weles took her last time. He said a god could bring another back if they were related by blood." I looked back at the two goddesses. "She's not dead, so one of you could give her *żityje*, right?"

My voice came out pleading, but I was desperate. If they couldn't wake Otylia soon, then what hope did we have? How long would she be gone for?

"I have given her all I can afford to keep her even in this state," Mokosz replied with a bowed head. "As I have told her, my power is dispersed among so many people, so I have little to grant at any time."

Dziewanna remained still, fists clenched by her side and her head tilted away. "I would give anything to wake her, but I lack both the *żityje* and the worshippers to have enough strength to do so. Weles is far more powerful than me."

"How many do you need?" I asked. "A hundred? A thousand? We can appeal to the Krowikie, Vastrothie, Simukie, and Zurgowie alike! Many worshipped Otylia for what she did in Huebia, and they could do the same for you."

"Wacław," Dziewanna replied. "Otylia has started another war, and traveling to Jawia now would only leave her vulnerable. Neither Weles nor Perun will forgive us for maiming their prized heir, and that will only create a greater opportunity for Czarnobóg and Marzanna."

"Then we beat them!"

"It isn't that simple."

"You're a goddess!" I yelled, staggering to my feet until I stood before her. Despite my superior height, I suddenly felt small, but that only made me more furious. "You once warred for the crown of Prawia because you knew Perun shouldn't rule. Why do you cower now when your daughter and all of the Three Realms hang in the balance?"

Dziewanna's eyes narrowed. They were reddened from what I assumed was her own weeping. "You are a heartbroken child! Contain the demon in your soul before I do it for you."

My legs gave way, and I collapsed at her feet, drained and beaten. "Goddess, tell me what to do. I can't lose her."

"Otylia will recover over weeks and moons," she said sharply, "but if we want to wake her quickly, there is only one option."

"What is it?" Ara asked, rising.

"Lipiec. Jaryło still holds this moon's Moonblade, but it has enough *żityje* to bring her back, like Wacław did for his mother."

I took a long breath, thinking through our options. "What if we stick to the plan? We have six Moonblades. You said Jaryło is weak, so we go to Perun and Weles, offering a deal of some sort. Surely, they have to listen to your story of what happened on the equinox, right?" Foolishly, I let myself garner some hope. "Maybe they will let us use Lipiec to wake her once they realize what Jaryło has done."

"Nothing is so simple." Dziewanna sighed, then offered me her hand. "Get up. We'll find you an offering to regain your strength. Then, we go to the only god with enough strength to match my father before this war ends like my last against him."

I rose with her help, but before I could ask what she meant by that, she turned and left. Ara and Sabina looked to me for guidance. I had none. So I said nothing, stepping into the hall with one last glance at Otylia over my shoulder.

We'll bring you back, I promised her through our bond. *Whatever it takes.*

40

Otylia

MY SOUL ROSE THE MOMENT AFTER I BLACKED OUT. I floated like one of End's wisps, staring down at the three shocked gods before me as Jaryło cried out.

Lipiec's red blade seemed to catch fire in his grasp. Black vapors spewed from his hand and crept up his arm. Decay followed in its wake, puss oozing from his skin as it contracted and curled upon itself like leather.

"What… What have you done?" he stammered down at my body.

"I've made you eat your words," I replied, despite him not being able to hear me.

Perun and Weles jumped into action, taking the Moonblade and holding their glowing hands over the expanding wound. But no *żityje* could mend the damage. Jaryło himself had described breaking a blood pact as worse than death, and I reveled in his agony as he dropped to his knees, bloodied, broken, and screaming.

The prince of Jawia had fallen.

Perun lifted him quickly in his arms as Weles grabbed Lipiec. "This changes everything," the thunder god's voice boomed, even at a whisper.

A force struck the pair before Weles could reply. Jagged pieces of stone sliced their skin as Ta rushed into the room with Sabina wielding my moonlight at her side, but that moonlight flickered in her grasp. I had no *żityje* left for her to channel. Their distraction worked enough to keep them from grabbing my body, and by the time Mother arrived with Narcyz and Andrij, the gods were already running for the balcony.

The Threads of Life burst into my vision without my command. Mother knelt next to my body and spoke, but I never heard her words, because the Thread tying me to Wacław tightened suddenly.

One blink I was in the palace. The next, I floated in a thunderstorm beneath one of Prawia's islands, surrounded by Perun's ginormous eagles and Weles's wooden servants climbing on tree-like spires that twisted from Jaryło's island below. Wacław fought among them with Grudzień in one hand and Kwiecień in the other. His gaze seemed distant, lost, and I felt his burning rage until I reached with my wispy form and touched him.

"I'm here," I breathed.

Lightning snapped from the eagle's beaks, but something shifted in him at my touch. His demonic veins shone blue the moment the bolts struck. Then he spun and screamed, slashing away the nearest servants and shooting upward with lightning cracking from his fingers. I sensed the winds battering him with Perun's storm, but he flew on anyway, his renewed determination flooding through our bond.

The gales only grew without Wacław to fight them. They encircled me, pulling me away from Mokosz's island and deeper into their embrace. All of Prawia was light, but at the storm's center was darkness that swallowed me whole.

A figure moved there, or more, dozens of them did.

Small, skittering creatures crept through the clouds as if they were the interwoven branches of a forest, meeting at the shadowed center. They formed legs and a torso, and I staggered back as the dark being I'd met once before took shape before me. Death.

"Do you remember your promise, child?"

He spoke with a viper as his tongue and spiders as his lips. The creatures upon his body crawled constantly, creating an ever-shifting form full of misplaced fangs and claws, but the talons at the ends of his fingers remained unmoving. They stretched as long as my forearm with blood dripping from their ends. I tried to stand strong beneath his gaze. Except he had no eyes, as there were only empty holes.

"I remember," I said, my own misty form barely taking shape.

"Yet you did not expect me to come for it so soon, did you?" Death stepped closer, walking on the storm with ease. "Of course not. One so young never believes their consequences will come due."

I gritted my teeth. "I know what you want."

"Then Rod has foreseen his end." When I gave no reply, he grinned. "He has likely told you that Czarnobóg is soon to arrive, and your trick against Jaryło has only made his path simpler."

"I'll do what I have to do."

He raised his hand to my cheek, and it took all my strength not to move as spiders and snakes I recognized as venomous climbed down my neck and over my torso. I had served Dziewanna for years. Wild animals had never scared me before, but this monster before me was fear itself.

"This is not your pact with Perun's foolish son," he hissed. "Do not believe you can thwart me, child. You will help Czarnobóg end Rod's life, or you will suffer as I take everything you love, torturing them for every agonizing moment of their futile existence." His grip tightened, his fingers tearing through my wispy body. "Do you understand?"

"I told you I'd do it!" I snapped. My voice came out shaky, but he released me anyway.

"Then go. I spare you from a god's finite death so that you bring me another's permanent one."

He vanished with the storm, leaving me drifting in a vast emptiness. The wispy body I'd taken dissolved around me too. I was nothing, yet I still had my mind and my connection to End. Its Threads of Life burst into brilliant colors around me, and I sensed those I loved within them. Wacław's sky blue, Mother's now swirling deep green and vibrant red, Ara's the silver of her arrows and my moonlight, Sabina's the bright colors of spring, and Ta's clear with streaks of every color within. When I willed myself to draw near, I felt each of them in my soul. The pain they felt for my apparent death. Their anger at Jaryło. And the care they had for each other as they endured.

"Take me back to them," I said to the void.

No reply came, so I pulled upon the Thread binding me to Wacław. The one that had always brought us back to each other.

"Take me back!" I shouted again. "I am not dead, and I'll make Jaryło wish he never lived!"

A *pop* struck my ears. I fell back, wisps shifting around me to form my fingers and toes. Slowly, they crept up my limbs, and sensation returned to my body as I dropped endlessly through the darkness. Colors shot past like time had in the Trials of Will and Destiny. Images formed within them, but I fell too quickly to see what happened within. I lost all understanding of time's flow there. I could've fallen for minutes or weeks.

Then the pain struck.

I bit my cheek so hard it bled just to stop myself from screaming. The taste of dried blood had already filled my mouth, but now it grew as I forced open my eyes, only to instantly regret that decision. Prawia's endless light was blinding. Even when I closed my eyes again, bright spots flickered across my eyelids, and a bursting headache joined the ache shooting through my skull.

Maybe it was better to be dead.

"Otylia?" someone said. It sounded distant, but then a warm hand touched my arm. "Otylia, are you awake?"

I could only groan in reply.

"The others are gone," the person replied. Ara… I recognized Ara's voice. Some deep part of me took relief in her being safe, but the rest of me was too busy just holding onto consciousness. "They went to see Simargł, but I wanted to stay with you."

How long has it been? I tried to ask her through my Moonmark, but there was nothing on the other end. How?

She took my hand. "I'm so happy you're alive. Can you hear me?"

My lips refused to move. I tried to squeeze her hand back, but a fresh stab of pain struck my head where Jaryło's blade had hit. It ripped my mind from my body. I tried to hold on. I tried to call out for her through my voice and for Wacław through our bond, but as a warmth washed over me, those thoughts drifted away until it all went blank.

41

Wacław

How much will we regret this?

SIX TENSE DAYS AND NIGHTS PASSED before Mokosz managed to arrange a secret meeting with Simargł. Otylia and Dziewanna had seen his servants clashing with Swaróg's when they climbed the World Tree, but the fire god hadn't shown his face. It wasn't a surprise, given the fact he'd broken free of the gods' imprisonment only a moon before.

I'd waited by Otylia's beside each day, only leaving to help plan or defend against the other gods' servants. Perun and Weles showed no signs of stopping their war to avenge Jaryło, and we had Mokosz to thank for the protection we had.

From what we could tell, Jaryło wasn't dead, but his servants were few and the foliage on his island was slowly withering. If only Otylia could wake and see her victory over the god who'd manipulated her.

She'll wake soon, I told myself as I followed Dziewanna through Mokosz's garden and toward the World Tree.

Only Ara remained in the palace along with Mokosz—who had refused to engage with Simargł besides sending her servants to organize a meeting. We had given Otylia whatever blood that refilled in her altar's bowl each morning. It was little. Despite the worshippers she'd gained, she was still a minor goddess, but I hoped the *żityje* would be enough to replenish her soul while we worked toward taking Lipiec.

I gripped Grudzień and watched the skies as we stepped into Mokosz's gardens, the others doing the same with their Moonblades. Dziewanna led with an arrow nocked. We'd offered her one of the Alatyr shards to mold into her willow wood bow, but she'd refused. There had been an odd look in her eyes—a familiar temptation.

"Maybe they'll give us a break for once," Narcyz said, scanning for Perun's eagles before glancing down at his blade. He'd been in awe of Kwiecień when I'd first taken it from Jaryło moons before, and a smile crossed his face now as he faked a swing. I could only imagine how exciting it was for the son of a smith to wield a god's sword as his own.

"I doubt it," Andrij replied. "If they're staying back, it just means they're planning."

Kuba walked by my side, a hand on the hilt of Maj. He'd returned the Thunderstone dagger to me since he preferred the sword. "They've got to know. Eagles have good vision, right?"

"They do," Vlatka replied from overhead with a flap of her wings. "I would know."

Dziewanna raised a hand to stop us as we reached the end of the gardens. "Best we be silent from here on. My mother has done well to keep most of Perun and Weles's servants at a distance, but the less attention we draw near the World Tree the better."

We left the cover of the gardens, heading across the soft ground that formed the exterior ring of Mokosz's island. Anyone watching would see us now, but it was a risk we had to take. Flying everyone would strain my already limited *żityje* and send us directly into Perun's hands. That wouldn't stop me from intercepting his servants if any of them tried to stop us.

As if the open edges of the island weren't exposed enough, we then had to take the branch to the World Tree. It was round like an actual tree branch and narrow enough to make me uneasy. Ironic because I could fly, but the drop below went on forever. One slip for anyone in the group who didn't have my abilities could put us in a difficult situation.

Otylia had told me about the many servants who she and Dziewanna passed on the way to Rod. The branches had been full of life then, but now we were the only travelers foolish enough to cross the battle lines. The conflict hadn't descended into an all-out war yet. That didn't mean anyone was willing to test Perun's anger by reaching out to Mokosz.

Vlatka swooped down once we were halfway. "The eagles perched up there are watching you."

Sure enough, a pair of giant eagles were perched near the normal-sized birds that often roosted throughout the levels of the World Tree. Neither seemed all that interested in being discreet. They just stared at us as Vlatka returned to scouting, her eagle form tiny in comparison to the servants.

Dziewanna continued on, and when I hesitated, she glared back at me. "Keep moving. We were always going to be spotted, but Perun can't see through their eyes. He'll learn of their discovery soon, though. We need to be deep in the World Tree by then."

So on we went.

Our destination was far down the trunk of the tree where only spirits and minor gods lived according to Mokosz. Few of them were present at any time, and fewer still had the *żityje* to fuel servants, unlike among the major gods. Even those islands would be exposed. Luckily, the trunk itself held hidden rooms that few knew—or cared—about. Simargł would be waiting for us in one of them if all went well.

It felt like an eternity before we finally crossed the branch. I took a long inhale when we arrived, unaware before of how little I'd been breathing. I could handle combat's rush after years of training with Xobas. Waiting for an ambush was another story entirely.

We rushed through the cavernous room inside the World Tree, full of altars that formed a ring around the interior of the trunk. A few of Mokosz's servants carried baskets to them before hurrying away. What had once been Simargł's island lay across the tree at this level, but there were no servants at his altars. How many other islands were uninhabited? And where was Dziewanna's?

There was no time for answers as we headed down a spiraling staircase lined with crystals streaked with every color. Prawia was miraculous in many ways, and even those little details I could have spent so much time admiring. It was a shame war had come to such a beautiful place. Well, it was a shame war had come anywhere, and now it seemed no place, no matter how sacred, was immune.

We descended level after level, my head growing dizzy with all the stairs turning me around. Each had the altars like the one before, but newer layouts appeared the deeper we went. Uncut areas of the trunk formed rooms and halls. The number of branches grew as well, some levels having as many as eight islands connected to it. Only the rare servant—or what looked like servants—occupied these levels. They came in odd shapes and forms, some resembling animals and others having disjointed limbs that looked like something out of my nightmares.

Then Dziewanna stopped at the bottom of yet another set of stairs. The crystals on either side of us appeared duller here, more worn. It was uncomfortably quiet, the only sound beyond our bated breaths was the winds outside, and even they were weak with Strzybóg's absence.

"This is it," Dziewanna whispered. "Stay alert. I trust my mother, but this is still Perun's realm."

She crept down a series of short halls, still clutching her bow and darting her head about like a deer that heard a twig snap. I sensed why soon. A vast amount of *žityje* lay in a room ahead—so much of it that I couldn't identify how many people or gods there were. Based on Dziewanna's cursing, it seemed she did.

"He brought his family," she said. "We agreed—no other gods."

I shrugged. "We're not gods, but you didn't come alone either."

"Point taken." She shouldered her bow and straightened her posture. "No one speaks unless I say so."

Without waiting for a reply, she started toward a wooden wall, then disappeared through it. I exchanged looks with Kuba, but he just shrugged. "You and Otylia are the ones who get the sorcery stuff. I'm just here to die for you guys."

He meant it jokingly, but my heart ached knowing what he'd sacrificed for me. I patted his shoulder. "I'm not going to let that happen again. I promise."

He smiled. "The fern feather doesn't say you're lying, but even you don't know the future."

We joined Dziewanna in the room, stepping through the wall and receiving a tingling across our skin. Kuba giggled at the sensation until he saw what lay beyond.

A burly, bald man with a round face sat upon a throne of ashes, flanked by three women and a man who exuded enough *žityje* themselves to make me want to flee. Simargł wore only trousers and an open vest. Scars covered his exposed chest and massive arms, and the room seemed to burn as he stared at us with reddened eyes.

"Your wildfire is a welcomed sight in Prawia, Dziewanna," he began, stroking his graying beard. "As is the conflict you've brought among my enemies."

Dziewanna smirked. "It has been far too long. So, too, has it been many years since I have seen your children. Kostroma, I'm sure Simargł's escape was your doing." Otylia's vision had shown us the truth, but I doubted Dziewanna wanted to expose the extent of her daughter's powers. Better to act ignorant and see if they tell the truth.

One of the young brunette women to Simargł's right smiled. She was beautiful, wearing a deep-necked indigo dress and a matching flower wreath that wove through her hair, but there was a threat in that smile, devious. "The gods rejected both you and me, but it seems we found our ways without them. Yes, I freed my father and killed Strzybóg for the suffering he put me through. I will do the same to Perun, Swaróg, and your husband when we're finished."

Years of pain filled her voice. Many of the gods had helped trick Kostroma and her twin brother Kupalo, who I assumed was the blond man on the other side of Simargł, into marrying through the tradition of the flower crowns. The pair had then killed themselves when they discovered the truth, turning them into demons. Her anger felt justified.

An odd feeling hit me when I looked from Kostroma to the

hooded woman beside her, the woman's face covered in shadow—familiarity. She held great amounts of *žityje* too, but nowhere near the gods. Had I seen her before?

"Know that we do not seek to kill the rulers of the Three Realms," Dziewanna replied. "But I know their flaws as well as you. Weles is no husband to me, and my father and grandfather would rather have used me for power than have me as their kin."

"No," the middle-aged woman beside Kupalo replied. With her deep black hair and robes broken by her eyes of silvery blue, she resembled darkness itself. Kupalnitsa—goddess of the night. "You seek peace for your precious daughter, as I have for my own children. That can only come when our enemies are tossed from their thrones."

I tensed at that. The god of fiery destruction and goddess of the night ruling the Three Realms hardly sounded better than Perun and Weles.

Dziewanna shook her head. "I cannot give you the Three Realms. What happens in your pursuit of vengeance is not my problem, but I will help you weaken them if you help us capture the final two shards of Alatyr from Jaryło. He is weak, tricked by Otylia into breaking their blood pact."

"I do not need your help," Simargł replied.

"But see, you do." Dziewanna crossed the room to them, her steps echoing. "We have six Alatyr shards, six Moonblades capable of putting Perun in Death's embrace far longer than you could without them. We also have the means of arranging a meeting with your enemies away from their islands. We all know even you cannot siege Perun's palace when he has Swaróg and Weles on his side. They must be divided from this new alliance they've formed."

Simargł huffed. "You've learned well from your father."

"Perun once believed I would amount to something. He was right, but he did not understand my goals."

Kupalo stepped to his father's side. "This is foolish. Perun fears us, especially now with Prawia divided. We should petition him ourselves and negotiate for you to retake your island and for our family to rule Jawia. Such a deal would prevent a war, allowing us to focus on destroying Marzanna."

"He speaks wisely," Kupalnitsa said.

But Simargł stamped his foot. "I have not endured hundreds of years of imprisonment to not have my vengeance. The gods tortured my children and stole everything from our family!"

"Father," Kupalo replied. "You promised you would give them a chance to prove that they've changed. Perhaps this is it."

Kostroma nodded. "At the very least, attempting negotiations would bring us closer to them as Dziewanna said. We attack if they go poorly."

I managed a sigh of relief at the cooler heads around Simargł. The fire god was ready for war, but his family's arguments were sound. Though Perun and Weles were furious with us, they would likely prefer discussions over continuing to waste *żityje* on a war, especially one that could spill over into the other two realms.

"I am outnumbered," Simargł grunted. He pushed himself to his feet, and at full height, he was twice as tall as Dziewanna. If the ceiling hadn't been the World Tree's high dome, he his head would've struck it. "When do we move?"

Dziewanna loosened her posture. "When Otylia wakes. She hasn't recovered enough to channel until we take Lipiec, but we need her for this. Weles and Perun won't accept us speaking for her actions."

"It is done." Simargł held out his hand.

Dziewanna grabbed his forearm as he did the same to her. "Mokosz's servants will arrange the meeting. We were spotted on our way here, but that was some time ago, so hopefully they won't know we met."

"Let them know. They'll just cower for longer."

We turned to leave, but before we could pass through the portal door, the hooded woman called after us, "Wait. I... I need to talk to Wacław."

I know that voice.

I bit my cheek when she pulled down her hood. "Vida?" Otylia had mentioned the appearance of the Frostmarked szeptucha we'd known as Minna in her vision of Simargł's escape. How had she come back to life *again* after Otylia revealed her true past to her? And what was she doing here?

The Frostmark once sliced over her left eye was gone, replaced by a symbol resembling a flower. She'd lost her cutting frown too, and she actually smiled as she crossed the room to me. "Could you tell Otylia that I wanted to thank her for helping me regain my memories? I would still be trapped under Marzanna's control if she hadn't shown me mercy."

"I… I will, but how are you alive? There were rumors you had died before, but it was hard to know what was true about the Daughters' stories."

She winced. "I'm not sure. Kostroma thinks Marzanna let me die during the szeptucha initiation ritual, then brought me back as some kind of mix between a demon and szeptucha."

"It is not surprising she would resort to such measures," Dziewanna replied. "Many kingdoms and tribes were exiling or killing her szeptuchy, so apparently this was her solution."

"Vida has told me about the two of you," Kostroma said to me, joining us in the center of the room. She held a regal confidence about her, but it was different than the other goddesses, her voice sounding more mortal than godly. "Krowik was her home too, and it will fall if you don't stop the Horde. Solga will too."

I raised my brow. "What does Solga have to do with this? They're at war with us."

She chuckled, her girlish smile again revealing the time she'd spent with mortals instead of the gods. "Rolika is a long way from Dwie Rzeki, but I am sure you have heard of The Lady?"

"I haven't, but I flew over Rolika once. It's unlike any other city I've seen." I remembered the buildings on wooden risers over the floodplains below, smoke columns drifting above as people in fine white clothes scoffed at slaves who hauled stone toward a massive wall.

"Well, then." She lifted her chin. "I am The Lady of Rolika, queen of Solga. Now that our peoples' petty border dispute is finished, I will send my armies to the aid of Krowik and your allies against the Horde. It's better we work together against the Horde than separately."

My chest tightened. "You're the one that enslaved all those people?"

"Prisoners of war, yes." She looked back to Simargł. "My father taught me that war is an ugly game in which you must use every piece you can to survive. When Solga expanded, we captured our enemies' men. Would you have preferred me to behead them when I could instead use them to ensure Rolika had a wall strong enough to hold back the Horde?"

"Why build a wall and then help us outside of it?" Andrij asked from behind me. It would take some time for me to get used to him being a szeptun, his eyes remaining hazy from the battle but his clothes mirroring Dziewanna's greens, browns, and reds.

"I will leave a garrison in Rolika," Kostroma replied. "Should the rest of Jawia fall, my family will use it as our bastion to recover before pushing back against the Frostmarked."

I crossed my arms. "So you don't actually care about Krowik or Jawia at all."

"I care about my family and my people." She stepped closer, meeting the intensity of my glare. "My responsibility is to them. I will do what I can to help you, but it is good war strategy to have a fallback. Do you?"

She turned away before I could reply. I considered calling after her, but Dziewanna tugged on my sleeve. "Come. We've done what we sought to do."

As we made our way back up the tower, there was a tug on my soul. Gentle at first, followed by shooting pain in my head. I dropped to a knee in the middle of a staircase with my head in my hands. It was the same pain I'd felt a week before when Otylia had tricked Jaryło, and though it faded until my connection with her was barely present, I took heart that its reappearance could only mean one thing.

Otylia was waking. She'd be all right, and once we got Lipiec to heal her, we could finally leave Prawia's problems behind.

42

Otylia

What is reality, and what is a dream?

MY WAKING MOMENTS MERGED with my unconscious ones. End's wisps carried voices and visions in each, forcing me to question whether my thoughts were even mine. The world seemed to spin through it all. Whether lying on my bed or falling through time's flow, pain and nausea endured.

"You can never kill the Deathless Sons."

Czarnobóg's deep, ominous voice followed me no matter how hard I tried to flee. I leaped into wisps at will to experience any story that wasn't mine. Death filled many as war swept across the living realm. Horrors from the past, present, and future met, crying for me to stop it. But I couldn't. Each vision pulled me deeper into the destruction of Koschei's Horde, and each brought me further into despair.

"Jaryło is crippled, but we grow stronger with each defeat. While you cling to the light, we thrive in the darkness, learning the truths that hide in the shadows."

"Shut up!" I screamed into the void, throwing my arms out. No moonlight answered. I was lost and powerless. My Threads of Life anchored me to reality, but even they lacked strength here.

A dull wisp drifted by. I reached for it but had nothing to push off. Still, I stretched further, desperately grasping at my only escape from the dark dragon's haunting. The wisp spun around to dance around my fingers, as if it were a child's game. But this was no game, and my patience was up.

"Stay still!" I commanded it. My voice echoed, carrying over and over until my throbbing headache dug deeper into my skull.

The wisp slowed. It twisted around my middle finger with only the slightest tickle across my skin before plunging into my palm.

I fell into the vision, the dark void surrendering to morning light that spewed through a cracked window. Three people filled a one-room house the size of Wacław and Lubena's. A small fire burned in the stove, but the cold seeped through the window and every crack in the house.

"I need air!" the woman lying on the bed shouted. Sweat dripped from her brow as she held a baby in her arms.

The younger of the two men rushed to the window and pushed the shutters open further. "We let much more of this in and we'll freeze the babe."

"Not much air to be had," the older man replied. "Strzybóg's winds haven't blown since the solstice."

"I don't care about the gods right now," the woman said, finally calming as she planted a kiss on the child's forehead. "The Great Mother has given me a daughter, and that's all I ever needed from them."

What ending is this? I silently asked my force to no reply. Of course not. If End could speak, it certainly had no intention of doing so with me.

I remembered Rod's explanation of my power during my Ascension. Everything was a cycle. Even at the beginning, there was another end. What was this child's birth then? The end of a pregnancy, a time of the woman's life, or something else?

The baby cooed as I drew closer to see if there was anything special about her. She had a normal amount of *žityje* for a mortal and wasn't particularly beautiful or ugly—not that any newborn looked much better than a wet piglet. So End had decided I needed to see a normal baby in a normal house during an incredibly not normal summer. Why?

Then the baby's gaze met mine, and something clicked. Maybe this was a reminder that life was a cycle too. Mortal souls traveled to Nawia when they died, only to return when they chose to.

What did that mean for Rod?

"You can never kill the Deathless Sons."

I didn't know whether it was actually Czarnobóg's voice this time or just an echo of it, but a shiver ran down my spine. Who were the Deathless Sons he was talking about? Rod had referenced Death—maybe Czarnobóg through him—as well as Jaryło and Wacław. Were there others who'd returned from death? Koschei? Simargł? And why had he mentioned them in line with *the* end? End gave no answers.

As the vision faded, I whispered a blessing for the little girl. It would likely have no effect since I was without *żitye*, but it felt right. I was a goddess. Wasn't blessing children and stopping bad ends my responsibility?

Reality's pain struck away any further thoughts. I'd once considered warriors' complaints unjust when they talked about wounds from battles long ago as Mother and I covered their cuts with poultices. I took it all back as I returned to my body, lying useless in bed. More voices surrounded me this time: Ara, along with Mother, Wacław, Sabina, and Ta. I hated it. My friends looked to me to lead them like a goddess should, but instead I'd thrown myself into Jaryło's blade to free myself from a pact. I'd threatened our timeline in Prawia so that I could be free. Jawia would suffer if we were too slow because of it.

And that taste of blood… It had filled my mouth long enough for me to think it normal. I knew Wacław, Ara, and Sabina had been feeding me my worshipper's sacrifices from the altar, but I wanted to plead for it to stop. Taste had never been a motivator for me. Now, though, I could only think about the sharp flavor of the oranges Sabina had given me in Nawia.

I focused on that thought, trying to remember the oranges' smell.

Strong, it reminded me of a strong storm in summer and the times I would run with Wacław through the puddles in the forest outside the village walls, free. Ironic that I'd only eaten them in prison.

"Otylia? Otylia, are you there?"

Wacław's voice was gentle through our bond. It soothed enough of the pain for me to regain my wits, but my thoughts threatened to drift away with every moment that passed. An old vision from my Ascension flashed before me. Wacław stood amid a whirlwind, destruction and death surrounding him. Even Kwiecień's light weakened in the shadows until I fought through the gales to him. My light pierced the darkness but couldn't defeat it, and our touch only strengthened the storm. Then a force burst between us. Stronger than even Perun's thunder, it tore me from the vision, returning me to the void.

I can't wake up, I told Wacław, the weight of the vision sapping my will. *The pain's too much.*

Liquid trickled through my lips. I fought back against the blood, refusing to swallow. They were only trying to help, but I didn't want it. I wanted to be free of this torture. My body defied my commands, and the blood's *żityje* seeped into my soul. Not enough. Lipiec's strike had damaged my body and soul enough that it had taken my pact with Death to keep me alive. It would take far more worshippers than I had to return me to full strength.

"We have a way to Lipiec and its żityje," Wacław said. There was a flicker of feeling across my hand, and I assumed he was holding it. No matter how hard I tried, I couldn't squeeze back. *"Simargł and his family are going to help us, but we need you awake first."*

I can't.

"You can. It's been over a week, Dziewanna says you never truly died. You have enough żityje to wake, but not channel or heal your wounds." He paused, and I felt his regret. *"I'm sorry. I shouldn't push you."*

Was he right? Could I wake up if I chose to? I hesitated to try. It would mean waking to pain, trial, and likely a war that I'd started by tricking Jaryło. Staying asleep was cowardice, but Czarnobóg's whispers awaited me in the depths of my mind. What did I fear more?

No, fear was the wrong focus. I'd let myself loathe everyone around me because of it for almost five years. Friends surrounded me now, waiting for my help. They cared about me, and I cared about them. I loved them. Some part of me tensed at that admission, but it was more than the romantic love I felt for Wacław. These people were my family. I couldn't leave them.

I took a long breath in my dreamscape, then pushed myself awake with every bit of strength I could muster. The pain was instant, and I lacked the energy to even curl into a ball. But beyond the darkness of my eyelids was reality. It stayed this time as a sea of voices called my name.

"She's awake!" Ara cried out in relief. Her footsteps departed, and I heard her shouting down the hall before she hurried back. My headache drummed louder with every word.

"She'll fall back asleep if you deafen her," Sabina replied softly. "Best we be quiet."

My breaths turned shallow as I clung to Wacław's hand, warm in mine. His palms were calloused from years of working the fields, but they were softer than the embrace of the finest blankets Mokosz could offer.

Slowly, I opened my eyes. Light burst into them, forcing me to squint as Mother sat beside Wacław with a smile across her face. "Welcome back, my *mała dzikq*. We missed you."

An unwelcome tear slipped down my cheek. I'd missed her for years, and despite the struggles we'd faced since rescuing her, seeing her meant everything to me. Even after the horrors I'd seen in my last vision before Jaryło's attack.

"Where's Jaryło?" I managed to say, my voice raspy and my throat dry.

"Suffering because of you," she replied. "Your deception worked, but we have to clean up the mess it has created."

Wacław sniffled and forced a smile. "You broke the pact, and that's what matters. Once we have Lipiec, we can heal you and go back to Jawia. We'll finally be able to stop the Horde. Otylka, you're free."

I shuddered at the memory of Death's creatures crawling over me. "Not yet."

"Yeah, I'd say killing the world's creator is pretty big too," Ta said as she hopped onto the end of the bed, shifting the entire thing. "I mean, that's gonna cause problems, right?"

Insightful as always.

"It will," Mother said, "but that is a problem we will face *after* we get Lipiec. I will have my mother send word to Simargł that Otylia is awake. It will take a day or so for them to arrange a meeting with Weles and Perun."

"Meeting?" I asked with a cough. Wacław hopped to his feet at that, returning moments later with a clay cup full of water that I drank greedily.

"We'll fight if we have to," he said. "There's enough death with Marzanna's war, though, so we're hoping to convince them that giving us the last Moonstones and letting Simargł's family rule Jawia is better than another war among the gods. We don't know what state Jaryło's in, but I doubt he'd be strong enough to claim Jawia now."

I tried to sit up, only to sink back at the rush of pain. "I saw him after Lipiec drained me. Whatever the blood pact did to him was terrible. He looked like he was being eaten alive by some force."

"Yet you smile," Mother replied.

Was I? I took another sip of water, my throat finally starting to feel normal again. "It's hard to smile when I feel like what he looked like."

"Then take the day to rest some more. Your friends have some work to do in the meantime fending off servants and szeptuchy they send our way. They seem to have realized we are planning something, since their attacks have grown since we ventured into the World Tree to meet Simargł."

Wacław patted Grudzień on his back. "We'll make sure it's safe for when you have to leave. Not that you need your powers to make someone flee."

Then he kissed me softly and left with the rest of them. I watched each of my closest friends go before my gaze fell on that sword.

Grudzień, the black blade of the twelfth moon, streaked with lines of color—not the gold Moonblade of Kwiecień that he'd wielded in my vision of our end. Had our destiny changed? And if it had, could I prevent the destruction I'd seen?

I clung to that hope as my energy waned. Destiny had woven her story. The Sudiczki had told our fates. But I was the goddess of endings, and I would have the final say.

Part 4
Darkness Ascends

43

Wacław

The top of the Three Realms. How many have ever stepped foot here?

THE SKY STRETCHED INFINITELY IN EVERY DIRECTION as we reached the highest level of the World Tree. Everything here was made of gray stone marked with white and black, but no matter how colorless the land, it couldn't change the majesty of Prawia. From the islands branching from its trunk below to the birds and servants flying through the gods' skies, it was unlike anywhere else in the Three Realms.

Narcyz huffed by my side as I stood at the edge, my toes hanging over. "How can you stare at the sky when we're literally about to face the most powerful gods?"

"I'm reminding myself what's still beautiful when all I've known has gone to Oblivion," I replied with a sigh. Even the air was different here, pure and still, as if waiting for our breaths to stir it. I wondered if it was different when Strzybóg wasn't dead, forced to recover after Kostroma's vengeance finally found him.

He crossed his arms. "Yeah, fine. I get it. Ever since that charger nearly killed me in that first skirmish with the Horde, I've been thinking a lot too."

"Whoa," Kuba quipped, leaning over the edge and staring down with a whistle. "Now we know the world's really ending."

Narcyz put a hand on Kuba's back. "One push."

Kuba snatched Narcyz's pantleg and smirked. "And we both hit Jawia at full speed."

"Are you really that dumb?" Ara called over, arms crossed and hip out. "I'm sure everyone left alive would love to watch you idiots tumble to Jawia, but we're kind of doing something important."

"Have you met a boy with a brain?" Ta replied.

"Hey!" Kuba furrowed his brow, then proceeded to stumble back into Narcyz, the two of them falling in a heap. "Okay, point taken."

"And we're the group Jawia's relying on to stop the Horde," Otylia muttered from beside Dziewanna. "If you're going to fight, can you at least not dangle over the edge with an *Alatyr shard?*"

I laughed and joined her. Her head wound remained, mostly covered by a white and silver kokoshnik crown she wore, but sarcasm was a good sign she was feeling better. It had been another two days since she'd woken enough to speak. Each day was an improvement. Even though she needed my help to climb the steps, it was remarkable that she'd managed to go from Death's door to this in just over a week. *Żityje* was an amazing thing.

Jaryło had been in even worse condition than her after I'd sent my Thunderstone dagger through his heart. He'd been crippled in Nawia until Maj's moon arrive, allowing him to use its Moonblade to recover. How long would it have taken him to return otherwise? Other gods like the northwest wind Kyustendil and now Strzybóg had died in the last moons, and we'd seen no sign of them since.

"Are you ready for this?" I asked Otylia, taking her hand.

"No."

My heart ached, and I lacked any more words of comfort than I'd given in recent days. What could I say to her after all she'd suffered and what she would soon have to do to answer for Death's oath—a pact she swore to save my life?

"Where are the rest of the gods?" she asked her mother.

Dziewanna tapped her fingers against her bow. "They'll be here soon. I wanted us to arrive first, since your group is unfamiliar with the World Tree and obviously needed the time to get used to its oddities." She raised her gaze to the sky. "Apparently, my father decided to be early as well."

Perun appeared amid storm clouds, giant eagles, and eight shirtless men with feathered wings, each wielding a different object: a massive ax, a golden apple, a bolt of lightning, a bow nocked with a thunderstone arrow, a fist sized acorn, a shield bearing his Thundermark, a small statue of a mountain, and a balancing scale that swayed back and forth before falling still. A winged nymph flanked him with the Lipiec in her grasp. We'd come to speak. The thunder god had brought an army.

Our friends formed ranks to separate Perun from Otylia, spurring a laugh from the god.

"You act as if she is the one who needs protection, but it is she who has laid ruin to my son through her treachery." He raised his arms at his sides. "I am the god of justice. We need not make war if you give what is rightly due."

"The only treachery is Jaryło's," Dziewanna replied. "*He* helped Marzanna bring about Czarnobóg's return. *He* is the reason for Marzanna's rage. You're just too blind to realize your favored son has fallen to corruption in his pursuit of power." She looked at Ara. "Show him your Springmark."

Ara stepped forward, pushing back her hair to reveal Jaryło's mark with its blackened veins reaching across her neck. "I'm Otylia's szeptucha, but he kidnapped me and covered her mark with his."

"End showed me the truth when Jaryło forced me into his blood pact," Otylia added. She stepped through the group to glare directly at her foe, her fury burning through our bond. "He needed Czarnobóg and Marzanna to threaten all of Jawia. It was the only way for you and Weles to unite behind him as king of Jawia."

A cane thumped against the stone. The rapid beating of wings followed, and Weles emerged from the stairs with nymphs, serpents, and wooden servants filling the space behind us. "You speak of visions only you have seen," Weles said. "What proof have you of such deception?"

"What else could have opened the veil between Oblivion and the Three Realms?" Dziewanna replied. Flames curled down her dress's sleeves to her skirts, still in the windless air as she nocked an arrow.

"The shards of Alatyr united to free the dark dragon. That did not happen by accident."

"Give me Lipiec and I'll show you," Otylia said. "My force should allow me to show you the vision from my mother's memories. He admitted the truth to her before leaving her to die in Marzanna's palace."

Weles hummed and stroked his deep brown beard. "You speak sense."

"Weles, you are hardly impartial," Perun replied. "Your wife and daughter threaten *my* son."

"Yet he calls me 'Father.' "

They aren't as united as we thought, I told Otylia silently. *We could use that.*

The lords of Prawia and Nawia had been bitter rivals for hundreds, if not thousands, of years. It wasn't surprising that Jaryło—who didn't even favor his blood father—could only unite the two when all was going well for them. With him down, what kept their fragile alliance together at all?

Weles shuffled toward Otylia, leaning heavily on his cane as his bear pelt hung over his chest. His frail form was just another trick. I'd seen his power firsthand, and I would not underestimate him again.

"I advocated for this marriage from the beginning," he said far more quietly than his counterpart. "Jaryło brought Otylia to me as an insolent child who knew nothing of the Three Realms beyond her worship of Dziewanna. Recent moons have changed much in her, however, and I cannot say her accusations surprise me, given Jaryło's pridefulness."

Thunder rolled, dark clouds swirling through the otherwise clear sky as Perun bared his teeth. "My son suffers, yet you insult he who has been wronged! Nothing can mend him. I demand reparations!"

"You demand reparations?" a rough voice replied as another group appeared on the far edge of the World Tree. Simargł led his family with flames swirling at his feet and smoke billowing from his mouth. He was a giant, and his fiery wings stretched five strides in either direction. "Look what forest your lightning has burned before you insult the girl's embers."

"YOU!" Perun tore the Thunderstone ax from his closest follower. Lightning snapped up its handle before arcing across its head. "You dare to enter my domain after killing Strzybóg and the Zorza sisters? I will sever your head from your body and place them as far across the Three Realms as possible."

So much for avoiding war.

"My father did not slay them," Kostroma said, her river blue dress and kokoshnik contrasting heavily with Simargł. "I killed Strzybóg for throwing my wreath from my head with *your* storms. Wieczorna and Poranna were not our targets, but they refused to release Father." She looked from Perun to Weles. "Both of you wronged my brother and me, stealing him away to Nawia and then manipulating us into marriage upon his return. I have despised you for centuries, but enough war rages across the Three Realms already."

Golden Kupalo stepped to her side. "Each of you has caused more destruction than you wish to remember. Perun and Weles, your wars have laid Jawia to ruin more than once. Dziewanna's revolution turned the living realm feral. And it is well known that my father loosed his flames upon each of the Three Realms after the gods of Prawia betrayed us." He surveyed the gods, hands held behind his back, but he bowed his head despite his accusations. "What wrongs have been done in the past must be addressed, but the alliance of Marzanna and Czarnobóg threatens all of us."

"I will not trust those who only speak lies," Perun growled.

"Then let's find a middle ground," I replied, joining Otylia at the front of our group. "We don't need to be allies, but if we wage war among ourselves, Czarnobóg wins."

Weles stamped his cane. "I have lost enough fighting many of you. It tires me." He extended a hand toward Perun. "You call Jaryło your son. If you care about him and the realm he seeks to rule, then is an agreement not for the best?"

The gods stared each other down for a long time until the World Tree shook beneath us. It swayed to and fro, forcing me to catch

Otylia as she stumbled. Three figures emerged from Rod's island in the distance, and though it tilted, they walked across the angled surface with ease.

"What is this?" Perun demanded of the other gods. "Simargł, what have you done?"

The fire god shook his head, calling flames to his fists. "This is not my doing."

"Nor mine," Weles said.

We all looked to the figures approaching from Rod's island. Two elderly men led a beautiful woman, the first draped with gray robes trimmed in red and the second cloaked in scarlet, a long war hammer hung over his shoulder. The woman was pure light. She wore flowers over the headscarf of a married woman as Prawia's glow radiated down her dress of white and gold.

"What is Rod doing?" Otylia said in my head. *"I thought he stays out of the gods' wars?"*

Who's with him?

She glanced at Dziewanna, then silent Mokosz. *"Probably the only major gods not Frostmarked, dead, or already here: Swaróg and Łada."*

As the three approached, Swaróg's Forgemark became apparent on the end of his hammer. The former king of Prawia was patron of smiths and the god of celestial fire. Dariusz's stories claimed he'd surrendered most of his roles to his favored children, Perun and Dadźbóg, but everyone present bowed their heads at the sight of him and the creator god. I did so too, in part because those same stories claimed his wife Łada could hold a man's gaze until he died.

"The dark dragon has come," Swaróg announced when he reached the branch's end. He swung his hammer and set its end upon the World Tree, then looked at Simargł. "You killed my granddaughters who opened and closed the evening gates. Marzanna seduced Dadźbóg while he remained trapped in Nawia, and he has opened Czarnobóg a way into our realm."

Just as we'd expected when the sun never reappeared after the solstice. Without the Zorza sisters who both guarded Simargł and opened Dadźbóg's path, there had been no way for the sun god to leave the underworld and Marzanna's whispers within it. Now, she possessed a god with an island in Prawia.

"The Deathless Sons will rise," Rod said, his voice barely more than a whisper as he looked straight at Otylia. "I warned you this would come." He extended his arms and closed his eyes. "The fall of Prawia has come if you all cannot unite against the foes you face."

"You would have me fight beside the destroyer and the deceiver?" Perun asked. Despite his resistance, he signaled to his servants, and many dove toward the World Tree's base. Weles did the same, his nymphs and servants descending the trunk instead. Simargł did not move.

The World Tree shook again, and Otylia gripped onto me as the gods shouted among themselves. "We have to do something before they tear each other apart," she said quietly.

"Or before Czarnobóg does it for them," I replied. "Rod is the god of balance, right? He has to have some idea how to fix this."

She grinned up at me. "I knew I fell in love with you for a reason." Then she pushed her way toward Rod with my help, speaking as loudly as she could. "You created the Three Realms. Who should rule them? How do we stop another war before it starts?"

Rod smiled at her, folding his arms as the others fell silent in respect. "You ask how to prevent wars that began ages ago. There is only a single way: balance."

"Mend the blood pact, Otylia," Mokosz said insistently.

"I'd fix Jaryło if there was a way," Otylia replied.

"That is a beginning," Rod said with a nod. "To mend a severed blood pact, you need only touch him and say that you free him from it."

She looked at Perun. "Then I'll do it. Give us Lipiec and I'll heal him. Guilty or not, we can punish him once we've beaten Czarnobóg."

The thunder god shook his head. "You ask for too much."

"Then Jaryło will suffer for eternity!" she snapped back. "And you will lose your precious realm. We both know the servants you sent will only delay Czarnobóg."

Dziewanna joined us, her voice losing its usual aggression. "This will take compromise, Father. I know it is not your strength, but we need the Alatyr shards. We ask nothing else, and it won't matter what deal we reach if Jaryło is not healed. Neither you nor Weles can break your own pact and take Jawia for yourselves."

"Accept," Weles said to Perun, "and I will renounce any claim to Jaryło. My wife's testimony rings true to my ears. I need no son who would break the veil for his own power. All I ask is you accept that the golden cattle belong to me."

"And what of you, lord of fire?" Rod asked of Simargł. "What do you demand?"

A roar echoed over Prawia, and the World Tree twisted, cracks running through its trunk. "Hurry!" Otylia shouted. "We don't have time for this."

"Each member of my family will have their palace restored in Prawia," Simargł replied, "and when the battle is done, I will fire whip a thousand times the back of every god who betrayed my children. In return, we will defend Prawia against the dark dragon, and I will renounce any claim to rule over the realm of the gods. For now."

Kuba winced nearby. "A thousand times," he said at his version of a whisper, which wasn't quiet at all. "That's a lot."

"It is the least they deserve for what agony they have inflicted upon Kostroma and Kupalo," Simargł replied. Kuba blushed and turned away, mumbling at himself to shut up.

"The demands have been made," Rod said. "To my ears, there is balance in them, as all have found compromise between their desires and those of others. Do any oppose these asks?"

"You take from me and dare call it justice?" Perun replied with a stomp that sent the World Tree shaking again.

Simargł flared his fires. "We could help Czarnobóg kill you instead, then take your place when he turns his attention elsewhere."

Perun scowled and turned to Weles. "Free me from our blood pact and I will accept. I cannot allow Simargł to roam Jawia freely while I am forced not to intervene."

"You risk another decimation," Weles said. "I am willing if it is necessary, but I will not tolerate you suffocating mortals beneath your rule again."

"It is a risk I must take."

"Then so be it."

Rod clapped his hands at that, and the World Tree shifted around us, the whites and black twirling within the gray as wisps surrounded each god, Naw, nymph, mortal and servant alike. "A new agreement is forged among the gods," he announced. "Let Destiny hear your words and write them upon your souls."

The wisps dissolved as quickly as they'd come. Rod walked to the center of the trunk, then knelt to place his hand upon the ground, which bore his Wheelmark. "Go and defend the realm. One Deathless Son has fallen. So must another."

Perun motioned to the nymph holding Lipiec. She brought it forward, then knelt, holding the blade flat in her hands for Otylia to take. "Do not betray me, granddaughter," Perun said. "I have tolerated much, but this is your final chance."

Then he launched off the World Tree with the rest of his allies in tow. The nymph followed once Otylia took the deep red Moonblade by the handle, setting the point of the blade down onto the stone below. I felt her strain from its weight, but I also sensed the bountiful *żityje* filling the Moonblade—an Alatyr shard ready to be channeled during its moon.

She took a long breath, then chanted in the old tongue as the markings upon Lipiec began to glow white. Energy burst through our bond. Pure, it forced me back as Otylia's skin pulsed with moonlight. The silver streak in her hair emanated a wisp, and she began to float, her eyes flashing white and the brilliant colors of the Threads of Life appeared around us. Only visible to her and those of us who bore her Moonmark, they connected all of us. Her green one was blinding.

Otylia's gaze fell upon me, and she landed with a familiar smirk. One that said she was ready to fight even Czarnobóg himself.

She took my free hand, squeezing it tight as I drew Grudzień. "Come, Wašek, and let's go slay a dragon."

44

Otylia

What does it mean to defy Death?

DEATH'S OMEN HAUNTED ME AS I LEAPED from the World Tree's trunk. The sky below was a sea of burgeoning darkness split by fire, lightning, and sunlight. Not Prawia's light but the familiar glow of the sun that had been absent from Jawia for a moon since the solstice. A battle of the gods, and for once, I felt small.

I transformed Lipiec into the tip of my silver spear, which I gripped tightly with my friends falling beside me. The Moonstone's *żityje* had mended my wounds in seconds, and more of its energy still remained. This was why Jaryło had fought so hard to hold the shards of Alatyr. Of all the power I'd felt in the Three Realms, nothing could compare to the immense reserve now available to me. I just hoped it was enough to defeat Czarnobóg.

"What's the plan?" Wacław asked through our bond. He held only himself with the weakened winds, my moon powers able to control the others' falls. *"Do we let Czarnobóg get to Rod to appease Death?"*

Czarnobóg's voice and Death's threats echoed in my mind. Even Rod had accepted his demise, but as I grew closer to the darkness below, the fear faded. We'd rescued Mother. We'd outsmarted Jaryło. We'd united three rival gods to defend Prawia. We'd taken control of eight Alatyr shards. Why couldn't we beat Death too?

"Kill Czarnobóg!" I shouted to all who could hear. "And when Death comes for us, we'll kill him too."

Both cheers and worried glances met me in reply, but there was no time for more conversation. We descended into storm clouds and darkness, pushed back only by my moonlight and the cracking of Wacław's lightning. The demons soon followed.

Chały shrieks filled the air, their female forms shooting toward us on shadowy wings and bolts of lightning. I hoped they hadn't learned their lesson about Wacław. Near me, he could absorb their blasts, but that didn't make their claws any less deadly against anyone who was unprepared.

"Go!" Ara shouted at me, wielding Październik's gray Moonblade awkwardly as she sparred with another chała. Unlike a goddess, she couldn't morph it into a bow that she'd be more used to. Her Moonmark already pulsed brightly upon her neck now that I'd returned, though, and she fought with a warrior's determination. "Find Czarnobóg. We'll handle the demons."

There was no time to worry about her, as chały struck at me with their strzygi and nymph-like wiły cousins close behind. I sent my spear through the first attacker and dissolved her into mist. "Make sure no one's fighting alone."

Sabina appeared at her side, releasing a moonblast before sending Czerwiec through a wiła's throat. She was no better with a blade than me, but at least she and Ara could channel my power to protect each other and keep our friends aloft.

"I promise I won't leave her," Sabina said with a smile far too cheerful for the disaster around her.

Wacław repeated my command to the others but never stopped guarding my back. Grudzień spun and slashed in his grasp as if it were a practiced dance, deflecting chały's claws before cutting them apart with the blade's jagged edge. Lightning arced between the fingers of his off hand. I felt his soul though, and for now, the demon was quiet. Now that our shared marks were emblazoned on each of our forearms, I could give him *žityje* like a szeptucha to keep it that way.

Further down, a roar revealed Czarnobóg. The World Tree continued to rock, pulled by the dragon's force as he clashed with the other gods. A thunderbolt illuminated one of his three heads near the level holding Mokosz's island. He'd risen quickly, and there would be no stopping him from reaching Rod if he got farther.

We dropped toward the rest of the gods with Mother, and I had to fight a new wave of fear as Czarnobóg's full form came into sight. *What have we gotten ourselves into?*

When I'd faced him in the Trial of Death, he'd been massive. He had grown since, his dragon torso and wings covering the entire distance separating Jaryło's island from Mokosz's. His three maws were each the size of the Dwie Rzeki longhouse, and the flames billowing from them could have burned half of Huebia in a single fireball. Everywhere he flew, heavy shadows fell. Spirits took form from them and clawed at anyone who came near. Demons followed close behind.

"Surrender your realm and be spared," the dark dragon roared as he slammed into the World Tree. Pieces splintered off and cascaded below, over a quarter of the trunk's width broken. "A new age has begun."

Perun released a war cry in response, signaling for his allies to charge as he launched a golden apple toward the beast. Weles, Simargł, and many other gods and spirits surrounded Czarnobóg, but the dragon laughed and unleashed his flames upon them until the golden apple struck.

A deafening *BOOM* rocked the World Tree as lightning scattered over Czarnobóg's hide. The blast spread like a wave that threw us back a hundred strides. I gripped Wacław's hand, never letting go as another roar echoed through the gods' realm. Dark blood seeped from between the dragon's scales near its front right leg. That golden apple would've torn any demon and many gods to pieces, but Czarnobóg was unfazed as light split through the shadows below him.

Three horses emerged with the light. Gold, silver, and diamond, they pushed through the sky with a chariot behind. A man stood in the chariot with bright light radiating from his skin. White wolf furs hung over his robes of bright oranges and blues, and he glared up at the gods with a single golden eye, the other covered with scarred slashes.

"Dadźbóg!" Swaróg called out from the World Tree above, his hammer raised. "My son, what is this foolishness? I heard rumors of your infatuations with Marzanna, but I dared not believe them until now."

Czarnobóg didn't wait for his ally's reply. He leaped up the tree with a single flap of his wings and slashed at Swaróg, forcing him to retreat. Only Mother's foray of arrows drove the dragon back, but now he fixed his gaze upon her.

"They need us," Wacław said, pointing toward the spirits below. Dadźbóg and his blindingly white wolves were tearing through the minor gods and spirits with demons in his wake. Kostroma and Kupalo worked in tandem to cover our allies, but they were falling back, even with Simargł's aid. "If we stop him, we can get everyone focused on Czarnobóg."

"No," I replied. "Mother's fighting Czarnobóg! I can't leave her."

He looked toward the others with regret before nodding. "Let's go."

We charged into the fray again, striking and dodging as demons surrounded us. How did Marzanna have so many? I feared what the answer would be, so I turned my focus to reaching Mother. I hadn't fought across Nawia and Jawia just to lose her when I was finally free from Jaryło's pact.

Wacław covered my back as I pushed ahead. I was being reckless—I knew it—but *żityje* would heal me if a demon got a lucky strike. Mother would fall to Czarnobóg without my help. She was leaping from branches to the World Tree and back, shooting a dozen flaming arrows in a blink before Czarnobóg crashed into where she'd been moments before. Most gods from what I'd seen could fly in some way, but without a specific force connected to flight, she relied on different sized jumps that forced Czarnobóg to switch directions faster than his giant body allowed. He grew more annoyed with each leap, and with a roar, rolling black vapors spewed from one of his mouths as another released a stream of flames. They rushed toward Mother from both sides.

Until wings sprouted from her back.

She shot away faster than the attacks could come. Her wings resembled a falcon's with speckled brown on the back and streaks of white on the front, and she had the speed of one too. I rushed to try to take her side, but even my moon-powered pull couldn't keep up.

"Remember Ira!" she called over her shoulder as she loosed another set of arrows. "No matter how many heads, a żmij is a żmij."

I moonblasted away the vapors that drew near me and then studied our foe. Heavy scales covered even his underbelly, unlike Ira, but despite the wound upon his right shoulder slowly healing, it still bled. "Got it," I replied before circling the opposite direction to her.

Wacław was at my side moments later, launching balls of lightning at Czarnobóg's wings but doing no visible damage. "Beating Ira meant me sticking my arm in his mouth. Do we have to do that again?"

"She means look for the weakness," I replied, sending moonblasts as Czarnobóg swung about to keep one head focused on Mother and the others upon Perun and Weles above. "Look where Perun's apple hit on the shoulder."

He nodded. "Stick together?"

"Always."

We dove toward the dragon's back. His jagged tail swept toward us as we finally caught his attention, but I swung Lipiec as a spear, cutting through his scales and drawing more blood. The wound was far too small to take advantage of on a moving target, and scales reformed over it as Czarnobóg roared in displeasure. Still, I took heart in hurting him, if only a little.

"Stab the shoulder itself," Wacław said as we neared the wound. *"I'll hack at the leg and see if I can stop him from damaging the World Tree."*

He'd said it silently, but Czarnobóg acted as if he'd heard, spinning away and sending flames washing over us. Wacław dove away with a windblast that did little. I cursed. Why had Strzybóg fallen when we needed to wield his power more than ever?

Luckily, I wasn't far, and I shouted in the old tongue, *"Prl"* to summon a shield of moonlight. The flames rolled over it, pushing against my *žityje*, but this wasn't the Trial of Death. I'd Ascended and gained far greater strength than I'd had then.

I hoped that drawing the attention of a head would give the elder gods a chance to strike. Weles sent wooden spears shooting from the World Tree as Perun tried to get an angle to thunderbolt the same weak spot we saw, but they were distant, blocked by Czarnobóg's wings and demonic allies. *Cowards.* They claimed to be the most powerful gods in the Three Realms, yet they left the most dangerous fighting to an exiled goddess, a newly Ascended one, and a Naw.

When the flames ceased, I dropped the shield. Wacław bolted forward, not toward the wounded shoulder that was now turned away from us, but the neck of the head that had just attacked us. Lightning pushed him with greater speed than any wind. It drowned out my calls for him to stop, but it was too late anyway.

Grudzień's teeth dug into the neck just as the head that had been focused on Perun now turned its gaze to Wacław. Its eyes turned pure black, and though I moonblasted the face, Czarnobóg's entire body shook before a ray of pure darkness shot from the maw. It hit before Wacław could even see it coming.

His pain surged through our bond as the strike threw him toward an island below. Forested, a river ran through its center and beneath a cabin before cascading off the edge. Wacław seemed to have no control over his fall, but I hoped he would land in the cushion of the river instead of the trees and brambles.

He didn't.

I followed him, wincing at his pain the moment he struck a spruce hard enough to send the whole thing toppling. It broke his fall, but his bones broke too. He struck the thorny bushes below as it tumbled, then groaned and closed his eyes as *žityje* stitched his wounds.

He wouldn't have enough to heal. That much was obvious from the way his legs were bent, so I dropped beside him with a lot more grace than he'd possessed, placing my hand on his check. "You'll be all right," I assured him as I sent my *žityje* into his soul.

Visions threatened to come at the touch, but I could mostly control End's power now. With Lipiec replenishing my own *żiłyje*, that strength was more potent, and I focused on helping him heal as the battle raged above. Czarnobóg had let Mother go for now, turning his focus to a group of minor gods.

The short goddess who led them rounded the side neck that Wacław had wounded. Her flowing dress trailed behind her with a drizzle of rain, and she extended her arms, appearing to windblast as the rain filled the wound. Her allies joined her, but their attacks lasted mere moments.

The center head released its dark vapors as the wounded one launched a fireball. The two collided, and the gods tumbled, their skin charred and eyes frozen open in fear as the World Tree shook from yet another blast.

It can't take much more.

Wacław grabbed my arm. "I can fight," he said through a cough, "but I need the demon. It knows how to beat him."

"No," I said sharply, yanking him to his feet. "I don't need the demon. I need you to not just attack a head because it launched flames at me. We have a plan, Wašek. Use the weakness, and if you feel the demon pushing, tell me. I refuse to lose you again."

With a deep breath, he placed his wide-brimmed płanetnik hat back on his head. "Then it's time to call in our friends, because we're going to need every Moonblade we have."

45

Wacław

The legends said fighting a dragon is fun.

TERROR GRIPPED MY CHEST AS I FLEW from the forested island with Otylia by my side. Together, we called our friends through our marks, hoping they could help turn the tide against Czarnobóg, who had even Weles fleeing up the World Tree after a series of strikes with his mighty claws. We needed to have too many allies up close for him to fight at once. Unfortunately, the gods all kept their distance.

It wasn't long before Narcyz and Kuba appeared, slashing through the strzygi as Ara pushed them with the moon. Their clothes were tattered and blood of both red and black tainted their skin, but they were alive. No doubt their Moonblades had played a role.

"What's the plan?" Narcyz said. His eyes were as wide as an owl's as he stared at the three-headed żmij. "Cut off his head, right?"

"Listen," Otylia demanded. "There's a wound on his right shoulder. It's healing, but if we hit it quickly, we should be able to do damage."

I raised Grudzień, using her confidence to push back my fear. "Use your Moonblades. They can pierce his scales. Otylia and I will hit the shoulder hard, and we need you all to distract the heads. Stab at them all you can, but watch out for the fire and rays of darkness they can shoot. We've lost enough friends." I glanced at Otylia and forced a smile. "And keep to pairs. No one's getting left alone in this realm."

Kuba thumped his chest. "Let's do this!"

"You're way too excited to die," Vlatka muttered with embers cracking in her maw.

We scattered, Otylia and I leading the group as Dziewanna landed on the branch connecting the forest island to the World Tree. She reached down to touch it, and *žityje* swirled around her as she chanted. I had no chance to see what happened next. Czarnobóg noticed our advance and turned two of his heads, launching fire and vapors.

Our friends dodged to either side, but we continued on behind Otylia's *pri* light shield. Lightning scattered overhead, a golden apple exploding as Czarnobóg deflected it with his tail. Yet another wound the dark dragon suffered. It would do little, though, as he moved his tail too quickly to strike. The shoulder was our best option, but as we neared, slashing through dark, wispy spirits that rose from Czarnobóg, it was obvious even that wound was nearly healed.

"Now!" I shouted. "There's no time."

Narcyz and Andrij attacked first. Kwiecień's golden light sliced through the scales upon Czarnobóg's far leg as Andrij shot his burning arrows directly into the wound. The rest followed with their own attacks, and my heart ached knowing I couldn't be there to protect them. But Czarnobóg was a threat to everyone. Stopping him was the best way to protect those I loved, and that started with targeting his weak shoulder.

For the second time, Otylia and I dove between Czarnobóg's enormous wings and approached the shoulder. The middle, darkness wielding, head turned to meet us again. This time, though, Kuba was there. Ta crafted hovering stone platforms that let him run up the neck, dragging Maj through its scales.

Their teamwork both distracted the head and sent black blood pooling down Czarnobóg's torso. It was another weak point, but there was no time to question our plan. We needed to strike.

So I dove.

Lightning snapped blue across my veins with Otylia by my side. It shot from every finger, giving me more speed than ever and surging up Grudzień's blade as I crashed into the wounded leg and swung. No scales protected him here anymore, and Grudzień's jagged edge ripped through the exposed muscles until it hit bone.

Czarnobóg's reaction was immediate, rearing back and turning over with a flap of his wings. They were so large that the resulting gust knocked me away from the leg. Otylia, though, held on with the moon's pull. She'd landed on the shoulder, and she raised her silver spear before driving its bright red Lipiec point into the wound.

All three heads were focused on us now, but they turned slowly from our friends' distractions and the thunderbolts of Perun. The leg wasn't far. One more strike could take it off…

I'm going to sever the leg, I warned Otylia through our bond instead of foolishly attacking alone again. *Cover me.*

She offered no complaint, so I called my lightning again and charged toward the flailing leg. Czarnobóg's tail swung past too slowly to hit. I took the chance to send a bolt toward the second golden apple wound. It missed, but I was heartened by the attempt, balling lightning in my free hand and launching it into the wounded leg before stabbing with Grudzień at full speed.

The lighting nearly did the job itself. When Grudzień arrived, it cut right through the bone and through the other side. I rushed away as only Otylia's shields stopped me from being charred to bits by the incoming flames.

"*Lipiec is drained,*" she said as we swept out of range of the heads before preparing to attack again. "*I have plenty of žityje, but we'll need to be careful from here on.*"

Let's go for the head Kuba sliced.

She furrowed her brow. "*You mean the place flames and death smoke come from?*"

Yeah, that.

With a swing of her spear, she sighed. "*Fine. We need to finish him.*"

We messaged our marked friends about the new plan, then swooped to join them.

Weles shouted from higher up the World Tree as we charged again. His vines grew from the tree, wrapping themselves around Czarnobóg's climbing limbs and wings, pinning him in place for a few precious moments. The dragon's heads unleashed his fury upon Weles, but though they further damaged the tree and forced Weles to flee yet again, his vines had done their work. We neared the center head just as Czarnobóg broke through the first of them.

I'll distract him, I told Otylia.

She nodded, so I darted toward the head as she drove her spear into the chink in the scales that Kuba had made. Much of it had closed, but her Lipiec-tipped spear pierced it with ease. Czarnobóg tried to turn his heads to challenge her. I met each, slashing Grudzień across the nearest one's nose and sending a bolt into another's mouth as it readied its flames. A bolt wasn't enough.

"Shield!" I shouted, hoping Otylia could protect herself as a fireball burst at us. Lightning shot me barely over it, and the heat singed my legs, melting my boot's soles. But Otylia wouldn't have the same speed.

I scanned the smokey darkness for her as Czarnobóg finally freed himself from Weles's trap and lunged upward, toward Mokosz and Simargł's islands. Our bond didn't reveal any pain from her, but I held my breath regardless. Where was she?

Then her silvery moonlight appeared. A shell of calm amid a storm of fire and death, she held the shield with one hand out, her other clinging to the spear she'd impaled into Czarnobóg's neck. Based on the black blood covering his scales, this head was nearly finished.

"Meet me in the center," Otylia said, glancing up at me before yanking out her spear and taking flight.

I nodded before shouting to our friends. "Back away! It's only going to get worse."

The darkness wielding head flailed in pain. Rays of pure black shot from its maw at random, forcing me to dodge carefully. The first ray had nearly killed me when I fell to that forest island, and if any of our friends were hit, they wouldn't heal as easily as I had.

Otylia was out of Lipiec's *žityje* to pull from. My reserves as a Naw were even smaller than hers, and each burst of lightning took more.

Once our friends were clear of immediate danger from Czarnobóg, I readied my stab to then drive down the neck, but a ray caught me off guard moments before I arrived. With my focus turned to the neck instead of the head, I didn't realize my mistake until the pain struck my shoulder. I dropped, barely holding onto Grudzień as I fell to Czarnobóg's back. *Žityje* rushed from my soul to heal the wound. Dangerous amounts.

"Keep going!" I shouted to Otylia as I dug my free fingers into the scales.

Czarnobóg spun through the pain of her strikes. They were working, and the dark rays were fewer and fewer with each stab she sent through the neck. Perun's thunderbolts and Simargł's flaming javelins were steadily damaging the other heads too, but the dark dragon did not slow his rise. We'd reached Mokosz's island now. Czarnobóg seemed to know, as he turned one of his heads from Perun and release a spout of flames that seared the gardens and turned the front of her hill palace to ash. Simargł's own island across the World Tree was already demolished from his exile long ago, and now, the Great Mother's began to resemble the fallen god's.

Until then, I hadn't seen Mokosz anywhere in the battle, but she emerged from the World Tree then with hundreds of her wispy servants around her. They held swords and rounded shields. More appeared below, taking more silvery forms than their more violet allies near Mokosz. She raised a hand, and together they charged.

I pushed myself to my feet, then stabbed Grudzień into Czarnobóg's back. He didn't even flinch, but every bit of a distraction from Otylia would help her finish the head. She was halfway up— where I was supposed to have met her—and the dragon weakened with each of her strikes.

Above, the violet servants raised their shields, locking them together as flames rolled over them. Their shield wall held, and when Czarnobóg prepared another blast, they swarmed the open maw.

The final head turned to unleash the same flames on the silver serv-ants. They moved in far less unison than those above, and as I looked for our friends, I realized why.

Ara floated near the World Tree below with her arms held out toward the servants. Moonlight spun at the ends of her fingers, and the servants moved with each twitch. There were thirty of them at least, so she struggled to control the motions of each illusion. Czar-nobóg appeared not to know the difference in the chaos, though, and released another fireball into them. His expression shifted when it passed right through.

"Deception!" He laughed. "Foolish little szeptucha."

"Run!" Otylia shouted down to Ara as Czarnobóg's demons charged Ara and Sabina by her side. The two dove into the World Tree, and my chest tightened hoping they would be all right.

Ara's distraction of the final head gave Otylia a chance to finish her climb up the center neck. She raised her silver spear, and with a war cry worthy of the mightiest warrior, drove it up through the jaw and into whatever dragon brain lay above.

Czarnobóg's other two heads arched back and released roars that shook the air, throwing both Otylia and me off him. I fell toward the World Tree and landed upon the closest level with the winds' aid. Otylia landed beside me soon after, and we both stared up at the dragon with labored breaths. I sensed her *żityje* draining slower than mine, but neither of us had much left. Had killing the center head been enough?

My hopes disappeared as Czarnobóg extended his wings and rose toward Swaróg's island and Perun's above it. He was nearly to Rod now. We had to stop him before he made Otylia complete Death's demand. But how?

"Where did my mother go?" Otylia asked as she scanned the sky. Dadźbóg's sun sorcery shone below to dispel much of the darkness Czarnobóg left behind, but Dziewanna was nowhere among it.

"I haven't seen her since we left that forest island," I replied.

Her eyes flashed white, and Otylia's Threads of Life appeared before us. The ones connecting her to Ara, Sabina, and me were obvious, but she focused on the two that went straight down the World Tree's trunk. The first was likely Dariusz back on Jawia. The second twisted and shifted, its angle changing until a figure jumped from the World Tree below.

Dziewanna swept upward on her falcon wings as a small army of strange animals flocked behind her. Winged bears and foxes, mares with flaming manes and the antlers of deer, and orange wolf-like beasts with black stripes. They all flew at her back as she closed down Czarnobóg, whose only real remaining foes above were the three rival gods we'd convinced to fight together.

Otylia grinned. "It wasn't like her to run. C'mon. Let's join her."

We took a running leap together, bounding up with the wild swarm. Dziewanna shot her flaming arrows into the wound I'd made upon Czarnobóg's back before smiling at her daughter. "You have done well. Let us hope it is enough." Then she shouldered her bow and began to change. Her antler crown grew as fur ran up her arms, her hands changing to claws and her teeth turning canine until she resembled a massive flaming bear.

The wild goddess was unleashed.

As one, we landed on Czarnobóg's back with the animal army, and our flurry of attacks began. Dziewanna's power must have flowed through her creatures, because their claws and teeth pierced the scales with some effort. The goddess herself ran on all fours toward the nearest head. She swiped down at the scales as we went, leaving a trickle of black blood in her wake. Combined, it was a series of scratches for a monster this large, but Czarnobóg took notice.

Flames erupted from his nearest mouth, meeting Otylia's *pri* shield as she pushed up between Dziewanna and me. A few of the animals were caught in the blast. Most, though, fought on after us, and even the elder gods took notice.

Perun launched another golden apple at the nearest head. It didn't strike as true as ones before, but its sparks scattered down Czarnobóg's neck and delayed his next fireball. Weles followed his rival's lead, sending a giant wooden spike from the World Tree into the same neck and through the other side.

For the first time, the dragon faltered. The far head burst flames over Perun's island, which he scrambled to protect, but the nearest one could only produce spits of sparks.

Czarnobóg's massive body careened toward the World Tree as we switched our target to the final head. His strikes before had been on the tree itself, leaving flames cascading up its side and gouges along every level, but this time, what I'd thought to be an uncontrolled fall was targeted at someone inside the tree. Weles stood on an exposed ledge. He continued sending blasts of *žityje* at Czarnobóg but realized too late the dragon was focused on him.

As we reached the third neck, driving Alatyr shards and claws into its base, Czarnobóg changed directions. He grabbed Weles instead of slamming into the tower. The god fought back, but even the lord of Nawia had used much of his *žityje*. Czarnobóg's grip held, and with a spin that sent us flying off his back, he descended amid flames and darkness.

"Weles! No!" Dziewanna shouted. She tried to chase her husband and the dragon who'd stolen him, but strzygi blocked her path. Even with our help, no matter how fast she slashed them aside, more demons arrived along with Dadźbóg's bright sun rays.

"Send me to Marzanna," Czarnobóg's voice rumbled toward his chariot-riding ally. "Nawia's god shall be hers."

Dadźbóg swept toward the dragon, his horses' fury knocking aside servants and demons alike. Gouges covered his arms and face. With the scar over his eye, he'd hardly been handsome before, but now he resembled the gruesome demons he fought beside. He raised his staff, chanting in the old tongue as light gathered around them.

But Swaróg burst to his son with his hammer raised. Czarnobóg vanished as he swung, striking Dadźbóg square on the back of the head and throwing him out of his chariot. The sun god tumbled, eyes closed, but no demons came to his aid.

We stopped, watching the fall as Dziewanna clenched her fists. "Czarnobóg took him…"

"Weles had me killed," Otylia replied. "Marzanna can have him. I'm more worried that the god of darkness just escaped a battle with basically every god."

"Barely," I said, trying to be positive. In truth, though, doubt gripped my chest. Would we ever have the chance to fight alongside all the elder gods again? And what would happen to Weles and Nawia?

Below, Swaróg's servants chased down Dadźbóg. They wore heavy metal armor fixed in interlocking plates across their bodies, and each of their movements clanked as fire burned from their joints. No matter how cumbersome, they reached Dadźbóg regardless, one catching each of his limbs before they dragged him back to their master.

We regrouped with our battered and bloodied friends as the remaining gods rose to the World Tree's top again. Kuba held his left shoulder gingerly as Ta wiggled a few teeth that hung loose.

"Think the Earth Mother's servants will give me a copper arrow for it?" Ta asked, head cocked, before yanking a tooth free. "She's still alive, right? Didn't see what happened to her."

"You show such great concern for your goddess," Ara quipped with a roll of her eyes. "Just be glad *we're* all alive. The gods can at least come back."

Kuba shrugged and held up the fern flower. "Hey! We can too. Just not so easily."

"Enough of your squabbles," Dziewanna snapped. "Prawia has nearly fallen and Czarnobóg has taken my husband. There is work still to be done."

Their heads hung, and mine did too. Battle brought a thrill with it, but it always faded quickly once it was over. Every sore muscle pushed through. Every kill, friend or foe, flashed through my mind. How many minor gods had fallen? I had seen Czarnobóg kill at least Dogoda, the goddess of the western wind who'd helped me on my journey to Nawia, but there had been so many gods and spirits that I didn't know. Jawia already suffered under Marzanna's endless winter. How much worse would it get with fewer gods to maintain nature?

We rose on the winds and moonlight until we joined the other survivors. Flames had covered much of the World Tree, and only

Kostroma's waters—along with other water spirits—had kept it from burning further. Still, Czarnobóg had destroyed many islands and levels of the tree itself. The result was a slant on Rod's level that required channeling to keep us all from falling off. Though the gods didn't seem to mind the effort, our friends scrambled as Otylia and I did our best to keep them upright.

Rod awaited us at the place where his island's branch met the tree. He'd never looked young, but the eldest god seemed to have aged significantly since we'd left. The gods gathered around him in their various states of woundedness and weariness as he took a long sigh, his palms pressed together before him.

"This is the darkest day Prawia has faced for many years," he said. "It brings great sorrow for me to say it is only an omen of what is to come. Each god, spirit, and mortal acts as part of the cycle of the Three Realms and the balance within it—even Czarnobóg; however, that balance has been disturbed. In truth, it has been since the shattering of Alatyr millennia ago, and each moment since has shifted us further from the balanced forces I wished to create."

Rod glared down at Dadźbóg, who knelt at Swaróg's feet with his father's servants holding his arms. "There has been disloyalty and betrayal among even those untouched by the corruption of Oblivion. So too, have chosen heirs fallen to such corruption, seeking their own power over the responsibility they hold as the bearers of the Three Realms' forces. For balance to be restored, these Deathless Sons must be defeated." He extended his arms toward our group, his gaze falling first on me and then on Otylia. "Eight Alatyr shards rest in the hands of these gods, Nawie, mortals, and nymphs. Only through the mending of Alatyr can this damage be mended in full."

Perun thumped his chest. "We cannot allow a group such as this to wield such power! Jaryło and Marzanna held the Moonstones as my children. Let me restore them to my possession so that order may be restored."

"Your children are what caused this war," Simargł replied, arms crossed. "If any family should hold Alatyr, it is mine. We have been trodden on for far too long."

A smile crossed Rod's face. "Perun is correct that tradition dictated the passing of the shards from Prawia's rulers to their children. Simargł, you have fought well, and the pact you have forged with the other gods this day must be completed, but despite the corruption of two of Perun's children, there is another."

"No…" Dziewanna stepped away, stumbling back into our group. "I told you I don't wish to rule. Last time I sought the Moonstones—"

"Was millennia ago," Rod said. "You have changed, Dziewanna, and so have the Three Realms. I decree you to be the rightful holder of Alatyr and ruler of Jawia. None can challenge my word."

Otylia and her mother gasped together as Perun raged. "My heir is mine to choose!"

"Yet your choices have allowed this crisis," Rod said without a bit of scorn in his voice. "Dziewanna discovered Jaryło's betrayal before any other, and it is through her daughter that this group has come to hold eight shards. Who else has a greater claim Jaryło's Moonstones than the sister who sought to end his plot?" Simargł opened his mouth to appeal, but Rod had expected it. "Your family has gained much this day, Simargł. The question of whether you should hold Alatyr has long since been decided."

Kupalo whispered something to his father. Simargł's face still burned bright red, but he just grimaced, silent.

"I will free Jawia," Dziewanna said, her shoulders low and her neck bent. "Thank you, Rod. This is an honor I have not earned."

Rod gave her a slow nod, then turned backed to Dadźbóg. "Now that the matter of the shards is settled, Swaróg, do what you will with your son. He is not the first to fall to the whispers of those seeking power, but he does not bear the mark of demonic corruption, only lust for a fallen goddess. The sun must rise again in Jawia."

Swaróg bowed. "I will ensure he sees the truth and that his daughters reopen the gates."

"Very well. Then go your separate ways and rebuild what Czarnobóg has broken." Everyone began to leave, many grumbles spreading among the gods, but he was not finished. "Otylia, we must speak."

She tensed at my side, putting my hand in a death grip as she spoke in my head. *"We got rid of Czarnobóg. Death's pact is over, right?"*

I don't know, I replied with my own stomach twisted. Prawia was all but destroyed, the World Tree mangled and its connected islands burned. *Do you want me to come with you?*

"No. I have to face this myself."

Her hand slipped from mine, and all I could do was watch as she joined Rod and retreated toward his palace.

46

Otylia

Do I have to kill the god who created everything?

ROD'S ISLAND TILTED. Lopsided and difficult to climb, it reflected the state of the World Tree. Czarnobóg had burned much of Prawia, but he hadn't done it alone. Marzanna had freed him, Jaryło had allowed it to happen, and Dadźbóg had opened a portal for him into Prawia.

Were their errors any worse than mine?

That thought consumed me as I nervously fiddled with Lipiec, transformed into a red crescent moon hanging from my headband over my right temple, mirroring the silver one on the opposite side. It couldn't be dismissed with my silver spear, and I'd decided not to hide it. Better my foes fear me from first sight. This was no battle, though.

I stared at the gray palace ahead. Darkness seemed to reach across the island toward it, like creeping vines choking a tree. I'd gifted Death a key to my power in return for Wacław's life. Now, I had to pay the price. My mind argued with my heart whether it had been right.

It didn't matter. What had been right couldn't change my choice. I still had the boy I loved because of it, and if Rod's stoic posture gave any hint, I feared I would now have to kill the eldest god. Chiefs and warriors spoke often about their legacy. Would this be mine? Nemiza, Calamity, slayer of Rod and destroyer of the eternal balance.

A spirit still guarded the door. Its head was down, not in a bow but in a deliberate aversion of its gaze when I neared. A deep, low hum rose from it as Rod passed and waved his hand.

The spirit dissolved into wisps, and Rod rested upon the threshold for a moment, staring at the spot where it had stood. It was a mournful look I recognized from Father's moments holding the mortar and pestle Mother had once used to make her potions. Then he ran his fingers lightly over the crude Wheelmark etched into the wooden door. They traced each crevice and crack in the wood's grain, and a faint glow followed until the whole mark pierced the gray with pure white light.

He chuckled to himself before dragging his hand down the door and stepping into the throne room beyond. "All things are a cycle in the Three Realms," he whispered, his words echoing against the stone.

Unlike the destruction behind us, the throne room remained untouched, not crooked with the rest of the island or charred in the slightest. It felt as if I'd stepped into another realm entirely. Having seen only the slightest bit of Rod's power, it was a real possibility.

Rod stopped at the center of the room. Light was everywhere in Prawia, but his face seemed in shadow at the peak of his creation. He kept his head raised, fixing his gaze upon me. Before, his eyes had been a deep brown, but they were inconstant now. One moment gold. Violet another. Then back to brown as he summoned a wooden cane, which he leaned on. "The time has come."

I gritted my teeth. "We beat Czarnobóg! Death can't demand I kill you without his help."

"When you look into the power of the force you call End, what do you see?" His voice was calm, almost amused.

"The Threads of Life or colored wisps that show people's ends and worries about them."

He grinned. "Have you ever looked into your own?"

Fear struck me. A void in my chest, stealing my voice. I'd never thought about whether I could see my own ends beyond the few terrifying visions I'd seen through Rod and Wacław. Now, the thought of it alone paralyzed me.

"How can you hope to understand those you face if you do not first seek the truth within yourself?" He folded his hands up his sleeves and tilted his head back. "Take a long breath and then touch your own Thread. No matter the fear that holds you now, it will be far greater if you do not foresee what will come."

I did as he said, opening my eyes to the Threads of Life. My green Thread wrapped around me tightly before stretching toward those I loved, but I paused at the sight of Rod's. A spiral of white and black joining to a center of gray, so many Threads connected to him that I lost sight of the god himself. One tied him to me, despite mine not doing the same. Many more extended out the door, and more still bound him to every piece in the throne room. Every column, slab upon the floor, and piece of the throne received one of his winding Threads. They were supposed to connect us to what we loved. What did that mean for Rod?

"Rod…" I stammered, stepping back in awe. "Your Threads connect you to everything."

"Yes, they do," he said softly. "What craftsman does not love his creation, no matter how flawed? Take hold of your Thread. You may touch mine if you wish, but I must warn you that it is unlikely you will gain anything but terror from the experience."

The warning only made me curious what I'd see in his memories. Hadn't I learned not to mess with ancient beings? Such knowledge came at a cost, and seeing the worry in Rod's eyes was enough to dissuade me. He remained distant from mortals and even gods often, but I saw the care he had for the Three Realms and everything within them. My heart ached as I grabbed my Thread.

End took control, throwing me through time's flow and into a vision on the other side.

I stumbled into a familiar bedroom within Mokosz's palace. A bow, quiver, and various clothes hung over the chairs throughout.

The gray Październik Moonblade lay beside Ara on the bed, unsheathed as old tongue symbols pulsed on the flat of its blade. Doubts stirred within me about Rod giving Mother reign over the Alatyr shards, the memory of her destruction flashing before me, but I shook them away. Rod demanded I see these visions. Why?

A breeze swept through the room, and wisps of darkness appeared on the balcony outside. I summoned my spear out of instinct, but dismissed it quickly. Our time in Vastroth had taught me that I couldn't stop what happened in these visions, only try to stop them from coming if they hadn't happened yet.

So I stood, helpless, as the darkness took the shape of a man's shadow, sprinting across the room and landing upon the bed. Ara awoke with a scream, but she had no time to reach for Październik. The shadow covered her mouth as it raised a dagger.

Ara stabbed it first.

She'd slept with a hunting knife strapped to her thigh ever since we'd left Dwie Rzeki. The shadow had expected her to go for the Moonblade, but she'd drawn her knife instead, driving it into the shadow's throat… and going straight through. The iron blade did nothing, and her hand drifted through her attacker's body as if it wasn't there. Then it struck.

I cried out, turning away the moment the dagger plunged into her skull. End wanted me to see, but I didn't need any more. The message had been sent.

End pulled me into the next vision anyway.

My feet found soft earth that sucked in my boots up to the ankle. I staggered, then found my footing beneath a leafless aspen tree beneath the late-night moon. Snow covered the ground, but the swamp thinned much of it to create an odd combination of terrains as a weak wind blew from the west. It carried weeping from nearby.

Sabina knelt beneath another aspen, her hand pressed to its graywhite bark. I drew closer. My connection with the moon gave me better than normal sight at night, but it wasn't until I was only a few strides away that I saw the black strands reaching up the tree's trunk. Like Mother's altar and Heart of Jawia, corruption had taken hold.

I knelt by her side and laid my hand on her shoulder. She wouldn't know it, but it felt right to be there for her. A nymph was bound to their element, and as a tree nymph, her aspen's death would mean hers too.

"I wanted to return to you for so long," she whispered to the tree. "I never got to find Mother…"

She began to sing in the nymph tongue as the tree creaked. Soft and warm, it rose through the swamp and hung in the windless air. Each word grew quieter than the one before, and her body became translucent, fading. Tears rolled down my cheeks as I held her, but there was nothing I could do. Death strangled her aspen. And soon she dissolved into nothing.

"I get it!" I shouted to End. "I understand Death's punishment!"

My force tried to pull me deeper, but I tore myself free, falling to Rod's feet with a cold sweat stinging my skin. I knew what would've come next. I'd seen enough. Losing Mother once had been hard enough, and the last thing I wanted was to see her and Wacław suffer Death's wrath for my decision. That didn't make what I had to do any easier.

"Have you drunk enough of the truth?" Rod's voice carried through the hall.

"Too much."

He laid a hand on my shoulder. Firm but not heavy enough to hurt. "Few have defied Destiny's will as much as you in such little time, Otylia. The balance has shifted—how, even I cannot say. It is clearer to me than ever, though, that it is time for the cycle to begin its next shift."

I huffed. "Without the god who created it."

"Indeed."

"What will happen without you?" I asked, rising. "Imbalance? War among the gods for the Three Realms?"

"Has my presence prevented either of these events?" He gestured to the throne room, as if it somehow represented discord instead of being a shred of peace in the battle's aftermath. "The Three Realms will change, but they always have been and always will be. It is the way of things, the *right* way of things." Slowly, he nodded to himself. "Guilt surely weighs heavy upon you for your deal with Death. Let me free you of it."

I shook my head. "You can't."

"Is it harder to calm a young woman's heart than to create the world from an egg?" He laughed with his hands over his stomach. "Perhaps it is. Nonetheless, it should give you peace that my death was inevitable. Destiny foresaw it many years ago, and events have only hastened its coming. I have lived longer than anyone. I have allowed Death and subjected all others to him. Now, it is right that I endure the same."

My hand drifted to Lipiec at my temple. Moonstone was capable of killing any god, even him. "Will you ever return?"

"That would require Death to agree to a deal with me. As you have seen, he is a shrewd negotiator." Rod raised his brow. "What say you? Should I make a pact with Death?"

"I did to save Wacław."

"You love him, yes. The heart guides us more than we wish, but we would be lost without it."

I stared into the Threads of Life again, studying each strand that stretched from him. "And you love the Three Realms. What would you give to save them?"

"All I have. All I am."

"I'm the evil one who's taking that." Tears threatened my eyes again, but I held Rod's gaze. This was my doing. I wouldn't look away from my failure.

"Hmm." Rod pursed his lips for a moment, then replied at a whisper, "Then we are all evil." He closed his eyes with a long breath. "You have asked enough questions, child. Jawia withers without your haste. Strike strong and true."

Rod's palace burned red as I removed Lipiec from my temple ring and embedded it in my spear once again. The god did not move. Even his breaths were silent, and it felt like my heartbeat echoed through the throne room. A dull, heavy drum. It was the funeral march for a god, and I prayed it would not mark the same for the Three Realms.

Lipiec pierced Rod's ribs, driving straight into his heart. He didn't scream. He didn't flinch. As I pulled back my spear, there was only the smallest exhale, the last air escaping his lungs before he dissolved into a rainbow of wisps that floated to the ceiling.

The building shook.

I reeled away as cracks ran across the columns and walls. They covered the entire hall before I could blink, splitting the throne into eight pieces. Rubble crashed around me, and by the time I reached the door, the far half of the palace had caved in completely. Outside was no better.

Rod's island broke apart, each chunk floating into Prawia's endless sky as only a narrow path to the branch remained. It resembled the shattered islands in Nawia. Chaos breached Perun's realm of order, and I stood at its epicenter. Nemiza. Calamity. The eldest god was dead, his island destroyed with it, and a sixteen-year-old goddess was the only one to witness it.

A single rainbow wisp floated along that path before stopping within reach. Rod had warned me against seeing his memories, but this one acted like it *wanted* me to touch it. It drew nearer as I raised my hand, and when my fingers brushed the colors, Rod's voice spoke in my head.

"Jaryło is broken, Czarnobóg repelled, Dadźbóg captured, and Wacław mended. Yet another Deathless Son remains."

I found myself standing in a shallow swamp of misshapen trees. Before me, a fence topped with human skulls surrounded a misshapen house of wood and bone. A wrinkled woman with mangled gray hair sat on its doorstep, and though her features were indistinct from this far, I sensed *żityje* bursting from her soul. She seemed to stare at me, a smile creeping across her face. Then she stood and entered her house as it rose with her. Legs like a chicken's sprouted from either side of it to carry the entire building as high as a tree.

"Only the crone knows how to kill Koschei the Deathless," Rod said. *"Go to the place in the Mangled Woods where the two rivers meet. Pass Baba Jaga's tests and she will show you the truth. This is my last gift to the Three Realms, and I pray to each of my many children that it is enough."*

The vision faded, and I stood once again at the edge of the island. It had split behind me, now a hundred fragments. Part of me wished to stay there and protect that remnant of Rod. He had created the Three Realms. Why shouldn't a piece of his island survive longer?

His Thread held the answer. Likely, he'd never needed an island. Rod had been bound to everything, so even in his death, the Three Realms themselves were his remnant. Each god had their piece of the realms. He had them all.

With every step I took, the dissolution continued until the island and branch connecting it to the World Tree were all but dust. I no longer feared what lay on that island. The true battle lay ahead, as the gods awaited me on the World Tree's peak. Their servants were gone, leaving only my friends and Prawia's surviving immortals, and I knew each of them would question what I'd done.

It didn't take long for Perun to yell, "What is the meaning of this?" He snatched my arm as I tried to make my way toward Mother. "Girl, where is Rod?"

"Dead." I muttered. Why hide it? They'd figure it out eventually, and I had enough problems without being known as a liar. "I made a deal with Death to save Wacław moons ago. When we arrived here, he demanded in return I kill Rod or watch as he destroyed everything and everyone I loved. Rod told me to do it."

Perun roared into Prawia's sky. His thunder boomed, and I barely saw the golden apple he threw before it exploded, knocking me off the World Tree.

Mother's curses broke through the gathering storm as I caught myself mid-air. The apple hadn't been a direct hit. Still, my entire front burned, and blood trickled down my face until *žityje* stitched the wounds shut. My instincts told me to summon my spear again, but I didn't need End's visions to know that would lead to my death. Few could match the elder gods. I wasn't foolish enough to think that I was one of them.

That sentiment didn't stop Mother from staring down Perun with an arrow nocked and her bowstring pulled back to her chin. "Hurt my daughter again. I dare you."

"Mother, stop," I shouted, still airborne with my waning *żityje*. "End showed me what happened last time you warred with Perun. I won't let you fight again because of what I've done."

"Brave words, child," Perun replied, "but you have brought war from the moment you stepped foot in Prawia. First you ruined Jaryło, and now you slay Rod. How like your mother you are. Destroyers, the both of you."

"Then treat me as you did her."

Mother looked at me with shock. "Do not do this."

"There may be another way," Mokosz added, stepping between father and daughter. That same calming tone filled her voice, but words couldn't fix this. Even the Great Mother's.

"There is none!" Perun roared. He slammed his ax into the World Tree, lightning cracking around its head. "Weles's spawn has defiled Prawia, and I will tolerate it no longer. The agreement we all forged to defeat Czarnobóg stands, but she is banished." His gaze fell upon me. "Take your shards and leave this realm forever. Neither you nor any of your descendants shall ever return to Prawia."

"What about Marzanna?" Wacław asked. I felt his panic, but Grudzień did not shake in his grasp as fury broke through his fear. "You can't just let her take Jawia! Thousands of people will die!"

"And their deaths will be your lover's crime." Perun yanked his ax free and swung it over his shoulder. "I have fought to rebuild mortal civilization from ruins many times before, and I shall do so again once my son has recovered. Uphold your oath to forgive him and begone."

I bowed my head. "I will do what I promised.

Perun huffed, then waved for me to follow. "Then come. Let us be done with this madness."

47

Wacław

She actually did it…

IT WAS DIFFICULT TO COMPREHEND OTYLIA and my emotions as we descended through the air toward Perun's palace. Neither of us understood the ramifications of Rod's death, but Death had tricked us both. He'd won.

You had no choice, I told her silently, taking her hand.

She looked at the World Tree. Burned, scarred, it was nothing like the majestic sight we'd seen upon our arrival. Czarnobóg had retreated, but he'd left great destruction behind. The realm of gods was dead, and it was all our fault.

"End shows me there's always a choice," she replied. "I chose the people I love."

I squeezed her hand tighter. My heart yearned for a way to fix the pain that came with her admission, but I couldn't. What was done was done. Now we had to live with the consequences.

"Before he died, Rod showed me where the witch of the Mangled Woods lives," she whispered. "Baba Jaga knows how to kill Koschei. We just need to find her. Then we can figure out what Czarnobóg and Marzanna are planning to do with Weles."

"How can you focus on Koschei right now? We're about to give Jaryło his power back just minutes after you…" I cut myself off, realizing how sharp my tone had gotten, but it was too late. Otylia knew exactly what I'd meant to say.

She pulled her hand free, drifting away as we approached Perun's island. "I chose you when Death demanded it, and I've feared my nightmares ever since. Yes, I put my spear through Rod's heart. Don't make that haunt me too."

Perun's eagles and cloud-formed servants scoured the mountainous island. Massive oak trees covered the slopes all the way to the edge where we landed, far below the palace of rock built into the mountainside. Part of me wished to cower beneath their branches. Knowing I'd hurt Otylia was so much worse than a rebuke. I had grown used to her sharp words, but she'd never been one to ask for pity.

A black crater filled the island's center courtyard before the trail up the mountain. As deep as a canyon, it charred nearly a fifth of the island. Perun gave it a look of disdain, then led us toward the palace. I'd believed him to be invincible before, but seeing the king of Prawia's home under siege had changed that. Though Perun was mighty, no one was invincible.

The servants turned their attention to us, forming a loose circle. Was Perun afraid of us trying to flee? Dziewanna had stayed back to guide our friends down the World Tree, and even with Grudzień and Lipiec, there was no way we could fight Perun by ourselves. Besides, each god had upheld their end of our agreement, so we would do the same. Banishment from Prawia was enough punishment for one day.

"It's amazing compared to our homes," I said to Otylia once we reached the base of the mountain and stared up at the grand palace above. She and Dariusz had bedrooms at least, but Mom and I had spent my entire life in that one-room house.

"A palace filled with nothing," she muttered. "Just servants of his creation."

Storm clouds gathered around Perun as he took flight, this time pulling us along with his storms. It felt wrong to fly under another's power, but when I called the winds to see if I could wriggle into control, a force pinned my arms to my side. Perun didn't even give a glance.

"You may channel the winds, płanetnik," he said, "but I am lord of the skies."

He carried us to a balcony along the left edge of the palace. Any further and we would've struck the mountainside. In a way, Perun's palace resembled his wife's through its position within the rock, but Mokosz's humble earthen hill couldn't match the towering columns and walls here. I suspected that was intentional.

"Jaryło's chambers lie within," Perun said with a hand on the immaculately crafted door. Bolts of lightning crackled across the wood, meeting his glowing Thundermark in the center. "You will enter, free him of this blood pact, and leave. Speak nothing more."

Otylia nodded slowly, and Perun led us into the chambers beyond.

Sharp angles met us everywhere. From the golden chandelier hanging from a sloped ceiling made of triangular designs to the bright metal furniture, not a single line was misplaced. It somehow felt brighter than the eternal light outside, but there had been life and vibrancy around the World Tree. Here, it was stale, empty, and the light seemed to fade as we turned to the figure on the gold sheeted bed.

Jaryło sat with his legs tucked to his chest, the exposed skin upon his hands and face decaying and flaking to his sides. An empty hole filled where his left eye should have been, and darkness stared back from it as puss oozed from his wounds. He opened his mouth to speak. Only a whimper came out, but the curl of his lip exposed his disdain.

Otylia grinned as she paced along the bedside. Despite Perun's glare, she didn't hold back the satisfaction I felt through our bond. Jaryło had sought to use her for his own gain, but unlike Death, he'd lost. Otylia had outsmarted him at his own game, and though she had to heal him, she reveled in her victory.

"He deserved this," she said silently. *"I wish he could suffer longer."*

He's lost everything because of you, I replied. *He'll never rule Jawia, nor will Weles ever call him his son again. All you're mending is his body, nothing else.*

"It's too much."

She placed her hand on his shoulder, spurring a grunt from him. "I free you of the bond you forced upon me. Heal, and with two good eyes, look upon the destruction you have brought to your father's realm."

When she stepped away, Jaryło coughed and squeezed his legs tighter. Skin shifted upon the ends of his fingers and stitched itself back together. Slowly, the changes crept up his hands before disappearing beneath his clothes. His bottom lip trembled, but relief soon crossed his face as his eye socket mended and a new eye formed within it. It had taken only a few heartbeats. The god of spring's body was reborn, but the corruption in his soul remained.

"It's done," Otylia said to Perun as she tightened her autumn leaf cloak over her shoulders.

"This agreement is the only reason you are not imprisoned for eternity," Perun replied. "You may have mended my son, but nothing can change the chaos you have wrought by killing Rod. As long as he is dead and Weles captured, there can be no stability among the realms."

Otylia stopped at the door, and I kept myself between the two. We'd come too far for either him or Jaryło to change their mind and ruin everything. "I know," she said before stepping out.

Then we left, leaping from the balcony with her moonlight and my winds to catch us. There was freedom in it. Otylia's pacts were finished, and we could leave this realm forever. Despite her exile from it, I doubted Otylia wanted to return anyway. Rod had named Dziewanna as queen of Jawia, and everything we'd worked to save lay in the living realm. Prawia would recover without us. Jawia wouldn't be so lucky.

Otylia took my hand again as we descended toward Mokosz's island. Moonlight rose from her dress of white and silver in wisps, like it had after her Ascension, and her sorrow flooded through our connection. She laid her head on my shoulder.

"Tell me it's over," she breathed.

I nuzzled her head with my cheek. "You're free from the gods and from Death. We can go home." All of Prawia could probably see us flying from Perun's palace, but I lacked the energy to care about privacy. We'd survived a battle with Czarnobóg and avoided another war among the elder gods.

"Not yet."

"But you wanted me to say it's over?"

She forced a laugh. "I know it's not, but you're the one who always thought the best could happen. I need your optimism, even when it's wrong."

"I'm sorry about before." I sighed, remembering what she'd said about Baba Jaga. "Returning and stopping Koschei is why we did all of this. It makes sense to keep our focus forward."

"I can't keep living the past. I focused on Mother's death and you leaving for so long, and then my life became about finding her again. We've seen and done horrible things to get to this point. Now that I have you both back, I just want to move on and live again. It's selfish—I know—but the faster we kill Koschei, the faster I can have that real life."

"You deserve that life," I said as Mokosz's island drew nearer. Like Perun's, its gardens were burned from Czarnobóg's flames, but the entire front of the palace was demolished too. "I promise, Otylka, that I'll do whatever I can to give you it."

She pulled her head back, brow furrowed. "Don't promise what isn't yours to control."

"Then I promise I'll be with your side until the end, whatever it may be."

Voices rose from below before she could reply. Sabina and Ara rushed toward us with Otylia's moon power, asking a hundred questions about what had happened.

"Jaryło's healed," Otylia replied sharply. "But he's finished, and I'm finished with this realm."

We landed in the heart of the burned courtyard, where the statue had once stood. Dziewanna replaced it with her heels dug into the ash and her arms crossed. She was the eye of a storm, wispy servants rushing around her with baskets full of rubble instead of offerings.

Mokosz was walking away, so I assumed they'd had yet another argument.

"Ready to begin your exile and leave this awful realm behind us?" Dziewanna asked as we arrived. "The others are inside, and my mother will send us back through her Heart of Jawia when we give the word."

Nothing about Jaryło. She gave only a momentary glare at Perun's island before turning toward the palace, barely waiting for Otylia's confirmation. Rod had named her queen of Jawia, but she scowled like she'd been insulted.

"Dziewanna, before we go," I said, pulling Grudzień from its sheath. "Rod gave the Moonstones to you, but you don't actually hold one."

Marzyana stepped from beside what had once been the palace entrance. She held the orange sickle blade of Sierpień out. "You are kind, Wacław, but keep your sword. Jawia needs you. I am simply a forgotten goddess who's trapped in this realm. It would be a waste to leave it with me."

"People are already starving, and it will only get worse," I replied. "You're the goddess of the grain. Who better than you to help us restore our crops?"

She bowed her head. "Very well, but I am no fighter. Dziewanna, you should bear the harvest shard."

"Put the blades away!" Dziewanna snapped, turning away and sending her cape of leaves spinning around her. "I have no desire to hold the Alatyr shards. Not again…"

I cocked my head. "But Rod—"

"Is dead, and my husband is gone." She looked at Otylia with a softened expression. "You saw what happened when I pursued power. I did not ask for this, but neither did you ask for anything you've had to do. Leave the shards with those whom you trust. They will be great tools in the battles to come—just not in my hand."

Silent, we followed her up what remained of the steps and into the rubble of the foyer. Our friends awaited us in a nearby round room, their bags slung over their shoulders and their gazes weary.

They hadn't needed to come, but they'd chosen to anyway. Otylia had rescued Sabina, protected Ta, and always fought for Ara. What had I done to deserve such friendship from the others?

"So the old god made you do it?" Ta asked. "Rod?"

Otylia shook her head, and I felt the pain in her chest. "No. End showed me what would happen if I didn't give into Death's demand." She scanned the group, meeting each of their gazes. "I don't say this enough, but I care about all of you. Death threatened to take you all from me. It was you or Rod, so I gave Death what he wanted." She clenched her fists so tight her nails dug into her palms. "And I'd do it again."

"Didn't think you had a heart," Narcyz quipped. "I mean, that's why you ended up with Wacław, right? He's got enough feelings to make up for all of us."

She went toe-to-toe with him. "Go to Oblivion, brute."

He grinned. "Good. Would've hated to think you got all soft on us."

Then she hugged him, and he just stood there, rigid as a board with his hands by his side. Kuba laughed and embraced them both. I joined in too, and our laughter spread as Narcyz gritted his teeth.

"Not letting go until you hug her back," Kuba said.

"Guess we'll all die here," Narcyz replied.

Most of the others joined the hug, and Andrij reached over the top to mess up Narcyz's hair. "Oh, come on. I know for certain you give the best hugs. Best you do it so Nemiza doesn't send you to Weles too!"

"Fine…"

A cheer erupted as Narcyz finally hugged Otylia. It was for a moment at most, but I took heart that we could unite, even after the horrors we'd witnessed. We all parted moments later to find Mokosz waiting with her hands held before her. Tears stained her cheeks.

"I weep for the creator," she said, barely louder than a whisper. "I also weep for you, who must face the darkness alone."

"We aren't alone," I replied, pulling down my płanetnik hat before finding my strength and meeting her gaze. "We have each other, and we have thousands of allies on Jawia. Come with us, Mokosz. Your Daughters fight by our sides. Your *daughter* stands before you, needing your help to protect Jawia."

Her head dropped. "I have done all I can. My palace lies in ruins, my people in Vastroth suffer despite the freedom Otylia granted them, and my husband despises me for protecting you as long as I have. As always, I am with every woman, mortal and not, but I do not have the strength to push further." She stepped toward Dziewanna. "However, there is one more fragment of my power that I can offer."

"I am sick of gifts," Dziewanna replied, wrinkling her nose. "I don't want Jawia. I don't want Alatyr."

Mokosz took her hands and slipped something into her palm. "You did not wish for a daughter either, yet now she is your everything. Dziewka, my dear, you are the one hope I have left for Jawia, and you may be our only hope of securing your husband's realm again. Do not let your hatred cloud your judgement."

"Convince Father that Jawia is worth his effort." Dziewanna deposited whatever the item was into a pouch at her hip. "Is that all?"

Mokosz nodded.

"Then we will be on our way."

With a deep breath, Mokosz drew a pattern in the air. She chanted in the old tongue, and the air became light. Our feet lifted off the ground, and Mokosz's final words barely met my ears before Prawia's light vanished.

"May Destiny guide you home."

Part 5
The Mother of Death

48

Wacław

Did we take too long?

DWIE RZEKI WAS FULL TO THE BRIM. Hundreds would travel to our village during festivals, but that was nothing compared to the flood of refugees now inhabiting it. Tents and hastily built cabins lined the trails inside the walls and beyond, making it difficult for us to get anywhere in the days after our return from Prawia, as their inhabitants swarmed us at every opportunity.

Sierpień, the eighth moon, was nearly upon us now. We'd spent enough time at home to mostly recover from our battle with Czarnobóg, but each moment we rested was another for the Horde to advance. And advance they had.

I held my head in my hands as I waited at the table in Mom's house. Despite my half-brother Mikołaj being away with the army, his mother, Natasza, had not allowed the rest of our group to stay in the longhouse's empty rooms. Instead, we all piled into the houses of those of us who called Dwie Rzeki home. Narcyz had brought Andrij into the smithery. Ara's family had hosted Sabina. Kuba's had taken in Ta. And Dariusz had argued but eventually allowed in Marzyana. That had left Dziewanna, Otylia, and me to somehow fit into Mom's house.

"We're falling back to Dwie Rzeki. We can't hold this open ground."

Xobas's message from two nights before echoed through my head. I looked up at Otylia, still asleep on my bed. Mom had offered Dziewanna the other one, but the goddess had chosen to sleep on a bedroll next to the stove instead. She'd woken earlier than even nightmare-riddled me today and was somewhere off in the woods.

Time had been difficult to track in the perpetual darkness caused by the deaths of the two Zorza sisters, but Swaróg's push for their return gave us much needed light now, even with Dadźbóg in captivity. Still, Jawia stayed beneath the moon each night, and the shadows of the day were a sharp contrast to the boundless light of Prawia.

Simargł and his family had caused weeks of darkness, but they were also some of the only gods willing to aid us against Marzanna. If Kostroma and Vida's promise held, Solga's armies would meet us here to fend off the Horde. I didn't know what to think of the fire god or his daughter. As long as they fought with us instead of against us, though, I would take the help. I was nervous to leave home again to find Baba Jaga. Knowing there were armies and gods alike to protect it brought some calm to my heart. Not enough.

So I waited with only the stove's crackling and restful breaths of Mom and Otylia to break the silence. Even with the fire, my breaths fogged the air. It amazed me how quickly I'd gotten used to the comforts of Prawia. Reality was like a frigid smack to the face, and this was just the calm before the storm. When Koschei arrived, my home would be under siege, and the lives of thousands would be at stake.

How far out are you? I asked Xobas. It was still early, but I knew my old mentor well. He wouldn't sleep much in times like these.

"We'll reach Dwie Rzeki soon," he replied. *"Tell me they've prepared fortifications."*

I glanced at the door. A hundred strides beyond it lay one of the earthen barricades the refugees had built in case of the Horde's arrival. Three rows of them protected the outskirts of the village before the wooden palisade itself. I feared it wasn't enough.

They've tried their best, but it's no Mothermarked wall.

"You saw how little those did for us."

They gave us time to escape.

Xobas sighed. *"There will be no retreating this time."*

He was right. Dwie Rzeki was as far west as we could go in Krowik. Fleeing into Solga would mean abandoning our tribe's lands in their entirety. I had seen Rolika's massive wall for myself, but I had my doubts that Kostroma would be to accept our refugees. She saw our armies as her best chance to stop the Horde. Without them, we were a burden.

I stood, pacing over to the stove and placing my hand upon its warm stone. Today would be our last day in Dwie Rzeki before heading east to find Baba Jaga. Mom had expressed her usual concerns and pride, but this day was more significant than most. It was Otylia's seventeenth birthday, making mine tomorrow. Celebrations of age were mostly connected to the jumping of the fire on the spring equinox and declarations of relationships at Noc Kupały, but Mom had never been apart from me for a birthday. I felt how much it weighed upon her.

When Otylia and I had been little, we would gift each other something we found in the woods, exchanging them as close to midnight as our parents would allow. I smiled to myself as I pulled a spiraled seashell from my pouch. A fisherman from Klist, a city on the far northern shore, had been wearing it around his neck. The patterns upon it reminded me of our shared marks, so I'd traded for it. It was hard to think of something Otylia hadn't seen in our wilds, but neither of us had reached the North Sea besides when we'd rescued Dziewanna. There had been no time to search the beaches for shells then. I hoped she'd be surprised.

I slipped it away as Otylia stirred. Wrapped in furs with her hair draped over her face, she was adorable. She could intimidate the most fearsome demon when awake. Beautiful but fierce. Asleep, she had no walls against the world, and the girl inside those barriers was the one I loved most. The real her.

"Where's Mother?" she mumbled through half-opened eyes. A stray hair found its way into her mouth, and she fought to spit it out before I sat on the bed beside her and helped the effort.

"She went into the woods for something a while ago," I whispered, rubbing her head in hopes she wouldn't spring awake. Her body could heal faster than any of us with her and Lipiec's *żiłyje*. Prawia had hit her hard mentally, though, and she needed more time away from the constant fighting than she would admit.

But she shot up anyway, nearly smacking her skull against mine. "She went without me?"

"Shh." I held her and pointed to Mom. "I'm sure Dziewanna will be back soon. It's still early. Rest for a bit longer."

"Says the one who's been up already."

I climbed into bed beside her. "Will you give in if I rest too?"

She tensed. "Where do you think she went?"

"I don't know. She's your mother."

"She didn't tell you *anything?*"

I chuckled. "Well, she told me one thing…"

She spun around, frowning as any bit of adorableness faded. Yes, she loved me, but that glare was enough to make me doubt it. "I'll call down Simargł on you, Wašek."

"Really? That would be great, because he'd be *very* useful against the Horde."

She jabbed me into the stomach hard enough to make me wheeze. "Stop it! Just tell me where she went, please."

"Fine, fine." I held her cheek, running my thumb across her crescent scar. "She told me that you'd come after her, so I should distract you as long as possible."

Fury burst through our bond. She leaped out of bed, furs still half draped over her. Her white underdress seemed to burn in the dull light from the stove as she stormed toward the door.

Otylia, wait! I pled silently.

She didn't. Barefoot, she rushed into the snow outside, her own light now rising from her skin with wisps of silver. I rushed after her once I'd put my boots on first—like a sane person.

"Dziewanna always has a plan," I told her once I'd caught up, our breaths fogging the air between us. "Let her do what she needs to. Xobas and Zakir will arrive with the army today anyway, and she'll need to help them while we search for Baba Jaga."

Otylia clenched her fists, then looked at me with pain in her eyes.

Their usual deep green flashed white, and the Threads of Life appeared around us. "Why does she keep secrets from me?" Her voice cracked. "Why can't I just have her back?"

I took her in my arms again. "I'm sorry."

"I don't want your pity," she said, her head buried in my chest.

"You have it anyway. Believe me, I know what it's like for a parent to not be what you'd hoped them to be."

"But you hated Jacek."

I closed my eyes, remembering back to a time moons before, when I'd spent each waking moment trying to prove myself. "I didn't. At least, not then I didn't. All I'd wanted was his approval, for him to see me as something more than a failure. I loved him, even if he didn't love me."

She looked up at me with a grip on my tunic. "Then why'd you choose me over him so easily?"

My heart grew heavy. I looked away, unwilling to admit my pain, though she'd feel it through our bond. "Telling Yuliya to take his life instead of yours was the hardest thing I'd ever done at the time. It didn't matter how much Father had abused me. Some foolish, hopeful part of me still thought I could make him love me. Maybe he deserved to die. Maybe he didn't. But I killed him without looking him in the eye and letting him know it was me."

"Marzanna killed him."

"Her power did, yes, but I made the choice. It's the same one Death forced you to make with Rod."

She pulled my chin back toward her and kissed me. "You wanted to deserve his love, but he never deserved yours. All you've done is show he was nothing but a coward, too afraid of having a demon for a son that he made you one. His failure made you stronger, and now you're his heir's only hope of defending the tribe he built."

"You're the hope. Dziewanna is." I tried to step away, but she held me tight.

"You save the people I've given up on." She looked toward the village. "We need that when everything's falling apart around us. I need that."

I kissed her, then quickly picked her up before she could fight back. "And you also need to let Dziewanna do whatever it is she's doing." She tried to kick free, but it was half-hearted and I carried her back with ease.

Mom was awake inside. A wry smile crossed her face at the sight of Otylia in my arms. "Quite the pair, you two. Wacław, if you could do me a favor and go collect some firewood once you've set your infuriated betrothed aside."

She'd taken the news that Otylia had given me her flower wreath with glee. We weren't officially betrothed, but it didn't matter to her. For likely my entire life, she'd hoped for me to wed Otylia, and I wouldn't spoil her joy with formalities. That didn't stop Otylia and me from blushing.

"Collecting wood was what started this whole mess," I replied with a chuckle, setting Otylia down and receiving a deserved elbow to the stomach in the process. "I wonder if Marzanna's leszy is still out there."

Mom raised her brow. "You never replaced that ax."

"I…"

"Was off fighting demons, gods, dragons, and gods know what else." She laughed and reached under her bed, pulling out another ax. Its head still glinted like new iron. "Luckily, I traded for one while you were gone. Go on. Take it and chop up one of the fallen trees. I'm sure Dziewanna will need the ones still standing once this is all over."

I took it. "Thank you, *Matka*. Otylia, do you want to come?"

Mom was a step ahead of me. She locked arms with her and waved me off. "If you are to leave today, then the two of you will need supplies. I will take Otylia into the market and scrounge together whatever food we can find."

"Help me," Otylia said in my head, but I just chuckled.

"Have fun!" I turned to leave, glancing back at them at the last moment. Otylia met my gaze. There was a deepness in it that filled my heart, and I held onto that warmth as I stepped out into the tundra beyond.

49

Otylia

Is this her attempt at bonding?

LUBENA LED ME THROUGH DWIE RZEKI like a predator dragging its kill. She held my hand lightly, but there was no letting go. Wacław's mother was hardly a threatening woman, but she'd made it clear this was something I had to do. It didn't take long for me to learn why.

"You know by now that Wacław can be sensitive about some things," she said as we passed a group of refugee tents. Children poked their heads out from them to stare at me. Apparently, I was enough of an icon now to be noticed in even the simple gray dress I wore. Or was it the lack of a braid? I'd almost forgotten how important that had once been for me.

"He is," I replied, trying not to cringe. *Am I really having this conversation right before leaving to find the witch of the Mangled Woods?*

Lubena continued with stories and tips about how to deal with Wacław, but to my relief, Ara joined us once we reached the village center. People were gathered everywhere, sitting with their wares on blankets or constructing shop stands that looked ready to fall at the slightest gust. Ara was even more excited than Lubena to rush between them. Her hair was more well-kept than ever, her cheeks striped with the paints of her Zurgowie clan.

"Looking forward to seeing Zakir?" I asked at the first opportunity to change to a topic other than stories from Wacław's childhood that would've made him blush deeper than a ripe apple.

Ara beamed. "Are you kidding? I thought I was going to die. Then I stumbled into a battle with a three-headed dragon. Yes, I definitely want to see Zakir and forget about all this for a few minutes at least!" Her expression soured as she surveyed the merchants' near empty offerings. "Not easy to forget when it's freezing during the day in summer, but at least the sun is back."

"It is good that you have friends and lovers to support you in these times," Lubena said, buying a stale half-loaf of bread and forcing me to take it. "My mother told me long ago that it is better to live for a short time with those you love than to experience eternity alone. Let us hope that, instead, you all live for many more years."

I closed my eyes and focused on the moon in Nawia, its power pulsing in my soul. Focusing on it calmed my nerves. "I don't have a choice when it comes to that."

Ara wrapped her arm around my waist and walked by my side to the next stand. A middle-aged woman stood behind it, selling apples that were suspiciously golden. Just the sight of them made me wince in expectation of them exploding.

"You might live forever," Ara said, "but Wacław still needs you to keep him alive. Even he can't survive being cooked alive by Czarnobóg's flames."

"Thanks for making me imagine that." Wacław's death had become all too common of a nightmare for me. The last thing I wanted was to see those same visions when I was awake.

"Aww. Is that your way of saying you actually care?" Ara giggled. "It's still so new to me to see you like this!"

As the only one of us keeping any focus, Lubena bought a few apples and shoved them into my bag. "Otylia was once a little girl who obsessed over every creature that crawled through the brush." She gave me a knowing smile. "You cared about people too, but I doubt you'll ever break your mother's habits. That's probably for the best."

Lubena knew me like I was her own daughter, and now that the attention was on me, I almost wished we could talk about Wacław's stories instead. There were many things I'd done as a child, twigs stuck in my hair and an unyielding desire to see everything Dziewanna's wilds had to offer. Bones had replaced twigs, but I'd never lost that love of the forests. Until now. Marzanna's monsters lurked everywhere, tainting my secret hideaways. I liked having companions to rely on. Still, part of me missed being alone with the animals and trees.

"I'm sorry, little one," Lubena said, taking my cheek softly. "I meant it in the best way."

I let myself smile. "You always do." Then I swung my bag over my shoulder, hoping she'd stop buying us food with the little she had. "We don't need more than a couple days of supplies. Wacław and I can both fly."

The two of us were going alone with only Kuba to join us. Our friends held Moonblades and other powers that Dwie Rzeki would badly need if they had any hope of holding out until our return. Mother believed Kuba's fern flower would help guide us toward the "treasure" we sought with Baba Jaga. I wished she'd come with us, but she was adamant that her rekindled force of the wilds would be better served here. Rod had named her queen of Jawia. Despite her not admitting it, I knew she felt that she needed to prove herself worthy.

Lubena gave a disappointed sigh. "You're right. I just… I had hoped there would be something worthy of me buying you for your seventeenth year. Has Dariusz said anything yet? I doubt so."

"My birthday was always a sore topic for him." I wrinkled my nose, remembering his muttered rambling about "youthful obsessions with age." Wacław and I had always exchanged little treasures we'd found in the woods. I felt guilty not having a gift for him this year, but we were too old for it now, right?

"All the more reason for us to celebrate," Lubena replied.

"It feels wrong." I stepped beneath false Perun's Oak. Bones rattled in its branches, as if their clanging were the last breath of the trees killed by Marzanna. "People are starving."

"It is the little things in the darkest times that remind us why life is worth struggling for." She looked past me, her motherly smile returning. "Ah, Wacław has returned. I won't keep you from him, as I know the armies are to return soon. See me at the house before you leave, please?"

I returned her smile. "Of course."

Wacław joined us then, hugging his mother before shooting a glare at the oak. I took satisfaction in knowing he hated Jaryło as much as me. He wore a ragged cloak, his black blood-stained płanetnik hat, and a spare brown tunic that he'd grown out of years ago, but he held himself differently now. The demon had pushed away the shy, frightened boy from moons before. For that, I was grateful. He'd regained the spark I'd seen in him when we were younger, and he was far more confident now that the demon was quieted.

"I hope she didn't say anything too embarrassing," he said with a kiss on my cheek, Sosna appearing at his heels and yapping for my attention too.

Ara laughed. "No, definitely not."

His cheeks turned bright red again, and I couldn't stop myself from grinning. "It's okay," I said, scratching Sosna under her chin. "I'm *sure* it's common for little demon boys to wet the bed."

"*Matka!*" he cursed to himself, his blush deepening. "I can never leave her alone with you again, it seems. Did you at least get the supplies while you were gossiping?"

I patted my bag. "We did. Lubena insisted on giving us more than we needed, but your mother has always been that way."

"She has." He looked toward the eastern edge of the village center. "Xobas says the armies will be here soon. They'll probably take camp outside the walls, so we should meet them near the gate."

Ara took off at a sprint. "Zakir's here!"

Wacław watched her go, then looked back at me with a wince. "I meant they'll probably arrive in an hour or two."

"Let her be excited. Remember how desperate you were to see me after only a moon?"

"Yeah, but you were trapped by Weles in the *realm of the dead.*"

I furrowed my brow. "And Zakir was fighting the *un*dead."

Kuba scampered up before Wacław could reply, crouching to pet Sosna. "You two fighting again?"

"Do we really fight that often?" Wacław asked.

"Nah, but it's fun to watch when you do. You get all red and can't find somewhere to put your hands. Otylia just looks like she's ready to blast you to Oblivion, her nose all scrunched like a pig."

I punched him in the gut, hard.

"Ack!" He crumpled and dropped to a knee. "What's that, Sosna? You think Otylia should be nicer to me?"

"Shut up," I muttered.

He covered the fox's ears. "Shh. She's sensitive. Just because you and Dziewanna brought her to us doesn't mean she likes the harsh tone."

"What's it like, understanding animals?" Wacław asked with a chuckle. Why was he enjoying this?

Kuba stood, still holding his stomach, and pulled the fern flower from his pouch. It still glowed a fiery red that spread up his hand and arm. "It's weird. I didn't get the chance to listen much before, with us going to Prawia and everything, but now, most of them are scared or starving. Some of 'em still want to find another one to bed, but that's less common than I thought."

"You wanted to hear animals seduce each other?" I asked.

"Hey, ya never know where you might learn some good lines. Too bad then that animals aren't all that good at sentences."

Wacław threw his arm over Kuba's shoulder and pulled him toward the east edge of the village center. I followed behind, shaking my head. "Luckily for you," Wacław said, "you're not one to speak properly anyway."

The boyish mockery continued as the rest of our group found us along the way toward the gate—all of them except for Mother. We were hardly discreet, and we drew plenty of stares.

"It sucks that we missed fighting the Horde," Narcyz said as we neared the gate. He'd cleaned up remarkably well since our return home, keeping well shaven and his hair no longer in knotted bunches. No doubt it had to do with Andrij.

"You kidding?" Ta replied. "We got to fight a dragon with *three heads!*" She held up a black circular object. "I grabbed one of his scales when we were heading down the World Tree. Could be fun in one of my blades."

Sabina pursed her lips. "Perhaps there is a more decorative use of it? A dark dragon's scale could cause other effects, right?"

She looked to me for an answer, but I just shrugged. "Ta, you can stab Czarnobóg with it for all I care."

"Better to stab him with a blade." She huffed. "It's got a good enough pointy end."

Marzyana smiled in a cream dress embroidered with waves of grain across the sleeves and trim. She had been nervous in Prawia, unsure, but she seemed to be enjoying Jawia. Ironic, considering it was a frozen wasteland unfit for a harvest goddess. "You are young, Ta-naro," she said. "In time, perhaps Dziewanna will choose you to wield one of the remaining Alatyr shards."

Ta crossed her arms, burrowing her head into her chest. "Fine."

We passed through the gates, waiting anxiously as we stared down the winding trails beyond. Sightlines were better without leaf cover, but a light snowfall had begun. Our armies were somewhere in the haze, but where?

A figure burst down the southeastern trail. Ara, tucking her coat tight around her as snow covered her boots and trousers, but she smiled like a child. "They're here! And Zakir is leading them like a true king. I knew he could do it."

I grabbed hold of her to wipe off the frost that covered her. It was sprinkled all throughout her dark hair, giving her the look of a graying woman. "You want him to see you like this?" I asked. "You should've kept to the more worn paths. A steppe girl like you will freeze to death like this."

She bounced to keep her blood moving. "He'll keep me warm."

Kuba and Narcyz snickered, but Ara gave them no care as the horsemen appeared. Like she'd said, Zakir rode at the front beside Xobas with one hand on his reins and another reaching into his saddlebags. He pushed into a trot before stopping when he reached us.

Ara rushed toward him as he leaped off his horse with more excitement than I'd ever seen from him and pulled a flower from the bag, handing it to her. "I missed you."

Ara practically squealed as she kissed him, grabbing the flower and then kissing him again. "I'm so glad you're okay."

"Our young marzban is a tactical mastermind," Xobas said from atop his own large mount. He sat tall, back straight, with a long tan cape draping from his right shoulder. With leather armor under simple robes that just covered the cavalry blade sheathed at his hip, he appeared to have taken to the role of Simukie general well. He smiled at the pair before dismounting and patting Wacław on the shoulder. "We've fought many battles since you left, but I'm sure you have stories of your own. Let us share them around a fire. I lost feeling in my fingers weeks ago."

50

Wacław

We need to end this war.

OUR GROUP GATHERED AROUND A CAMPFIRE southeast of the Dwie Rzeki walls. There were thousands of warriors from Krowik, Vastroth, Simuk, Vastroth, and the remnants of Astiw spread throughout other camps. With the village already bursting with refugees, they would have to make due inside the earthen fortifications instead.

Xobas paced before the fire, his gloves removed as he recounted the battles they had fought since we'd left for Prawia. Each had been a loss. The Horde advanced relentlessly no matter how well our alliance's warriors fought, and if it hadn't been for Zakir's ambushes with makeshift bombs and other traps, the entire army would've been destroyed. Still, what remained was a skeleton force compared to what we'd once had. Some refugees had joined the retreating army, but most able men had already joined the fight. What we had now—plus the Solgawi if they showed up—was all we had to work with.

"Your bravery has saved Krowik, and likely all of Jawia too," I said, sitting beside Otylia on a log. It was a small thing, but having her there with our shoulders and legs touching eased my fears. "We needed the time in Prawia. Now, Otylia is free from her pacts, and Dziewanna has regained her force. Once we reach Baba Jaga and learn how to kill Koschei, we can destroy the Horde."

"It won't be easy," Otylia said. "But Wacław's right. You've given us a chance."

Zakir bowed his head, resting against Ara as she ran her hands through his curled hair. "I did what I could."

"You did well," Xobas replied. "I can't say yet whether it was enough, but the Solgawi could change the tide of battle." He looked at me. "When will they arrive?"

"I don't know," I answered.

"The gods weren't happy with me killing Rod," Otylia added. She kept her chin raised, but I felt the pain that still came with that admission. "Simargł didn't confront me like the others, but it could threaten the alliance we'd made with his family."

Snow crunched outside our campfire ring. Half of us shot up immediately, weapons raised, only to see Dziewanna entering with a grin. "Simargł is as unpredictable as his flames," she said, circling behind Otylia and laying her hands on her daughter's shoulders. "But he will come. At the very least, Kostroma is as headstrong as myself. She will bring the armies without him if he refuses."

"Will it be enough?" I asked as Otylia tensed beside me. She'd been obsessed with Dziewanna's disappearance all day, and here she showed up without a warning.

Xobas stopped pacing with a heel dug into the snow. "It must be. We have no other choice than to stand and fight with what allies we have."

"How long do we have to find Baba Jaga?"

He closed his eyes, tilting his head back in thought. "Two days and nights. Three if they took time to recover from the last battle."

"I'd hoped for more."

"Hope won't win this." Otylia stood and extended her hand to me. "Let's say goodbye to Lubena and go. You too, Kuba."

"You too, Kuba," he replied in a horrible mockery of her voice. She glared at him, but he just stuck out his tongue. "Yeah, yeah. I'll shut it instead of ruining your romantic trip to the Mangled Woods."

Ara hugged Otylia. "Stay safe."

"I'm the immortal," Otylia said, returning it. "I'm more worried about you."

"Jaryło couldn't kill me. What's a few thousand demons led by an immortal sorcerer?"

Ta raised a fist. "That's the spirit."

"If you want to die," Narcyz muttered.

We finished our farewells with only a smattering of extra quips, finishing with attention for Sosna. She whined at Otylia's departure, but when Dziewanna called her name and told us she'd be with us soon, the fox yapped and sprinted to her master with all the grace of a toddler who'd just learned to walk. My heart ached walking away. Having them with us in Prawia had meant everything. We'd needed them then, but Dwie Rzeki needed them now. Though all the gods who cared were with us already, I whispered a prayer they'd survive long enough for us to kill Koschei.

Otylia noticed. "I used to pray so often," she said. "It's sad how much that changed when I met the gods."

"I think people just need to feel like someone's listening," I replied, running my free hand across a tree's bark. Its texture grounded the thoughts that threatened to escape. "You hear the prayers, right?"

"Sometimes. I wish it was that simple, but they either come in dreams or End's visions. Neither are fun for me."

The laughter of warriors disrupted my response. Groups of them roamed through the deep snow away from the trails, some reuniting with family and others trying to forget their sorrows for a few minutes. More still sat around their own fires with empty gazes and slumped shoulders. For them, camp would offer warmth, but it couldn't change what they'd experienced. I reminded myself that it didn't matter how much or little power people had. We all suffered in war, and we were the ones who'd survived this long.

"You listened to Darixa in Huebia, and now she's a queen," I said once we reached the trail heading towards Mom's house. "You heard Ta when her own goddess couldn't save her parents, but they're back now, fighting in the army to defend Jawia. She came with us because you cared. General Mesfin's entire Vastrothie army did. The gods failed us, but you didn't. Dziewanna didn't. Even Marzyana didn't. When the eldest and most powerful cower in Prawia and Nawia, you're fighting to stop the suffering."

"I wish I could run too." She walked closer to me, our strides falling in step. "Why do we have to save everyone who hated us?"

I wrapped my arm around her waist. "Because it's the right thing, I guess."

"You don't think about running into the woods like we did as kids, never returning this time? We could take our families and friends and just pretend the war isn't happening." She gritted her teeth. "What if it's the only way they survive?"

"Would we ever forgive ourselves if we left?"

Mom's house came into view. She was out front, shoveling away the latest batch of snow that had covered the steps down to the door. Her cheeks were bright red, and her heavy breaths fogged the air as I jogged to help her.

"I'm nearly finished," she said, shooing me away. "Go on inside. I want to give you something before you go."

"*Matka*, please!"

She huffed and swung the shove's handle at me softly enough not to hurt. "Wašek, I'm not old until you make me be old. Any of the grey hair I have is because of you being gone these last few moons, not because I can't shovel a bit of snow."

Otylia grabbed my arm and dragged me inside before I could protest further. The warmth hit me instantly, a wave of relief that made me want to lie down next to the fire and stay away from the Mangled Woods forever. We'd stayed long enough, though, no matter how much Mom hated to see me go.

The delicious smelling stew on the table only added to the comfort. Still hot enough to send steam spiraling over each bowl, it pulled me to a stool as Otylia joined me, but I couldn't eat until Mom finished. She obviously wanted the short time we had left to be special for Otylia and my birthdays, so I'd let her have it. It was the least she deserved.

She stepped through the door a few moments later, but instead of her usual smile, her lips flicked up nervously for a moment before she scrambled to grab her food. When she sat, she averted her gaze.

"Mom, what's wrong?" I asked, reaching for her hand. "Did something happen?"

"I…" She cleared her throat and forced a smile. Like me, she was a terrible liar. "It's nothing. I hate that you have to leave again so soon."

"I wish I could be back here more than anything."

She squeezed my hand back. "You've grown. Both of you have, and that's good… that's good. I tried to think of something that would represent how far you've come in the last year, but with the blizzards and the refugees to help feed…"

"You don't need to give us gifts," I said with a soft smile. "You've already given me everything."

"Well, I did anyway." She rose without having taken a bite of her stew, then reached under her bed to retrieve a pair of wooden necklaces. "Odeta—Dziewanna—helped me make them."

As if hearing her name, Dziewanna walked in with a wry smile. "My apologies for my tardiness. I needed to tend to my friends."

"Where were you?" Otylia asked, pushing to her feet. "You've been gone all day, and now you have to meet with *friends?*"

"I cannot temper the fury I gave you." Dziewanna rounded the table to sit beside Mom. "With the army's arrival, I decided they could use what help the wilds can give. I've called the surviving animals, nymphs, and spirits from the area to assist when battle comes. I should have told you this morning, but you deserved your rest." She sighed, weariness replacing her smile. "Before you, I worked alone for so long. It takes time to replace centuries of habits… But today isn't about me."

She nudged the necklaces Mom had set down. "The idea for the gifts was all Lubena's. I admit, she is far better at this than me."

Otylia and I each picked up a necklace. Crafted from light willow wood, mine resembled her silvery white Moonmark, and hers my deep red Eclipsemark. Each marks' lines were burned into them by what I assumed was Dziewanna's fire, and they looked meant to fit together. When I raised mine to Otylia's, the crescent moon rested perfectly in the gap missing from the eclipse.

"They're beautiful," Otylia said, smiling at me before looking at our mothers. "Thank you."

"Now you don't have to wear my Bowmark," Dziewanna said. "You have Wacław's mark to bear now."

Otylia wrinkled her nose, then removed her Bowmark necklace to add the new amulet onto it. "It doesn't matter if I'm not your szeptucha anymore. You're with me as long as I've got your amulet."

I did the same, adding Otylia's Moonmark amulet beside the Mothermark one Mom had given me when we'd left moons before. "We're never far from home then."

Tears wetted Mom's eyes as she held a hand over her heart. "That's all I could ever want."

"It's not all," Dziewanna said with a raised brow at her. "Is it?"

I cocked my head as Mom seemed to tighten again. "What is it? This is wonderful, Mom. What are you afraid of?"

"I don't wish to sit here and wait for the Horde to kill me." She stood, straight-backed. "You two are defending our tribe, so why can't I?"

"I love that you want to help," I said, "but you've never held a weapon before."

Otylia nodded. "Lubena, these demons won't hesitate to kill you."

Mom rolled up her sleeve, taking a deep breath. "Then give me your mark. Everyone says your Eclipsemark let Narcyz call lightning from the sky, and you can talk to me if I have it, right?" She shifted rapidly from foot to foot as the words tumbled out of her. "Please, let me do this!"

Otylia grabbed my arm. "I'm not sure—"

"It's okay," I said softly before looking at Mom. "It makes sense. I just never thought you'd want to fight."

"This village cast me out, but it's still my home," Mom said.

"You know that Narcyz can't channel my lightning, right? My

mark won't give you any abilities, so if you want to channel against the Horde, Otylia would be better."

Dziewanna drummed her fingers across the table. "That may not be true. I know Nawie have marked people before, but whether it resulted in channeling like with the gods, I'm uncertain. Forgive my blasphemy against my own father, but I highly doubt Perun would have violated his blood pact with Weles to save Narcyz. I will push him while you're gone to see if I can't get a bit more lightning out of him."

"So Lubena could do the same?" Otylia asked.

"In theory, yes."

Mom extended her arm toward me. "Then I am ready. Please, Wašek, let me have this."

I stood and rounded the table to her, but instead of taking her hand, I wrapped her in a tight hug. "I don't want to lose you. Not like this."

"Now you know what I have felt each moment since you left." She sniffled and stepped back, her motherly smile returning. "The Frostmarked Horde is coming, whether I bear your mark or not. Give me the relief of knowing I can use your power, and if that fails, then at least I can hear your voice a few more times before my end."

Tears threatened my eyes, and I had to wipe them away before taking her arm. "This won't be your end." I glanced at Otylia, looking for confirmation but only getting a nod of encouragement. "We *will* be back to kill Koschei."

I closed my hand around Mom's arm and reached into my *žityje*. Lightning burst through me, cracking at my fingertips, and no matter how light I tried to be with the mark, she cried out anyway. I released her as fast as I could, catching her as she dropped to her knees, clutching her forearm.

"I'm all right," she huffed. The Eclipsemark pulsed red, surrounded by streaks of irritated skin. I hated hurting her.

"I'm sorry," I whispered, but she shook her head.

"No, thank you. The pain will pass, as all things do."

I helped her back to the table, so we could sit and finally eat our rapidly cooling stew. Despite her agony from moments before, Mom looked much calmer. She ate eagerly with us and shared stories from my childhood birthdays. It was embarrassing how foolish I'd been, but I laughed through it. We needed those moments. Lately, they had been far too few. As Mom had said, though, all things pass, and we soon had to leave.

We bid our mothers farewell and joined Kuba near the eastern village gate. Like us, he was bundled up tight in a heavy woolen coat, but he left one hand ungloved, clutching the fern flower with it.

"You're going to get frostbite," Otylia said, rolling her eyes at him. "The air is colder than the ground."

He carefully placed the flower in his bag. "Yeah, well… You're right. It just feels good when I've got it. I don't even think it matters, since I've got the powers anyway, but I like holding it."

"Enjoy seeing Maja again?" I asked. She'd returned with the armies, and the smirk across his face answered for him.

"Wish it could've been longer, but of course I did. She's just happy I'm not a dog anymore."

"Jackal," Otylia corrected.

"Yeah, that."

Small talk done, we leaped into the air, Otylia on her moonlight and me carrying Kuba on the winds. Strzybóg's death had weakened them already. With Dogoda and others dying in the fight against Czarnobóg, they were fractured, difficult to control with any precision. That hadn't been as much of a problem in Prawia's perfect conditions. Amid Marzanna's snow, it soon became a nightmare, and a couple hours into the flight, I had to give up.

"We're heading straight into a blizzard," I shouted into the storm. The winds were working against me as much as for me, leaving us in an odd hovering position that left us exposed to all the pricks of hail. "Otylia, you need to take over before it steals my control."

She extended her hands, moonlight wisps rising from them. "Fine, make me do all the work."

Under her power, we pushed onward, and she guided us beneath the clouds. It was a risk, but Kuba was only a mortal. Taking the storm's battering was easy for Otylia and me. It had already done its damage to him.

"You were right about that frostbite," he said to Otylia as the frozen Wyzra River became visible. "Didn't expect it on my face, though."

Any quip I had disappeared at the pillars of smoke rising ahead. Every village, large and small, smoldered. I recognized Małe Wzgórze, whose people had helped me recover after we'd escaped the Battle of Kynnytsia, but nothing remained of the circle of buildings atop its hill. A few shadowy figures moved within the space.

"Demons," I told the others. "Is it worth fighting them?"

Otylia pointed behind us. "You think killing those three is going to put a dent in *that*?"

I spun around, and my stomach sunk at the darkness moving to the west. Not an army's march, but a mass of snarling, scrambling beasts that covered the ground and much of the sky. Even the blizzard couldn't obscure the thousands of them. We'd been lucky to fly clear of their chały and strzygi.

"Let's get 'em!" Kuba exclaimed, drawing the Thunderstone dagger.

I readied Grudzień. "Better we deal with them quickly than let them join the Horde."

Otylia shook her head but relented. "Fine. I'll guide the two of you down, but I'm staying up here in case we're noticed. Be quick."

As we dropped, I thought about Mom. She'd be fighting with the armies in Dwie Rzeki once the Horde arrived. They were already badly outnumbered, so what could three more demons do to shift the battle? Maybe killing them would change nothing, or maybe it could save a few of our allies' lives. If there was even a chance of the latter, it was worth it.

The demons were spread out, but we kept together as we landed behind the rubble of what had been the house of Beata the healer. The nearest one reacted to our arrival. A lumbering, snarling thing, large boils covered its bloated torso as noxious vapors surrounded it.

"Careful," Otylia said through our bond. *"That's a nezhit. It'll give you a terrible disease if it catches you."*

I repeated the warning to Kuba through my mark, but he just scoffed.

"Wasn't planning on it."

Then the fool charged. Darting to the right, he threw a snowball into the nezhit's face and attempted to round it as I hopped the broken wall and attacked the opposite flank. The snow didn't even bother the beast, and it swung out at Kuba, forcing him to retreat.

"I was sure that would work," he said.

"Maybe vocalize your ridiculous ideas before trying to get yourself killed."

The nezhit snarled, looking from Kuba to me. With the blizzard snuffing what little winds I had, I relied on my swordsmanship. Kuba was far less experienced with the dagger, but he showed no interest in using the javelins he had strapped to his back. He was a kid with a shiny toy. There was no use telling him not to use it.

I'll draw its attention, I told him. *Once it turns its back, aim for the head. The Thunderstone will drain its żityje.*

When he nodded, I lunged with a slice of Grudzień's jagged blade. It raked across the nezhit's torso, but it was quick enough to avoid a killing blow. The demon released a flurry of claw strikes in response. Otylia's voice echoed in my head as I pulled back, hoping to avoid the diseases that the nezhit could inflict. It followed my retreat, and Kuba took advantage of the opening. He missed the head, but a stab into its spine followed by another in the neck was enough.

Kuba laughed at his victory, but I kept my blade raised. The demon in me sensed the approaching *żityje* of the remaining demons. Two zmory, their nightmarish bodies cracking with each movement as they crawled toward us on all fours.

"You've had your fun," I said, going back-to-back with him. "Throw a javelin first this time and then use the dagger. Even a stick of wood can hurt them."

"Excuse me," he quipped. "It's a *sharp* stick of wood, thank you very much."

I chuckled. "Even better."

We split, each of us focusing on a zmora. It was amazing how different it was fighting them now. On the equinox, it had taken my newfound wind powers to give me any chance, but lacking them now only made me cautious. A Moonblade was more than enough to defeat a demon without the winds.

A shriek came from Kuba's direction, and I hastened a glance to see a javelin sticking out of his zmora's chest. It slowed the beast enough for him to take the advantage. I had to block a strike before I could see the result, but the fight didn't last long. The zmora managed a scrape across my leading leg, then I cut off its head with a two-handed slash.

"Uh, Wacław?"

I turned from my kill as Kuba dashed over to me. His zmora was close behind, the dagger now gripped in its mangled hand.

"How'd you let it take the dagger?" I asked, pushing him behind me.

"Simple. Got sweaty hands."

The zmora charged, but it was no better with the blade than Kuba. A few wide strikes from it later, I shoved Grudzień through its chest, the Moonblade absorbing the demon's *żityje* until it collapsed.

I spun back to Kuba once I pulled the blade free. "You've got to be more careful with Thunderstone."

"I just wanted to help," he mumbled.

"You did." I picked up the dagger and returned it to him. "Just be confident."

He snatched it. "It was easier when we had our matching shields."

"Oh... You know we can make new ones, right?"

"You mean it?" he said, looking back at me. "It's just been so different since you found out you're a płanetnik. I'm glad you've got Otylia, but don't forget about us mortals."

"I'm sorry. I—"

He looked up at Otylia. "Don't apologize. A promise is a promise with you. It's just a piece of wood, but it feels better with one in my hand."

I scanned the snow around the ruined buildings. Had the Horde left bodies? "There was a battle here, so there have to be a couple spare shields, right?"

"What's taking you so long?" Otylia said through our bond. *"I'm using my illusions, but I don't want to stay in the open forever."*

We're grabbing some leftover shields, and then we'll be right there.

"Whatever. Just hurry."

So we did. Once I ate the dead demons' hearts to replenish my *żityje*, we ran through each of the buildings in search of slain warriors. Whatever battle had taken place was small, though, and after a few minutes, I was ready to give up. Then Kuba called from near a patch of burned trees.

He pulled two round shields free from the snow. Neither looked damaged beyond a few nicks, one bearing the commonly used red symbol of the fern flower, and the other a spiraling pattern of greens. There were footprints leading away from the spot, one of the legs dragging behind the other—a fallen warrior turned to a demon without anyone to burn his body.

"They're not matching," Kuba said, "but it'll do. I'm taking the fern flower one for obvious reasons. You good with this one?"

I took the spiral shield, gripping it in my off hand. Ever since we'd left the Mangled Woods, I hadn't used a shield so I could focus on the winds. The blizzard had shown that strategy could leave me exposed without them, though. It *was* just a piece of wood, but it could save my life from a stray strike.

"Brothers in arms?" I said once I'd strapped the shield over my back.

He grabbed my forearm as I did the same. "Always."

Ready, I told Otylia. *The demons are cleared.*

"Good, because the Horde's spotted us."

51

Otylia

They just had to go digging for shields.

NOW THAT THE BOYS HAD FOUND THEIR SLABS OF WOOD, we could continue our journey east. Except the Horde had a different idea.

Ten lightning chały burst through the blizzard in my direction. I'd used illusions to cover myself, but we'd lingered long enough to draw attention. The demons Wacław and Kuba had killed were likely Frostmarked anyway, so they'd have made the army aware of our presence. Light rose from my hands as I readied a moonblast.

But the chały stopped as Wacław and Kuba reached me. Their slender female forms flickered between lightning and storm clouds. They never took their gazes off me, but when I summoned Lipiec as my silver spear, they wavered.

They didn't know we took Jaryło's blades…

Czarnobóg had seen us fighting with them, but had he assumed Jaryło was on our side? The Frostmarked had likely heard of my arranged marriage with him. If they hadn't discovered our blood pact's breaking, then they would have no reason to believe we were enemies. Apparently that frightened them, because the chały glanced back toward the Horde, and after a moment, all but one bolted away on their lightning, gone as quickly as they'd come.

The final smirked as her misty form solidified. "Jaga will not save you, Nemiza. Lord Koschei will destroy what remains of your pitiful tribe, and then all will bow to Lady Marzanna."

She left before I could give Koschei any reply. I exchanged looks with Wacław. Could we trust the sorcerer's words, or was he hoping his warning would turn us away?

"What choice do we have?" Wacław asked, wiggling his jaw in thought. "If we can't kill Koschei, the Horde will overrun Dwie Rzeki."

"Rod wouldn't have lied," I said. "Besides, Ivan's story in Nawia said Baba Jaga had magic to help defeat Koschei. He just failed to kill him forever."

Kuba sheathed his dagger and gave an exaggerated nod. There was a new confidence in his gaze, his chin raised into the moonlight. "Then into the creepy woods we go."

I forced myself not to look back at the Horde as I carried us further east. What happened in the battle was out of our control. All that mattered was reaching Baba Jaga's hut in time for us to return and finish this. So on we flew for hours, destruction evident below as the blizzard pelted us from above. There had been thousands of refugees around Dwie Rzeki, but worry crept over me about the number that hadn't escaped. Marzanna and Czarnobóg could transform those whose bodies weren't burned into demons or the soulless husks we'd seen in Huebia. Every loss for us was a potential soldier in their undead army…

The Mangled Woods came into sight as we passed over the village of Bustelintin. Snow covered the Frostmarked cultists we'd slain there moons before, but my heartache only worsened remembering how many of our group had died in the ambush. Kajetan had been arrogant and the other warriors brutes. They hadn't deserved that end, though. I saw that more clearly now.

"This is where I killed my first man," Wacław said, drifting closer. I felt the knot in his stomach. "It's become too easy now. I barely feel anything when I swing my blade."

I looked away. The opposite was true for me, as I'd slowly let myself care for those around me. Even in many of the demons, I saw the lives they should've had instead of the ends they got. I couldn't admit any of it to him. "It's them or us. The living made their choice, and it's mercy for the demons who I can't save."

Since Huebia, that had been most of them. Marzanna and Czarnobóg's corruption ran deep in their servants. I would do what I could to save the redeemable, but there were those whose only possible end was Oblivion.

Wacław pulled away at my aggressive tone. I didn't reach for him. With all that had happened, and all that I'd done, I needed the time to think. To push forward meant accepting the past. Even the pain.

"We need to go more north," Kuba shouted from ahead as we neared the edge of the woods. He tried to flip toward us, but he wasn't all that used to flying and ended up turning all the way around. "I've got a feeling in my gut."

I raised my brow. "Is it a feeling or the fern flower telling you where Baba Jaga is?"

"Dunno. They feel the same."

Great…

Wacław shrugged and adjusted his hat as he looked toward the north. It looked no different than the rest of the twisted, warped trees that consumed the woods. "We brought Kuba to trust the fern flower. If he says it's the right way, I say we follow. We don't have any other leads unless you want to jump into the Lake of Reflection."

"You just want me to take my clothes off again," I quipped.

His cheeks flushed. "I… Never mind. Let's just go north."

Wacław's embarrassment was always adorable, whether with his mother or now, and it brought a smile out of me. I'd liked seeing the tougher side of him in recent moons—when the demon wasn't baring its teeth—but that gentleness was what made him *him*. We'd all changed. It was a relief to see he hadn't too much.

The blizzard vanished the moment we passed over the Mangled Woods, replaced by curly mists. I glanced back, curious at the near perfect line dividing Marzanna's storm from the corrupted lands below. This was where her cultists had hidden for years. Why was it rejecting her power now?

"You see that?" I asked Wacław.

He held out his arms, pulling himself free from my moonlight with a somersault on the winds. "See it? I feel it. The woods weren't free from Marzanna before. What changed?"

"Jaga…"

Kuba scoffed and held his hands behind his head in another attempt to manage himself in the air. Instead of leaning back, he only managed to flip backwards until Wacław caught him with the winds. "No way one witch can keep Marzanna out of this entire forest. It's massive!"

"She isn't just a witch," I replied.

"Then what is she?"

I shook my head, fists clenched by my sides. "Dangerous. We're close, but we need to be careful. There's a reason she has a fence made of bones."

"Do we know what she wants?" Wacław asked. "You said Ivan couldn't get the real way to kill Koschei out of her, so why would it be any different with us?"

"Ivan wasn't a goddess." I looked at Kuba. "Lead the way. I'll keep us low and covered as best I can with my illusions. We're looking for a flaming river according to the legends."

Wacław cocked his head as we continued on. "Why didn't we see the river last time we were here? You'd think one on fire would be hard to miss."

Something was off about the woods. Beyond the creaking dead trees and creepy mist, End's force seemed both present and distant at the same time. I focused on it to see the wisps of things both living and undead.

Blackened wisps formed around me in the gray, terrified faces screaming as their arms reached out for me. Dozens of them. Hundreds. They appeared from nothing and rushed to join the sea of demons surrounding us, but neither Wacław nor Kuba noticed. This was End's power. What did it mean?

"What's wrong?" Wacław asked, noticing my distress.

I pushed away End's power, and the demons vanished with it.

"There are a lot of demons here. They're screaming. I… I had a dream like this, but I thought they were people then."

He swallowed. "Maybe they were."

"It doesn't matter. We need to focus on finding Baba Jaga. No more distractions."

"What if they can help us? If they're demons and maybe even Nawie who have been trapped here, they've been suffering. We could help them, and they could be powerful against the Horde."

Kuba closed his eyes. "I hear them too. It's fainter than the animals, like a vibration against my skull. Thought I was going crazy." He opened them again and glanced at me. "Maybe I am if I'm hearing the same things as you."

"You *really* like getting punched, don't you?" I said before looking to the north. The mists seemed to continue forever. "It could be a trap. Koschei knew we were coming."

Wacław crossed his arms, that gentle voice of his giving way to insistence. "We can follow the voices but keep a distance when we think we're close. If they're too corrupted, they won't have any Thread of Life left to touch, right?"

"You're right," I muttered. "We could use the help too."

The demons' wisps returned as I opened my eyes to End's power again. Even expecting them, their grabbing and screaming startled me, but this wasn't Vastroth anymore. I was in control.

"Silence!" I shouted, my voice echoing through the woods.

They quieted and reeled back as if I'd sent a moonblast. All except one.

"Goddess, you see us! Answer our plea!" it said in a deep voice, the wisp taking the shape of a man's square face.

"You are demons?" I asked.

"Survivors!" he replied with the others joining in with excited agreement. "Or we once were."

Another leaped forward, forming a narrow face. "An army of the dead drove us from our homes," the voice squeaked. "We tried to hide anywhere else, but they found us everywhere… except here."

I reached for them. "Where are you? Show us."

My fingers brushed the first's wisp, and visions flashed before me. They showed a village not much different than our own, surrounded by farms and rolling hills. Then came the riders. Mortal men at first, they resembled the cultists we'd fought at Bustelintin, but when the villagers fought back, the demons arrived.

The man, Florian, fled with his family instead of trying to fight back with his farming scythe. He carried his daughter, Aneta, in his arms with heavy breaths as he tripped through the deepening snow. Somewhere behind, his wife cried out, but by the time he turned to try and aid her, it was too late. So he ran with the girl until they eventually reached the Mangled Woods. They'd stopped by a stream—*not* a flaming one—and slowly starved.

I pulled myself from the vision with a gasp. Cold sweat stung my skin, and I cursed End for never making the visions easy to move in and out of. "I'm sorry about your wife." I huffed, regaining my breath before pointing to the other wisp. "Is this your daughter?"

Florian nodded. "And there are others from many villages. We are Krowikie, but some are from the eastern clans. Even got a couple Astiwie."

Another delay. I internalized that for a moment, but this was what was right. Even if it wasn't the immediate goal, these were people trapped in the woods. The Mangled Woods had taken their lives, but I was the only one who could give them another chance.

"We'll help you," I said.

"Thank you, thank you!" Florian replied. "Be careful when you come to us. Our bodies are broken, and I fear we may attack you no matter your intentions."

I grinned. "Don't worry. Surviving demon attacks has become our specialty."

I followed the path from his memories, dropping into the trees near the stream. The mists were thicker here, and the eerie feeling in my chest deepened as my feet met the snow. Ankle deep, it didn't swallow my legs like in Dwie Rzeki. It was still supposed to be summer, but Baba Jaga couldn't keep Marzanna's power out entirely.

The Threads of Life burst to life around me as human-like forms moved near the stream. Like in Huebia, I reached for each of them, allowing the Threads to wrap around me. Wacław drew his blade, but I raised a hand. "Let them come."

Frost covered the demons that emerged. Male utopiecs far smaller than the beast we'd fought the night of the equinox, rusałki with their long green and brown hair, and miawki like Kostroma, their skinless backs exposing the decaying muscles beneath. They were swamp demons I had once fought to repel, but with their Threads in my grasp, I saw their past lives. These weren't demons who'd been corrupted through their own choices. Life had been cruel to them, and only I could give them a second chance.

"The Horde drove you into these woods, corrupted you through the darkness," I called to the gathered demons. Their undead groans grew louder with their approach, so I raised my voice. "Let my light lead you out."

Then I plunged my power into the Threads. Light spiraled from my fingers, encircling us and banishing the darkness for a hundred strides. My feet lifted from the snow as *żityje* coursed through my veins. It was power greater than anything, and I reveled in it as the demons stopped. The darkness in their eyes faded. Their bodies remained decayed and decrepit, but color returned to their Threads of Life, soon replacing the black entirely.

I dropped into the snow, my legs wobbling until Wacław helped me gain solid footing. Redeeming so many demons took much of my *żityje*. My worshippers and szeptuchy would give me offerings to replenish it, but I now had far less than I wanted as we neared Baba Jaga. Fighting her wouldn't get us what we wanted. That didn't mean I intended to be unprepared for her tricks.

More and more of the demons neared us as a utopiec and young miawka knelt before me. Their wisps were no longer dark, but I recognized them. "Thank you for showing me here," I said to Florian and Aneta.

"No! Thank you, giver of light!" Florian touched his forehead to the snow before me. "What do we call you? How do we spread your name?"

I hesitated. My Vastrothie worshippers called me Nemiza, but Rod's words echoed in my mind. Did I want to be Calamity? Did I want to cause the same destructive ends as my mother? I took a long breath. *My name is my own.*

"I am Otylia, daughter of Dziewanna and goddess of endings and moon." I surveyed the hundreds of demons, all of them now bowing before me. Their corruption had been simpler to correct with darkness and starvation bringing their deaths, but I felt bits lingering in their Threads. They needed revenge to be truly free. "Follow us and we will lead you from these woods. You have the bodies of demons, but your minds and souls remain. Use the powers you've been given to help us destroy those who took your homes."

"We can't take them out right now," Wacław said through our bond. *"Do you really want to take them to Baba Jaga?"*

As the demons began to rise, most voicing their approval, I grinned at Wacław and spoke aloud. "Baba Jaga's sorcery made these woods a prison instead of a sanctuary. Let's show her how we mended those she broke."

52

Wacław

*We face the witch of the Mangled Woods with an army of demons in our wake.
Oh, how things have changed…*

KUBA LED US NORTH FROM THERE by foot. He thought we were
close, and though Otylia could likely lift all of us with her moonlight,
we would be vulnerable in the air. Baba Jaga was infamous for a reason. The last thing we needed was to be attacked before we had the
chance to even speak to her.

Still, I kept Grudzień unsheathed, held low at my side as smoke
began to sting my nostrils. I signaled for everyone to get low and
then grabbed hold of Kuba's arm. "We're close to the river of fire,"
I whispered.

Otylia nodded. "I don't know if it's the same one as the Smorodina, but I'd rather not be pulled to Nawia again."

"I would investigate with my invisibility," I replied, "but I doubt
it would be much use against a witch as powerful as her."

She thought for a moment before snapping moonlight to her fingers. "She'd more easily sense my *żityje* than yours. I'll give you an
illusion, and you're faster with the winds pushing you anyway."

The light encircled me, running up my body until I resembled a
smaller leszy, my legs branches and my clothes dried leaves stomped

into snow. It followed me when I made larger motions. Each movement of my fingers, though, remained hidden beneath the illusion.

"All the trees are dead, so maybe just drop onto the ground if you think she sees you," Otylia said.

Kuba snicked. "Ah, yes, the best defensive position."

"Maybe we just throw you to her instead," Otylia quipped, her brow furrowed. "I'm sure your skull would be a worthy addition to her fence."

He backed away.

"That's what I thought."

With Kuba quieted, I kissed Otylia on the cheek and crept forward, Grudzień now sheathed. The mists were thicker here, and I could barely see a few strides in front of me as trees and boulders seemed to appear from nothing. That would hopefully work in my favor. Unless Baba Jaga could see through her mists, that was. We knew next to nothing about the witch's power, and each step I took brought me deeper into her territory as what I assumed was the flaming river gave the mists an orange hue ahead.

More and more smoke joined with the mists until I couldn't breathe. Risking the use of my power, I created a small whirlwind to create a gap of air around me. It wasn't much, but it was enough for me to get a few needed breaths before my foot slipped on the edge of a steep slope.

Snow gave way to melting ice. I scrambled for a foothold, but there was none as the heat struck. Flames danced below, sending waves of smoke over me. Only a quick push with the winds kept me from falling into their embrace, and I launched myself onto the opposing slope. This time, my boots slipped until I grabbed hold of a branch and pulled myself onto flat ground.

That was too close.

Sweat dripped from my chin as I stood and surveyed what lay ahead. Faint traces of smoke drifted here along with the mists, but they kept far more to the southern bank, leaving my view of a bone fence unobstructed. I shuddered but resisted pulling my blade. There was no motion except from the river, so I advanced through the trees, crouched.

The bones clattered against each other beneath the weight of the wicked northern wind. Chorna, we called him, bringing his devious and chilled gales whenever he pleased. Death's stench hung in them as I searched for a way through the fence, but all I found was hundreds of arm and leg bones bound together by some unseen force. Skulls sat upon each post. Though I tried to look away from their empty eye sockets, I swore I could feel their gazes following me, and the hairs upon my neck raised when a gate came into sight.

I found her fence and a way through, I told Otylia and Kuba silently. *But I don't know a safe way across the river. I'll turn back and—*

A chill struck my shoulder, creeping through my back muscles until it struck my spine, freezing me in place. Fingers dug into my collarbone as a thumb jabbed into the base of my neck. My illusion dissipated.

"If it is not one as deathless as my offspring," a sinister, elderly voice said from behind me. Her grip tightened further, and each of her knuckles cracked with the motion. "It has been so many years since I have had visitors as *special* as you, dear child. Come, call Otylia, Kuba, and the uncorrupted ones you have brought to my door. Have them cross my threshold so that they may feast upon my hospitality."

I tried to turn and face her, but I couldn't. It was as if every muscle in my body was locked tight. So I did as she said.

Jaga found me, I told the others. *She wants all of you to come.*

Otylia's fear met my own. *"All of us?"*

Even the demons.

I opened my mouth to ask about the flaming river, but before I could speak a word, Baba Jaga raised her other hand beside my face. It was wrinkled and gray, and discolored nails arced from her fingers like claws. When they flexed, *cracks* echoed from the river until she raised her arm. Stones followed, fixing themselves onto the near bank and expanding across the river until a narrow bridge crossed it.

Otylia appeared not long after. Her silvery gray dress blended into the smoke and mist, but the autumn leaves on her cape offered a rare dose of color in the dreary woods. As her eyes met mine, they shone brilliantly green in a stray streak of moonlight. There was no fear in them.

"Baba Jaga," she said from the other side of the bridge as Kuba and the others emerged from the mists behind her. "I am Otylia, goddess of endings and moon. Release Wacław and let's talk."

She spoke with all the confidence of a war chief, and surprisingly, Baba Jaga loosened her grip upon my shoulder. Pain lingered as I staggered forward, dropping to my knees. *Žityje* seeped from my soul to heal the wound, but it wouldn't close.

I risked a glance at the witch as she grinned back at Otylia. She wore a loose brown dress embroidered in dark greens upon the sleeves and collar. Her sunken eyes were the gray of a walnut tree's bark, black swirling within them beneath thick brows that seemed to encompass her entire face. Only her long, pointed nose with a mole upon its end could distract from their oddity as she extended her arms like a mother wishing to hug her child.

"You are my guests," the witch said in the aura of the flames. "Join me within my gate, and do not be late. The bones may call, but I assure you that these are only those who sought to intrude on my hall."

Her words carried the rhythm of song as she turned and muttered something with her hand pressed upon the bone gate, arched with an impossibly large skull implanted upon its peak. When her incantation was finished, it swung open, and she glanced at us over her shoulder. "You did not seek to intrude, did you?"

My eyes widened as I stuttered, "I... I..."

"No," Otylia said, suddenly beside me as she grabbed hold of my cloak and pulled me to my feet. "We only want to talk."

"Good. I would have *hated* to punish the daughter of the wild goddess for failing to respect my realm."

Realm?

Otylia and I exchanged questioning glances, but there was no time to talk. Baba Jaga was already hobbling through the gate. Despite her limp, she walked faster than most, and we had to jog to catch up while still keeping a reasonable distance.

The pathway beyond the gate was hardly that. Twisted trees covered the landscape here too, but unlike the other side of the fence, leaves filled their branches. Gray and brown things, they *looked* dead, but they didn't hang loosely like autumn ones. They just flapped in the wind, as if they lived but had only lost their color.

"Weird," Kuba mumbled, picking a low-hanging leaf.

"Don't!" Otylia exclaimed as she tried to intercept his reach, but she was too late. The leaf plucked off the branch like any other, then promptly dissolved in his hand.

He dropped his shoulders with a huff. "Well, that's disappointing."

Otylia snagged his wrist. "You're lucky you didn't…" She rolled her eyes and threw down his arm as the streaks of rashes upon his palm became visible. "Kuba Piotryk, you are a fool."

"Oh Oblivion," he muttered to himself before waving his hand about. "That really itches! Anything you can do about it, mighty goddess?"

But she just stomped after Baba Jaga, so he turned his attention to me. What could I do? I was just a storm Naw, not a healer.

"Better hope she gives you a potion later for that," I said. "Though she might make you work for it."

My dread returned when I continued on to see the hulking shadow lurking in the thin mists ahead. I'd thought it to be a group of trees or a hill. No, it was a misshapen house, bits of its roof overhanging in sections and its base stretching in directions that didn't make sense. All of that paled in comparison to the fact the bottom of its door was at twice my height, because massive chicken-like legs propped it up. And they *moved.*

The house came running in our direction when Baba Jaga held her fingers to her lips and whistled. A disjointed hobbling like the witch herself, its stomps echoed through the woods and fell hard enough for the ground to shake. What channeling could turn a building into such a beast? I didn't know, so I just gawked at it by Otylia's side until it came crashing down strides before Jaga.

"Well, that's new," Kuba said, itching his palm so aggressively I worried he would take the skin off.

Otylia ignored him. "It's just like my vision." She took my hand and gave it a tight squeeze. "All the legends about her are true."

"And none of them are good," I added.

Florian approached with his hands on his hips. Utopiec slime dripped from his fingers, and his entire body had just odd enough proportions to feel wrong while still being operable. After suffering demonic corruption for moons, though, he didn't seem to mind now that he was free. "Err, I doubt all of us can go in there. Might be best if we stay back and let you have your talks with the witch."

"Nonsense!"

We all staggered back at Baba Jaga's sudden appearance. One moment she'd been by the house's door. The next, she was standing between us, her eyes wild as she looked from Florian to me and then back. "There is plenty of space for all in my house," she said. "Plenty for all…"

Then she headed into the house at a run. How her legs moved shouldn't have allowed for her to go that fast, yet she did anyway, and based on the displays we'd seen, we had no choice but to follow.

"Don't leave my side," Otylia said through our bond. *"As long as we're together, we can help the others if they get into trouble."*

I held her tight. *I didn't need an excuse.*

The house lurched as we stepped upon its threshold, and when I looked back, Kuba and the landscape behind him were distorted. Some features on his face were too big and others too small. When he followed us through the door, though, he looked normal. I assumed the same would happen with the demons, but Baba Jaga insisted we keep moving through the narrow wooden hall that greeted us. An embroidered runner covered it. Otylia squinted in the low light as she studied those markings, but we passed quickly. Her panic met me moments later.

"My moonlight is gone!"

I reached for the winds but found nothing. *Same with my power.*

She twisted her grip on my hand, glaring at me as we continued on for far longer than the house appeared from the outside. *"We shouldn't have come here."*

Rod said this is the only way.

Baba Jaga suddenly smiled back at us and turned a corner at the first intersection we'd seen. From what I could tell, the house was even bigger than Father's—Mikołaj's—longhouse. It seemed to carry on forever with only the sparse candles to offer light. I looked back to see how Kuba and the others were doing.

They were gone.

"What's going on?" I yelled, pulling Otylia to a stop before snapping my gaze to Baba Jaga and reaching for Grudzień's hilt. "Where are our friends?"

The witch cocked her head. "What of the gifts?"

"They aren't gifts!"

"Why, of course they are." She gave Otylia that same terrifying smile. "All the gods who visit me bring gifts. If only your mother would have come."

Otylia threw her hand to the side to call her silver spear, but it didn't come. "They are not gifts!"

"Foolish child…"

The stinging wound from Jaga's nails began to deepen. I cried out as it spread across my chest, but kept a grip upon Otylia and the Moonblade. If I lost either, we were doomed. "Let them go," I snarled, "or you'll regret it."

Baba Jaga was in front of me in an instant, her hand against my cheek with her nails digging below the ear. "Unleash the demon, oh Naw of the storm. You could be like me, shape the world to your will and defy the men who seek to dominate it."

"Like you shaped those people who sought refuge in your forest?" I shook with the effort just to stand as her strange power pushed against my mind. "We saved them from the gods trying to dominate it!"

Her hand pulled back. "Is this true?" she asked Otylia as I caught myself, then raised Grudzień.

Lipiec disappeared from its moon amulet on Otylia's ear and formed as a Moonblade in her free hand. "It is. I ridded Wacław of his demonic corruption, and I've done so for hundreds of other demons. Your house blocks my power, but if you're corrupted, I can help you too."

"I have lived hundreds of years in these woods!" the witch replied. "Why would I need a child's help now?"

The demon burning inside me, I moved to raise my blade to her throat, but Otylia yanked me back. "Because it's not too late to mend what you've broken," she said. "Your son is destroying all of Jawia, and we need your help to stop him."

As Baba Jaga sneered, the house warped around us, walls becoming chairs and the hall turning to a table that stretched for thirty strides. A chandelier of candles and bones hung over its center, and its light revealed that the room had no doors. Otylia and I found ourselves sitting near the table's end, near the witch.

Voices filled the room as our friends appeared in the rest of the chairs. Relief crossed their faces. Kuba tried to stand across from us, but he frowned as the chair refused to release him.

"Welcome, freed ones," Baba Jaga said from the table's head, raising a cup and then gulping its contents. Blood trickled down her chin as she set it back on the table. "I have been informed by Otylia that you are not offerings for me, which is a shame, as each of you would make fine additions to my forest."

"What do you want with us?" Kuba demanded as he rocked back and forth to unsuccessfully free himself.

Baba Jaga dragged her long nails over the table and circled it to him. The scratching stabbed at my ears, giving me a pounding headache as she stopped at Kuba's side. "What a brave boy. Have I not been hospitable when you have come into my home, seeking a way to kill my only child?"

Her gaze shot to me. "You and I are the same. We were called demons by mortals, but they failed to understand that we were much greater. Even the gods have forsaken their Nawie now. I see it as an opportunity."

She's a Naw?

The demon's anger faded within me, replaced by greed. "What opportunity?"

"To rid the gods of their influence." She appeared at my side, gripping my chair's arm so tightly that it crushed beneath her grasp. "Marzanna and Czarnobóg are no better than Perun or Weles. They seek to manipulate Jawia beneath their wills, while I wish to free it and all the forces they have squandered."

"You destroyed these woods," I said. "How is that freeing Jawia?"

She looked at Otylia, one end of her mouth curling. "The goddess who ends corruptions can shake that which has tainted my power. Without it, I can protect what the realm of the living should be and rid it of what *infects* it."

Otylia's glare sparred with Baba Jaga's. "Koschei is a Naw like you, isn't he? He's hidden his second soul somehow, and you know where it is."

"Perhaps…"

"If I redeem your soul, then you'll tell us where his is?" She gripped her own armrests, unable to stand and face the witch.

Baba Jaga vanished from my side and appeared at Otylia's. She held her hand lightly to Otylia's cheek. "I will do more than that, little goddess. A dragon guards his treasure, and I can temper his flames long enough for you to do what you must."

"We can't do this," Otylia said through our bond. Her presence pushed back upon the demon's hunger, especially with Baba Jaga no longer touching me. *"We helped Simargł, but what if she's even worse?"*

We can free her from her corruption and then save Jawia, I replied.

"We'd just be handing it over to her then."

"What will you do afterward?" I asked. "You're a Naw like me, but even with my demonic corruption weakened, it's still there. What will you do with your power?"

Baba Jaga just tilted her head, her fingers waving through the air.

"That is not your concern. I am proposing a trade that benefits both of us. Agreeing is in your best interest, as those who reject my offers always learn to regret it in the end."

Kuba clicked his tongue, his eyes wide. *"I got it!"* he said through my mark. *"She called his soul treasure. What if the fern flower can help me find it?"*

It's a stretch, I replied. *And there's still the dragon.*

"Which you've fought before."

As I relayed Kuba's idea to Otylia silently, Baba Jaga loomed over us. She seemed to grow with each passing moment, the light dimming as her smile widened. "Well, what will it be?" she asked menacingly.

Otylia took a long breath and replied in my head without looking, *"Do it."*

I swung Grudzień at the witch. The Moonblade's jagged edge ripped through the flesh at her shoulder, sending her reeling with a shriek. Whatever magic controlled the house broke too, and the room spun around us until Otylia and I stood again in the maze of halls with Baba Jaga. Finally, we could move, but the others were gone again.

"You will suffer for this!" Baba Jaga's voice echoed.

Another great wave of pain struck my unhealed wound as I tried to strike again. It slowed me enough, and her magic threw me back into the wall, pinning me there. Otylia already had Lipiec ready. By the time Baba Jaga turned to counter her, she sliced through the witch's extended arm.

But Baba Jaga only laughed. Though blood seeped from the wound, her arm remained intact, and it stitched shut in less than two heartbeats. "I built this place to be immune to the gods' powers. The shards of Alatyr are mighty, but this is *my* home!"

Rattling filled the hall as she vanished, reappearing at the dead end far ahead. Dark wisps spiraled around her and poured from her mouth and eyes. They reached for the bones built into the walls and ceilings, and when the witch chanted in the old tongue, the bones stitched together. Otylia and I stood back-to-back with our blades raised as hundreds of skeletons formed from every inch of the house besides the roof and exterior wall.

Kuba and the other demons were scattered throughout the now open house ahead. Skeletons blocked them from us, so with a silent command to Otylia, I charged toward the nearest group, sweeping and slicing with Grudzień like a madman. She kept at my heels to protect my back, and despite her lack of training with a sword, she held her own.

The skeletons were far from smooth with their bone swords and spears. Together, though, they threatened to overwhelm our divided group, and when I glanced back to check on Otylia, my stomach dropped at the sight of the downed skeletons re-forming.

"We can't kill them!" I shouted to anyone who could hear. "Fight toward the door!"

Except that was where Baba Jaga hovered on what looked like a large alchemist's mortar, a pulsing broom clutched in her hand. She looked plenty distracted by controlling the skeletons, but she still cast spells at any of our allies who drew too near. We needed to push forward as one.

Black blood already covered the ground by the time we reached the nearest group of our demonic friends. Kuba was with them, slashing away with his Thunderstone dagger in one hand and a bone sword he'd stolen from a skeleton in the other.

"About time!" he grunted, rolling to the side before severing a skeleton's ankle and sending it tumbling.

"The house is still suppressing my power," Otylia replied. "All I need is a moonblast..."

I eyed the roof before parrying a skeleton's strike. It was far easier now with the demons covering our flanks and crushing the skeletons that came near. "Kuba, how many javelins do you have left?"

He tapped his back. "Two, why?"

"Throw one through the roof. I want to see what happens."

Though he gave me a questioning look, he didn't voice his objections. We fought forward to connect with another dwindling group of demons as Kuba drew a javelin and let it fly. Florian and Aneta were in this group, falling back into our protection and then staring up in awe as the javelin struck the roof. Shards of wood rained down upon us. I grinned for a moment, but my hopes dropped as only the tiniest hole opened between the odd arrangement of boards above.

Then the light appeared.

Otylia rose into the room's center with moonlight shooting from her hands. "Get down!" she commanded, and as we all ducked, she threw out a moonblast so powerful that my ears rang from the force. The main wave passed over our head, straight through the skeletons and into Baba Jaga.

I whistled my approval at her, then tried to reach for the winds. Only the tiniest breeze slipped through the hole in Baba Jaga's magical barrier, so I stuck to Grudzień instead. The skeletons were already rebuilding themselves. We rushed through them as Otylia sparred with the witch's sorcery, clearing us a path, but her *żityje* waned.

When we neared the door, I leaped with Grudzień raised, slicing at the base of Baba Jaga's mortar. Moonstone struck bone with a mighty *boom* that shook the entire house. Baba Jaga wobbled, falling out of the way before catching herself away from the door.

"This is our best chance!" I called to the others. "Go!"

Their decrepit bodies ran through the door like a nightmarish stampede. A few skeletons had managed to catch up to the back of the group, but Kuba and I slashed them to pieces as Otylia landed by our side. Sweat dripped from her brow.

"I can't hold her off much longer," she stammered.

I nodded to the now cleared doorway. "You did great. C'mon."

We sprinted through the door with the skeletons' rattling at our heels. The house was beginning to stand, its massive chicken legs pushing us into the air, but with Baba Jaga hurt, our powers returned in full force. Otylia's moonlight and my winds steadied our fall until we hit the ground at stride. Our allies had pushed through the gate ahead. We were almost there, but then came the witch's cackling.

Baba Jaga rushed overhead on her flying mortar, sweeping her broom at the side like a paddle. The freed demons had all made it through the gate, but it slammed shut just as Kuba arrived.

"Go!" Otylia shouted to the demons. "Run west until you find Bustelintin. We'll find you there and show you to safety, I promise!"

Florian held a fist over his heart and bowed his head. "We'll wait for you, my goddess."

His daughter repeated the motion, her beady eyes wet with tears or miawka swamp water. It didn't matter, their sentiment was true, and they escaped over the stone bridge as Baba Jaga kept her gaze on us.

"You enjoy my hospitality, reject my wish for gifts, and now do this?" She smacked her lips together. The skeletons closed in behind as the three of us raised our weapons and prepared for a fight. "Now, I am forced to show you what happens to those who mistreat their host."

53

Otylia

What now?

I SCANNED THE BONE FENCE BEFORE US. Baba Jaga blocked the only gate out of her lands, and her skeletons were closing in fast. We couldn't fight them off forever, but I was running out of *žityje*. Carrying Wacław and Kuba all the way across Krowik and the Mangled Woods had taken more than I'd hoped.

There were no breaks in the fence, but I eyed a section near where the flaming river turned away. Would it give us space to run if I could moonblast through? I gritted my teeth without answers or time.

"Godly blood makes for a *wonderful* stew," Baba Jaga cackled from above, *žityje* pouring from her fingers as she pointed at the nearest trees. Their warped branches began to move and their roots broke through the earth.

Time to go, I decided.

With the witch's chants echoing through the forest, I released my own channeling into the fence near the bend in the river. The moonblast was directed instead of all around, saving *žityje*, and the condensed push shattered the bones with ease. I ran toward the opening as Wacław struck down the first skeletons to arrive.

"Follow me!" I shouted at him.

His winds whipped past to shove away the skeletons. We couldn't down them permanently, so putting some distance between us and them was our only option until we could fly without worrying about Baba Jaga. But the witch was quick. She arrived over the river by the time we hopped through the hole in the fence. I raised Lipiec, now at the end of my silver spear, cursing her. "Let us go, witch, or next time you see us, we'll have an army ready to slay you."

"Were those cowering demons not one?" she said as she waved her broom about. More trees shifted around us, their branches reaching for our limbs. "The three of you are alone, little one, and there is nothing—"

A miawka streaked from the opposite shore. Long black hair dangled over the creature's exposed back as she latched onto the bottom of Baba Jaga's mortar. The witch swung at her with her broom, but more demons followed, fueled by their demonic strength and speed.

"Find Koschei's soul!" one of them called to me. "We'll distract the witch."

I held a fist over my heart in thanks, but before I could turn to flee, Wacław grabbed my arm. "We can't leave them!" he exclaimed.

"You've seen the sacrifices that happen in war," I replied, trying to be as understanding as possible despite the panic burning in my chest. "We gave them a second chance, and they're using it to help us."

"But the others…"

I pulled him along. "They'll be safe in Bustelintin. Baba Jaga hasn't left the Mangled Woods in centuries, and I doubt she'll start now."

His disappointment was obvious through our bond, but he relented, following me along the riverbend with Kuba just strides behind. We took flight once Baba Jaga was out of sight. Her cackling and demonic shrieks carried on longer, though, clawing at my thought as I tried to focus on what lay ahead.

Smoke curled around us like Weles's snakes as we rose to the treetops and beyond, into the nightscape. The clear view of the moon filled me with new hope, and it trickled *żityje* into my soul. Not enough to face the dragon that guarded Koschei's soul according to

Baba Jaga. It would hold me over as we flew to safety, and for now, that was enough.

That effort was made easier by Wacław using his winds to fly himself and Kuba for now. Marzanna's blizzard clouded the skies to the west, but whatever Naw power Baba Jaga possessed still kept the storms out of the woods. It was ironic that the forest known for inflicting death upon all who enter was the only sanctuary from the eternal winter beyond. Now, instead of having to freeze to death or endure demonic attacks until you starved, you could choose which happened first. Lovely.

Below, I caught sight of Florian leading the remaining demons toward the western edge of the forest. It wasn't far, and I hoped that meant they'd have plenty of time to escape Baba Jaga's wrath.

Kuba pulled the fern flower from his bag and took a long breath. "Show me the way to the treasure," he told it. "If, you know, a super dead sorcerer's soul can be considered a treasure."

"Great confidence," I quipped.

"And he's technically super *undead*," Wacław replied. "At least I think he's undead."

"Shh!" Kuba waved his arms like a child throwing a tantrum. "I feel something. It's different than before, but it still wants us to go north. Well… that way." He pointed northwest, toward the Klist Bay that connected to the North Sea.

I sighed. "Great, so back into the blizzards."

"Hey, I don't choose where the treasure is. I'm just really good at finding it."

Wacław chuckled, staring over the water. "My last experience with the sea led me to Nawia. Let's hope this one is less… I'm not sure the right word. Eventful, maybe?"

Kuba smirked as he sliced the air with his dagger. "Better be eventful if we're fighting a dragon."

"No way you're going anywhere near the thing," I said with a stern shake of my head.

"But I fought Czarnobóg!"

I furrowed by brow. "Yes, while he was distracted by the elder gods, hundreds of spirits, and a bunch of other people far more worthy of focusing on than you. You did well with that stab to his neck, but it'll just be the three of us this time."

"I don't want to lose you again," Wacław added, patting his friend's arm before smiling. "Besides, someone is *going* to have to open the treasure and deal with Koschei's soul while we handle the dragon."

Kuba tapped his chin as we neared the edge of the woods. "Hmm. That's a good point. Fine, I'll do it, but just because *you* asked me. Not her!" He pointed at me with his tongue stuck out. Oh, how easily I could've sliced it off and silenced him forever, except he wouldn't have been silent. He'd just make awkward moaning noises while he pointed at his tongue.

"We should rest before heading north," Wacław said. "The question is: Do we camp in the woods or outside of them?"

"I'll take a snowstorm over that crazy lady any day," Kuba said with a scoff. "No way I'm dealing with that again. What was she anyway? Witch? Naw?"

"Probably both," I replied.

He frowned. "Aren't you supposed to be the one who knows things? I mean, you're a szeptucha, goddess, and all that stuff."

"I'm not a szeptucha anymore."

"You got what I meant."

I took a few long breaths to temper my annoyance with him before thinking back to what Baba Jaga had said. She claimed to be a Naw. Was that true? If so, how had she become powerful enough to create a cursed forest large enough to house a tribe of its own? The answer weighed heavily in my gut as I looked from Kuba to Wacław. "Whatever spirit or demon inhabits your second soul affects what power you have, right?"

"That's how it was with Bidaês too," he said, "so it seems so."

"Then whatever took her second soul was terrifyingly strong. Czarnobóg probably wasn't the only dark thing created when Alatyr shattered." I shuddered at the thought there could be others. "Let's talk more once we land. We're going to need all the *žityje* we can get."

Baba Jaga's power hadn't kept out the cold, but entering the blizzard felt like a blade slicing across every inch of my exposed skin. I pulled up my hood. It didn't help, and my face went numb by the time we found a low area between a few hills to make camp. The hills would protect us from at least part of the wind and also keep us out of sight of any stray Frostmarked. Still, it was frigid there as Wacław and Kuba began digging out a small shelter for us to sleep in.

I focused on creating a blood altar for me to refill my *żityje* from offerings. My stomach churned already as I wove the moonlight into a basin and thin silvery spirals that held it. Drinking blood had become easier since my time in Nawia, but not *too* easy. I hoped it stayed that way. Even if my szeptuchy and worshippers weren't giving me offerings of mortal blood like some gods demanded, the taste of blood and the feeling of it coating my throat were revolting.

"You're getting better at that," Wacław commented over his shoulder as the pile of snow behind the two boys grew. "It used to take you an hour to summon an altar."

He was right, but even now, it wasn't a quick process. The altar had a shape of its will. I had to craft my moonlight to match that form, pushing my control over it to my limits. Most of my time channeling had been large strikes in combat, so my training in the intricate details of spell weaving was difficult. I'd believed once that gods had it easier than szeptuchy in that regard. Unfortunately not.

Eventually, I managed a complete altar amid the barrage of snow. It was translucent, warping the light that passed through, but it did its job. Blood filled the basin, which was solid enough as I took it in my hands and raised it to my lips.

Think about anything else.

I closed my eyes, picturing Mother with her flaming arrows and crown of antlers. No, she hadn't been exactly as I'd expected. She wasn't a goddess who knew every secret of the world. She wasn't an all-powerful champion who could easily defy her father's demands. Her past wasn't unscarred by pride and destruction. But I loved her despite those things, and because of some of them.

To have a perfect mother would've made the weight of becoming a goddess even greater than that I already had to bear. Dziewanna *was* powerful and defiant, but she had her own flaws too. Some of those same ones I saw in myself when I dared to look inside. She'd learned from those flaws over the centuries, and now, I needed her to teach me how to overcome mine if I was going to somehow help her defeat Marzanna and Czarnobóg.

First came Koschei.

Mother, Ara, Sabina, Ta, and thousands of others would die if we didn't find where his Naw soul was hidden. I hated relying on Kuba and the fern flower, but we had no choice. Even if Baba Jaga hadn't planned to kill us after we helped her, she was too powerful to unleash. Something in my gut told me that corruption kept her in the Mangled Woods. Maybe it was better she stayed that way.

Blood covered my tongue as I lowered the empty bowl. My thoughts had pulled me away for a moment, but there was no avoiding the aftermath. *Żityje* filling my soul didn't stop my urge to vomit, and it took a significant portion of my waterskin to get rid of the bloody taste.

"Otylia the blood-drinker." Kuba laughed and drank too, wiping a bead of sweat from his brow. "Hope you enjoyed that while we dug you a place to sleep, oh mighty goddess."

I rolled my eyes. "Thanks, Kuba."

He nudged Wacław. "You hear that? She was actually nice to me."

"I suspect that's because you're the only person standing between Dwie Rzeki and destruction," Wacław replied.

"His flower is the only thing," I corrected.

Wacław took off his płanetnik hat and extended his arms to the side, sending a breeze through our little valley. "My demonic soul gives me power, and your godly one does the same for you. If anything, Kuba's is more important. He at least earned it."

I didn't like the feeling that he was right. Kuba saved me from admitting so, as he scratched the back of his neck. "Well… You see… I didn't do it alone."

"Oh?" I said, smirking at Wacław. Had he hidden his help from me?

"Not him!" Kuba said with a dismissive wave. "He was too busy off doing whatever a couple does in the woods when no one's looking." He yelped as I threw a snowball at him, striking him in the shoulder. "All right, all right. There was this demon at one point that I couldn't beat, but an archer shot it dead before it could kill me."

Wacław raised his brow. "Who?"

"Dunno." Kuba looked at me. "But I coulda swore it looked a lot like Dziewanna, which is weird because I was sure no one followed me."

"Because you're *so* observant," I said, heading toward the shelter.

"I am!"

I glanced back at him with one foot stuck into the slit in the snow. "Great, then you can take first watch. Make sure my mother doesn't come to haunt us."

Wacław chuckled as he followed me in, ignoring Kuba's complaints. Kuba could be a fool, but I couldn't resist grinning when he was around. He had a lightheartedness that was contagious, despite him resorting to humor at inappropriate times. Worries still gripped me. For a few moments, though, it felt good to joke like people our age were supposed to.

No amount of joking could cover my exhaustion as I threw down my bedroll in the tight shelter. Wacław squeezed in next to me, wrapping his arm around my waist. Another calming presence. But he hadn't been like that around Baba Jaga.

"What happened to you back there?" I asked him. "One moment you were ready to slice Jaga's head off, and then the next you wanted to help her."

He was silent for a few breaths. His were warm against my neck, banishing the cold from at least a small part of my body. "I'm sorry."

I turned to face him. Worry covered his face as I furrowed my brow. "I don't need an apology. We can disagree on how to respond to things, but that was the demon speaking in the hut. It sensed her Naw power."

"It did…" He looked away, then returned his gaze to me. "Controlling the demon is so much easier around you, but it was like Baba Jaga could dampen your presence."

"Tell me when you're struggling. I can feel when something's wrong, but I need you to be honest with me."

"I promise."

I placed a hand on his stubbled cheek and kissed him. "Good. Because if we're going to face Koschei's dragon, we need to be in control of both our powers. Ira survived and Czarnobóg escaped. This one we'll have to kill."

"We'll be ready," he replied softly, brushing my hair from my face. Gods, his voice was so much different when the demon was gone. Even when he was fighting by my side, not acting so gentle, he was still him when he was in control, but the Płanetnik lingered. I accepted that it likely would forever. "I'm worried about Kuba, though."

"He's faced a lot with us. He's clumsy and foolish, but have faith in your friend."

Wacław smiled, then pulled me close. "If my goddess commands it, then I'll have faith."

54

Wacław

I prefer land to sea.

THE ENDLESS WAVES OF THE NORTH SEA STRETCHED BEFORE US as we passed into the moonlit bay just east of the village of Klist, where Chief Serwacy had once ruled. It lay in ruins now, smoke curling from its houses and charred longhouse. Like Dwie Rzeki, it had a wooden palisade, but such a simple fortification hadn't stopped the Horde. I wondered if even Huebia's great walls of stone could.

Marzanna's blizzards weakened here, and I finally took hold of the winds again. Though Otylia had taken her offerings last night, her *żityje* supplies weren't infinite. We'd passed into the Sierpień moon. Her Lipiec Moonstone would no longer have its vast reserves, and she'd used most of it in the fight with Czarnobóg anyway. We needed her as strong as possible to face the dragon ahead.

"How far?" I asked Kuba. He led the way with his fern flower clutched in his grasp, staring to the north.

"Hard to tell." He glanced back at me. "Maybe a couple more hours? The feeling's getting stronger, but it's not like the flower tells me how close we are."

Otylia wriggled her jaw in thought, so I flew up next to her. "What are you thinking so hard about?"

"I just heard from Ara," she said, her voice tense. "Zurgowie and

Simukie scouts spotted the Horde not far from Dwie Rzeki. We thought we had a couple of days, but she's not sure anymore. Xobas and Mikołaj have ordered the warriors to be ready for an attack before the next nightfall."

That's not enough time.

Neither of us said it, but we both knew what this meant. We would be too late to stop the Horde's siege against Dwie Rzeki. Our only hope now was to arrive before it was finished.

I checked in with Mom, Narcyz, and Xobas through my mark, and each of them confirmed Ara's story. Mom worried about me. Everyone else worried about themselves as an undead army bared down upon them. Morale was low, and any attempts by Mom and Narcyz to channel my powers had been failures. They needed us there.

So we pushed faster into the clearing sky. Being over the sea made me uncomfortable, having never even seen so much water until I'd flown to the evening gate far to the west. Dwie Rzeki was called the village of two rivers because of how much the Krowik and Wyzra's waters defined us, but we lived on land. What lay in the sea was unknown and frightening. If rusałki and utopiecs could haunt rivers and swamps, what beasts lurked beneath the surface of the North Sea? I hoped never to find out.

The sight of land soon disappeared behind us, and nothing replaced it ahead. Still, Kuba remained insistent. The fern flower hadn't led us wrong in our pursuit of Baba Jaga, and though we hadn't directly learned from her how to kill Koschei, the little information she'd given had led us this far. It would be enough. We would find Koschei's second soul and end this. We had to.

It felt like an eternity before the first hint of green emerged on the horizon. Otylia caught sight of it first as the sun rose, and she grinned as she pointed toward it. "You were right, Kuba. There's an island ahead."

A small, lush paradise amid the Oblivion that had consumed Jawia, the island was covered in lush forests. It appeared uninhabited at first. As we drew closer, though, we spotted a few large buildings adorned in gold that seemed to be molded from the forest itself. They nestled into the side of a small mountain that rose toward the far end of the island. Half of the mountain looked as if it had been cut off at the coastline, as it stretched no further than the peak before dropping off into the sea at a sheer cliff.

"What is this place?" I asked, catching my hat as the winds suddenly escalated as we neared the island. They didn't defy my commands, but I had the familiar sense that someone else could command them here.

"I don't know," Otylia replied. "But whatever it is, it has held back Marzanna's winter."

That was a relief. The air wasn't warm, but it was far from the frigid environment we'd left. Feeling my fingers and face without enduring the burning cold was a simple but powerful sensation. It was hard to realize how bad I'd felt until the reminders of comfort returned, and I wished that comfort would last longer than the short period we hoped to stay here.

Once we succeed, I reminded myself, *we'll feel the world's warmth again.*

To defeat Marzanna, first we needed to beat her Frostmarked Horde. I kept my focus on that as we landed amid the trees. Kuba believed the "treasure" was near the base of the mountain, but with the buildings there, I urged us to land farther than Otylia wanted to. Who knew who lived here and what power they had? The last thing we could afford was to be trapped on a distant island as Jawia fell.

Oaks filled much of the forest, and my heart lightened as creatures scurried through the underbrush nearby. Our lands had felt dead ever since the snow arrived. We weren't the only ones struggling through the extended winter, and I hoped Dziewanna's return could bring nature some relief until we defeated Marzanna.

We pushed north with our weapons ready. This island had been inviting so far, but Baba Jaga's warning was fresh in our minds. She may have been lying about the dragon, but we weren't taking any chances. Being ambushed by such a powerful foe could easily be our deaths.

The trees creaked beneath the weight of the winds as we reached a stream that we forded with a patchwork of logs. Only chały had managed to create such gusts outside of my control before, but we hadn't seen any demons. Even Otylia's Threads of Life and wisps didn't reveal anything until a figure shot over us, landing on a branch overhead with a long navy blue coat flapping behind him. He played a cheerful tune on his wooden flute, and birds perched themselves upon his light gray hair as he stared down at Otylia.

"Oh, Lady of Endings, Lady of the Moon!" the man exclaimed, wincing as he lowered the flute. "I did not expect to see you on Buyan, but what a sight you are."

"Kyustendil?" Otylia covered her mouth in shock. "You're alive?"

The lord of the northwest wind huffed and hopped down from the tree, then promptly fell. Otylia rushed to him and helped him up as he brushed off the dirt from his elaborate clothes. "Excuse my lack of dexterity," he said. "Jaryło's blade had me drifting for moons, and I have only just returned to consciousness. Fortunately, for we minor deities, recovery is quicker than the elder ones, but it will be many moons before I am well enough to wield my power to any great ability again."

"I didn't expect you to be that brave against Jaryło," Otylia said, smirking.

"I surely hope that is not an insult!" He straightened his coat and shirt beneath. Old tongue symbols ran along the shirt's collar, pulsing a deep blue. "Nor is your expectation any surprise. I hardly display myself as a fighter, because it is not my skill of choice. However, I sought to escape Nawia, and so did you and your friends whom Weles trapped. It was a natural alliance. It seems that we both succeeded in the end; though, I would have preferred to escape without rendering myself infirm for so long." He nodded in my direction. "I am glad to see as well that you have not lost yourself to demonic madness."

I stared at my feet. "Well, it wasn't a smooth process."

"It never is with your kind. And you, Kuba, found the fern flower? Wonderful!"

Kuba grinned. "I'm just happy to have a body again."

"They are quite useful, yes." Kyustendil clapped his hands and hopped onto the winds before slowly descending again. "Now, what brings the three of you to Buyan?"

"Koschei the Deathless," Otylia said, her joy disappearing. "Baba Jaga said she's a Naw, so we assumed Koschei is the same. We think the fern flower is leading us to his second soul somewhere on this island."

Kyustendil drummed his fingers together, eyes wide. "Fascinating... Fascinating... Buyan, if you are unaware, is the island where Alatyr first landed in Jawia, making this a place full of mystery and wonder with secrets that even I do not know. We winds reside here when we are not elsewhere, and when Dadźbóg wishes to rest, he and his Zorza daughters make this his home. My siblings say they have not seen the three of them for some time."

I pointed up. "The sun was gone because Kostroma and Kupalo killed the Zorza sisters to free Simargł. Marzanna seduced Dadźbóg while he was in Nawia, and he helped Czarnobóg attack Prawia, stealing Weles and taking him back to Marzanna. For now, Dadźbóg is imprisoned. Seems like Swaróg at least forced him to give us light again, though."

"Oh, dear. I have missed much."

Otylia crossed her arms. "You're telling me you didn't realize the sun hadn't risen yet?"

"Time becomes meaningless after centuries," Kyustendil said with a dismissive wave. "Besides, I choose not to wonder much about the other gods."

"Do you at least know if a dragon lives here?" Otylia asked. "Baba Jaga said one guards Koschei's soul."

Fear crept over his face. "Ah, yes. From what I know, there were two creatures created to guard the resting site of Alatyr on Jawia before its pieces were removed and divided. The first was the wonderous bird, Gagana, formed from the powers of Swaróg and Perun. The second was the wise serpent Garafena, formed from the power of Weles. For a time, they were aligned in this, but their purpose faded without Alatyr. Gagana has not been seen for many years. Garafena… well, she lurks somewhere. It would not surprise me if Koschei had found a way to convince her to guard his treasure. Those żmije and their treasures…"

"If Garafena was meant to guard Alatyr," I said, "then we could convince her that we're trying to reunite its pieces. Maybe she'd let us take Koschei's soul then?"

Kyustendil shrugged. "That question is for much greater gods than me."

"It's worth trying," Otylia said. "We should just be ready in case that plan doesn't work."

"You're Weles's daughter," I said. "She'll have to listen."

She scoffed. "Not if Weles refuses to."

"There is always the Indrik too." Kyustendil pointed to the peak of the mountain, forests climbing up its side. "It is an odd creature that many have tried to tame to no avail, but is *not* in good relations with any serpent. Perhaps the daughter of the wild goddess will have greater luck?"

"So we find the Indrik and then search for Koschei's soul?" I asked. "It shouldn't take too long to fly there."

Otylia crossed her arms. "Are you sure we need the Indrik?"

"If you believe yourself capable of killing a dragon created at the beginning of time," Kyustendil quipped, "then go on your merry way and fight her alone."

"I think he means that's a bad idea," Kuba said.

"Thanks for that," Otylia muttered.

"Any time!"

Kyustendil agreed to follow us but not fight due to his limited power, so he kept to the back as we flew over the wind gods and Zorza sisters' homes. Oak branches and roots wound through their exteriors, working as one with the roofs and walls to form flowing structures. Beautiful, they were a part of the forest instead of separate from it. I wished more of our villages had been built like that. Still, we'd at least allowed nature within our walls, unlike Huebia.

We passed the homes quickly and began the climb up the mountain. The oaks here were massive, bulking things that were far taller than any others I'd seen on Jawia. Leaves covered them in a canopy so thick that it was impossible to scan the woods for the Indrik, so we descended near the mountain's peak, landing on a cliff ledge that would give us a view of everywhere below.

"Tricky creature, the Indrik," Kyustendil said, meticulously fixing his bangs that drooped over his forehead.

"What is it anyway?" Otylia asked as I sent the winds out to search for animals. Unfortunately, I didn't really know what I was looking for.

The wind god leaned up against the cliff, staring at the sky. "Some would call the Indrik miraculous. Others would likely label it as a horrific beast. It is unlike any other creature in the Three Realms, having a body resembling that of a bull, legs like that of a deer, and its head a horse's with a single horn sticking from above its brow. Quite the steed, I say."

"You've seen it, then?" Otylia asked.

"I have, but I was never foolish enough to try and catch it."

"You were the one who convinced us."

He winked. "Was I? See, this is what you deserve for listening to me."

With his better description, I honed in my search on larger animals. There were fewer this far up, and soon, one of the winds brushed against a singular horn on top of a horse-like head. "It's further up the mountain," I said, standing and drawing Grudzień.

But Otylia pushed down on my arm. "No swords. We want its help, not to kill it."

"This is where I leave you," Kyustendil said with a deep sigh. "Alas, you have been wonderful company, but I cannot allow the Indrik to know I revealed its secrets. It may never forgive me. Besides, I am a *horrible* animal tamer—even worse in my current state."

"So much for brave," Kuba whispered to me.

Kyustendil wagged a finger. "It is not I who called myself brave.

That was Otylia. I am no hypocrite, merely aware of my great limitations."

"Thank you," Otylia said, offering him a hug that he eagerly accepted. "We'll make sure you have a realm to return to when you're recovered."

"Dear child, you have changed." He looked her up and down. "All the determination with only a portion of the spite. Remember not to lose of all of it, okay?" Then he gave another wink and leaped off the cliff, catching himself on his wind and disappearing into the forest below.

I watched him go before grabbing Otylia's hand. "Well then. Shall we tame a magical beast?"

55

Otylia

What kind of malformed monster is this thing?

KYUSTENDIL'S DESCRIPTION OF THE INDRIK HAD MY SKIN CRAWLING. It felt like an insult to all the wild beasts Mother held dear, but then again, Buyan was apparently the first island on Jawia. Maybe the Indrik was the origin and the animals we knew were its descendants.

I pushed away those wandering thoughts. Our time was short, and finding the Indrik had only added another step in our journey. Kyustendil was a bit like Kuba in his joyfulness through everything, but I'd learned to trust his word when he was being serious. He'd sacrificed himself for all of us in Nawia. If he said we needed the Indrik, then we needed it.

Wacław led us to where his winds had found the Indrik, not far from the mountain's summit. We landed on one edge of the cliff that marked the northern edge of the island. Birds roosted along the sheer drop, but there were few places for them to do so. It looked as if a warrior had run their blade straight down it in a single slice. The mountains of Perun's Crown were far more rough and uneven, but if Kyustendil's story was true, there was likely another piece of it that explained why the mountain ended like this.

A rustling came from the bushes nearby, and I had to fight my instinct to summon my spear. Many had failed to hunt the Indrik. How many had tried to befriend it?

"Indrik of the ancient island," I called to the forest. "I am Otylia, daughter of Dziewanna and Weles, and I come seeking an alliance."

There was only the whistling of the winds for a long time. I feared we'd lost it, but just when I was ready to head further into the woods to continue our search, a creature bounded from behind the nearest patch of oaks. A long white horn glistened on its head, and from its horse head to its deer hooves, it was a deep gray with its mane and tail white streaked with black. Somehow, its narrow legs supported the weight of its bulky torso and allowed it to move gracefully toward us.

"Welcome, Otylia of the end," a slow, pronounced voice said in my mind as the Indrik stopped strides away. It was larger than any horse I'd ever seen, its head reaching to nearly twice my height. *"Why does the daughter of the wilds come to me when her home falls to Marzanna of the ice?"*

I bowed to it. "Marzanna's Frostmarked Horde is led by a sorcerer named Koschei the Deathless, whose soul rests on this island under the guard of the serpent Garafena. We seek to kill his soul, so that we can stop his attack on our home."

"A worthy goal, but that does not explain why you have come to me."

"We were told that you could help us either defeat Garafena or find a way to convince her to let us take the soul."

The Indrik glanced down the mountain, exhaling sharply. *"By Kyustendil, yes?"*

Kuba laughed, and I glared at him, only realizing then that I wasn't the only one who could hear the Indrik. "He is a friend," I said.

"He is one of the few who has not sought to kill me for glory. Dziewanna is the mistress of the hunt, but she honors the forests when she does so. It seems like you are like your mother in this." It stepped closer, studying me. *"Garafena was not always my foe, as she was created to protect Alatyr, but like all others who lack purpose, she became lost. I see you bear Lipiec on your ear and your*

companion wields Grudzień as a blade. What is your intention with the Alatyr shards?"

I smiled at Wacław, then looked back at the Indrik. "We want to reunite the Moonstones and fix the veil separating Oblivion and the Three Realms. After that, I don't want anything to do with the shards. Alatyr is too powerful for one god, or even one group, to have."

"Garafena would not believe you, but I have traveled the underworld and this one. I know deceit when I hear it." It took one step closer, now standing directly before me, lowering its head to meet my gaze. *"I will help you, Otylia of the end, if you swear to return Alatyr to its rightful place when Marzanna of the ice and Czarnobóg of the dark are defeated."*

"I swear."

In truth, I didn't know what promise I was making. We had no idea how to use Alatyr once it was reunited, and that assumed we could even take the final shards from Marzanna. But my intent was honest. I had no desire for the immense power that the united Alatyr Stone held within it.

"Very well." The Indrik turned so its side faced me. *"You are to be my rider, and I will aid you in your pursuits as long as they remain true. I do not know if Garafena will honor even my word, but should we come to blows, I will do my best to protect you."*

I carefully touched its side. Despite Mother's attachment to the wild mare, I was far from an expert rider, and mounting a normal horse without stirrups was hard enough. It took a pull from the moon for me to jump and get a leg over its side, but once I was on its back, I felt a rush of confidence. There was power in this beast that it hadn't shown.

"Lead the way," I said to Kuba, who held the fern flower as he and Wacław rose on the winds.

He grinned and pointed down the mountain. "This'll be fun."

At first, I was worried I wouldn't be able to keep up with their flight while riding the Indrik. That changed quickly.

The Indrik leaped over the tops of the trees without even tensing its muscles beneath me. We were at least as fast as my power could push me, and it felt like a blur as we shot down the mountain. An earthquake shook the entire mountain when the Indrik's hooves hit the ground. I couldn't resist a giddy grin each bound. Ascension had given me all the power of a goddess, but riding an ancient magical mount was a special feeling.

Kuba led us to a massive oak near the bottom of the mountain. Golden apples hung from its branches, resembling those Perun had wielded in Prawia. Its trunk was three strides wide, and Kuba swore that Koschei's soul was buried in its shadow.

"Where's the żmij?" Wacław asked, Grudzień ready as he scanned the woods.

The Indrik huffed. *"Garafena has remained hidden for many years, but you must remain vigilant. She may awaken should Koschei's soul be disturbed."*

"I'll keep watch," I said. "You two did well digging the shelter, so how different can unearthing an immortal sorcerer's soul be?"

Kuba grinned. "I'm not even mad at that jab. Well done."

"Then dig."

The boys both nodded and got to work. While they tore at the dirt with their fingers and the winds, I kept alert, gripping my silver spear so hard my fingers ached. I could handle another dragon fight. We'd fought two already. But the wait ate away at me as I anticipated Garafena's ambush. The minutes felt like hours, and when Wacław called out that they'd found something, I nearly jumped off the Indrik's back in shock.

They dragged a chest through the winding roots of the oak, groaning from the effort. It appeared like nothing special. Just a locked wooden box covered in dirt from years beneath the surface.

"I'll break the lock, so get ready," Wacław said, raising his blade as Kuba drew his dagger.

The lock clattered to the ground after a single swipe, and for a moment, Wacław and I stared at each other, holding our breaths. Maybe Garafena was gone. Maybe we wouldn't need to fight my father's dragon.

That hope faded at the sound of a mighty roar echoing through the forest. Smoke stung my nose as flames rose from nearby, but the thick foliage blocked my sight.

"The żmij has awoken," the Indrik said. *"Hurry and kill Koschei's soul as I speak to her!"*

Kuba flung open the chest. "What the—"

A pure white rabbit jumped free and hopped into the underbrush before Kuba could react. He muttered to himself, then looked to me for help. "The chest's empty now."

"Go get it!" I demanded, waving for Wacław to help him. How hard could it be to catch a rabbit?

"But that's not his soul," Wacław appealed.

"Whatever sorcery separated his soul from his body was strange magic," the Indrik replied as Garafena's rumbling grew closer. *"The rabbit may hold the answer."*

So the two took off with the winds, beginning what had to be the most consequential rabbit chase in Jawia's history. That left Garafena to the Indrik and me.

Gods, this is ridiculous.

Fear replaced that thought as Garafena rose through the trees, her maw sending flames into the sky. She looked more like a brown snake with wings than the dragons we'd faced before. Her body wriggled as she flew, and her only teeth were two fangs as her eyes turned to slits. They were focused on me.

The Indrik charged without warning. I slipped, forcing me to grab hold of its mane as it weaved through the trees. "I thought we were talking to it?" I asked with each of my words jarred by the heavy strides.

"If I have judged your allies correctly, then they will need some time to find the rabbit." Amusement broke through the Indrik's stern tone. *"Let us guide the serpent away."*

I sent a moonblast at Garafena to draw her attention, but she'd already caught sight of us. The blast hit harmlessly against her scaled hide as she tucked in her wings and dove. Flames followed, and I winced at the heat against my back.

The Indrik expected the move, dashing to the side and forcing her to change direction. Żmije were powerful dragons, but their size made them cumbersome. The Indrik's agility allowed us to evade the flames with ease as I released moonblasts at Garafena's underbelly.

"This young goddess is your master's daughter," the Indrik said to her before hopping off the edge of a small cliff and landing without the slightest hesitation. *"She seeks to reunite Alatyr."*

Garafena's roar answered it. "Weles left me to protect a stone that was no longer here."

"He betrayed me too," I yelled over my shoulder, my arms straining from my hold on the Indrik. "And I can give you a purpose again."

"Listen to her before you strike," the Indrik pleaded. *"She is wise for one so young."*

Garafena swooped around us with her green eyes studying me. There was intelligence behind them, a comprehension beyond a beast's. Our legends spoke about żmije like mythical animals of great power, but Ira, Czarnobóg, and now Garafena had all shown they were more than animals. Dragons could burn down villages and slaughter armies, but they acted more like gods than anything else, leading and manipulating to get what was in their interests. Like anyone mortal or immortal, they had desires beyond just survival.

The serpent's body crawled through the air as she spoke. "Koschei has tasked me with the defense of his soul. That is purpose enough."

I raised my spear, Lipiec shining red through the night. "You were created to protect the most powerful artifact in the history of the Three Realms. Rod is dead, so Alatyr is all that's left of the earliest forces. I want to bring the shards back together… I *will* bring them back together. But we need Koschei dead before that can happen."

"You are a child. How can you reunite all twelve Moonstones?"

"We have eight already." I pointed to the sky and crafted moonlight into an illusion of Jaryło's seven Moonblades and Grudzień. "Jaryło kept them as swords, and we took them when we discovered his betrayal. He is the one who helped Marzanna release Czarnobóg. We already have one of her shards too."

Garafena's fire lit the sky as she reeled back and roared. "The dark one is free?"

"And allied with Koschei."

"No! You must speak lies."

The Indrik jumped suddenly, launching us near to Garafena before landing with a massive quake that sent cracks in every direction. *"Otylia of the end does not lie. You know Koschei is a deceiver, yet you assist him anyway because he reminds you of your master."*

Garafena rumbled but dropped toward us slowly, her body slithering through the treetops and her fangs dripping with venom. I shuddered just thinking about the bite of Weles's serpents. "You are lucky that the Indrik speaks favorably of you, child. Weles has gifted me with an understanding of people's true intentions, but it seems even I can falter in this."

"Thank you, Garafena," I said with a bow of my head. "I will honor this promise."

She stopped above us, her head large enough to block out the entire sky. "Words are not enough. Give me Lipiec to guard, and I will take this as a showing of good faith. None shall touch it until you return with the other eleven shards."

I tensed. Lipiec had already helped in the battle against Czarnobóg, and its Moonstone at the tip of my spear would ensure I could kill anyone and anything. But its moon had passed. Its *żityje* reserves would be inaccessible for another year, and I had no desire to fight an ancient dragon. Weles had wronged me. Garafena was no different in that. She didn't deserve to be slain because he'd left her alone on a distant island with no reason to live.

"It's yours to protect, then," I said, touching the end of my spear and drawing Lipiec into my grasp as a stone. Jagged, it represented the shattering of the Alatyr Stone thousands of years ago, and I took a long breath trying to imagine how powerful the united stone would've been. I promised I'd see it in my lifetime.

Garafena lacked arms, so I just tossed Lipiec toward her head in hopes she'd catch it. As it neared, she opened her mouth, and a beam of *żityje* shot from it to the stone, holding it before her. "Thank you, Otylia. I shall seek your return with impatience."

"And you'll let us take Koschei's soul?"

She nodded. "If the sorcerer has allied himself with the worst of my kind, then I have no desire to aid him further. Do with his soul as you wish." Then she turned, flapped her wings hard enough to shake the trees like the mightiest storm, and flew off toward the mountain.

The Indrik bobbed its head. *"You have done well. For the daughter of the wild one, you know well how to tame the untamable."*

"It takes one to know one," I said with a grin as I scanned the woods. "Let's go find the boys before they awaken another spirit. I'm done with żmije."

"Oh, little one, no one is ever done with dragons."

56

Wacław

I'm chasing a rabbit with an immortal sorcerer's soul in it. Wonderful…

I HAD CAUGHT PLENTY OF ANIMALS during my hunting trips. While I was hardly Ara, I considered myself decent. That made Kuba and me scrambling through the woods of Buyan feel all the more foolish.

"I saw it over there!" he shouted in my direction, pointing toward a patch of underbrush nearby. We'd run further down the slope, and the foliage had grown thicker with each step.

"Where?" I asked as I threw out the winds in hopes of sensing it. "There are a hundred bushes where you're pointing."

"That one! Or that one? Gods, I don't remember…"

I groaned and rushed toward where he was pointing. Even the winds struggled to find such a small animal in the thicket, so Kuba's mumbling was still our best lead.

He ran after me, yapping with each thorn that scratched his legs. "Why are you complaining? You've gotta admit that all these bushes look the same."

"They do, but that doesn't make your random comments any more helpful."

"Yeah, well… Okay, you've got a point."

A roar echoed over the island, and I glanced over my shoulder to see a massive winged snake flying over where we'd come from. Garafena's brown scales seemed near black in the moonlight. When she unleashed her flames, they shimmered like precious stones.

Be safe, I silently said to Otylia.

Honestly, I would have preferred to fight the dragon, because this rabbit had me wanting to lightning strike the entire island. Kuba and I were panting messes as we slipped and slid through the ever-wetter ground. *At least it isn't snow,* I tried to tell myself, but it didn't help.

The winds finally brushed against the rabbit nearby. It had stopped too, the winds carrying its small, quick breaths to my ears.

Don't shout this time, I told Kuba through my mark, *but it's close.*

I sprinted after it with my power pushing me with each stride. Stealth wouldn't work—we'd tried that already—so I had to catch it with speed. My rush startled the rabbit, though, and it bolted from its bush and toward a stream that crossed ahead. Lightning arced from my fingers. I could keep the demon's rage back, but my own anger had run my patience dry.

One strike was all it took.

The charred rabbit skidded to a stop at the stream's edge as Kuba caught up behind me. "Coulda left some fun for me."

"This was your definition of fun?"

He shrugged, then picked at the burrs coating his trousers. "Better than being burned to death by a dragon."

We approached the rabbit, weapons drawn just in case there was a trick involved. "I don't get it," I said as I crouched and poked at my kill. "Why hide your soul in a rabbit that's in a chest on an island in the middle of nowhere?"

"Gave us a good runaround, didn't it?" He cocked his head. "Lucky you had your winds and lightning. No way I would've caught it."

"Well, we got it either way."

Kuba stepped away, a disgusted look on his face. "Uh, did we?"

I looked back at the rabbit as something inside it began to move. The rabbit itself remained still, but an object moved through its stomach and up its neck until a bird's head poked through the rabbit's mouth. How, I didn't know, because in the moments after, an entire duck appeared out of the rabbit—at least as large as the animal it had been within.

Kuba and I swapped looks. "Your turn," I quipped.

So he dove, slicing and slashing with his Thunderstone dagger like a kid with a wooden sword. It shouldn't have been hard. But he was Kuba, so he tripped on a root and faceplanted as the duck fled. Still, he waved me off as I moved to make chase.

"I got it!"

He did miraculously have it. Despite the duck taking flight, Kuba burst after it faster than I'd ever seen him run, then leaped as high as my head to snatch the bird before crashing to the ground with a thud. The duck squirmed, but he drove his dagger into its chest before it could escape.

For a moment, we both took a long breath as another roar jarred my heart. I worried, but I hadn't felt any pain from Otylia. Instead, she felt proud, confident, so maybe her and the Indrik's plan had worked. Not having to kill every beast we faced would be a first.

"Think that's it?" Kuba asked, not letting go of the duck in case something else happened.

I reflected on what had just happened. "Kuba, did you fly?"

"Whatcha mean, fly?" He smirked. "I've always been a better jumper than you."

"Yeah, but never *that* good."

His eyes widened, and he rolled up his sleeve to expose his glowing red Eclipsemark. "It never did that before!"

He'd dropped the duck in the motion, and before I could reply, a *plop* came from it. I grabbed it without a second thought, not ready to go on another chase. Nothing moved within the duck, though. It remained limp and bloodied, but the duck hadn't made the sound. A chicken egg lay at my feet. Unlike its predecessors, it didn't flee, but Kuba snatched it anyway, then took a sigh.

"So an egg inside a duck inside a rabbit inside a chest guarded by a dragon?" he said. "Am I missing anything?"

I dropped the duck and wiped the blood off my hands. "It depends on whether there's something else in the egg."

"There better not be."

A gust rushed through the forest, nearly knocking us off our feet. I reached for Grudzień as Garafena appeared again, her long wings pushing her slithering form through the sky. Except she was heading up the mountain. I could've sworn she glanced at us out of the corner of her eye, but she made no effort to stop us from holding the egg. Otylia's voice entered my head moments later.

"We handled Garafena. Did you catch the rabbit?"

And the duck, I replied. *The egg too.*

"What?"

It's better if you see for yourself. We're down the slope by a stream, but I'm sure the Threads can show you to me anyway.

Kuba held the egg as we waited for her arrival, his eyes full of wonder despite it looking no different than any other egg I'd seen. "The egg makes sense. Sure, it's not a duck egg, but at least it could fit in the duck. How in Oblivion did Koschei get a duck in a rabbit? You think he…" He proceeded to mime someone sticking a duck up a rabbit's butt.

I laughed. "No, I highly doubt he did that."

"Makes ya think though."

"At least Koschei could make you use your head for once."

We spun at the underbrush shifting nearby, but Otylia appeared moments later, the Indrik carrying her at its equivalent of a gallop. It stopped quicker than any horse. Those legs shouldn't have been able to carry it, yet the motion was smooth unless it wanted to create the earthquakes we'd seen when it charged down the mountain.

"That explains the egg," Otylia said, dismounting, then examining the scrapes along both of us. "Ironically, you two were hurt more chasing a rabbit than I was facing a dragon."

"Not fair!" Kuba appealed. "That little bastard was quick."

"But we caught it," I said, stepping to Otylia's side. "Then a duck somehow appeared out of it, causing Kuba to accidentally channel my power and fly to catch it."

She grinned. "Kuba with storm powers. Surely that couldn't be dangerous at all."

"I'm going to ignore that sarcasm," Kuba said before holding out the egg. "I caught the duck without even trying, and it dropped this egg when I killed it."

"What's inside?" Otylia asked.

"I… Wacław said to wait for you."

She huffed and grabbed the egg. "Of course he did."

"Careful!" Kuba tried to snatch it, but she pushed him back.

"You wanted to wait for my help, so you're getting my help." She raised the egg into the moonlight emanating from her skin. "Keep your blades ready. Obviously Koschei has a knack for trickery."

Once we nodded that we were ready, she cracked the egg, but nothing spilled out. There were only the bits of egg shell left in her hands and a thin metal object.

"What is that?" I asked.

She picked the object from the shell. "It's a needle. Something's glowing on it."

I drew closer, trying to tell the difference between Otylia's light and the needle's, but she was right. The tip glowed softly with warm light. It didn't pulse or seem to give off any power, but we kept our guards up anyway.

"Is that it?" I asked. "His soul?"

"The soul is not a physical object to behold," the Indrik said as it stepped closer, looking closer while carefully keeping its horn from stabbing any of us. *"It is rare that one exists beyond Nawia in a form of its choosing instead of inhabiting another, but Koschei appears to have discovered a way for his soul to rest on this needle's end."*

Otylia smiled, her excitement rushing through our connection. "How do we kill it?"

"You must return it to his body, then kill him with a final blow."

"All of this for a little needle?" Kuba asked before pulling out the fern flower and giving it a kiss. "Well, at least we found it after I found the magical flower."

I punched him in the gut. "It's more than a needle. That is his soul, and it's our way to finally end him and the Horde."

"You hit softer than Otylia at least," he mumbled as he clutched his stomach.

"It's because he's too nice," Otylia said before wrapping me in a hug and whispering, "Are you sure we can trust him with—"

I kissed her forehead. "Don't worry. I'll give him some tips about using the winds on the way back. He'll be great."

"I don't need to hear, Otylia," Kuba quipped. "Thanks for asking."

"No, you don't," she replied.

Kuba rubbed his neck. "Feels weird. We came all this way, and now we just go home?"

Otylia rolled her eyes and pointed to the mountain. "I can call Garafena back if you want to fight her alone. That way you can have a more dramatic ending before we go home and save the tribe. You can stab Koschei with the needle yourself if you want."

"Yeah, I guess that's important, but probably better if you do it. I kind of die if I get stabbed."

Otylia slipped the needle into her bag, and as they grabbed water from the stream, I drained the rabbit and duck before we left. There wasn't much *żityje* in them, but we'd need all we could get. The Horde hadn't shown mercy before. They surely wouldn't again.

As we took flight, I reached out to Narcyz through my Eclipsemark to hear how Dwie Rzeki was faring. Ara and Xobas had confirmed before that the Horde would arrive soon. I held my breath as I waited to hear if the attack had come. The reply came soon after, but it wasn't what I'd hoped for.

"Hurry!" Narcyz shouted in my head. *"The Horde's here, and... gah... I don't think we can hold them."*

57

Narcyz

They better have figured out how to kill Koschei.

SMOKE STUNG MY EYES and screams had my ears ringing. But Wacław's voice was clear in my head as I stabbed and blocked in the shield wall our survivors had managed to muster.

"We're coming," he said. *"It'll be a while, but we've got a way to kill Koschei. He's still immortal, so if you see him——"*

Slit the old man's throat, I replied, sending Kwiecień's golden blade through a disgusting demon's chest. Wacław and Otylia knew the names of the types. Didn't matter to me. If they wanted me dead, the feeling went both ways.

"I meant: keep your distance."

I dug my boots deeper into the snow as the winds sent hail over my face. Just another curse from Marzanna. "They found Koschei's soul!" I shouted to the others in my formation. There were around a hundred of us, or there had been last I checked. The Horde had come from every direction, so it was impossible to know how many of us were left. "Kill these bastards, and when they return, we'll separate the sorcerer's head from his neck!"

A cheer rose through the army. News would spread quickly, but Wacław and Otylia would tell the others marked anyway. That meant

Dziewanna and the others with actual powers could get to him while we held the line.

Another wave of demons charged over the earthen wall a hundred strides ahead. All but the last of the defenses beyond the village palisade had fallen in minutes. I'd never forget our last battle against the Horde, but their charge today had been the bloodiest thing I'd ever seen.

Five hundred chargers had hit our lines at full speed as lightning demons and ones with sharp fangs attacked from above. Even with six Moonblades, a wild goddess, szeptuchy, and demons all fighting on our side, we were outmatched in the darkness. Couldn't see the stupid things before they appeared out of nowhere and tried to slice you to pieces.

Footsteps approached from behind me, pushing their way through the formation to my side. "I told you our friends would succeed," Andrij said with literal flames at his fingertips. It was strange, but his devotion to Dziewanna had been rewarded. He had regained sight despite his smoky eyes and could wield fire. I just had a fancy sword.

"I also told you that you're better on the wall," I muttered. "Better angles up there."

He drew his bowstring and shot a burning arrow into a demon. As big as a bull, it roared before collapsing as the flames spread to its allies. "Seems good enough for me right here."

I grunted to myself and raised my shield as Andrij stepped back, allowing the shield wall to form up. We needed to stand firm, and I readied myself for the impact as that voice in my head decided it wasn't loud enough.

"Narcyz, are you listening to me?" Wacław yelled.

Kinda busy!

"You can channel my power! Kuba managed to do it on accident, so just try not thinking about it."

What a load of—

The demons arrived, crashing into our shield wall with a deafening echo of shrieks and snarls. Our men—and a few women that had decided to pick up weapons—stabbed back, but we lost ground. Holes formed in our lines where the largest demons hit. The smaller ones followed and ripped into the deeper ranks until entire sections of the formation were separated. Andrij burned groups of the attackers, the firelight exposing the masses of them waiting behind, but it wasn't enough. Soon came the horn for retreat.

Andrij and I ran with the survivors, swinging and shooting wildly to clear a path through the chaos. Nowhere was safe as arrows rained from both armies. Too many had already embedded themselves in my shield, and a crack ran along it as I blocked another from striking the back of Andrij's head.

"We need to get to the gate!" I urged him.

But my heart dropped when the eastern gate came into sight. Hundreds… no, thousands… of our warriors tried to flee through its narrow gap. They piled up, not forming a defensive line in their panic, and the demons tore through those trapped outside. Hundreds more like us hadn't even reached the gate.

"We hold here!" Andrij commanded, unleashing his flames at another charging group of demons.

I gritted my teeth, but joined him. His flank was badly exposed, and if staying here kept him alive, then so be it. "You'll run out of *żityje* eventually," I warned him.

He loosed an arrow far over his target's head. "I know."

"Wacław says I should be able to channel his power." I dodged a diving strzyga, then slashed across her owl wing with Kwiecień. Her black blood joined the sea of it that melted the snow at our feet. "I don't know how."

"This would be the perfect time for you to figure it out."

The demons had closed around us now. With the rest of our formation dead or caught at the gate, we were far from our allies and encircled—any warrior's worst nightmare.

I bit my cheek and tried to reach for that same feeling in my head that came when Wacław talked. It was like something pulling tight. The same thing happened when I reached out to him, so maybe if I tried…

Three demons lunged at once. I stopped one with my battered shield, slashing at another with Kwiecień, but the third snuck to my left before I could turn. Right when I tried to reach out to Wacław, its claws ripped into my shield arm. I yelled with all the rage my tired body could muster and threw the shield. The demon was unfazed by the yell, but the shield knocked it back enough for me to gain the space I needed. By the time it recovered its footing, I was already thrusting my blade through its forehead.

That move had felt *good*, better than any other I'd done in the battle so far. Another set of demons tried to use the gap between Andrij and me to surround him, but I got there in two quick strides, sending them sprawling with a low strike and following up with a stab through each of their skulls.

My heart raced with the thrill. I'd never killed so many demons that quickly. They couldn't keep up with my motions, but my shield was gone, broken. It didn't matter. Kwiecień's hilt had plenty of room for a two-handed grip, and it swung even stronger that way. The most massive beasts fell like they were leaves in the wind. I lost count of the demons and cultist riders I killed, slashing away until I found myself standing on an ever-growing mound of demonic corpses.

"What happened to you?" Andrij called over the noise of battle, backing into me as his flames dimmed. "I've never seen you fight like that."

I grinned, then pushed deeper into the thrill in my chest. Power rushed through me—the same one I'd felt when Mieczysław tried to kill me moons before—and a tickle ran across my fingers as little zaps of lightning arced from them. "I think I'm channeling. Huh. No wonder Wacław got so good with his sword." It was cheating, but against a demonic Horde, we needed every advantage we could get.

"Think you can get us out of here?" Andrij replied.

I hopped as I sliced down another set of demons with strikes so fast I couldn't even see Kwiecień move. Nothing pulled me into the air. "I still can't fly, but I can try to clear a path to the gate. Cover my back."

We swapped positions, and I clenched my jaw as I held out my free hand toward the gate. Demons swarmed the fifty strides between us and it. For better or worse, whatever warriors had been trapped were gone. I didn't know how many had made it through, but I wasn't going to let us join the dead.

Lightning shot from my fingers in an uncontrolled blast. Splitting in every direction, it bore through the closest demons and knocked over those further away as that rush of energy left me. I stumbled, struggling to stand, but I'd cleared most of the demons between us and the gate. I grabbed Andrij and made for the gap.

Demons swarmed us as we fought our way toward the gate, and my injured arm hurt worse with every swing. We were only halfway before I had to switch back to a one-handed grip. It was faster, but that speed I'd felt before was weaker now. My connection to Wacław's power felt looser, and that just made me more desperate to get to safety. Andrij's power had failed him too. We wouldn't last long as two powerless warriors surrounded by demons.

The winds stopped pushing me as we reached the last batch of demons. My legs felt like logs, my arms like anvils. We were so close! I tried to lumber on, but lightning demons shot from the sky as more surrounded us on the ground. There was nowhere to go.

Just as the demons struck together, a horn blast came from just inside the wall. The gate burst open moments later, and while we fought for our lives, I caught sight of riders, both their torsos and their mounts covered in chain mail. They charged through the demons with longswords glinting in the moonlight before dark blood coated their blades. Hope came with them, but it distracted me long enough for a demon to rake its claws across my back, forcing me to my knees in agony.

Andrij cried out for me as the riders reached us. They circled about, giving Andrij enough space to drag me free from the swarm and toward the gate with the riders covering our retreat. My head grew light as we passed into relative safety. The world spun around me, and I collapsed into a tree once we reached the makeshift camp the army had set up within the village.

"Who were those men?" I huffed, closing my eyes as a headache struck.

Andrij took a long breath. "Solgawi, based on their armor. Looks like Kostroma and Simargł kept their promise."

"Let's hope it's enough."

58

Ara

How does she do that?

DZIEWANNA STOOD BESIDE ME on one of the archery platforms mounted to Dwie Rzeki's south wall. She shot flaming arrows down upon the sea of demons so quickly that I could barely comprehend her movements. Meanwhile, I felt useless, managing to only craft a few illusions to misguide the demons before shooting them in the head. It wasn't enough, and the few shots I managed were disrupted by the blizzard's winds and hail.

Sosna yapped at my feet and wrapped her fluffy tail around my leg.

"Yes, I know they're trying to kill us," I muttered, loosing my second-to-last arrow before shouting over my shoulder. "I need more arrows!"

Xobas's runners had been supplying us with all that we needed upon the walls, but now, there was no reply. After the outer fortifications had fallen, the village grew more chaotic with each passing minute. Demons slammed up against the southern gate, and it sounded like the eastern one was no better. They hadn't broken through yet. I doubted it would be long before one of Marzanna's szeptuchy arrived, though, and demolished the wall like they'd done in the last battle.

Dziewanna dropped a new set of arrows into my quiver, then proceeded to shoot again without a moment's hesitation. "We need to find Koschei if we're to end this when Otylia returns," she said. "Marzanna must be channeling her power through him to control many of the demons. If he dies, they'll lose their organization."

I reached into End's wisps with Otylia's power, hoping to find some hint of his location. Instead, screams battered my mind as death after death passed before me on the wisps. I cursed and forced them away. Otylia had warned me how difficult they were to control, but End could be simple at least once, right?

"I'd fly overhead," I replied between shots, "but there's no way I'm going up in *that*."

Between the blizzard, strzygi, and chały, the sky was a deathtrap. Strzybóg's szeptuchy were all but useless with their god's death, and we had far fewer nymphs and flying demons than the Horde. Having Wacław and Otylia would've helped clear the skies. I doubted that even they could give us the advantage in the air, though.

A rumble shook the wall, and I grabbed hold of it to avoid falling off the platform. Screams followed to the north, near the confluence of the Krowik and Wyzra rivers.

"They've broken through," Dziewanna said after only a glance over her shoulder.

"How can you tell?" I replied.

Her determined frown turned to sorrow. "The animals I've called are connected to me. They fight alongside your warriors, but they are falling quickly."

Wings flapped nearby. I turned, ready to loose an arrow until Vlatka appeared.

"Marzanna and Czarnobóg's szeptuchy are attacking the north and east," she said to Dziewanna. "They must've realized you are here."

"Of course they would avoid me," Dziewanna replied. "Cowards."

"Czarnobóg has szeptuchy?" I asked.

Dziewanna loosed another round of arrows as the gate cracked below. "They're all men, szeptuny, surrounded by darkness that chokes people. Is there any sight of Koschei?"

"He's launching his sorcery against the walls from deep within the Horde's ranks," Vlatka said, "but he keeps moving. Seems like he's content to let the demons do the work."

"Where was he last?"

"North gate. His blast blew open a huge chunk of the wall."

Dziewanna shouldered her bow and looked to the north. "Then that is where I must go. Ara, come with me while Vlatka keeps scouting."

We rushed across the village to the north gate. I would've carried Dziewanna with Otylia's moon, but my *żityje* was running low from the illusions and moonblasts I'd used. Luckily, even with my arrows running low again, I had the deep gray Październik Moonblade, which I drew at the sight of the demons pouring through the north wall. The entire village was panic, but the generals had organized a real defense here. Warriors from every tribe had created a shield wall as Solgawi riders and armored infantry tried to push forward.

"Make room for the goddess!" Xobas shouted from horseback nearby. Blood dripped from his curved cavalry blade. While other commanders would keep to the rear, it didn't surprise me to see he'd been involved in the fight.

Dziewanna burst forward, her entire body aflame as she struck the first line of demons. I followed as the warriors surged behind her. Even a goddess was only one fighter, but I'd seen how momentum shifted areas of the battlefield. Her presence alone had given the warriors hope, and watching their enemies burn from Dziewanna's touch was enough to ignite a spark in any defender's heart.

It amazed me how easily my Moonblade sliced through the demons. I still had little experience in melee combat, but it was lighter than any blade should've been and natural in my hand. It allowed me to not only help the charge behind Dziewanna but lead it. Warriors covered my flanks without command and cut down the smaller demons while Dziewanna and I focused on the upióry that had feasted upon the dead. Some towered nearly twice my height. Moonstone cut them all the same.

What felt like an eternity later, we reached the destroyed gate, allowing Mothermarked szeptuchy to push into the cleared space and create earthen walls where the wooden ones had been. It wouldn't hold forever, but the choke point allowed the defenders to build another shield wall multiple lines deep.

"Do you trust me, Ara?" Dziewanna said over her shoulder, unleashing her flames in a semicircle before her and turning the ground to a shin deep muck. "I need your help if I am to reach Koschei."

I nodded, but my arms trembled as I raised my Moonblade. "Let's kill a sorcerer."

Despite the power Dziewanna obviously had now, I feared she'd run out of *żityje* as we fought our way through the demons. She still had few worshippers, and she hadn't stopped channeling her flames since we'd arrived at the north gate. So I reached out to Otylia for advice.

How far away are you? I asked. *Dziewanna is going to burn through her żityje at this rate just getting to Koschei.*

"We're close!" she replied. *"It's taking all my żityje just to get everyone there."*

I parried a cultist's ax as he rode past, then circled away with ice covering his veins. *Everyone?*

"I redeemed enough demons in the Mangled Woods for a small army." She seemed hesitant yet hopeful. *"Will it be enough?"*

Just hurry. We don't have much time.

Dziewanna switched tactics as we fought through the swamps near the Wyzra, pushing toward where sorcerous blasts lit the sky. She controlled roots and branches instead of flames. They entangled, then crushed anyone who came near, and others shot straight through the demons' heads like arrows.

When a few upióry rushed by her defenses, she danced between the impossibly quick beasts with fur crossing her skin. Her teeth turned sharp, her whole body growing until she looked half woman and half bear. The upióry never stood a chance.

She roared when she was finished, and a hundred calls responded.

We fought on as wolves, foxes, hawks, and countless smaller animals cut through the Horde to join us. They guarded our flanks, but we were still surrounded. Every step was perilous, each stab a risk to get caught out. There was a joy in fighting beside Dziewanna, though. I felt her deific strength in my soul. It urged me to be better, faster, and I channeled that will with Otylia's power, moonblasting when the sword wasn't enough.

Koschei appeared after yet another of those moonblasts cleared a path ahead. Riding his white horse with a dark crown on his head, he looked like the king of death. His black eyes sucked away the moonlight around him, and darkness seemed to cover him and his elite riders, who wielded massive bone spears and watched the battle from behind skull masks. Unlike the sinew and muscles exposed beneath Koschei's skin, the elites appeared alive, not bearing any god's mark.

The sorcerer turned toward us with a crooked smile. I tried to get Dziewanna's attention, but she was busy fending off a swarm of strzygi as Koschei pointed a finger of bone at me. Though his mouth moved, I couldn't hear the words.

Black tendrils burst from his hand.

I yelped and dove away as they crossed the space between us in a blink, but they snatched my legs out from under me. Październik slid from my grasp. My only weapon was gone as the tendrils crept up my legs, stabbing me like a hundred daggers. I called the moon's power to my hands, but what could I do? A moonblast would hit my legs, and illusions wouldn't help either.

As I dug my fingers into the snow and screamed for help, a blur of orange sprinted over me. Sosna dug her teeth into the tendrils, growling and shaking her head violently. I hated that she'd put herself at risk. But gratitude soon replaced that fear, because the tendrils released me and retreated to their master. Sosna yapped and licked me across the face as Koschei ushered on his elite guard.

"They're coming!" I shouted to Dziewanna as I scrambled back, my legs all but useless from the pain.

The goddess leaped over me, flames dancing around her bear-like form as she glared at the advancing riders. Few of our animal allies were left, but they fought with everything they had. My heart raced watching it all happen so fast. I was little use with my Moonblade now, so I crawled over to a tree and climbed it until I was nearly standing. Sosna kept watch as I pulled my bow again, my hands shaking with each movement.

Do it for Otylia, I told myself. *She wouldn't be scared, so neither should I.*

Dziewanna ripped through the first two riders as I tried my bowstring to no avail. It was impossible to aim while panicking. I needed to focus. I needed to find the calm Otylia had used to tame her power. So I did what no one should ever do in the midst of battle. With three long breaths, I closed my eyes and pictured myself as a proud huntress. Master of the forest. Expert of the bow. Fearless.

Then I pulled back the bowstring and aimed, holding my breath as I willed End's wisps to show me the immediate ends—where the riders would be.

Every color emerged from the darkness. The riders were living, and their wisps were vibrant against the blackness Koschei wielded against Dziewanna. I focused on the nearest one, who was rounding a tree to flank her. Archery was usually a guesswork with a moving target, but the wisp showed exactly where he'd be.

The bowstring snapped against my bracer when I released it, a familiar sting that told me I'd managed enough power behind the shot. Dziewanna didn't notice the rider, but the wisp had been right. My arrow met the rider right where it said he'd be, hitting right in the heart.

I staggered and caught myself against the tree's trunk. My *żityje* was all but gone now. Looking into the immediate future took more of it than calling the wisps normally, and it gave me a sickly feeling.

Luckily, I'd done enough to help Dziewanna defeat the elites, as the last dropped from his horse with a mighty bite from her bear maw. Darkness covered the space between her and Koschei. Sosna and the other remaining animals protected me, but the demons all kept their distance as Koschei's dark tendrils consumed the trees for a dozen strides. Threads of *žityje* spiraled between his deathly fingers as he stared at the wild goddess.

"I know what your offspring has done to my soul," he said, his voice hollow and airy, echoing upon itself. "You have come to finish me, but another has claimed you as her foe today."

The already frigid air cooled further. It seared at my exposed skin as darkness circled Koschei's hand, expanding until it spiraled across the ground before him. Dziewanna wasn't going to just let him cast his spell, though, and she charged, her growl of frustration smothered by the growing storm.

She was too slow.

White and blue climbed from the snow and consumed the darkness until a woman stood in Dziewanna's way. Clutching a scythe in one hand and a skull in the other, she was deathly pale and dressed in robes of black trimmed in red. Her cheeks were painted in crimson warpaint, and a line of it ran from her thin lips to the bottom of her chin. She raised the scythe and smiled with her eyes flickering from black to a pure white. Above, the Frostmark woven into her arcing kokoshnik headdress pulsed as ice pyres rose around her.

"Hello, dear sister," Marzanna hissed. "You did not believe I would allow you to ruin my fun so easily, did you?"

59

Wacław

We're too late…

Dwie Rzeki burned.

The Horde covered my home from its once lush forests and rivers to its vibrant flowing trails. What defenses our army had managed to build had fallen, leaving the dark mass of slithering, snarling beasts to ravage the lands beyond the village walls. Inside them was little better.

"Where are you, Mother?" Otylia asked the air as we surged toward the east gate on her moon power, Florion and our other newly allied demons into the fight below. Though the winds could hold Kuba and me, they were fickle in the blizzard and barely able to deflect the hail that had pelted us for the hours we'd flown.

It was impossible to tell living from dead. The swirling masses of snow, waves of arrows, and moonlit darkness obscured everything, so we swept lower, immediately finding chały.

Lightning cracked at their fingers, but as Otylia took my hand, I grinned. The storm was mine. All they could do was feed my power as their bolts shot into me, igniting my veins in a bright blue.

"I'll deal with these," I said to her. "Go find Dziewanna and end this."

Relief crossed her face, and her Threads of Life emerged as she followed the one connecting her to Dziewanna, bounding across the air on the Indrik's back. Ara had messaged her moments before that Marzanna had arrived. My stomach flipped at the thought of facing the winter goddess who'd tricked me all those moons ago, but with Grudzień drawn, I turned my focus to the chały. They reeled back at the realization I'd absorbed their blast. Too late to evade my own strike.

Thunder rolled as I raised Grudzień into the storm clouds. Then I pulled from Marzanna's storm, drawing lightning into the blade and spinning to send an arc of it through the demons. It cut through them like the sharpest sword. In a deafening *crack*, they fell with one final shriek piercing the blizzard.

Kuba smiled up at me. He still struggled to channel the winds effectively, but it at least allowed me to focus on my own fighting. "Can I do that too?" he asked, grinning at his hand.

"Not unless you want a demonic soul," I replied before turning my attention to the rest of the battle.

To the south, I caught sight of Sabina leading a group of nymphs through the clouds. Their songs echoed over the sounds of death below, occasionally replaced by the roar of fire from Vlatka's eagle beak. They seemed to barely have the better of the demons on that side of the battle, but the situation was far worse to the north, where Otylia had gone.

Dark spires stabbed from the ground to the clouds at random, surrounding an area resembling a crater from a powerful blast. They blocked my sight, but my tether to Otylia told me that's where Koschei and Marzanna were. Even the demons kept away from there; though, strzygi and chały circled overhead to ensure none of our allies drew near.

I motioned for us to go, but Kuba caught my arm as he pointed toward the east gate. It had fallen, and the demons were pushing back a thin formation of warriors. Dozens of tents and houses filled the trails just strides behind them. "Narcyz and Andrij are inside the walls, and I know Maja is too. I need to help them, please!"

I embraced him quickly before grabbing my shield from my back as he thumped his own. "Go. Protect the village, and use my power to keep our friends safe, even if it means using it to flee with them."

With half-a-smile, he turned and flew toward the eastern defenders. Panic filled my chest watching him go. The countless bodies of people and demons covering the ground told enough of a story how the battle had gone, and I hated putting another friend in harm's way. There were still thousands of demons charging the gates. How long could we hold, even if we forced Marzanna to retreat?

A snap of pain from Otylia tore me from my thoughts. There was no time for sentiment, so I pushed all my strength into the winds and flew toward the spires. The sky grew darker here, the moonlight fading as an unbelievable frost struck me. It became difficult to even keep my eyes open, and I had to blink rapidly out of fear of my eyeballs freezing.

Then the goddesses appeared. Marzanna, robed in black and red. Dziewanna, much of her body morphed into a ferocious bear. And Otylia, riding upon the Indrik's back with her light banishing tendrils of darkness that sprouted from the rider in the circle's center.

"Koschei!" I shouted, pulling the storm clouds with me as I dropped with lightning at my back.

The undead sorcerer grinned up at me with the battle's flames reflected in his soulless eyes. Another fire burned in my heart—hatred. Naw or not, Koschei had slaughtered my tribe and so many others. He'd enslaved and corrupted. He'd sworn himself to the gods of death and darkness. And I swore I would ensure he never saw daylight again.

60

Otylia

Mother won't fight her alone. Not this time.

THE AIR ITSELF LASHED OUT AT ME as I landed beside Mother with my spear ready. It shouldn't have been possible to be so cold, but Marzanna was winter itself.

"You have come to witness your mother's death?" she cackled. "I have no use for her now, so why not rid the Three Realms of her? The only one who'll miss the wild goddess is you."

Mother growled in response, slamming her bear arms into the icy ground. Blood dripped from her fanged teeth and fury filled her gaze. But she was wounded too, slashes tearing through her dress and exposing the cuts beneath. I didn't get a chance to tell how deep they were, because she charged, colliding with an ice shield Marzanna summoned at the last second.

Shards scattered in every direction, but the Indrik saw them coming. As Mother clashed with the ice goddess, we rounded them to Marzanna's rear. I released a moonblast moments before the Indrik plunged its horn into her back.

Ice exploded from Marzanna. It threw me off my mount with blood dripping from a dozen wounds, but the Indrik seemed unharmed as it landed beside me.

"We must wear down her žityje," it said. *"A thousand cuts are greater against a god than a single blow, especially one without an Alatyr shard."*

I cursed my deal with Garafena as I rolled to dodge an ice spear that shot from the ground. It had needed to be done, but how could I kill Marzanna without Moonstone? We hadn't expected her. Now, her appearance had us on the back foot until we could send the needle into Koschei's head.

Mother's flames seared the ice as they grew across her entire body. Like a torch in the night, she was blinding as she charged Marzanna again and again. Marzanna extinguished the flames each time, but then Mother would circle away and bring them back. Burns spread across Marzanna's exposed skin, joined by knicks from the Indrik's horn and my spear as we mirrored Mother's attacks.

The Indrik's earthquakes threw Marzanna off balance as I mounted it again. If it wasn't careful, the same happened to Mother, though, and a crevice opened beneath her foot. Marzanna had fallen to her knees, but she chanted in the old tongue, filling the crack with ice and freezing Mother's foot within it.

"Jawia has fallen!" Marzanna hissed, charging Mother with her sickle blade ready. "And now you'll fall with it."

I pushed the Indrik faster, but we were too far. Marzanna slashed the sickle toward Mother's throat as she flailed her bear arms in defense. My scream echoed through the woods. I couldn't lose her. Not again. Not forever.

I poured all the *žityje* I had left into a moonblast.

A *boom* shook the woods as light flashed before me. I slumped onto the Indrik's neck, blinded and unable to hold myself up from exhaustion. The sounds of the fight continued ahead of us. Marzanna's laughter, followed by Mother's roar.

She's alive. That's all that matters.

My vision slowly cleared as a surge of pain came from my bond with Wacław. I cried out with no *žityje* to dull the impact. From the cracks of lightning ahead, he'd arrived to face Koschei.

Take the needle, I told him silently, throwing it toward him. *We need you. I need you.*

His power wouldn't be enough to defeat Marzanna if mine wasn't, but between him and our friends, they had seven Moonblades. We only needed one.

The Indrik sprinted toward a patch of trees and set me down. *"I will aid Dziewanna. Do not fall in this battle, Otylia of the end. The Three Realms are not yet finished with you."* Then it sprinted off.

I could only grit my teeth and watch Mother continue her fight against Marzanna. Her roots tried to entrap her sister now, but Marzanna's ice shredded them like they were nothing. Even fire couldn't do any real damage.

I spun, spear ready as footsteps approached. But it wasn't a demon.

"Ara?" I said with a gasp. "What are you doing here?"

She hobbled to me, using her deep gray Moonblade as a crutch. Father would've considered such use of a godly artifact an insult, but I didn't care. Seeing her brought hope to my heart, if only for a moment.

"Dziewanna said she needed my help," she said before leaning herself against the tree. With a sharp breath, she nocked an arrow on her bow. "Now I know why."

"You can't be here!" I snapped. "My *żityje* is out, so you won't be able to channel."

She smirked. "I never needed channeling to shoot a beast before. Why would I need it now?"

Then she loosed the arrow, the force of it throwing her to the ground. I caught her, then looked back at the goddesses. Ara's arrow had somehow pierced the flying spells and embedded itself in Marzanna's ribs—right where her heart would've been if she'd had one. It was only a distraction for someone as powerful as Marzanna.

A distraction was all Mother needed.

She dropped her bear form, grabbing her bow and shooting a series of flaming arrows faster than I could comprehend. Marzanna glared at Ara and missed the greater threat for only a blink. By the time she realized it, three arrows burned deep in her torso as another buried itself in her skull. Her ice shield blocked the rest, but the damage had been done.

Koschei shouted from the center of the spires as Marzanna reeled back. Darkness spun around her, and she collapsed with the Indrik shaking the ground.

A thousand cuts.

I ran toward Marzanna. My head spun. My soul was drained. But I kept my gaze on the fallen goddess who'd taken everything from me.

Marzanna launched wild ice spears at Mother and the Indrik, forcing them back for a moment, but she'd lost sight of me. I was nothing without *žityje*, right? A mortal with a silver spear was no threat to the queen of eternal winter, but it plunged into her stomach anyway.

Her eyes flashed from white to black as my spear vanished without my *žityje* to fuel it any longer. It had served its purpose, and the darkness grew around Marzanna as her wounds failed to close. All around us, the frigid cold returned to winter's normal chill. We'd won, yet Marzanna only smiled.

"Oh, child," she said, staring up at me. "You should know better than to have such hope."

The dark spires shattered, and thousands of sharp stones fell upon us. I raised my arms to instinctively call my *pri* shield. None came. I feared the stone shower's damage without *žityje* to heal, but moments before they struck, Mother appeared over me, covering my body with hers.

Each stone struck her with a horrifying noise, like that of a dagger driven into someone's chest. It was over in seconds, but when Mother dropped to the ground beside me, her blood stained the snow. Only a few of her wounds began to close.

"I really should get more worshippers," she muttered with a wry smile. She stumbled, and I had to throw her arm over my shoulder to keep her from falling.

"Why'd you do that?" I asked, shaking as memories of her death five years before ran through my mind. *Not again…*

She pressed her hand to my cheek. "I would give anything for you, my *mała dziką*. But do not weep. Though I will need some *žityje* to mend the wounds, these stones are not enough to kill me. My work is not done yet." Wincing, she turned with me to face Marzanna, whose dark gaze fell upon us.

"Your pathetic cities and villages burn," Marzanna muttered, nearly upon us. "I possess your husband! I destroyed your precious forest and have my Alatyr shards to thrive no matter what you do to kill me. You have *nothing* left."

Mother pulled an arrow from her quiver and stepped toward her. "I have everything." Then she drove it into Marzanna's skull.

61

Wacław

I just need the needle.

KOSCHEI DIDN'T MOVE AS I SWUNG GRUDZIEŃ, but he didn't need to. A force shook the ground, sending spikes of ice at me before I could react. They struck me, and I tumbled to Koschei's side as *żityje* desperately worked to mend my wounds.

"So the young płanetnik chooses to show his face," Koschei said with a mocking laugh. "Such a shame it must end like this… for you."

Tendrils broke from the closest spires, but I hacked them away as they snatched at my limbs. One grabbed hold. I stumbled back at its touch, *żityje* draining from my soul until I slashed through it, careful to ensure another didn't follow. *Żityje* deprivation was more than torture, and in a battle like this, it was death. Otylia was too busy focusing on Marzanna. Our other friends were caught elsewhere in the battle, too far to help. I needed to take charge myself.

Pretending to dart to the side, I sent a ball of lightning at Koschei. He deflected it with a sorcerous shield, but the effort drew his attention away for long enough. I bounded above and launched lightning that he deflected with a shield.

I tried to catch a glance of Otylia's fight with Marzanna out of the corner of my eye. Between the creeping darkness, shattering ice, and blasts of fire and moonlight, it was impossible to tell who was winning. But I felt Otylia's pain. Her desperation came through our bond, and as she threw the needle toward me, I prayed to the Great Mother that she not take another strike.

"Many before have already tried to kill me!" Koschei said, pointing at me once again. Dark wisps drifted from his hand before sputtering and falling short. "What is this?"

I called the needle to me on the winds, catching and holding it up. "You mean this?"

"No!"

I charged, and the sorcerer cried out as he threw himself from his horse and into the icy ground with a *snap*. "Baba Jaga tried to help you," I said. "But she gave away just enough."

"It cannot be!" he shouted, but as he held out his arms toward the spires, they began to crack. "IT CANNOT BE!"

I charged, forcing him to use all his remaining power to block my strikes with Grudzień. He succeeded, but even the blades could only wound him. The needle was all that mattered. Though he knew that, he fought like a trapped animal, desperate for an escape. There was none.

His sorcery soon faltered for a moment, and I slammed the needle into his forehead. It carried his soul at its end and returned it to his body. He was vulnerable now, and as he staggered back, I ran Grudzień through his chest with lightning cracking across its blade.

"Suffer in Oblivion," I snarled. "It's better than you deserve."

The spires shattered as Koschei dissolved into ash. Thousands of black shards descended upon us, but I could only stare at the place he'd stood. The sorcerer who'd conquered Jawia, slaughtering as he pleased, had died at my hand.

Why wasn't I happy?

Marzanna cried out from the circle's edge once the shards had fallen. Darkness surrounded her like a whirlwind, and when Dziewanna drove an arrow into her head, she began to dissolve like Koschei.

"No!" Otylia screamed. "She can't escape!"

Dziewanna stepped back with tears in her eyes as Marzanna vanished in her grasp. "You'll pay for what you've done!" the wild goddess roared. "Jawia is mine, and with every force in its grasp, I will uproot you from that hole you've dug yourself in Nawia. I will slay Czarnóbóg, and then I'll come for you."

No response came. The darkness faded from the clearing without Koschei's power, and the air warmed to that of a usual winter without Marzanna's. But beyond the ring the sorcerer had created, thousands of demons awaited us, their groans and shrieks all the more obvious without their leaders to deal with.

I landed by Otylia's side, her frustration evident without need of our bond. "That was our chance," she grumbled.

"If Koschei summoned some part of her, then she'll be weakened," I replied.

Dziewanna staggered into a tree, huffing as a series of wounds bled across her back. "We wounded her badly, but there was no way to kill her through such a spell. My sister will be back."

In the pause, Kuba spoke through my mark, *"Uh, did you guys do something? The bloodthirsty monsters just stopped and are kinda just standing there."*

Koschei's dead, I replied with a sigh of relief. If the demons had stopped attacking, then Mom and everyone else still alive were safe for now.

"Oh good. Does that mean I can take a nap and try to forget any of this ever happened?"

I ignored him, repeating what he'd said about the demons aloud. Ara stayed tense, holding her bow tentatively while leaning against another tree to keep weight off one of her legs. "Think they'll let us get back to the village?"

Dziewanna raised a hand. "Wait. Koschei must have held them under some sort of spell. I would ask Otylia to search their Threads, but she is without *żityje*."

"Easily fixed." I grabbed hold of Otylia's arm where our marks met. "I don't have much left, but it's better than nothing."

For once, she didn't protest, and I gave her all the *żityje* I had, stopping before my reserves became dangerously low. Our time in Vastroth had been terrible. I was grateful, though, that whatever ritual she'd used to calm my demonic soul had tightened our bond and ensured we no longer needed to transfer *żityje* through blood. That had always felt uncomfortable, no matter how necessary.

Otylia gave a weak smile in thanks, then looked into the Threads, her eyes flashing white as thousands of them emerged around us. Each beyond our group was blackened, but some held the dullest streaks of color. Did that mean not all of them were truly lost? We had believed they couldn't be saved, but had Koschei's sorcery altered their Threads?

"They're not all fully corrupted," Otylia said, shuddering as she often did when seeking End's power. "I can't save demons who were corrupted by their own actions, but many of these were corrupted by others, especially Koschei or earlier demons in the Horde."

"What about the ones who are fully corrupted?"

She scanned the woods, where many of the demons were moving now. I readied Grudzień at that, but they were lumbering *away* from Dwie Rzeki and toward the Wyzra River.

"There's no saving those who are so far gone," Dziewanna said, "but we are too few and too weary to defeat all of them. Our best route would be to redeem those with some semblance of a mind left before their demonic hunger overtakes them."

"There are at least a thousand of them," Otylia replied, her eyes wide. "I don't have enough *żityje* to save them all."

Marzyana stepped through the crowd of demons with a gentle smile. "I did not intend to eavesdrop, but I was on my way to help when the demons fell still. Did you say you are in need of *żityje*, Otylia?" She held out the orange sickle-like Moonblade of Sierpień, transforming it to a Moonstone. "It is because of you and your friends that I have found a purpose. It is Sierpień's moon. Use it as much as you need, as I have not tapped much of the Moonstone's *żityje*."

Otylia accepted it—again, surprisingly without resistance. "Sierpień is yours, Marzyana. You saved Ara and then all of us when you helped take the Moonblades."

She closed her eyes, and the light returned to her skin as a new calm came through our bond. Then she returned the stone to Marzyana and took to the air.

What happened next was one of the most miraculous things I've ever seen. I'd only heard how Otylia saved the demons in Sheresy, and there had been many in the Mangled Woods. Now, though, she glowed as she grabbed every Thread within reach, pulling others to her with the force of endings until they surrounded her. A thousand strands. Their darkness succumbed to her light as she chanted in the old tongue, and color crept along each as the demons who'd stayed began to shift. What had once been horrific sounds turned to mumbles and then confused whispers. No longer were their eyes blackened and dead, and though their bodies remained scarred by their demonic forms, many smiled with their gazes fixed upon Otylia.

"She freed us!" a former zmora exclaimed, dropping to her knees. "Gods, what have I done?" Others knelt too, and tears followed the initial joy as they realized the horrors they'd endured as demons.

Light fading, Otylia kept herself aloft as she shouted through the forest, "Marzanna and Czarnobóg controlled you through Koschei. They destroyed your homes and your lives, but you're free to choose your life now. Stay with us and fight to free Jawia from their grasps, or pass on to Nawia as your souls should have."

Then she descended to me. Her eyes were normal again and her expression was stern, focused, but I couldn't stop smiling. "That was amazing!"

"I felt all their pain," she breathed, stepping into my arms and burying her head into my chest. "I thought it was bad in Vastroth, but the things Koschei made them do…"

I held her tight. Waking from the Płanetnik's control and realizing what suffering I'd caused had been one of the hardest things I'd ever endured. Moons later, I still had nightmares about it, and these people would be no different.

"You freed them from that agony," I whispered. "I know that pain. Otylka, you didn't just save Jawia from their attacks. You saved them from an eternity of enduring their demonic hunger and the end they'd face in Oblivion."

She shuddered. "I wish that made it easier."

The crowd of demons parted as we headed back toward Dwie Rzeki, helping along Dziewanna and Ara. A few of Dziewanna's wild animals followed with Sosna, and I patted her head as the little orange ball of energy yapped at each of us.

"She saved my life," Ara said. "I don't know how you thank a fox, but I owe her."

Otylia grinned through her sorrow. "Sosna has a habit of that. Give her meat and belly rubs."

Ara chuckled. "I think I can handle that."

Otylia and I held hands as we neared the northern gate. Our emotions stirred, switching between pride and anguish after what we'd gone through. We'd ended the greatest threat, but the bodies lying in heaps around our village told of the sacrifice it had taken. Mortal men and women who'd held spears and swords as their nightmares descending on their homes. Thousands of them had already fled their villages in fear of the Horde, and this had been their last place to turn. They had no powers, nor an understanding of how we could defeat the Horde. It didn't matter. They'd fought for themselves and their loved ones to the end.

Weles, give them paradise in Nawia if you're still alive. It's the least they deserve.

We would need countless funeral pyres to free their souls and prevent them from becoming demons, but that would come later. First, we had to reunite with our friends and comprehend our losses. Those of us who'd survived now stood in the aftermath of the largest battle for centuries. Elders would one day speak of our victory to their grandchildren, and then those children would do the same to their grandchildren when they were grown. Eventually, stories and myths would replace the truth.

None of the songs that would be sung about us mattered to me then. I had been the one to slay Koschei the Deathless. A Naw. A once exiled demon rejected by his father. But I hadn't done it alone. Otylia had fought beside me, for me, and even against me when she'd needed to. My friends had kept us going, giving us the support and aid we'd needed through the darkest of days. And Dziewanna had restored hope to us all. The goddess of the wilds, the queen of Jawia.

The lines of demons extended past the remnants of the north gate. They hung their heads and whispered prayers to Otylia and Dziewanna as they passed. A sinking feeling struck my chest as we finally reached the defenders and townsfolk behind them, far fewer than the numbers we'd seen in the village only days before.

Mom came rushing from the crowd when I called for her through my mark. She nearly tackled me with her hug, tears streaming down her cheeks as she cradled my head. "Oh my son! Thank the gods you're alive. Thank the wild goddess!"

My heartache only deepened seeing her pain. Besides Otylia, no one meant more to me than her. I didn't know what I would've done if she'd died. "It's okay, *Matka*. It's over."

"I… I felt your lightning," she stammered. "I didn't want to kill them. They're demons like you, and I saw your face in each of them, but they left me no choice. When I dropped my spear, I got so scared."

My power had kept her alive? That struck me hard. Relief and sorrow both washed over me as I wept with her. "I'm sorry you had to fight. I'm sorry I wasn't faster."

"He's gone?" she asked, stepping back and wiping the tears from her eyes. "The sorcerer's dead?"

Otylia rested a hand on her shoulder. "Forever."

She joined us as we headed toward the village center, where the rest of our friends awaited us. Kuba, Xobas, Narcyz, Andrij, Ta, Zakir, and Sabina all had their share of wounds, but they rushed toward us nonetheless to exchange embraces. Even Narcyz accepted my hug. It lasted far longer than I'd expected, and when he released me, tears wetted his eyes.

"Your lightning saved me again," he said in my head. *"Thank you."*

I smiled and punched him lightly in the shoulder. *No, you did that yourself. I knew there was a reason the east gate held better than the north.*

"You two going to kiss or just stare at each other like a couple on Noc Kupały?" Kuba quipped, leaping onto me with a laugh. "Gods, it's good to see you not torn to shreds."

"Good to see you too," I replied before glancing behind him. "Is Maja okay?"

He nodded. "She kept to the back with the other women who don't know how to fight. Probably for the best."

"She's alive, and that's what matters."

He smiled, but before he could reply, Dariusz called for us from the base of Jaryło's Oak. I scowled at the tree, then the priest, before relenting and approaching with Otylia and the others. Defenders and demons alike filled the village center around us. Eager, they watched us closely as we stopped before Dariusz and Xobas, the rattling bones in the oak feeling more ominous than ever.

Dariusz bowed. "After the longest night ever known to Jawia, you all have brought us the first light we have seen for too long. I speak for every person in the living realm when I say that you have our eternal gratitude."

Otylia's jaw dropped at the sight of her father bowing to her and her mother. He'd always been pious to Swaróg, but no one would've ever described Dariusz as a humble man. Yet here he was, yielding to his daughter, the wife he'd sought to control, and the boy he'd tried to sacrifice at birth. Oh, how times had changed.

"Thank you, Dariusz," Dziewanna said, then raised her voice. "But our work is not finished. Weles remains captured, his realm likely bleeding under the grip of Marzanna and Czarnobóg."

"It isn't finished here either," Xobas replied. "You all have done well to defeat Koschei and the Horde, but we all saw thousands of demons escape. They will attack again if we don't find them."

Dziewanna nodded. "And the fields will remain fallow as long as Marzanna's winter endures. We must face her in her home on the black sands of Nawia's edge, ridding the Three Realms of Czarnobóg, ending my sister's corruption, and restoring my husband's rule to Nawia. Weles betrayed my daughter and abandoned me, but the dead have little hope without him."

I noticed then that it was Dariusz leading the discussion, not Mikołaj. "Where is my half-brother?" I asked him. "Where is the high chief?"

A murmur spread through the crowd as Dariusz's shoulders slumped. "Not long has passed since your brother was named high chief of these lands, but he united us in that time, allowing us to be prepared for this day."

"What happened to him?" I snapped, grabbing his priestly robes at the chest.

"High Chief Mikołaj has fallen."

I released him and fell back on my heels. "Miko…"

My elder half-brother had mocked me my entire life, but his opinion toward me had changed since my return from exile. We had never been the closest of brothers. He still shared my blood, and I was the one who pushed for him to overthrow Mieczysław as high chief. Though he'd succeeded in organizing the final defense of Dwie Rzeki and uniting our allies behind his army, I couldn't help but feel responsible for his death.

"Who will lead us now?" I asked, choking on my words.

Dariusz cleared his throat. He almost stopped his lip from curling when he spoke. "Only one village remains standing among the lands of Krowik. As Mikołaj bore no children, Dwie Rzeki passes to you as Jacek's next oldest son, so unless any of the surviving chiefs from the razed villages object, you are the heir, Wacław."

My head spun. I stepped back, shaking my head as it felt like a boulder filled my stomach. "I can't be high chief."

"Should not, I agree," Dariusz said, "but you are the heir to Dwie Rzeki. Unless you defy tradition and choose someone who is not a chief, then you are the main candidate."

"Dziewanna should rule," I blurted out. "Or Otylia! They're goddesses, not a Naw."

Dziewanna gave an understanding smile. "I appreciate your recognition, but if I am to honor Rod's wish for me to rule all of

Jawia, I cannot focus on a single tribe, no matter if it is one of the few remaining."

I looked at Otylia, but she just squeezed my hand, her gaze stern. "There aren't many of us left. Many of them are demons, and no one understands them more than you."

"*You* saved them," I insisted.

"And you taught me that they are worth saving. I can lead with you as queen, Wašek, but we both know I'm not the best at caring for people." She stepped closer and pushed up my chin, forcing me to look at the gathered people—mortal and uncorrupted demons. "You have the heart for this, and you are the heir. You've spent years trying to prove yourself to Jacek. Take his throne and prove he was a fool and a coward to reject you."

I bit my cheek, averting my gaze until I saw little Nevenka in the crowd. My little half-sister clutched a wooden toy tight to her chest. Though she'd likely been hidden away in Mikołaj's longhouse with her mother, Natasza, during the battle, she must've been afraid. If she was, she didn't show it as she smiled at me like she had every time she'd seen me since she was born. She noticed me staring and spoke. It was too quiet to hear, but I read her lips, "Do it, Waci."

A hand fell on my shoulder. Xobas's, and he gave me a shake as he said, "The greatest kings and chiefs don't want to lead. Zakir has grown quickly into the role. You will too. Jacek didn't see it in you, but you were always better with your words than your blade. And you're not half-bad with that sword of yours."

"Thank you, Xobas," I said, giving him a hug that ended with him squeezing me hard enough for me to lose my breath for a moment.

Dariusz pursed his lips as I looked at him again. "What'll it be?" he asked.

I didn't need to think any longer. The answer stirred in my heart, and I took hold of it as I stared out at the gathered crowd. "This isn't Krowik anymore, not really," I said with all the strength of my lungs. "Some of you are Krowikie like me, yes, but others are Simukie, Zurgowie, Astiwie, or demons who have found a new chance. Many

more of you are Vastrothie and Solgawi who have your own kingdoms to return to—probably two of the only ones that survived the
Horde. We've come from across Jawia. Some of us have different
names for the gods, and others had no names for them at all until
recently."

I glanced over my shoulder at the tree we'd once called Perun's
Oak, the weakened winds barely shifting its branches. "So many of
those gods have deceived us, no matter the name we call them or
how often we sacrifice at their altars. They saw us as divided peoples
to be used in their games or just ignored. But we aren't divided.
When faced with the greatest threat we've seen in countless generations, we put aside our differences and defeated Koschei and the
Frostmarked Horde. This last village east of the Krowik bore the
river's name as its tribe, but we're more than a single tribe now. To
stand defiant and finish our fight against Marzanna and Czarnobóg,
we must be more."

Dariusz huffed beside me. "What do you propose, then?"

"A united kingdom." I let that statement spread among the crowd
before continuing. "The Kingdom of the Wild Moon, made of all
the fallen tribes who Dziewanna and Otylia have protected. If they
refuse to take the throne and no one else wants it, then I'll do what
I can to ensure each of you has a place here. Mortal, demon, Naw,
or nymph. The time of scattered tribes split by our differences is
over." I raised my hands toward the crowd. "Let anyone who would
oppose me come so that the people here can decide who to follow.
I won't rule through fear."

Whispers spread as some applauded, but a few crossed their arms.

Zhaleh stepped forward, her chin held high and her green Zurgowie paint smeared across her cheeks. "I cannot stand idly by and
allow a Krowik to take my clan from me. I am high priestess of Zurgow, and my people will have the lands you promised to us."

I nodded, not surprised by the zealous priestess's objection. "The
southern hills are yours and Simuk's, as we agreed. If you don't wish
to remain in our kingdom, then those who wish to leave with you to
have independence may."

"I will stay," Zakir said quietly from Ara's side before raising his voice when she nudged him. "Simuk will join the Wild Moon."

"Then your clan is dead," Zhaleh replied. "We will live on." With a raised fist, she called the Zurgowie to her, but only fifty or so answered. A few led horses—far less than they needed as a nomadic clan.

"No matter how few," I said, "our agreement stands."

The priestess scoffed and mounted her horse, then led her followers out of the village, heading toward the south gate. Despite Zhaleh never being a friend, it hurt to see her leave. The Zurgowie had once been a clan with thousands of riders. Many had remained with us, but the clans had suffered more battles against the Horde than anyone else. That made Zakir's decision all the more meaningful.

"Does no one else believe they should have a claim on the throne?" Dariusz asked, pleading with the crowd. By choosing to declare a new kingdom, I was no longer the heir, giving him an excuse to support someone else.

No one spoke.

"Then who supports Wacław Lubiewicz to be the first king of Wild Moon?" Dariusz asked, again choking on his words.

My friends all shouted their affirmation, and thousands of voices followed. Each raised a hand to confirm their vote, but Dariusz didn't need to count for a majority. He raised his arms as he always had as a priest, drawing the attention back to himself. "Then it is decided. Go forth as people of a new kingdom and rebuild the realm the Horde has destroyed."

Many from the crowd came to greet the goddesses and me, smiling and weeping as they told their stories. There were far too many to remember, but I cried and laughed with them until I was too exhausted to stand. The last of the crowds returned to houses, tents, and makeshift shelters as others built the pyres for the dead. We'd created a new kingdom from ash. It would take time to recover even a portion of what we'd lost.

Despite Mikołaj no longer being high chief, I ensured my half-siblings and Natasza kept their places in the longhouse. There were plenty of rooms left over for our group and Mom. Like many others beyond the wall, our house was in ruins, but Mom took it as well as she could. We were all grateful to be alive, even if the ground remained covered in snow.

Once all the others found a bed to collapse in, I found Otylia standing beneath Jaryło's Oak, staring up at the moon. She'd found a simple gray dress to wear under her woolen coat, and her hair tumbled behind her in knots as I joined her.

"I can't believe the Horde is gone," I said, following her gaze. The waxing crescent of Sierpień hung in the sky, and I could've sworn the stars around it were dimmer. Each was a living soul. We wouldn't have a count of our dead for a long time, but I focused on the fact we'd protected the rest.

"I remember that vision on the equinox so vividly," she replied with an arm held across her chest. "Mokosz showed us what the Horde was capable of, but we were all too blind to understand it."

"You weren't."

She shook her head. "I took too long to figure it out and to find Mother. Jawia almost fell."

"So did Prawia," I replied, wrapping my arm around her waist and pulling her to my side. Both our hearts slowed at the touch. A rare moment when things felt right. "The gods couldn't stop this, so a girl who didn't even know she was a goddess definitely couldn't have. Besides, you would've found her faster without me ruining everything in Vastroth."

"I should regret saving you instead of following my Thread to her."

"You don't?"

She turned to me, holding onto my tunic as she stared at me with her green eyes as welcoming as the first blooms of spring. "I couldn't keep going if I'd lost you, Wašek. You needed to endure your demonic soul to become who you are. It was terrifying, but you're stronger because of it."

I dropped my head. "I swore to be your sword as you lead."

"Instead, you've given Mother and me a thousand swords in a kingdom named after our forces." She grinned. "I can't believe you did that in front of Father."

"I couldn't become high chief, not like that."

"So you became a king—just like the Sudiczki foresaw in your fate."

I held her hands against my chest, returning her smile in spite of my sorrow. "Then you'll be my queen like they said?"

"I told you at the Lake of Reflection that I don't believe in fate."

"Yet you've met Destiny."

She kissed me, and the worries of the world faded for a few wonderful moments as our souls met. Our bond gave us many gifts. With her, our emotions merging was the greatest one of all.

When we parted, she held her hand to my cheek. Ungloved, it was frigid, but I stopped myself from shivering with her in my arms. "I have met her," she said, "and she knows that my fate is my own."

Then she slipped from my grasp and headed toward the longhouse. I watched her go with awe and confusion fighting for my heart. "Is that a yes or a no?"

"If you don't know, then maybe you should ask the fates," she replied with a wry smile over her shoulder.

She disappeared into the longhouse with the others, but I stayed beneath the tree for a while longer, staring up at my lover's moon. Her mark on my forearm seemed to hum to its silent tune. Always present, just like her in my heart.

I dropped my gaze to the Jaryło's Oak. It had never been Perun's, and even if it had been in his honor, he'd kept to his realm's petty disputes instead of saving those who worshipped him. His son was worse, but I saw the resemblance now.

I'm king, I thought to myself. *It's my job to root out the deceit in my lands.*

Grudzień slid smoothly from its sheath with its own hum. Hungrier than the moon, it was like it could read my intentions and responded with its approval.

"The Deathless Sons are gone," I said to the world, to whatever essence of Rod remained. "And they'll never be welcomed back."

My blade struck the oak's trunk with a vicious *crack*. Swords weren't normally fit for cutting down a tree, but the Moonblade remained perfectly sharp. It had been Marzanna's Alatyr shard of the twelfth moon. Once, she'd asked me to kill Jaryło, and as I swung at his Heart of Jawia over and over, it seemed right that her lost shard would sever his connection to the living realm.

I lost count of the strikes by the time Grudzień cut through the last of the trunk. The village center had been all but quiet before, but the sound of the tree toppling echoed through the trails like the last cry of a mighty god. Except Jaryło wasn't mighty anymore.

With a long sigh, I rested Grudzień on my shoulder and marched to the longhouse without another look at my handiwork. Jaryło was disgraced. Koschei was dead. And Czarnobóg was repelled for now. Rod had named me as the fourth of the Deathless Sons, but despite the demonic soul clawing at the cage within me, I had risen from my darkness. Not because of me. Not because of my storms. The Płanetnik had sought power through himself, but the ones I'd loved had saved me time and time again.

I was never alone, and in the battles ahead, I was grateful to know that no matter what I faced, that would never change.

END OF BOOK 4

A Word From The Author

It is insane for me to think that this is the tenth book I have published since I began writing about five years ago. Every book is a journey of its own for me as an author, and *The Deathless Sons* has been incredibly rewarding as the culmination of many plot points I have planted in every book of The Frostmarked Chronicles. Though the series isn't finished, I've loved igniting a few of those storylines and sending Wacław, Otylia, and all the gang into the realm of the gods. It was finally my chance as well to show Perun and other deities (golden apple grenades for the win!), and I can't wait to dive into the final book of the series with you all soon.

Thank you as always for following my books. If you've read this far into the series, you have journeyed with me for over 2,000 pages, which is an amazing honor for me. I am so grateful for all of your support through these last five years and into the future.

If you have enjoyed reading this story, please take the time to post an honest review on whatever retailer you purchased this book from. Every review helps new readers discover the series.

To receive your free copy of *The Rider in the Night*—the prequel novella to The Frostmarked Chronicles—other side-novellas attached to the series, and exclusive first looks at upcoming books, join my newsletter at www.Brendan-Noble.com.

- Brendan

About the Author

Brendan Noble is a Polish and German-American author currently writing fantasy inspired by Slavic mythology: The Frostmarked Chronicles. Through these books and his "Slavic Saturday" post series on YouTube and his website, he hopes to bring the often-forgotten stories of eastern Europe into new light.

Shortly after beginning his writing career in 2019 with the publication of his debut novel, The Fractured Prism (Book 1 of The Prism Files), Brendan married his wife Andrea and moved to Rockford, Illinois from his hometown in Michigan. Since then, he has published three series: The Realm Reachers, The Frostmarked Chronicles, and The Prism Files.

Outside of writing, Brendan is a data analyst, soccer referee, and the vice-president of Rockford FC (Rockford's semi-pro soccer club). His top interests include German, Polish, and American soccer/football, Formula 1, analyzing political elections across the world, playing extremely nerdy strategy video games, exploring with his wife, and reading.

www.ingramcontent.com/pod-product-compliance
Lightning Source LLC
Chambersburg PA
CBHW030836190726
48285CB00004B/1246